Murder in Palm Beach
The Homicide That Never Died

Bob Brink

PEGASUS BOOKS

Pegasus Books
3338 San Marino Ave
San Jose, CA 95127
www.pegasusbooks.net

First Edition: December 2014

Published in North America by Pegasus Books. For information, please contact Pegasus Books c/o Caprice De Luca, 3338 San Marino Ave, San Jose, CA 95127.

Most of the settings in this novel are real. The characters are fictitious. Any resemblance to actual persons, living or dead, is entirely coincidental.

Library of Congress Cataloguing-In-Publication Data
Bob Brink
Murder in Palm Beach: The Homicide That Never Died/Bob Brink – 1st ed
p. cm.
Library of Congress Control Number: 2014956768
ISBN – 978-1-941859-11-7
1. TRUE CRIME / Murder / General. 2. LAW / Criminal Procedure. 3. FICTION / Crime. 4. FICTION / Political. 5. FICTION / Legal. 6. LAW / Ethics & Professional Responsibility.

10   9   8   7   6   5   4   3   2   1

Comments about *Murder in Palm Beach: The Homicide That Never Died* and requests for additional copies, book club rates and author speaking appearances may be addressed to Bob Brink or Pegasus Books c/o Caprice De Luca, 3338 San Marino Ave, San Jose, CA 95127, or you can send your comments and requests via e-mail to cdeluca@pegasusbooks.net.

Also available as an eBook from Internet retailers and from Pegasus Books

Printed in the United States of America

ACKNOWLEDGEMENTS

I want to thank Dana Hauser for her eagle-eyed proofreading of the manuscript. Thanks also go to criminal attorneys Valentine Gabaldon (retired) and Richard Lubin for their clarification of trial procedures.

FOREWORD

In January 1976, the doorbell rings at the Palm Beach home of a man and his wife who have just returned from a dinner party. He answers and is mortally wounded by a shotgun blast.

Rodger Kriger was a prominent citizen, and pressure on law enforcement to solve the crime grows. Police settle on a charismatic karate instructor named Mitt Hecher, well-known to police for beating people up for money and sport, then question his guilt.

But Assistant State Attorney James Scraponia despises Hecher and charges him with murder. A jury finds him guilty, and a judge sentences him to a minimum 25 years in prison. During Hecher's term at the brutal and anarchic state penitentiary at Raiford, an often-fatal disease strikes his loyal, loving wife. He is devastated.

Did Hecher kill Kriger? Some people, including a few criminal attorneys and private investigators, have their doubts. A number of scenarios cast suspicion on other possible perpetrators. Did the sons of a wealthy Cuban do it? Were the operators of a gambling enterprise out to get Kriger? Was a love triangle the basis for the shooting? Did a vicious underworld figure do the bidding of a criminal gang? Was a prominent politician behind the slaying?

Judges repeatedly frustrate Hecher and several attorneys working, without fees, to get a new trial for him. Will they ever succeed? If those who think he was innocent are correct, will the real killer ever be found? And what will happen to the politically ambitious prosecutor?

Murder in Palm Beach is the saga of a battle between a man whose swagger has sent him spiraling to the bottom and powerful, sinister forces determined to keep him there. It is a story of redemption wrapped in a mystery tale reeking with power, sex, violence, and romance.

Murder in
Palm Beach
The Homicide That Never Died

MURDER IN PALM BEACH
The Homicide That Never Died

By Bob Brink

PART I: SETUP

Chapter One

"Getcha somethin, mister?" asked the barmaid, the sex appeal of her tight, ultrashort shorts and a halter top diminished by a bulging midriff.

"Uh… yeah," answered the middle-aged man from behind sunglasses. He leaned sideways and turned his hard, pockmarked face from the patron two stools away. "I got a friend with big bucks who's looking for somebody to take him on a boat ride for some fun with a coupla babes. I heard I might be able to find what I'm looking for in this place."

"You heard right. See that good-lookin guy over at the table close to the stage, sittin' by himself with a beer?" The barmaid nodded in that direction, and the man peered into the smoky haze of the dimly lit room. "Go talk to him. He might be a little unfriendly at first. Be kinda tactful, okay? I don't want no trouble in here."

"You don't have anything to worry about, honey," he said, smiling. "I deal with surly guys all the time."

Standing near the guy's large square table, he gazed around as if determining whether to stay, doing a half turn that opened his navy blazer and drew the blue shirt tightly over well-defined pectorals, highlighting a lean body.

"Mind if I sit down?"

Davey Ross didn't reply for a moment. "You blind or just pretending like you're some Hollywood glamour puss?"

"Huh? Oh… the shades. That's funny. I must look pretty weird." He laughed as he pocketed the sunglasses. "I forgot to take them off when I walked in. I've got sensitive eyes and have to wear them in bright sunlight."

"So if you're not a Hollywood star, don't stand there like you're waitin for the cameras to roll. Sit down. You're makin me nervous."

"I'm Jack." He extended a hand while taking a seat opposite Davey.

"I don't shake hands with guys unless I'm sealing a bet."

"Okay by me. And since I'm not a betting man, we'll just keep our hands to ourselves."

Jack ordered a Jim Beam on the rocks with a splash from the waitress.

"But I do have some business on my mind. The sexpot sitting at the end of the bar—I'd guess she's a stripper and we're going to see her perform."

"Geez, you're a shrewd devil. Don't know how you figured that out. Maybe you got the brilliant idea that a woman wouldn't walk around town in a skirt showing her leg all the way to her ass. You're a fucking genius."

"Oh, hell, my mind is always coming up with amazing insights," Jack said with a straight face.

Davey laughed raucously. "So what's this business you got on your mind? You ain't thinking about any hanky-panky with the dancer, are you?"

"You mean the stripper at the bar?"

"Yeah. But you better quit calling her a stripper or somebody's gonna get pissed off. She's an exotic dancer."

"Uh-oh. She your gal?"

"Nope. She ain't nobody's gal, but she's got the hots for the Great Dane. He likes em all and treats em good—big bucks for big boobs." Davey laughed short and loud, and heads turned his way.

"Who the hell is he?"

"Guy named Rodger Kriger, and you don't wanna mess with him."

"Why? Is he her pimp?"

"No, and you better not let him hear you say that. He's big—about six-four. But that ain't what makes him dangerous. He's powerful."

"Body builder or something?"

"That ain't what I meant. Geez, what do I hafta do, draw a picture for ya? He's a big shot in this county. He's got a lota money, lives in Palm Beach. He's on boards and councils and whatnot. You know... he's in big with the movers and shakers."

"I getcha. Look, I'm not trying to get laid. I'll cut to the chase. I heard Republican politicians from Washington can come down here to this place incognito and get lined up with high-class prostitutes and go out on the ocean in a boat where they don't have to worry about anybody knowing what they're up to. I'm working for some people who sent me down here to make the arrangements for their young client. His old man ordered it. He's a pretty important guy. Pretty *damned* important. Let's just say that when we're talking power, he makes Kriger look like Mickey Mouse."

"Must be his son's graduation present or something, huh? Yeah, I can help you with that. Only thing, I don't know about this incog... what'd you call it?"

"Incognito. Means anonymous. It's secret."

"Oh, yeah. Well, politicians come down here from Washington all the time for a fling. They've heard about the Shore Club and the two Republican bigwigs who hang out here and set them up. And guess who one of them two fine citizens is. Rodger Kriger. Him and his buddy Barney Robbins. That guy Robbins is so crooked, I don't know how he walks without a crutch. He's on the board that runs Palm Beach—whatever it's called."

"You mean the town commission, or town council?"

"Yeah, town council, I think that's it. Let me tell you, that town is so full of phony bullshitting bastards, it makes you wanna puke."

Davey lowered his head for a moment, then raised it.

"But hey, why should I complain? These rich sleazebags fatten my wallet when I bring stuff to their parties so's they can get loosened up—if you know what I mean."

He looked slyly at Jack.

"Then they revel like them pagans did back in the Roman days. That's after they hold their charity galas where they show the world how wonderful they are to help the poor slobs who weren't lucky enough to have a rich daddy or never decided to get rich by screwing the other guy."

Davey stared hard at his beer.

"When these politicians come down here, they don't tell nobody they're coming and hardly go out in public, cuz somebody might recognize them and call the paper or TV. They're safe with Kriger and Robbins—Republicans like them. Those two guys set it up so the political big shots can go out on a boat with whores, and a good time is had by all out in the ocean. A lot of privacy out there."

Davey paused.

"So is that what you're looking for?"

"Exactly. I need two quality prostitutes and a guy with a cabin cruiser who can take my client out in the ocean with them for two or three hours."

"No problem. Of course, there will be a charge for my consulting service."

"How much do you need?"

"My fee is fifty bucks per item, and there are two items: the boat, and two hookers, which there's a two-for-one special on at the moment."

"That's not a bad price, considering how inflation's been skyrocketing," said Jack.

He pulled a wallet out of his inside sport coat pocket and withdrew two fifties, two twenties, and a ten.

"There. One-hundred-fifty smackers. Now keep your mouth shut."

Davey felt the power switching. "Oh, yeah," he breathed. "You just put a clamp on my mouth. But I've gotta ask you not to blab about our financial arrangement."

"Mum's the word."

"Okay. The guy you need to see for the boat is Johnny Traynor."

"Who he?"

"He's the captain of Robbins's boat, and he does the mechanical work too—used to be a race car driver. This boat is a fifty-foot Bayliner—a cabin cruiser big enough so's your young stud and his two wenches can roll around inside the cabin. He can screw em up and down with the action of the waves. A different kind of rhythm method." Davey let out a guttural laugh.

"So where do I find this Traynor?"

"He hangs out here once in a while. I can give him a call and tell him you want to meet him here. He's got an apartment a few blocks away. Traynor can get ahold of Robbins, and Robbins will let Kriger know about the plans for the politician's kid."

"Sounds good to me."

"Ask Traynor about the girls, too," said Davey.

"I thought you were going to provide them."

"I didn't say that. I'm just making the referral. Wait a minute and I'll go make a call to Traynor and see if he's home."

Davey walked to the phone booth in the corner by the restrooms. Ten minutes later, a tall man with a modicum of belly flab stood searching the dark interior with squinty eyes set in a narrow face.

"Is'at him?" said Jack?

"Yeah," said Davey, waving to Traynor.

He approached the two men.

"What's the limp for?" Jack asked.

"Vietnam. Got shot in the foot. Kept him off the racetrack for a while, but it finally healed and he won a few ribbons on the stock-car circuit in Georgia."

Davey introduced Traynor to Jack. The boat captain's head was lowered, eyes lifted in what seemed to Jack a weaselly, shifty look. He told Traynor about the boat. The captain went to the phone booth and returned, reporting that Robbins would be able to provide the boat. Kriger would come to the Shore Club in a couple of hours to meet Jack and make the arrangements.

"Go to a restaurant if you haven't ate yet, or just wait around," Davey told Jack.

"You going to introduce me?"

"Nah, I gotta go. It ain't necessary. Kriger'll be happy to talk to you. You'll know who he is—big blond dude, only one in the place dressed up."

"Where do I get the hookers?" Jack asked Traynor.

Traynor smiled smugly.

"I'm a man of several talents. I can see who's available. Give me your number where you're staying and I'll call you. Meantime, talk to Kriger, tell him the date you need the boat.

"Got it."

Jack and Traynor exchanged phone numbers, and Jack drove his rental car several blocks to the Blue Pelican restaurant on the Intracoastal Waterway. It was unusually balmy for a late autumn evening, and he sat on the patio to watch boats moor at the docks after heading in through the Palm Beach Inlet from short ocean excursions. After a leisurely meal of broiled dolphin, he returned to the Shore Club.

Kriger sat alone at a table in the middle of the room, looking a little bored as he watched a dancer strut her stuff.

"Hi. If I'm not mistaken, you're Rodger, Jack said, smiling while extending a hand. "I'm Jack. Johnny Traynor said you could help me."

"Johnny who? Oh, I know who you mean. That fella who comes around here once in a while. He's Barney Robbins's boat guy. So what do you need?"

"The son of a very important Republican politician in Washington is coming down here to celebrate an occasion, and I need to line up a boat with a couple of party girls to go out on the ocean for a good time. Traynor told me how to get the girls, and he said your friend Robbins could provide the boat."

"Sure can. We'd be happy to help out. Who's the pol?"

"Can I sit down?"

"Oh, sure. Sorry. Pull up a chair."

Sitting close to Kriger at a right angle, Jack turned his head to the left and right, then lowered it.

"This has got to be very discreet. Is that understood?"

"Oh, yeah," Kriger blurted. "All these Washington guys have to keep things on the q.t. That's no problem."

"I would appreciate it if you would lower your voice," Jack said with a little lilt to avoid sounding dictatorial.

"Ooh," Kriger cooed. "You seem pretty touchy about this. Sounds like your pol isn't anybody to sneeze at. How high up is he?"

Jack looked at Kriger hard for several seconds.

"Your lips closed?"

"Yeah, yeah, of course," said Kriger, lowering his voice further and bending toward Jack.

"The top."

Kriger jerked backward.

"You don't mean…"

"Yes. The president. Wallace Grey."

Chapter Two

"Hi. You must be Shane Grey."

The man's client stood next to the hotel registration desk.

"Yes. I guess I'm the only nineteen-year-old around here."

He was casually stylish in tan corduroy pants, a plaid shirt, and brown deck shoes. But his face had a rugged, outdoorsy look accented by sandy hair that hung over his ears and down his neck. His smile was warm and gentle, almost apologetic.

"I'm Jack Varner," the man said, thrusting a hand out without smiling. He looked sinister in dark green sunglasses. "How's your room? The Hilton's not great, but it's probably the best hotel on Singer Island. Didn't want you to be too far away from the boat dock."

"Oh, it's just fine. I'm used to camping outdoors a lot, so this is real comfort."

"So you're a sportsman? Let's go. My car is in the lot. You hunt?"

"No," Shane replied, following him out of the lobby. "Actually, I do just the opposite. I work in Texas for Save the Critters, the environmental group. I'm out in the hinterlands a lot."

"Interesting."

"Yes. I like the work. But it gets lonely. I spend a lot of time working by myself for long stretches. Actually, there are always people around—the Secret Service agents. But they just do their job, and we don't talk to each other."

"Well, you're not going to be by yourself this afternoon," Jack called over the roof of the Ford Mustang rental car. "We've got a little surprise waiting for you."

"Uh-oh. What's my dad up to now?" Shane's grin betrayed uneasiness as he climbed in the passenger seat. "I know he's looking out for my best interests, but he's got plenty to keep him busy in the Oval Office and flying around the world looking out for the interests of the country. Sometimes I wish he would just quit worrying about me and let me do my own thing. I'm legally an adult now, and I can take care of myself."

Jack drove out to A1A and headed south.

"Hey, you're here to celebrate your job promotion, right? What'd they move you up to?"

"I'm going to be the West Texas regional field representative. That'll mean a lot of traveling to check on operations."

"Is it all guys who do this kind of work, or are there some chicks you get to rub shoulders with—or rub something with?" Jack chuckled.

Shane forced a smile. "No, the girls all work in the office in Austin. I hardly have any contact with them."

"No contact?" Jack retorted with mock dismay. "Well, we'll see if we can help you make contact." He grinned at Shane.

Shane shrank in his seat. "That's okay. I'll be all right."

At the Sailfish Marina, a valet greeted the Mustang. The two stood by the docks and surveyed the scene.

"Wow, pretty impressive," said Shane. "A lot of money in those yachts."

"Yep. See that baby over there?" Jack pointed to a slip occupied by a fifty-foot cabin cruiser with Escapade in black Gothic script on the stern. "That's what you're going out on. Too bad it's overcast today. Oh well, I think you'll want to spend most of your time inside the boat, anyway." He turned his head to look at Shane and smiled. Shane looked back, bemused.

"Let's go inside the bar and meet the guy in charge of this little party."

A sidewalk led to the sprawling, plain white marina building and they entered directly into the bar through double glass doors.

"There's Johnny Traynor, the boat captain, over by the bar. I don't know who that guy with him is."

Jack approached Traynor, standing beside a stool.

"Johnny, this is Shane Grey," Jack said. "Shane, Johnny Traynor."

"Hiya dude," he responded coolly.

Shane nodded.

Traynor drummed his fingers on the bar. He quickly turned to Jack.

"Let's get this crate rockin, shall we?"

"Yeah, in a minute," said Jack. He turned to his client. "Why don't you use the head before we move out, Shane?"

"Probably a good idea," said Shane.

A casually dressed, middle-aged man followed him to the restroom. Shane, glancing over his shoulder, recognized the man as a Secret Service agent.

"I need to talk to you for a second," Jack murmured to Traynor, leading him to the end of the bar. "Who's that guy with you?"

"Oh, that's Richie Gatson." Traynor glanced at Gatson, who was gazing about the room, and turned his back toward him while moving closer to Jack. "He does some pimpin out of the Shore club. I had him help me line up the two girls. I didn't want him pissed off at me for cuttin into his territory. He's a tough guy. Been in trouble with the law so much they ran out of things to charge him with."

Jack looked out the corner of his eye at Gatson, who was rocking on his heels, looking impatient. He was built like a bulldog, and Jack perceived an air of hostility in his tense face and square stance.

"When he ain't pimpin," said Traynor, "he and a guy named Mitt Hecher operate a little sideline. Anybody's got a grudge against somebody, Hecher and Gatson get paid to beat em up. Hecher teaches karate and his students make up a gang. He supplies them with drugs, and they look up to him like a god, cuz he ain't to be messed with.

"I ain't shittin ya when I say you don't wanna fuck with them two dudes. Hecher… he's a genius at beating the system. That's why his students worship him. He's only gone to jail maybe a dozen times—short stints—but he's got a rap sheet as long as a fat man's grocery list. He holds the all-time arrest record for bar brawls. It'll never be broke, like Ty Cobb's lifetime batting average." Traynor's face brightened. *Eureka!* "Hey, now that'd be a riot—them both bein such mean bastards."

"What's this Hecher got to do with us?" Jack's voice hinted at impatience.

"Nothin," said Traynor, shrugging. "I just thought you might want to know who you're dealin with. Remember the dude in the Shore Club who set you up with me? Davey Ross? Him and Hecher are buddies."

Gatson walked up to Traynor and Jack.

"Hey, you guys gonna shoot the shit all day, or what? Let's get crankin." Facing Jack, he pointed to the other end of the bar. "See the two bitches over there? They look okay?"

The call girls chatted with each other and laughed, glancing occasionally at the men arranging payment for use of their bodies. Jack studied them, noticing how the younger one, with blonde frizzles, was vivacious, her face a continual parade of expressions synchronized with hand gestures. The other, eight to ten years older, had long, almost black hair and an olive complexion. Her smile, he could sense, hinted of guile and her demeanor was sensuous, with a worldly-wise air. Both wore short shorts, blouses unbuttoned to show abundant cleavage, and spiked heels. Jack assumed the canvas bag on a seat beside them contained lower-heeled substitutes they could switch into before boarding the yacht.

"I already looked them over," Jack said. "How could I not notice? Mighty fine."

Pulling out his wallet, he counted several bills and looked back and forth at Traynor and Gatson.

"Who gets the bread here?"

"Just give it to Richie," said Traynor. "He'll pay the girls and me out of it."

"You ready?" Gatson asked Traynor.

"Hell, I was ready before that last Jack Daniels. One more and I might forget how to steer this tub and we'll end up in Cuba. A little surprise for Fidel."

"Okay, wise ass, get sailin," Gatson barked. "You need to be back in three hours." He approached the two women at the bar. "Follow him, gals. He'll take you to the yacht."

"The party is about to begin," Jack bubbled as Shane returned from the bathroom. "Let's go."

They walked to the dock behind Traynor and the women.

"Have a ball, Shane," Jack chimed when they reached the slip with the Escapade.

Shane turned quickly at him, his face registering mild alarm.

"You're not going along?"

"Naw, this is your party. I've got business to work on."

"But... but... I don't know..."

"Hey, take it easy. There's nothing to be nervous about. You're in good hands. Traynor is an expert captain. And those babes will take very good care of you. You're going to have a real good time. Look. They're standing on the deck waiting for you. Get on over there... stud." Jack chuckled, then turned and walked away.

Shane started to follow him, stopped, looked toward the boat, and hesitated. Slowly he walked toward it.

"We thought you'd never get here," the blonde greeted cheerfully. "Can you make it okay?"

"Thanks, I can manage." Shane placed a foot on the side and nimbly propelled himself aboard.

"Ooh, so athletic," she hummed, catching him in outstretched arms as he landed on the deck. "What a hunk."

Shane turned pink. His eyes roamed over the craft.

"Nice boat. Who owns it?"

"Barney Robbins. He's on the upper deck. You won't see much of him. He just came along as a back-up pilot in case anything happens to Johnny."

She looked at the sky. "What a yukky day, huh? I used to live in Tampa, and it almost never is cloudy or rainy all day long over there, except when there's a storm. Let's go in the cabin."

She led him through the door and down three steps to a long section of L-shaped, tan, suede couches. An oak coffee table fronted them.

"Where is your friend?" asked Shane.

"Oh, Alexis is probably up talking with Barney. So your name is Shane, right? I'm Sharon. Pretty close. Shane and Sharon. Do you want something to drink?"

"If there's a 7 Up, that would be fine."

"Let me check." Sharon walked to the small kitchen. "Yup. This fridge has everything."

She popped the cap, handed the soda to Shane, and sat next to him. "Where do you live?"

Jack sensed her insincerity. "I've been working in Texas."

"You look like you've been working outdoors—so tanned and rugged looking. So manly."

"Yes, I spend most of my time out in the uninhabited areas—the plains, the Hill Country, the wetlands. You know, swamps. We're trying to stop developers from draining the wetlands, which causes fish to die from lack of food. And they're resting places for migrant birds. We're working on saving lots of different species, from the kangaroo rat to the jaguar."

"The jaguar!" Sharon exclaimed, her eyes popping as she jerked back. "Oh, that's scary."

"Naw, not really. Not as long as you don't threaten them. They're beautiful creatures."

"Do you ever get into the towns, where you can meet girls?"

Shane blushed and shifted in his seat. "Well, not very often, I guess. When you do this work, you have to sacrifice your social life."

She stretched her arm on the back of the couch behind his head.

"But I've become resigned to it," said Jack. "I enjoy my work."

"Don't you miss being with girls, though? I'd think that would be hard on you. I mean—oops." She giggled and put her hand over her mouth. "That was a bad choice of words."

Shane managed a smile. She leaned closer and rested her hand on his far shoulder. He tensed and pulled his shoulders in.

Sharon drew back. "I'm going to get a Pepsi. Is your 7 Up okay?"

"Sure, I'm fine."

She returned with the soda and sat a couple of feet away from her customer.

"Where did you grow up?"

"Washington, D.C."

"Oh, that's an exciting place. Was your dad with the government?"

"Uh... yes, yes, as a matter of fact. He worked for the government."

"What kind of work did he do? Or what kind of work does he do?"

"Well, he sort of... he had different jobs. He has an executive position. I can't talk about it a lot."

"I understand. I guessed he must have some kind of top-secret job when government agents checked out Alexis and me. "

Shane said nothing and took a swig of soda.

"You must have been real popular with the girls in school, good-lookin kid like you." She nuzzled up to him, her head against his chest, simultaneously placing her right hand high on his thigh.

His leg tightened

"Oh, what muscle," she exclaimed. "I guess that comes from so much climbing and tromping through those rugged places in Texas."

Shane's forehead moistened and he felt a drop of sweat slide down his spine.

"You must be very brave, all alone out there where a wild animal could attack you," Sharon purred, raising her face close to his while massaging his thigh, ever nearer to his crotch.

"Excuse me," Shane said, rising. "This soda is going right through me."

He looked back at Sharon with a smile that she could tell was forced as he walked to the bathroom. In a few minutes, he returned, looking less tense. He sat on the couch a few feet from her.

"You're kind of shy with girls, aren't you?" She wore an impish smile and slid closer to him. "I think that's cute."

Shane shrugged and looked at her with an embarrassed smile, then away. He began feeling feverish again.

"Just sit back and relax," she said softly, caressing the back of his head. "Close your eyes."

After a minute, she slowly drew her lips against his, placing her other hand in his crotch. She kissed him, but he made no response. Inserting her tongue in his mouth, she tugged on the belt of his pants and deftly unclasped it, then loosened the button and lowered the zipper. She ran her hand under his underpants and began to massage his penis. It remained limp. Shane twisted his hips.

"I don't think we should be doing this."

"What's the matter? Don't you find me attractive?" Sharon pouted.

"Oh sure, of course. It just seems to me we're getting overly familiar a bit too quickly. Maybe I'm just not in the mood today."

Sharon pulled the zipper back up and fastened the button.

"My soda is getting warm," said Shane. "Think I'll pour it in a glass of ice." He fastened his belt and headed for the kitchen.

"You sure you're not cool enough already?" Sharon muttered, snickering.

"Pardon?"

"Never mind. I was just thinking that with no sun today, it's not all that warm. Tell you what, you sit down and relax while I go up and see how Alexis is doing, okay?"

"Sure. Take your time. I'll just look through that art book I saw under the coffee table."

Sharon climbed the stairs to the upper deck and found Alexis sitting on a bench chatting with Barney Robbins.

"See those two small boats ahead of us?" Alexis said to Robbins. "They've been keeping the same distance from us the whole time we've been sailing. Two guys in each boat, and they're just sitting there, not fishing or anything. I wonder what they're up to."

"They're… kind of like bodyguards," said Robbins. "Those are the guys who frisked you earlier."

"You know, I can't make them out clearly from this far away, but the two in that one boat do look a little familiar." She pointed to the craft on their right.

"Yes. Your client's father is a pretty important guy. That's about all I can say."

"Aha. So that's it."

Alexis turned to Sharon.

"Wow, am I glad to see you. It's chilly up here in this breeze. I'm not dressed for this. Not that it took you very long. You must have gotten lover boy excited pretty fast."

Sharon rolled her eyes. "Are you kidding? I couldn't even get his pulse rate up, much less his dick. I wasn't even sure he was breathing. What a dud. A *dead* dud."

"Well, maybe he goes for older women," Alexis purred. "Let's see if I can charge his battery."

Alexis descended the stairs and opened the cabin door. She stood with arms raised, hands grasping the frame for support. She had long, olive legs, neither thick nor thin, and there was no space between her upper thighs, which made her body the more voluptuous.

"Hi handsome," she said softly.

"Oh, hi," Shane said, looking up from the book and over his shoulder.

"Hope I didn't disturb you."

"No, not at all."

"I was getting chilly up there in the wind," she pouted. "I need a body to warm me up. Mind if I sit next to you?"

Shane looked up at her, hesitation showing. "That's okay."

Alexis heard reluctance in his tone. Supported by rubber platform shoes, she walked toward him with lithe sensuality. She sat at an angle toward him, her legs crossed.

"I was just admiring some paintings by Georgia O'Keeffe," Shane piped. "Are you familiar with her?"

"I know who she is because I'm from New Mexico. I know she was a great artist, but that's about all."

"Really? I'm fascinated with her because she was attracted to New Mexico for its spirituality, which is related to its Indian history. She seemed to enjoy her lonely existence, driving around her ranch in her Model A Ford. Sort of like my life out in the deserted areas of Texas, where I get around in a Ford F250 Camper."

He pointed to the paintings *White Trumpet Flower*, *Jimson Weed*, and *Oriental Poppies*. "Look at those gorgeous flowers. They draw you in."

Alexis put her arm over his shoulder and moved her face next to his to see.

"Yes, they draw me in. There's something sexual about them."

"Hmm. I never thought about them that way."

"I think they look something like the female genitalia."

Shane pulled his head back a little. "That's interesting."

"Young as you are, you might never have even seen a naked woman."

"Well, I… I mean…"

"Oh, I'm sorry. That was awfully forward of me. I shouldn't be so personal."

"That's okay. I guess I've been too busy pursuing a career to spend much time with women."

"Excuse me. I'm tired of sitting." Alexis strode to the kitchen and opened and closed several cabinet doors. "Oh, look what I found. A box of chocolates."

She returned and stood in front of the table, holding a chocolate between a thumb and forefinger. She slowly drew the other hand across her breasts, down her torso and hips, and up her thighs to her crotch, which she massaged.

Shane peered up from the book and quickly back down.

Alexis sat next to him and moved her face near his. Inserting half the square piece of chocolate in his mouth, she closed her mouth over the other half and pushed her lips against his. Chocolate smeared around their mouths, and she licked it off him.

"Aren't you going to do the same for me?" she asked, feigning hurt.

"I guess I'm a little fastidious." He sounded apologetic.

She sashayed back to the kitchen and returned with several pieces of Kleenex and a clean face.

"Let's see what else this woman painted," she said, and began turning the pages of the book.

Shane put his hand on a page. "There's her other side in those stark portrayals." He pointed to the exaggerated antlers and skull in *From the Faraway, Nearby* and to *Cow's Skull: Red, White, and Blue.*

"Which side do you prefer?" Alexis asked.

"It depends on what mood I'm in. Right now, I prefer these."

"So sex and beauty are not what interest you at the moment."

Shane looked repentant, as though he'd stepped on a little frog.

"No, it's not that. I just go from one feeling to another and it's… you know… kind of unpredictable." He squirmed. "I run across skulls of wild animals out in the hinterlands of Texas, and those paintings make me feel at home."

"Why did you make the trip here all the way from Texas? How long are you staying?"

"I guess my dad wanted to help me celebrate my job promotion, so he set up the whole thing. I'll be returning day after tomorrow."

"So you came here by yourself?"

"Yes. He had the contacts for me. But I didn't come with any friends."

"Well, that's no good. I'm here to be your friend."

"You're very nice."

"I'm lucky to be with such a good-looking, interesting guy." She draped an arm around his neck. "Let's see some more of Georgia O'Keeffe's work."

With her right hand, she turned the pages, exchanging comments on the paintings with Shane. She tickled his ear with her left hand, and he began to blush.

"I want to do more than be your friend," she whispered in his ear. "I want to make you feel good. Very, very good."

Putting both arms around his neck, she drew his ear to her and inserted her tongue, swirling it. Dropping her right hand to his crotch, she felt for an erection, but there was none. She slowly massaged while nibbling on his neck.

Shane became increasingly agitated, turning his head right, then left, beads of perspiration forming on his forehead. But it was irritation he felt, not excitement.

Alexis straightened up.

"I'll tell you what. I brought a cooling body oil in my bag. Why don't I help you out of your shirt and you can lay that strong, masculine body right here on the couch? I'll give you a nice, soothing back rub. All of that crouching and ducking from those wild animals—I'm sure your back could use some loosening up." She reached for the buttons on his multicolored, plaid shirt.

"Oh, that's all right," Shane said, pushing her hands away. He squeezed his hands together and moved his legs in and out. "I'd have to shower afterward, and I don't feel like I want to bother with it. Thanks, anyway."

"Excuse me while I use the restroom," said Alexis.

A few minutes later, she emerged, naked except for her elevated shoes. Her eyelids were painted cobalt and her lips a dark red. She ambled toward Shane, hips swiveling. She stopped five feet in front of him and stood, one leg bent, hands on hips, head lowered in a seductive gaze.

"Ma'am... that is, Alexis... See, I don't even know you well enough to feel comfortable calling you by your first name. I don't want to do this."

"But don't I turn you on? Can't you just enjoy making love with me?"

"I... I don't... I'm not... I guess I'm just not cut out for this. Maybe it's the making love part. There isn't any love."

"Oh, I get it. You're saving yourself for somebody."

"Yes, that's it." Shane sounded relieved. "I'm waiting for the right person."

"Well, then, I'll just go and get dressed, and we'll call it a day." Heading for the restroom, she tossed a coquettish look over her shoulder. "Although I must say, it would have been fun—the easiest money I'd have ever made. You're quite a hunk."

The dapper, good-looking man—middle-aged, with a receding hairline—looked flamboyant in a shiny purple tie, lavender shirt with navy-blue pants, and a tan sport coat. Looking around the Shore Club, his gaze fixed on a group of men at a round table, watching a stripper perform.

"Hi Rodger," he said, sauntering up.

"Barney. We thought you'd never get here. You're missing the action. The dancer is almost through."

"Yeah, I got hung up with business. I see most of the guys were able to escape from their wives."

A few "Hi Barney"s rang out from the group, and Barney responded with little waves.

"Pull up a chair." Rodger Kriger was ebullient. "Let's have the full report on how it went with the pres's kid."

Robbins slid a chair over from an adjoining table and ordered a Wild Turkey on the rocks from a waitress.

"It didn't work out very well."

"What happened? Those girls were two of the best hookers around. You don't mean he got nasty or anything, do you?"

"He didn't do anything."

"Then what was the problem?"

"I just said what the problem was. He didn't do anything."

"Huh?"

"He wasn't interested. Nothing the gals did got him excited. They tried everything. He just kept his head in an art book."

"You gotta be kidding me." Kriger stared at Robbins, looking amazed, then broke into loud laughter. The other men at the table stopped chatting and looked at Kriger.

"Hey Rodger, what's so funny?" said one.

"The president's son…" he laughed some more… "is a fruitcake. Barney took him out in his boat with two whores and they couldn't even get his dick up."

He reared back in his chair and roared, laughing so hard that his torso heaved. The patrons in the entire room looked his way and the stripper paused in her routine.

"Come on, Barney, tell me the details," Kriger implored, wiping away a tear. "This is better than a dirty joke."

"The girls said they tried to seduce him and Alexis had her hand in his pants, but it was like squeezing a bowl of linguini. She got naked and he said he was saving himself for the right person. I think the right person for him is a two-letter pronoun ending in e. He drops the s."

Kriger looked perplexed for a second, then smiled.

"I get ya, Barney. Did ya hear that, guys? Barney says the pres's son wants a *he*, not a *she*."

"Geez, I wonder what Grey would think if he knew this," someone at the table piped up.

No one responded for a couple of seconds. Then Kriger's face brightened.

"Hey, you know what? I'll bet he already knows it. In fact, I'll bet that's what this was all about. Grey didn't send his kid down here to celebrate. He sent him here to get straight. He thought a couple of hookers could do the trick."

"Ya think?" another guy said.

"It makes sense. Why would he send his son here all by himself to celebrate a job promotion with nobody he knows? That's no way to have a party. That job promotion thing was just a cover."

"Hmm," the guy mused. "Now that you mention it..."

The other men set about discussing the possibility among themselves, the words "fairy" and "faggot" popping up amid occasional snickers.

"Well, we did our job," Kriger said to Robbins. "You can lead a horse to water, but you can't make him drink."

"Maybe Shane will follow in his father's footsteps, and one day he'll be president," said Robbins. "It wouldn't be the first father-and-son presidents. There was John Adams and John Queery, I mean John Quincy..."

Kriger let out a belly laugh.

"We'd do it the English way, and give the top job to a queen," Kriger said.

He and Robbins rose from their chairs and slapped each other's backs. They both shook with mirth, but Kriger's peals of laughter reverberated through the room. Everyone joined in the hilarity, having heard sufficient bits and pieces of the conversation to discern the reason.

The other men at the table likewise chortled. As the stripper finished her act, they rose and exchanged handshakes and expressions of goodwill before meandering toward the door.

"See ya, Barney," Kriger called. "I promised the dancer I'd buy her a drink after her act."

"Hi sweetheart," Jack Varner said.

The barmaid was the same one he'd spoken with on his first visit to the Shore Club. She still wore short, rose-colored shorts, but had switched from a halter top to a tight, powder-blue sweater that reached to her neck.

"I don't see Rodger Kriger. Think he'll be coming in tonight?"

"Oh, I don't know. He doesn't always make it in on weekends. And after the fun he and his buddies had three nights ago, he might need a rest."

"What happened?" Jack asked.

"You didn't hear? I thought the whole town knew about it by now. Seems Barney Robbins took President Grey's son out on his boat with a coupla the girls that work outa here, and all he wanted ta do was talk about art. I never heard anybody laugh so hard in my life."

Varner's eyes narrowed. "Who are you talking about?"

"Kriger and them other Palm Beach guys in the club. They come in once a week to see the show. Barney told Kriger what happened, and Kriger cracked jokes about it and got the guys laughin till everybody's sides was splittin. The whole room was crackin up. Everybody in this place has been talkin about it for three days."

"Let me have a shot of Beam."

"Hey, you don't look happy." The barmaid frowned as she poured the Jim Beam.

"No, no, it's just that I have some business to talk over with Kriger, and I have to catch a plane. Guess I'll have to give him a call."

Jack threw the shot back with one gulp, grimaced, and headed for the phone booth in the corner.

"I have to be getting back to Washington," he spoke into the receiver.

"So soon?" Kriger demurred. "Well, I know political life can be pretty hectic. It was good meeting you. I hope your client had a good time and everything turned out all right."

"Uh, Shane isn't very talkative and he didn't have a lot to say about the boat excursion before he left for Texas. But apparently others did provide a pretty clear picture of what happened on that boat. As a matter of fact, I'm given to understand that Barney Robbins and you spilled the beans to people at the Shore Club."

"Oh, well, we might have mentioned it in passing to a couple of friends who were there. But it was no big deal."

"I understand that everybody in the Shore Club, and probably beyond, knows what happened and thinks it's pretty funny."

"Hmm. You know, I suppose the two hookers might have talked about it, and maybe the boat captain, and it kind of got around."

"I think I made it pretty clear that this had to be very discreet. You may have thought the Shore Club was a comedy club and you were the headlining comedian, Mister Kriger, but I don't happen to think what you did was funny at all. In fact, it's a good thing you aren't here because I'd be very tempted to beat the hell out of you." Varner's voice had crescendoed almost to yelling. The barmaid and the smattering of patrons turned to look.

Kriger was silent for several seconds.

"I'm sorry if it got a little out of hand, Mister Varner. But I don't think it's anything to be concerned about. I'm sure in a day or two the whole thing will be forgotten and nobody will think twice about it."

"Too bad I can't agree with you. This is something that's going to stick in people's minds. I've got to run now. My plane leaves in an hour and a quarter."

"Have a good flight. And if we can make this unfortunate incident up to you in the future, please let us know."

The response was a click.

Chapter Three

Mitt Hecher and Davey Ross wore impassive expressions that hid machinations lurking behind eyes measuring every patron in the Unicorn Tavern.

"I see one," Hecher said. "The guy at the bar trying to make it with the bitch two seats away."

Ross looked worried. "Geez, he's pretty big."

Mitt, a veteran street fighter, stared at the guy a moment.

"The bigger they are, the harder they fall."

"Oh, man," Davey sighed. He semiconsciously patted the bulges under his jacket on either side of his chest jacket and took a deep breath. "Okay, let's go."

Mitt and Davey half-resembled a Mutt and Jeff team. Mitt was Mutt, five-foot-six in his bare feet, but with a strong build that was both muscular and wiry. Davey was Jeff, standing ramrod straight at six feet.

Davey's father operated a wholesale fish business and financed a bar in Lake Worth for his son. Hecher hung out there, and after Davey sold the business, they began making the rounds of other watering holes, getting into trouble.

The pair sauntered into the rectangular room, which had a bar on one side and dark wood paneling with Kmart-quality pictures of wildlife on the opposite wall. The room was less than half full. Two thirtyish patrons, a skinny fellow and his overweight, frumpy companion sat kissy-facing at one of two high-tops back of the staple-shaped bar. Two businessman types, one middle-aged and the other older, played cards at a small table. In an alcove that extended beyond the bar, two men dressed in worker's clothes shot pool on the only table.

In the middle of the long row of stools, the big guy half-stood and half-sat, turned toward the woman. Measuring at least six-foot-three, he was large-boned and obviously strong. His attire suggested a construction worker: flannel shirt with the sleeves rolled up to his elbows, scuffed jeans, heavy tan boots with thick rubber soles. Though perhaps only in his early thirties, his passing good looks couldn't disguise the effects of a hard life. A slight paunch had formed, doubtless from drinking a lot of the draft beer that he downed now while talking to the woman.

She wore tight-fitting jeans, sexy high-heeled sandals, and a white blouse with sleeves falling just below softly rounded shoulders. As he talked, she twirled a finger atop a cocktail glass while looking at him with head cocked away, a doubtful smile on a face that was pretty in a plain way.

Mitt walked nonchalantly up to the seat between the big guy and the woman. Davey followed several steps behind.

"My my, look what we have here?" Mitt said, breaking into a cocky smile. "What's a classy dame like you doin in the slummiest dive on South Dixie?"

The woman shot him a dour look and turned to face the bar.

"Hey buddy, quit buttin into our conversation," the big man snarled. "Scram!"

"Conversation? Seems to me a conversation has to have more than one person, and it looked to me like you were doin all the talkin, big mouth."

"What'd you call me, you little punk?"

"Ya know, you not only need your mouth washed out, but your ears need cleaning, too. I guess I have to repeat myself." Mitt leaned into the guy. "I called you a big mouth."

"Why, you fucking..." The guy jumped from the bar stool. Raising his fists, he came at Mitt, who had backed away and assumed the classic crouched position of a karate fighter: left arm forward at an angle, fist pointing upward, the right arm crossing the midsection, fist ready for action.

The guy threw a right cross at Mitt, who fended off the blow with his left arm and landed a chop in the solar plexus with his right, doubling the man over. Mitt came down hard on the back of the guy's neck, stepped sideways, and took a leaping kick at his kidney. That was the *coup de grace*, and the man fell to the floor like a spent bull at the hands of a matador.

One of the pool players and two blue-collar types at the bar rushed over and were about to pounce on Mitt. Davey pulled pistols from holsters covered by both sides of his jacket and pointed them at the interlopers.

"Hold it right there," he yelled. "Any of you guys as much as touch my buddy, I'll blow you away."

The three stopped in their tracks.

"Now, get back to what you were doin. The fight's over. Nobody's gonna get hurt anymore. Mitt's just got a little business to discuss with that poor dude."

The three men backed away. Everyone cowered, afraid to leave with Davey and Mitt still there. The woman at the bar sat staring at them, her hands holding her face in an expression of shock.

Mitt bent over the big guy. "How ya doin, dude?"

He grunted.

"You'll be all right." Mitt smiled at him.

"I'm gonna make you a proposition you can't refuse. You must feel like a real chump, a big lout like you letting a little guy like me beat the crap out of you, right in front of a gal you're trying to score with. Huh? Am I right? That's okay. You're in too bad a shape to talk much."

The big guy nodded and grimaced.

"So just listen to the great offer I'm about to make. You'll never have to worry about guys like me humiliating you in front of a woman you're hustlin again."

He helped the man to his feet.

"Let's go sit at that empty corner table and talk business. Now don't get any ideas about attacking me cuz I'll put you away again. And Davey here might just lose his temper and give you a pistol whipping that would make my karate chops feel like the teacher's ruler."

Holding his midsection, the guy stumbled to the table. Davey put his guns in the side pockets of his pants, his eyes darting from side to side as he watched over the entire room.

"What's your name? I'm Mitt." The karate expert reached out his hand.

"Bill, but I'm not in the mood to shake your hand."

"Okay, okay. You don't like me. You probably never will. Geez, I don't know why. But in time, you're going to appreciate me. Cuz I'm gonna help you. Of course, my services ain't free."

"What are you talkin about?"

"Here's the deal. I own a karate studio in West Palm Beach, only a coupla miles from here near downtown. Hecher Karate. You're gonna learn how to defend yourself with this great martial art and never have to worry about anybody bothering you. I have a special rate going at the moment: three lessons per week for fifteen bucks each. You can come in Monday, Wednesday, and Friday, or twice during the week and on Saturday.

"You might have to save some of that beer money, but you won't want to drink much after you get into this program. You're prob'ly gonna do pretty good after six months, but if you really want confidence about your ability to handle yourself, you might have to stick with it at least a year. Understand?"

Bill glanced at his nemesis and back at the table.

"Now, I'm gonna need payment for the first lesson in advance. So if you'll please dig into your wallet and pull out a twenty-dollar bill, Bill, we'll be all set."

Bill threw a sour look at Mitt, hesitated, and peered up at Davey, who rubbed the bulges in his pockets. Unhurrying, Bill pulled out his wallet and handed Mitt two ten-dollar bills.

"Bill, I got a feeling this is the start of a beautiful relationship. Now all I need is your full name and address and your phone number so I know where to contact you just in case you forget about our little agreement. You'll need to come in Monday to sign a contract."

Mitt looked around the bar. He walked up to one of the businessmen at their table.

"You got a pen and piece of paper I can borrow?"

The man shrank back, then scrambled in his pockets for pen and paper.

"Thanks, pal."

Mitt returned to Bill.

"Oh… uh, please give me the correct info, Bill. Don't mean to be hard-headed about this, but Davey and me will find you if it ain't right."

Bill wrote his contact information.

"I'm working on a construction crew and can't come in till after four o'clock on Monday."

"No problem," Mitt said. "We'll see you then."

The two jerked their heads toward the heavy walnut door as it clattered and swung open. Three cops whose uniforms bore West Palm Beach Police insignia charged in with billy clubs, stopped, and surveyed the scene. One walked toward the bar, and the barmaid gestured toward Mitt and his new client.

"Oh, I might've known," said a beefy officer with sergeant's stripes on both sides of his collar.

He strode toward the table where Mitt, Davey, and Bill sat, the other cops following.

"So whose kneecaps did you break this time, Hecher?"

"Excuse me?" Mitt replied with sarcastic innocence.

"Listen punk, don't get cute with me." The sergeant glared.

The street-fighting karate expert appeared not the least intimidated by the hulking form that stood close to him like a Florida brown bear ready to attack.

"What's goin on here?" the cop said. "This guy doesn't look like he's feeling too good. You beat him up or somethin?"

"Well, as a matter of fact, we did have a little dustup. Bill didn't take too kindly to my talking to the broad… uh, the lady over there at the bar, and I kind of let him know that I didn't appreciate someone trying to deny my freedom of speech. He apparently saw it differently and took a swing at me, so I had to defend myself. Then these other guys who prob'ly know Bill came at me, and my buddy Davey—he's got a concealed weapon license, and he pulled pistols on them. And that was the end of that. Bill and I are getting along just fine now. Right, Bill?"

Bill glared at Mitt, who returned the look.

"Everything's okay, officer," Bill said after a moment of awkward silence.

"You sure you don't want to press charges?" the sergeant asked.

"Naw, what the heck. Let's just forget it."

"See? I'm not even offended that he used my name in vain," Hecher said with a broad, cocky smile.

"Oh, you're a barrel of laughs," said the sergeant, rocking on his feet with arms bent as though ready to grab the man he despised.

Hecher had earned a reputation for trouble. Police throughout the Palm Beaches had come to dread calls to bar brawls and other fights Hecher was involved in, and would send three officers to restrain him. They'd repeatedly charged him with resisting arrest, along with such crimes as assault, minor weapons and drug violations, shoplifting, and petty larceny.

"You got off lucky this time, Hecher," the sergeant warned, pointing a finger at the cops' nemesis. "But one of these days your luck is gonna run out. It always happens to rotten apples like you.

Sooner or later something's gonna happen that'll put you in the big house for a long, long time, and you'll think those little stints in the county jail were Bahamas vacations. Mark my words."

Chapter Four

"Who the hell is she?" the Great Dane asked, the mop of blond hair flipping onto his forehead as he jerked upright.

"That's Stella Star," said a short, scar-faced guy seated opposite at the round table covered with a light-blue oil cloth. "She's new."

The tall woman sidling sensuously onto the stage of the Shore Club wore a gossamer sarong offering a peek-a-boo at bejeweled patches covering her pubic area and nipples. Silver, spiked heels accented impeccable legs that reached to heaven.

During the previous two years, Rodger Kriger had seen a bevy of beauties parade nude at the seedy joint across the inlet from Palm Beach. But *this* one...

In her heels, she stood five-foot-nine. Her mane of hair, a dark auburn, framed features in a proportional balance that lent her a beauty Kriger found neither hard nor soft. She was no youngster, but her body was as firm as an eighteen-year-old's, and she had gradually assumed the seductive guile of maturity, like copper that changes from a bright shiny tone to a burnished brown. She reminded Kriger of Rita Hayworth in an old movie he'd seen on television about fifteen years earlier, circa 1960.

He watched transfixed as Stella performed her routine, strolling in front of the fifteen or so men of rough or unsavory aspect at tables and a back bar that stretched across the room. The Shore Club was a hang-out for petty hoodlums, some with connections to low-ranking Mafia figures. Kriger, a former attorney in Washington and now a forty-six-year-old franchise operator, was the most respectable-looking, in a sand-colored sport coat and navy-blue slacks. His six-foot-four stature and large-boned frame, coupled with his ancestry, had earned him the canine nickname at the strip joint.

After a couple of minutes, Stella flung the sarong to one side and sauntered some more before releasing a snap on the string holding the pieces over her nipples. Giving the slack-jawed males time to appreciate her firm, more-than-medium-sized breasts, she then tripped the snap holding her pubic covering, pulled the loose string between her legs, and took long, slow strides from one end of the stage to the other. Returning to midstage, she did a one-hundred-eighty-degree turn and, like a hula dancer, swayed her rounded derriere.

Kriger felt his pulse quicken and swallowed the saliva that was forming around his lips. He grew hard between the legs. Stella pranced to the side of the stage, picked up a handkerchief, and walked mincingly, dabbing her face, then dropped the hankie as if by accident. Her backside facing the room, she slowly bent down to pick it up, looking back over her shoulder.

When other strippers bent to show their backsides, they would spread their legs and lock their knees in blatant displays of raw sex. Stella was different. She gracefully turned her knees to the right, forming an angle of thighs and lower legs, as she lowered herself. To Kriger, she was much more beguiling. Then she rose, walked in a circle, and lay face up on the stage, arching her back and running her hands over her writhing body. That was her finale, and she picked herself up and strolled off the stage, waving her hankie.

The men applauded and whistled, then began talking among themselves while a few paid their tabs and readied to leave. Kriger walked to the left side of the stage and opened a door that led up a short stairs to stage level and a small, open dressing room. He approached the room and saw Stella getting into her street clothes.

"Hey, how'd you get in here?" Her tone indicated surprise, but only mild offense. She appraised the Great Dane like a livestock judge at a state fair, her eyes moving up and down, taking in his smart attire, and stopping at his oxblood Gucci shoes. Looking up without raising her head, she broke into a coquettish smile. Kriger knew he'd won the blue ribbon.

"Oh, I just walked right by the manager," the Dane boasted. "He knows who I am and isn't about to bother me."

"Oh, do tell," Stella mocked. "And just who might you be?"

"Well now, why don't you put some lipstick on and I'll tell you over dinner? We'll run up to the Ocean Breeze in Jupiter."

"The Ocean Breeze! I've heard of that place. It's supposed to be really fancy."

"You didn't think I'd take a beautiful creature like you to a dive, did you?"

"Okay, big spender. Let's go."

"While you're freshening up, I need to make a quick phone call."

"I'm sure you do. I saw that gold ring on your finger."

"Hey, we're just having dinner."

"Sure, of course, that's all," Stella said coyly.

Kriger walked to the phone booth next to the men's room to the right side of the stage.

"Hi, Jan. Listen, that board meeting ran a little long and just broke up. I need to get together with a few of the members to discuss some things in private, so I might be getting home quite late. Don't stay up for me. I'll probably sleep in because I don't have anything scheduled with the business till afternoon. What? Oh sure, I'll help tuck the kids in tomorrow night. You know I do when I'm home. I'll see you all tomorrow. Yeah, love you, too. Night."

"I've got my car here, so I'll have to drop it off at my apartment first," Stella said. "And I've got to change into something nice. I can't go to a fancy restaurant in these slacks."

Kriger, in his brand-new 1975 black Lincoln Continental, followed Stella driving her 1968 blue Toyota Corolla over the Intracoastal Waterway and up U.S. 1 to a two-building complex near the Waterway in Lake Park. He followed her into a small, one-bedroom, modestly appointed apartment on the second floor, reached via a concrete staircase with a landing.

"Sit down." Stella gestured to a light-blue sofa. "I'll only be a minute."

Kriger did a quick check of the room and the kitchen for any hints of a boyfriend who could get him in trouble. Five minutes later, as he thumbed through a copy of *Cosmopolitan*, Stella emerged in a short black skirt and a lacy white blouse with a plunging neckline.

Kriger whistled. "Good thing we're heading up north. We're going to attract a lot of attention."

She smiled flirtatiously.

At the Ocean Breeze, Kriger ordered a Manhattan for Stella—her choice—and a glass of pinot noir for himself. He'd already had two drinks and was pacing himself for what he was sure would come after dinner—and to be sure he could come after dinner. He wasn't a spring chicken anymore, and his prowess was beginning to wane. She said she didn't eat much and selected a salad and small filet mignon, no potato. Kriger had eaten at home before the meeting but was hungry and ordered the same, with potatoes *au gratin*.

"So tell me all about yourself," Stella began.

"I'd rather hear about you. We can get to me later. What's your real name? I'm sure Stella Star is your stage name."

"Judy Gulkowski. Not too romantic, huh? Can't you just hear the guy announcing my act? And now let's hear it for the sexy, sensational Judy Gulkowski."

Kriger chuckled. "Yeah, I don't think that would work too well."

"Not much to tell. Grew up in Pittsburgh. Dad worked in the steel mills. Mom was supposed to take care of us five kids but she was usually too drunk to know what she was doin, so we were pretty much on our own. I just wanted to get out of the house as soon as I could. I stayed in school because I was cute and popular with the guys. I tried to get into modeling but they rejected me because I wasn't skinny enough."

"Yeah, I can understand that," Kriger said. "They want em with little tits and no ass. And you sure as hell don't qualify in either department. Otherwise we wouldn't be here."

"Oh, so you just want me for my body," Stella pouted.

"Aw, c'mon now, I was giving you a compliment."

"I'm just teasing."

"Yeah, as in strip tease." Kriger cackled.

"Very funny."

"So anyway, I took a boring job as a sales clerk in a lingerie shop. Then I saw an ad for a dancer on the same page where the shop was advertising. I went for an interview and found out it was for a strip tease dancer. I told the guy I'd have to think about that first, and tried doing it in front of the big mirror on the living room wall in my apartment. I realized I was pretty good at it and decided to give it a try.

"After a couple of years, the place closed and I figured Florida might be a good place to find work, what with all the guys down here on conventions, away from their wives. It's not turned out as good as I'd hoped. These strip clubs are run by pretty mean characters. They're kinda scary."

"Yeah, they're all bums." Kriger was about to say they didn't have the brains to make a legitimate living, but stopped himself, realizing Stella might take that personally. "They don't bother me."

"Now tell me about yourself," she said.

"Let's see." Kriger stroked his chin. "I was born in a log cabin."

Stella looked amazed. "You were? Where?"

"Upper Michigan Peninsula. My God, it was cold in the winter. We'd cover ourselves with fur blankets at night, but it got so cold our breath would freeze and we'd find little clouds of frozen breath on our pillows in the morning."

"Oh, that must have been awful," Stella said, wrapping her arms around herself as if to keep warm.

Kriger leaned back and let out a big horselaugh, prompting the few diners remaining at this late hour to turn and look.

"You..." Stella sputtered, and leaned over to poke him playfully in the ribs.

Their dinner arrived, and as they ate, Kriger related how he'd grown up in the Los Angeles area in a strict Catholic family, played football in high school, and completed law school at the University of Southern California. He decided to skip any mention of Jan, whom he met as an undergrad at the university. They married after she graduated and he completed one year of law school, and she worked to help pay the rest of his way through school. He figured that could be a touchy issue because of the sacrifice she'd made for him. He didn't know what Stella's reaction might be. Better to be discreet.

So he just told her about landing a job with the legal department of Land O' Gocean, a household name in restaurants. The chain of 8,200 mid-priced steak-and-seafood restaurants, spread throughout North, Central, and South America, was headquartered in Baltimore, with its legal entity located in Washington, D.C. While working there, he frequently rubbed shoulders with government officials and members of Congress. After eight years, he began acquiring franchises of the chain, and soon was too busy to continue working as an attorney.

"I saw an opportunity to open a bunch of franchises in South Florida, so we moved to Palm Beach a few years later." Kriger avoided mentioning that "we" included three children he and Jan had produced in ten years. But Stella would not let him off so easily.

"And who were 'we'?" she asked with a teasing smile.

"Aw c'mon, we want to talk about us, not about my family." Kriger's tone hinted of pique. In fact, three more children had been added since their arrival in Palm Beach.

"It's okay," she said. "I was just curious."

"I sold my franchises in the D.C. area and bought a slew of Land O' Gocean stores in Palm Beach and Martin counties. Got involved in local Republican government groups, some civic and business organizations, that sort of thing. Now I'm a big shot around here." Kriger broke into a haughty grin that covered most of his face.

While waiting for and paying the check, he talked about how the area had grown since he'd arrived eight years earlier, and various projects that planning officials foresaw in the coming years.

"How do you know all this stuff?" Stella asked.

"I'm a member of the Development Council of Palm Beach County." Kriger again flashed that imperious smile. "I told you I was important around here."

"Well well, I guess so," Stella said, leaning back from him and tilting her head in appraisal. "Okay, mister big shot, what's next?"

"Oh, I don't know." Kriger rubbed his chin and furrowed his brow. "Tell you what. We're not far from the Jupiter Hilton. Why don't we go and get a room where we can be alone and have a couple of drinks and get to know each other a little better?"

"A *little* better?" she asked with a mischievous grin. "Are you sure you don't mean a lot better?"

"*Moi?*" asked Kriger, spreading his arms in mock innocence. He laughed in a fiendish way. "Come on, beautiful, let's go."

The grounds of the Jupiter Beach Resort and Spa were lit well enough to reveal lush landscaping adorned with flower beds and palms that spelled tropical. In the luxuriously appointed lobby, Kriger checked them in as Rodger and Jan Kriger. He asked for a view of the ocean and was given a room on the eighth floor.

He laid his sport coat on the back of a chair, its dark wood matching the other furniture, while she dropped her faux-silk black purse on the seat. He opened the curtains to a sweep of the Atlantic coast twenty miles in both directions and the ocean beyond. Distant lights on the streets and bridges and a dim glow from an occasional boat a few miles offshore signified denizens of the night.

"Oh, my God!" Stella's eyes popped. "I've never been in a hotel like this."

Kriger flipped the lock on the sliding glass panel that opened to the patio. They walked out, and the balmy ocean breezes caressed their faces. He turned, and she allowed his long, strong arms to envelop her. They kissed passionately, and he led her inside.

Sex with Jan had become cold and unfulfilling. Now he was more sexually excited than he could ever remember. For a half hour,

Kriger indulged in erotic abandonment that left him sated. They showered.

"I wish I could spend all night with you." Kriger hunched his shoulders and held his palms up. "But you know my situation."

"Okay, family man. I understand."

Chapter Five

"Yo, Davey, what's up, buddy? You sound a little groggy."

"Yeah, I was snoozin." Davey cradled the phone on his shoulder. "Too much booze last night. Couldn't sleep too good."

"I've been thinkin. The big guy I beat up at the Unicorn—Bill. Remember?"

"Pretty hard to forget. A coupla guys looked like they was gonna jump you. Thought I might hafta do some shootin."

"Bill's been coming regularly to the studio. After the beating he took from me, he wanted to learn how to defend himself better. So that experiment turned out pretty good. That's a helluva good way to get students. We go to bars and I beat the crap out of guys, and they come to my studio to learn how to defend themselves. I give them a discount from the regular price, like I did Bill, and cut you in, since I need you to keep the customers in line with your hardware. You ready for another fun-filled night?"

"Why not? Let's go for it."

"We need to go to joints where babes hang out, cuz guys are more likely to want karate lessons if they get humiliated when they're trying to pick up a gal. I've been in Spanky's over in Northwood a couple times, and there's quite a few broads. I think a lot of them work in downtown West Palm and go there for happy hour. And then some stay and eat the bar food and party for a while. What say we go there tonight?"

"Okay. I know the place."

"We'd better take our own cars so you don't have to figure out what to do with mine in case the cops pick me up. We can meet at, say, nine."

"I hear ya. I'll meetcha out front."

Only two parking spaces were open when Hecher pulled into the lot for Spanky's on the near north side of West Palm Beach. Davey Ross stood near the entrance, smoking a cigarette.

"We'll just play it cool," Hecher advised, as Ross mashed his cigarette on the sidewalk.

The two men scanned the room, a large rectangle with a bar running along the left side and square tables set eight feet away. The patternless angles of the tables' positioning afforded ample spaces between for waitresses to move.

"Follow me," Hecher said. "There's two empty places at the bar next to the guy making it with that young thing. She looks like she wants to eat him alive."

Hecher led the way, surveying the patrons, looking innocent. A few feet from the empty spots, he stopped and stared at a table.

"Whatsa matter?" asked Ross.

"Get a load of that babe."

"Which one?"

"Which one?" Hecher sounded incredulous. "You don't know who I'm talkin about? Geez, man, the blonde. Who else?"

"Oh, yeah, I see who ya mean."

"Look, sorry about this, but our plans just changed. We're going over there. I'll hit on her and you can work on her girlfriend. She's cute, too. Long locks. Brunette. Her drapes match your carpet. You could get all tangled up in those."

"She ain't bad."

"Wait here."

Hecher meandered between the tables to the two young women.

"Hello, ladies." He affected a serious look. "I was walking by and noticed something quite alarming."

The two frowned and looked up at him quizzically.

"What are you talking about?" asked the blonde.

"Your glasses are getting close to empty, and if they aren't replenished, you might leave. And suddenly this place would lose its beauty and class."

The women's faces instantly broke into sheepish grins and turned pink. They looked at each other with heads lowered, chuckling.

"You're a real charmer, aren't you?" the blonde teased. "Or should I say BSer?"

"Now, ma'am, look at me." Hecher spread his arms wide and looked down at his body. "The picture of innocence. How could you suspect anything but the purest of intentions?"

Both women giggled.

"I can't let you leave. I'm Mitt."

"I'm Diane," said the blonde.

"I'm Cindy."

"Tell me what you're drinking, ladies."

"I'm having a strawberry daiquiri and she's drinking a vodka-and-tonic."

"Now you two stay right there, and my buddy Davey and I will be right back with the libations."

Both men's looks appealed to women in different ways. Mitt had a full head of thick, dark hair that complemented a southern-Italian olive complexion. Graceful contours softened otherwise prominent cheekbones. His nose hinted of a pug shape that tended toward those of battered white prize fighters, but not enough to detract from his good looks.

Davey was in solid physical shape and had chiseled good looks, the face descending from straight brown hair in a symmetry of lines and curves that culminated in a square jaw.

The two women smiled as Hecher ambled up to the bar, where Ross joined him. Hecher ordered Millers for himself and his cohort, and the drinks, and paid the tab. He handed the vodka to Ross.

"This is for Cindy. Let's go."

Diane and Cindy sat at right angles to each other, looking toward the bar. Hecher sat next to Diane, and Ross next to Cindy. The women thanked them for the drinks.

"So let's see," Hecher began. "You both work downtown and put in long hours. You came here to catch the end of the happy hour, and stayed for a bite to eat so you wouldn't have to cook."

"Wow," Diane said. "You must be clairvoyant. You got it exactly right. We work at the same place and didn't get out until six o'clock tonight. We needed to relax and were too tired to cook. Are you a psychic?"

"Did you say psychic or psychotic?" Davey chimed in, letting out a guttural laugh.

"That, too," Hecher said, straight-faced. "But I don't demonstrate my talent in that area in polite company."

The women laughed.

"What do you ladies do?" he asked.

"We're with a big security company," Diane said. "I'm in human resources and Cindy's in accounting."

"You make me jealous," Ross said to Cindy. "I ain't too good with numbers."

"You ain't too good with English, either," Hecher rejoined.

"Geez, how'd you figure that out?" Ross parried.

"I'm psychic. Or is it psychotic?"

"Touché, wise guy."

Both men took a swig of beer while the women eyed them cautiously.

"You guys seem to know each other pretty well," Cindy said.

"Yeah, he smarts off too much and I tell him to go to hell, and he does the same to me," Ross snorted. "Only thing is, he's a karate expert and he can beat the crap outa me. Unless I pistol-whip him first."

"Pistol?" Cindy remarked, looking startled.

"He's just joking," Hecher quickly interjected. "Davey is a marksman. He competes in shooting contests. Practices at the range a lot."

"And what do you guys do?" Diane asked.

Ross looked at his watch.

"Uh-oh. I gotta get goin. That plane lands in about a half-hour. I hate to leave this party, but I have to pick my brother up at the airport. He's comin in from California for a week."

"That's right," Hecher said. "I forgot."

"I'd better use the restroom before I go." Ross gulped down part of the beer remaining in his glass and rose. "Pleasure talking with you lovely ladies."

"We enjoyed it," Diane said.

Ross looked around the room, then headed for the corner.

"I really shouldn't stay any longer, either," Cindy decided. "I have a load of laundry to fold and put away, and I should do some ironing."

"Something I said?" Hecher joked.

"No, of course not. I've enjoyed the company of you and your friend. Maybe we'll see you two again. See you tomorrow, Diane."

"Okay, Cindy. Drive safely. This was our third drink."

"Yes, but we spread them out over several hours. I feel fine."

She walked to the door in her high heels with no apparent difficulty. Hecher watched Diane as her eyes followed her friend. He thought Diane bore a remarkable resemblance to the actress Tuesday

Weld, whose looks strongly attracted him. She had the same cascading golden tresses, though her face was a little broader and softer, less pert, the mouth a bit wider. She wore almost no makeup, exposing smooth skin with only two or three light blemishes. It must have mostly escaped the teenage pimple onslaught, he mused.

"So," she said, turning to Hecher. "Hello?"

"Oh, sorry. I didn't mean to stare. You caught me daydreaming."

"That's bad. You're not supposed to do that at night."

"I know. I guess it's something you don't plan."

"Now, where were we?" Diane resumed. "I was asking what kind of work you and your friend do."

"Davey kind of hinted at what I do. I own a karate studio. I teach karate classes, and if they can afford it, I give individual instruction."

"Oh, my. I knew you either worked out a lot or were in some kind of work that made you lean and strong. I thought maybe you had been in the service and were a drill instructor or something like that. Were you in Vietnam?"

"No. They don't take... uh, I mean, I had a high school football injury, a torn Achilles tendon that never healed right. You'd be surprised how they reject you for things like that. Even though it doesn't bother me much when I do karate."

"How did you get so good at karate?"

"I've been studying karate since I was a kid. Kids were always beating up on me because I was little, so I took karate and then I beat them up. But I want to talk about you, not me. Where'd you grow up?"

"There's not much to tell. I've had a pretty boring life. I was born and raised around here. Got two sisters, both still in South Florida, and a brother who's a senior at Florida State. Dad is a building inspector for the county, getting ready to retire, and Mom works in a doctor's office. I went two years to Florida State—wanted to become a teacher—but the bills were piling up, and I had to quit to take a job. I just never went back."

"Ever been married?"

"No. I went with a guy for two years after college. He got drafted and sent to Vietnam. When Ken came back, he wasn't the same person. He couldn't sit still. He was tense all the time. Loud noises made him jumpy, and he'd break out into sweats. He got angry real easy. He'd get violent and break things. I'd try to console him, but nothing worked. He lost his job and wouldn't leave his apartment. I finally had to give up. Try as I might, I couldn't help him. Last time I saw him was at an intersection west of town. He was homeless, holding a sign for food. It broke my heart."

"Oh, wow. I'm sorry."

"Excuse me. I need to use the rest room."

Hecher watched as her hips swayed the rounded bottom delineated by her close-fitting beige skirt. He noticed guys at the bar and tables turning their heads to look.

Would that make me jealous if I were dating her? He knew a lot of guys would, indeed, be jealous, and reflected on how that was ridiculous. They should be proud other men admired their gal, he reasoned. Jealousy didn't show their affection, only their fear of competition.

Diane returned with a fresh layer of lipstick and facial makeup. Her eyes were red, and Hecher knew she had been crying.

"You feeling okay?"

"Sure, I'm all right. I just got a little upset remembering how helpless I was to save Ken. I'll be fine."

"Can I get you another daiquiri?"

"No, thanks. What time is it?" She looked at her watch. "Oh, goodness. It's ten-thirty. I have to get going. I have another long day ahead tomorrow."

"I hope you're going to give me your phone number."

"Okay. I think I have a pen." She reached into her purse. "Yes. Here's an old business card I can write it on the back of." She jotted down Diane Berglund and her phone number.

"Berglund? What kind of name is that?"

"Finnish. My mother was Scottish. You must be Italian."

"Why do you say that?"

"You look Italian. Kind of swarthy. I think we look good together, don't you? Me being fair and you darker."

"Hmm. I guess so. All I know is, I think you're gorgeous."

"Oh now, come on," she said, her eyes downcast.

"Let me walk you to your car."

They reached her 1972 Plymouth, and she unlocked the door. Hecher put his hands on her shoulders and leaned in to kiss her. His lips met hers, and he wanted to linger, but she pulled away after a couple of seconds, smiling demurely.

"Night," she said, climbing in the car. "I had a good time."

"Me too."

Hecher closed the door.

———————————

"Man, I thought I'd never hear from you," Davey lamented, holding the phone in his lap as he propped his feet up on the coffee table. "That was like five days ago we was with them broads at Spanky's. I thought you'da called me the next day and tell me you fucked that gal's brains out. You was gettin it on with her."

"Nah," said Hecher. "She's a working girl—puts in a lota hours. She had to get up pretty early the next day."

"So you didn't get laid."

"No, but I got her phone number. Next time."

"You're slippin, Mittster."

"What can I say? Maybe I'm gettin old."

"Yeah. Thirty-one. You're over the hill. How old is she?"

"I'd say maybe twenty-nine."

"Well, I can't blame you for goin after her."

"Why did you take off?"

"The brunette didn't fire my gonads. I like em kinda raunchy. Know what I mean?"

"You ready for another adventure?"

"You mean like the one we was supposed to have at Spanky's?"

"Yeah. Only this time I'm not going to let any women sidetrack me."

"Got any place in mind?"

"How bout the Stop Inn on Military Trail, near the airport?"

"That should work. Hell, that place has my kinda women."

"Nope. No interruptions this time. Strictly business."

"I hear ya. When you wanna meet?"

"Tonight. I figure ten-thirty is good. These are night-lifers."

"See ya there."

Guys in jeans, T-shirts, and boots stood or sat at the bar, most with draft beers. They appeared to be men who worked with their hands: jobs such as construction and auto repair. A half-dozen or so better-dressed men, possibly clerical or sales types, sat at glass-topped wooden tables, talking over cocktails.

For every three men, there was one woman. They wore slacks or jeans, low-cut blouses or sweaters, and a couple of halter tops, and varied from trim to overweight to just plain fat. The age range of everyone was early twenties to late thirties. Two young men and a woman played pool in a back room set apart by a half-wall projecting three feet, on which the pool players rested their beers.

At the bar sat a stocky fellow in a navy-blue polo shirt with yellow horizontal stripes, and gray khaki pants, who appeared to be about twenty-five. He wore his dark hair in an unfashionable crew cut and had the light-brown complexion of a Hispanic. He chatted and laughed with a petite woman who wore a skirt that reached below the knees, and plain three-inch heels. Her expressions were soft, evoking kindness, and his happy expression showed affection.

Hecher and Ross strode up to the pair and sat at the two empty stools to the man's left. He was an inch taller than Hecher and much heftier. Before the short, young bartender could come to take their order, Hecher jammed his right foot down on the guy's left toes.

"Ow!" he yelled, whipping his head around at Hecher. "What the hell are you doing?"

"What d'ya mean, me? You tried to push me away, you son-of-a-bitch. I got as much right to sit here as you do."

"Huh? What are you talkin about? You stomped on my foot."

"No I didn't. You kicked me."

"Why, you lyin bastard," the guy growled, turning toward Hecher, who jumped off the stool.

"What are you gonna do about it?" Hecher challenged.

"Oh, so you want to fight, huh?" the guy said as he got off the stool.

"Come and get me," Hecher dared.

The guy lowered his head and charged. Hecher lashed out with two jabs, a left and a right, to the man's face. He staggered. Blood streaked his face next to his nose, where a gash had opened. He held his fists up to protect himself and moved cautiously toward Hecher, then swung in a wide arc at his opponent's head. Hecher ducked and delivered a powerful blow to the man's solar plexus, which caused him to hold his midsection and gasp for air.

Hecher moved behind his opponent and placed his left arm around the man's neck. He leaned close.

"Give it up. You don't want to get hurt anymore. You don't stand a chance against me. I'm a karate expert. Let me help you to a table and I'll buy you a beer."

While the guy coughed, Hecher nudged him toward a table.

"Sit down."

Ross had backed away from the bar, his arms crossing his chest and his hands gripping the handles of the holstered pistols under his jacket. But the fight happened so fast that nobody knew who was at fault. Several men came forward, but it was over before anyone had time to interfere. They gawked as Hecher and his victim sat, then returned to their activities. The woman of the victim's attentions slid off the bar stool and left, looking down and away from her former bar mate.

"Whatcha drinkin?" Hecher asked.

"Bud."

"Davey, here's a couple bucks. Get us a horse piss and a Pabst, if they got it, otherwise a Miller, will ya? Drafts. And whatever you want."

He turned to his vanquished table mate.

"Feeling better?"

"Yeah—asshole."

Hecher chuckled.

"You've got spunk. That's good. It'll help in the proposition I'm going to make. My name's Mitt. What's yours?"

He glanced at Hecher with a look both baleful and doubtful.

"Raúl."

Ross arrived with the beers, sat next to Raúl, and looked out at the room.

"So here you are, having a nice conversation with a pretty girl, about ready to close the deal with her, and then a jerk like me comes along and shows her you can't handle yourself. And what's she thinkin? If that guy can't take care of himself, how can he take care of me? What a chump you must feel like. If I were you, I'd be thinkin, I'm never gonna let that happen again. And I can help you make sure it doesn't."

Raúl's look softened, and revealed slight interest.

"In six to eight months, depending on how intensely you practice, I can have you skilled enough at karate to handle all but the biggest guys and the best fighters. You're already damned stout. Cuz stuff like this happens in bars, and you have to be ready for it."

Raúl gulped long on his Bud and wiped his mouth with the back of his hand.

"What've you got in mind?"

"What do you for a living?" Hecher asked.

"Bulldozer operator."

"Then you're no stranger to taking classes. You had to go to heavy-equipment school. I own Hecher Karate in downtown West Palm Beach. Take my classes three times a week, and before long you'll be able to defend yourself against just about anybody."

Raúl grunted and looked thoughtful.

"You got a card?"

"Yes, but if you don't decide now, you probably never will. I'm going to make it easier for you. I've got a contract in my wallet. Sign it and give me a small deposit, and I'll give you a fifteen percent discount—for an entire year. That should make up for the beating I gave you. All I ask is that you keep quiet about it because I don't want the regular paying customers to get upset."

"For a whole year?"

"Yeah, but you only have to sign up for six months now. If you want to renew after that, the discount will still be good for another six months."

Raúl ran a hand through his hair for several seconds.

"You think I can learn to fight pretty good?"

"Hell, yes. Strong guy like you. You're bulky, but you move fast enough."

"Okay, I'll do it. How much deposit you need?"

"You got a twenty?"

"Yeah, that's no problem," said Raúl, pulling a bill out of his wallet. "Can I start late Tuesday afternoon, say, four-thirty?"

"That'd be good. Tuesday, Thursday, and Saturday."

"I can do that."

Hecher withdrew the contract, and Ross handed him a pen. Raúl and Hecher filled it out, and Hecher said he'd provide a copy to Raúl on Tuesday.

"You're going to be glad you did this, Raúl." Hecher extended a hand.

Raúl hesitated, then shook it without squeezing while averting his eyes.

———————

Hecher returned to his apartment from the studio, made himself a ham-and-cheese sandwich, and plopped down in front of the TV. His mind wandered to Diane.

"Shit, I've got to get laid," he babbled aloud. He went to his desk and opened the lid of the plastic box where he kept business cards and personal phone numbers. He dialed.

"Hello, Diane. This is Mitt. Mitt Hecher."

"Oh. You mean from Spanky's. You never did tell me your last name."

"Didn't I? I guess not. Well, at least you remembered me."

"Yes, but it's been only a week. I haven't exactly been a social butterfly since then. Too busy working."

"Well, then, maybe you've got a place in your calendar for me."

"Oh, I think that might be a possibility."

Hecher could see her coy smile.

"How about I pick you up after work Friday and take you to Mama Gilda's for the happy hour, and then we'll have dinner?".

"Oh, I love Mama Gilda's. She makes the best Italian food. And of course it's only a few blocks north of where I work, which is good, because I probably won't get out of work until six o'clock. Is that okay with you?"

"Oh, for sure. Why don't you call me around four and let me know what time?"

"Sounds like a plan. I'm looking forward to it."

"Me too. Good night."

"Night."

They talked about her work and his karate students. He didn't tell her about how the young members of his classes worshipped him for his swagger, his defeats of much bigger opponents in bar brawls and street fights, and his defiance of the law. When happy hour ended, they left the bar and took a booth in the restaurant. She ordered the eggplant parmigiana and he the veal parmigiana, and they shared portions. They discussed how the area had changed over the years, with the construction of Interstate 95 uprooting homes and businesses during the eight or so years before it was completed in central Palm Beach County. And they noted the restaurants that survived all of this upheaval: this one on North Dixie, Fredrick's a few blocks up the street, Manero's and Okeechobee Steak House out west.

After dinner, they relaxed with a drink.

"My goodness, do you realize we've been here almost five hours?" Diane said, noticing her watch read eleven o'clock. "It's been a very long day. I think I need to wind it up."

Hecher stopped the waitress and asked for the tab.

"That was the absolute best eggplant parmigiana," Diane raved. "So tender, and the tomato sauce was so fresh and tangy."

"The only Italian food that compares with my mom's is Mama Gilda's," said Hecher, as the waitress returned with the tab.

He put money on the table, and they walked out the door. Diane stepped onto the sidewalk and into the path of a tall, portly, raw-boned man who appeared to be in his upper thirties. Several days' growth of beard covered his face. They collided.

"Hey, lady, watch where the hell yer goin," the guy snarled.

Hecher pulled her aside.

"You bullying son-of-a-bitch," he barked. "Apologize, or I'll flatten you."

"You?" the man said. "You ain't near big enough, you little shit."

Hecher went into the karate crouch.

"Mitt, no," Diane pleaded.

He moved in stealthily, then delivered, with lightning speed, a one-two combination to the guy's mouth and cheek. Blood covered his mouth.

"Mitt, please," Diane implored, louder.

The man swung with his right. Hecher caught his arm, thrust downward, and stepped behind him, pulling his arm back. Kicking the guy behind the knee, Hecher forced him to bend, then released his arm and landed a chop on the back of his neck, sending the guy face down onto the pavement.

"Stop!" Diane screamed, holding her face in her hands. "Mitt, stop it now!"

The guy lifted himself to his hands and knees and turned his head to look at Hecher.

"Follow us, you scumbag, and I'll give you the *coup de grâce*. And you don't want to find out what that is."

Hecher put his arm around Diane's waist.

"Sorry about that," he said, walking her to his car in the parking lot next to the restaurant. "I didn't mean to upset you."

They got in the car and Hecher drove off, heading for Diane's house in the Flamingo Park district.

"It's just that this violence is so unnecessary," she chided.

"But Diane, I couldn't let that guy get away with treating you like that. What kind of wimp would I be?"

"Do you think I would look at you as unmanly if you just took me away from that boor and let it pass? As good a fighter as you are? You don't have to prove anything to me or anybody else. If you have to beat up everybody who offends you, that's an unpleasant way to live."

"I guess I sort of have this code."

"You need to find another code."

"That's pretty hard to do."

"You should work at it."

"Okay, Reverend Berglund." Hecher smiled satirically.

"I don't mean to preach. And I know you were just looking out for me and defending my honor. I think that's wonderful and I like you for it. But I'd like you even more if you try to avoid fights like this. That would make you an even bigger man in my eyes."

He didn't respond, and they drove in silence the remaining few blocks to her home. It was a modest-sized, Spanish-styled bungalow in white stucco, set up on an embankment. He walked her to the door.

"Thanks for a wonderful evening," she said.

"Aren't you going to show me your cute house?"

"Well... okay. Just for a little while."

"Geez, you're quite the decorator," Hecher said, admiring wicker furniture draped with expensive-looking fabrics, *objets d'art* occupying niches throughout the combined living-dining room and the Florida room, and paintings adorning the walls.

"Come help me fix the drinks," she said, walking toward the kitchen. "What would you like? I have just about anything."

"I think maybe a rum and Coke, but hold the rum."

She laughed. "Really?"

"Yeah. I've had enough liquor for one night." He'd drunk a double scotch at happy hour and two Chiantis with dinner, and didn't want to jeopardize his performance prowess for what he knew would come later.

"I'm just going to have an iced tea, myself."

She took two glasses out of the cupboard. "Go ahead and put ice in these. It's in trays."

Hecher took her gently in his arms and leaned in close. He kissed her, softly at first, then twisting and turning his head. He'd gotten an erection and felt her getting weak. She pushed him away.

"Whew. Easy does it. I don't want you getting any ideas."

"Didn't you enjoy that?"

"That's not the point. I need to take it a little slower. Come on. Let's go sit down."

They took their drinks to the couch.

"So I was talking about your decorating talent," he resumed.

"I didn't acquire any of these things new," she said, waving a hand around. "I've gone—and still go—to auctions, flea markets, garage sales at nice homes, thrift stores…"

"You do that because you have to, or you want to?"

"Well, obviously I can't afford expensive furnishings. So if I want them, I have to dig around for deals on second-hand items. But I like doing it. It's a hobby."

"I sure like your taste. You know what else I like?"

"Tell me."

"Your body."

She looked at him demurely.

"But I'll bet your body is tense and taut from all of those hours hunched over a desk, batting at a typewriter, holding a phone to your ear. Why don't you let me massage your shoulders and soothe those muscles? Turn your back to me."

She complied, and he plied his hands over her neck and shoulders.

"Oh, that does feel good," she moaned.

He leaned over and kissed the back of her neck, then the side, and up to her earlobe. He sucked on it, pulled her head back onto his chest, and kissed the sides of her face. Her eyes closed and mouth fell open, and their lips came together in a wet, passionate kiss while his hands unbuttoned her blouse and massaged her bra-covered breasts.

He thrust his right hand under her skirt and up to her crotch, and began massaging.

She squeezed her thighs together and pulled her mouth away.

"No," she protested, breathing hard.

"What's the matter?"

"Not yet. Not on the first date."

"Oh, come on, Diane. This is 1975."

"I know. I'm a little behind the times. But I'm my own person. If you want me, you'll have to wait. I'm sorry."

"Well, if that's the way it is…"

He rose, and she walked him to the door. He turned and pecked her on the lips.

"Thank you for a wonderful evening," she said. "I guess the sound or silence of my telephone will tell me what you were after me for. I hope you do call. I like you—a lot."

Chapter Six

The Barracuda Bar on South Dixie was two-thirds full and bars with chattering patrons ran the full length of either side of the long rectangle. A plastic barracuda, dark green over silver, hung on the middle of the wall behind the south bar. On the north bar, directly across, a fish identical except for its blue top side faced the opposite direction, as though headed downstream. Their long, slender bodies enhanced the tavern's symmetry and order. But the sharp, fearsome teeth showing in their open mouths conveyed an uneasy sense that beneath this harmony lay the potential for bursts of discord.

Mitt Hecher and Davey Ross were bent on validating the message in those teeth. Hecher spotted a muscular, dark-haired young guy only a little bigger than himself, sitting at the south bar. He had his arm draped around the shoulders of a pretty woman wearing a red blouse that exposed her well-formed shoulders, and a tight skirt with slits.

"Perfect," Hecher said to Ross. "Let's go."

They moseyed up to the pair. Hecher slapped a hand on the man's shoulder.

"Hey, pal, what're you doin messin with my girlfriend?"

The guy whirled. "Huh? This your girlfriend?"

"Damn right it is, and I ain't too happy."

The man went back to the woman while Hecher folded his arms and turned his head, looking toward the north bar at nothing in particular.

"Is that guy your boyfriend?" the man asked the woman.

"Are you kidding me? I've never seen him before in my life. I haven't got a boyfriend."

The guy turned to Hecher.

"Hey, jerk, she doesn't know you."

Hecher had unfolded his arms and stared with intense interest at a spot at the opposite bar. He didn't move.

"Hey, asshole, what're you lookin at? You better face me or I'm gonna cold-cock you, and I don't like to fight dirty."

A blonde at the bar where Hecher was looking turned her head sideways, and Hecher mumbled.

"Oh, no, that's not her."

"What the hell's the matter with you, dipshit?" the guy said. "Quit talkin to yourself and face me like a man, cuz I'm gonna beat the shit outa you."

"Huh? Oh, sorry buddy. I made a mistake. I thought that was my girlfriend you were talking to. Let's forget it, okay?"

"Forget it, my ass. I ain't gonna let you off that easy, punk."

"Look, let's go outside and settle it, okay?"

"Good by me." He headed for the door.

"What are you doin?" Ross asked, moving close behind Hecher.

"I got a sudden attack of nausea. Must be something I ate. I'm not up to this. I'll just try to cool this dude off." Hecher talked over his shoulder, his eye catching the outward-facing barracuda, which seemed to be smiling.

They reached the paved entryway, and Ross stepped aside.

"This guy gonna interfere?" the man asked.

"No, I fight my own battles. But I don't want to fight. Let's just forget this happened. How about it?"

"Fuck, no. I didn't like your smart-ass attitude in there."

The guy lashed out at Hecher's face with his right fist. Hecher blocked the blow, locked the man's arm, and shoved it into his windpipe, holding it in place. He gasped and struggled. After several seconds, Hecher let up the pressure.

"Now, as you might have noticed, I'm a karate expert. I could hurt you real bad, but I don't want to. So why don't you just go back to that broad and tell her you made me promise to be a good boy from now on, and you can continue where you left off?"

He released his hold, and the man breathed hard and held his neck in both hands.

"Before you leave, let me give you my card." Hecher pulled out his wallet and a business card.

"Mitt Hecher, Hecher Karate," he read. "Let me have a pen, Davey."

Ross produced a pen from his coat pocket, and Hecher wrote, "15% off, good for 1 year. MH." He handed it to the guy.

"I did you a favor tonight. I was gonna make you look bad in front of the gal. And there's guys who'll do that. So you need to know how to protect yourself. I can sure as hell show you how. Think about it, and come on in."

The guy studied the card for a few seconds and put it in his shirt pocket.

"Maybe," he muttered, looking sideways at Hecher, and walked into the bar.

"Geez," Ross sighed. "You're goin soft, Mittster."

"Nah, my stomach's kinda upset. I'm just not in the mood. I figure what the fuck, let the dude make it with the bitch. Ten to one he still makes it to the studio. He'll just be less pissed off at me. Come on, let's get outa here."

Hecher drove home, fixed some peanut butter and crackers, and watched the late news. Then he went to bed. But he couldn't fall asleep. The tavern scene played over and over in his mind. It was uncanny how much the blonde at the bar across from where he was standing resembled Diane Berglund. Then, when she looked at the woman next to her, he saw it wasn't her, but someone less attractive. Even so, he'd felt her presence, and couldn't focus on his mission. And he'd lost his desire to humiliate his victim. It seemed odd—like becoming impotent. What was happening to him? Was he turning into an old man? Finally, a restless sleep overcame him.

At the studio the next day, the back view of the blonde at the bar popped into his head now and then as he conducted the karate classes. When she turned her head, he began to see Diane's face.

He felt tired that evening from sleep deprivation, and ordered Chinese take-out. Dinner over, he went to his phone file.

"Diane?"

"Who's this? Mitt?"

"Yeah. How's it goin?

"Just hunky-dory. I didn't know whether to expect a call from you, or not."

"Well, I... here I am."

"How's your week going?"

"Oh, pretty good. I was wondering if you wanted to do something this weekend."

"Well, since you took me out to dinner last time, why don't I have you over for dinner. I probably can't measure up to your mother's Italian cooking, but if you'll settle for some plain old American food, I'd love to have a go at it. Maybe I could do a German dish. I have a couple in mind."

"Oh, that'd be great. I get tired of Italian all the time."

"Terrific. How about Saturday night, around seven."

"Sounds good. See you then."

He greeted her with a bottle of semidry red Riesling, which a liquor store salesman had advised for German food.

"Thank you. That's sweet of you."

"Actually, it's dry."

"I like your dry humor."

"Oh, one-upping me, huh? A woman with wit."

"My goodness. So full of alliteration. I learned that word in... well, English lit."

"But I'm not lit-erate about wine," Hecher said, dragging out *literate*. "The store guy had to advise me."

"The Riesling should go well with the sauerbraten. Come help me make Manhattans. I hope you like that drink?"

"Haven't had it in ages. I love it."

In two glasses, they poured Canadian whiskey, sweet vermouth, and bitters, stirred, added ice, and dropped in orange slices and maraschino cherries. They took their drinks to the couch.

"Delicious," Hecher said.

Diane took a serving bowl of Caesar salad out of the fridge while they made small talk. Using long wooden spoons, she lifted it into salad bowls. They sat at opposite ends of the small cherry-wood table.

"Diane, you are a gourmet cook. This is wonderful."

"Come on now. You're exaggerating."

"I'm not. It's scrumptious."

"So where do you get your karate students?" Diane asked. "Is it just word of mouth? Do they just come to you, or do you do some sales work to bring them in?"

"Both. Davey and I go to bars and shoot the bull with guys. Sometimes they ask me to go outside and show em a couple of holds, just to prove I'm legit."

"Bars can get rowdy. I'll bet you've proved you're legit without going outside—probably more than once."

"I thought you said you were Finnish, not Deutsch. That sauerbraten is out of this world. What a feast."

"You're going to give me a swelled head. But you haven't answered my question."

"Was that a question? It sounded like a statement of fact."

"I guess it was. One that begged a response."

Hecher kept his head lowered and his eyes focused on his plate.

"Yeah, I'll admit I've been in a few scrapes."

"I hope you'll put that behind you and fight only when you don't have a choice. I don't want to see you get hurt. Now, how about some dessert?"

"Oh, lordie. What kind of spoiled black belt are you turning me into? I could get fat and lazy, and sluggish, and then how would I do leaps and kicks, and keep a step ahead of my opponents?"

Diane went into the kitchen while Hecher sipped the Riesling. She returned with two dishes of warm cinnamon apple dumpling à la mode. Hecher continually shook his head while making "mmm" sounds as he wolfed down the dessert, abandoning decorum.

"Oh, wow, that was heavenly. Let me help you with the dishes."

"No, no. I'll just run hot water over them and let them soak."

"Let's relax on the couch," he said. "The only thing more divine than that food will be putting my arms around you."

"You are a bad boy, aren't you? Let me use the bathroom first. You can use the spare one across the hall."

Hecher returned and waited on the couch. Diane came back wearing fresh lipstick, and Hecher got a whiff of sweet perfume, which always was a strong turn-on for him. He felt an overwhelming desire for her, driven by a consuming warmth that surged through him, something he'd never experienced before.

Embracing her supple body, he passionately kissed her on and in the mouth, the neck, and all over her upper body as he pulled her shift away, revealing a skimpy black bra holding delicate breasts. Unclasping the bra, he sucked on her nipples and ran his right hand under the loosely held-together shift to her bikini panties. Then he loosened the remaining buttons of the shift, lifted her arms out, and carried her without exertion to her bedroom, where he laid her on the queen-sized bed.

He tore at the buttons on his shirt and threw it on a chair.

"Wait," she said. "It's the wrong time of the month. You need to wear a condom."

"What? Oh, no," he protested. "That'll take so much of the feeling away. Besides, I don't have one."

"I do. I bought a few just in case this might happen. We can't take a chance."

"Geez, I suppose you're right."

She went to her bureau and pulled a Trojan out of a drawer.

"Be a good boy and put it on," she said, handing it to him.

He went to the bathroom, undressed, and rolled the prophylactic on. He put his J.C. Penney underpants back on and emerged.

Diane lay on her back. Hecher slipped her panties off, then removed his Penneys and lowered himself on her. He plied his tongue, teeth, and fingers over her entire body and into every orifice. Her breathing grew heavier, her body twisted, and she moaned. Sweat broke out over their bodies, heightening the sensuality as they slipped and slid across each other. Intermittent paroxysms of carnal sublimity evolved to a crescendo of ecstasy that culminated in a synchronized, orgasmic coda.

They'd been at it for forty-five minutes, and lay on their backs, exhausted.

"That was wonderful, Diane."

"Oh my goodness, yes. What a lover you are."

Hecher closed his eyes, and drifted off to sleep. Diane got up and turned the lights off in the living room and bedroom, pulled the blanket over Mitt, and crept in beside him.

They woke at dawn. Hecher nestled against Diane and kissed her on the cheek.

"Sleep good?" she asked.

"Like a bear in winter."

"So did I."

He positioned the pillow upright against the headboard, rolled onto his back, and propped himself up against the pillow.

"Diane, there's something I think I need to tell you."

"Uh-oh. You're married."

He laughed. "No, nothing like that. I have not exactly behaved like a choir boy. In fact, I've been in a fair amount of trouble."

"I know."

He jerked his head toward her.

"You know? How do you know?"

"Cindy told a friend at work about the night we met at Spanky's. The friend said you had quite a reputation for trouble with the law."

"You knew that and you still agreed to go out with me?"

"I didn't find out until after our dinner date, but of course I knew it before I invited you here."

"But why did you have me over? I don't understand."

"Because I look at people not for what they've been, but for what they are. I saw something good in you, something I liked."

Hecher stared at her open-mouthed.

"Hell, I don't know what to say."

"You don't have to say anything. Let's just move forward from here."

Chapter Seven

"Hi. Welcome to Land O' Gocean." The slender, young hostess beamed. "Are you having lunch?"

The man was in his late thirties, short with dark hair, a mustache, and a light olive complexion. He appeared to be Hispanic, probably Cuban.

"Rumba," he murmured, casting a furtive glance in either direction.

The smile evaporated from the hostess' face and she looked nonplussed. Then it hit her, and her smile returned.

"Oh, I'm sorry. I'm new here. I'm supposed to get the manager for you. Wait just a moment, please. Juan will be right here."

The patron stepped to the side of the hostess station. A man in a shirt and tie approached, his head lowered as he appeared to scrutinize the customer. They were about the same age but the manager was taller and his face had the same smooth, sallow skin and similar bone structure. He was well-built and had a grim look that suggested he was accustomed to dealing with belligerent people, perhaps as a bartender in a tough bar.

"May I help you?" he asked coldly.

"Rumba," the man said.

The two made eye contact for a second.

"Follow me."

The manager led the patron down an aisle past a row of booths, some unoccupied, to a door in a secluded corner of the restaurant. Pulling a set of keys out of his pocket, the manager unlocked the door. The two entered a small room, and the manager used a key to lock the door from the inside. Square tables identical to those inside the restaurant were arranged geometrically on one side, and cushioned chairs like those inside were lined against the perpendicular wall.

"Have a seat." The manager motioned to a chair. "What's your name?"

"Diego."

Part of a bar occupied the corner to the left of the door.

"I'm Juan," the manager said as he went behind it, ducked down, and made a shuffling noise. He rose and beckoned Diego to come.

"Keep your fingers crossed. But before you do, reach into your wallet and hand me twenty dollars, please."

Diego stared.

"*Veinte dólares.*"

"*Ah! Perdón,*" Diego said, smiling, as he pulled a bill from his wallet.

Juan bent down again and came up with a green canvas bag. He set it on the bar and leaned it toward Diego.

"Reach in and take one," he instructed, reverting to Spanish.

Diego withdrew a white ping-pong ball and inspected it.

"*Cincuenta y nueve no es mi número de la suerte.*"

"Oh, come on now," Juan responded, more friendly. "Fifty-nine is lucky as any number."

The manager reached under the bar a third time, and raised a chalkboard displaying the number forty-three in large figures. Diego looked at the board and nodded that he understood.

"Sorry. You win some and lose some. Better luck next time. Where do you live?"

"Delray Beach."

"Huh? You came all the way to Lantana to play bolita? Why didn't you go to the Land O' Gocean in southwest Boynton Beach? It's a lot closer for you."

"I didn't know about that one. Next time I go there. Same password?"

"Yes. Rumba."

"Okay. I'm going next week."

Juan let Diego out the door and returned to the bar in the corner. He reached down to a shelf, pulled a telephone onto the bar, and punched the keypad.

"Hey José," he said, continuing in Spanish, "I just sent a customer your way. He'll be there in a few days. I don't mean the restaurant—the back room. You doing much business?"

"Yeah. Word is getting around the Cuban community. The trouble is, I heard the word has reached Kriger."

"I was going to ask you about that. He came in two nights ago when I wasn't here and asked the hostess if she'd noticed any unusual activity. She didn't tell him about the password, but she said he seemed awfully suspicious."

"He came here, too, and talked to me, but I just told him I wasn't aware of anything wrong. He acted like he didn't believe me. I think we have a problem."

"Yeah," Juan concurred. "He's probably heard about what's going on."

"Carlos said he's been nosing around his operation in West Palm Beach, too," José added.

"Even Carlos? He's very careful. Oh man, the boss definitely is onto us." Juan paused. "So what do we do now?"

"Hmm." José went quiet for several seconds. "We might as well keep doing what we're doing. If the Dane is going to get rid of the management, he'll do it even if we stop the bolita. No way he's trusting us anymore. So let's take in as much as we can till the ax falls. Then…"

"What?"

"Kriger has always made life difficult for us. We got a couple friends who did time in Batista's rotten prisons, and they don't much like rich capitalistic bastards. You know who I'm talking about."

"Yeah, yeah. But where are you going with this?"

"Well, I'm sure they'd love to give Kriger a good scare. Maybe more. These guys are pretty rough."

"Umm… I don't know. That makes me a little uneasy. Why don't we just wait and see what happens? We'll keep up the operation, and decide later what if any action we need to take."

"I'm with you," José agreed. "Let's get together with Carlos. I think he'll like our plan."

"Okay. I have to get back up front now. I'll give you a call later and we'll set up a meeting with Carlos."

———————————

"Hey, Alberto, I got one," Kriger shouted. "He's a big sucker. I don't think this boat's going to hold him. He must be a whale."

"I coming!" Alberto answered from the bridge. He turned to his co-pilot. "Here, take wheel. I going down to help Rodger."

Alberto's navy-blue jacket matched the waters of the Atlantic. The stark contrast with his white chino slacks would have commanded attention if anyone were there, but in this vast, lonely expanse, fashion's statement was muted. As he descended the stairs in his Gucci deck shoes, only the sun seemed bedazzled as it smiled with equal brilliance on the slick, milky-white exterior of the luxury, eighty-three-foot Bertram and Alberto's slacks. Alberto hastened up to Kriger while pulling his Giorgio Armani sunglasses down from his forehead.

"Here. Give me rod. You go in fight chair, and I give rod back."

"Yeah, Alberto, good idea," Kriger grunted. He sat upright in a deck chair, pulling back on the rod. "I'm going to need a little extra support."

Alberto was at least a half-foot shorter than Kriger but rock solid. He firmly grasped the rod and reel from his friend and stood with legs apart, tilting backward, while the rod alternately bowed and slackened. Kriger sat in the fighting chair and fastened the belt around his waist.

"Okay, Alberto. I think I can handle it now."

The Cuban handed the rod back to the Great Dane. He barely had taken control when it straightened and the line streamed out against the drag on the reel. The pull nonetheless became so strong that Kriger struggled to keep his grip. The fish leaped out of the water and crashed again below the surface.

"Whew," Kriger gasped. "I almost lost the rod. What do you think that baby is?"

"Look like blue marlin to me," Alberto shouted. "I wish Jorge and Miguel here. They help bring fish in boat. He look ten, maybe twelve feet."

The fish surfaced again and thrashed its bill from side to side, and Kriger planted his feet farther ahead to gain leverage. Just as suddenly the tension slackened. But Kriger didn't relax, realizing this was a wily fish accustomed to dealing with predators in its neighborhood. The battle for its life might not have been its first against a member of the land species.

"Have the captain speed up," Kriger urged, pausing to catch his breath, "so this bastard can't fight as much, and then I can start reeling him in."

The Dane had exercised little and was in less than optimum physical condition. His strength was waning.

"Okay," Alberto assented.

He hustled up the stairs to the bridge and shouted to the co-pilot.

"More knots. Faster."

Alberto returned to the fishing station.

The yacht's speed prevented the fish from lurching, and Kriger only had to hang on until it was spent from trying to free itself. An hour passed, and he began to reel.

"I see him, Alberto. He's a beauty."

"I have captain come down—help pull fish in," Alberto offered when the fish was twenty feet from the boat.

He hurried up the stairs and returned with the co-pilot, ten or so years older than Alberto, slight, wearing a white captain's cap with a dark bill. He carried a gaff.

Kriger reeled the marlin in close to the boat. The captain swung the pole, burying the hook below the fish's head. Alberto grasped the line with Kriger, and the three men hoisted the blue fish up to the rail. It twisted and writhed like a belly dancer, and the sun glinted off its shiny body the way light reflects from a harem skirt's gold-coin sequins. When they had pulled it onto the deck, Kriger kept his hold on the line while the fish thrashed. The co-pilot attached a rope at the bottom of the rail and stretched it across the fish to the stairway post while Alberto struggled to hold the tail.

While the fish lay asphyxiating, Kriger and Alberto went inside the cabin to relax.

"What you want to drink, my friend?" Alberto asked. "I have everything."

"After that battle, all I want is a cold beer."

"Corona okay?"

"Perfect."

Alberto went to the kitchen and made a Bacardi and Coca Cola for himself. He took a long-necked Mexican brew and a lime out of the small fridge. He popped the bottle cap, cut a wedge of the lime, and pressed the lime onto the top. He placed beverage coasters on the oak coffee table and the two lounged on plush beige sofas. Kriger squeezed the lime into the bottle and took a long swig.

"Rodger," Alberto inquired, lowering his voice and leaning forward, "you want to sniff some coca?"

"Coca?" Kriger looked puzzled. "You mean cocaine?"

"I have the best. My supplier in Colombia make sure it pure."

"I've never done drugs," Kriger said.

"Oh, coca make you feel so good. You should try."

"I don't think so, Alberto. I probably wouldn't know when to stop. I think I'll just stick to booze. And sex. But not a lot of both at the same time. I tried that once and it didn't work too good." Kriger threw his head back and laughed coarsely.

"It can make you feel good even if you don't use it," Alberto said almost under his breath, a wicked smile forming.

Kriger stared, bemused.

"You don't understand?" Alberto asked, and sipped his rum drink.

Kriger crinkled his forehead, as if he were trying to comprehend.

Alberto rubbed the thumb and first two fingers of his right hand together.

"Oh, I get it." Kriger hesitated. "You deal in that stuff, Alberto?"

Alberto stared hard at his friend but didn't answer.

"Look, Alberto, I'm too visible around here. I've got too high a profile, what with all of the civic and government organizations I serve on. If anybody found out I was involved in a drug smuggling operation, my reputation would be destroyed—even if I didn't end up in prison. The risk is just too great for the return. As it is, I'm taking a huge chance with my affair with Stella. But I can't help myself. A man has to feel close to a woman. Know what I mean?"

"Oh, yes, Stella. She is so young and bootiful."

"She's a knock-out, all right, but not all that young—maybe ten years younger than me. That's not all what it's about, though, Alberto. We like being together."

"Does Jan know?"

"Oh, yes, she found out some time ago. We took a skiing trip to Squaw Valley last March. You ever been there?"

"No. I hear about it."

"It's gorgeous. Majestic mountains, with magnificent Lake Tahoe right in the middle. Anyway, while we were there she made me promise to stop seeing Stella. And I did, but not for very long."

"She ever say she want divorce?"

"No, but I wouldn't be surprised if she does. Two things are getting in the way of that. One, we've got six kids. And two, you know how difficult it is for Catholics to get divorced."

Kriger took another swig of Corona and wiped his lips with the back of his hand. Alberto swallowed a mouthful of rum and Coke, which had diluted as the ice melted.

"And I've got another problem that could hurt my business as well as my reputation. I don't know if I should tell you this because it involves your people."

Alberto looked startled. "My people? What you mean?"

"I'm sorry. I didn't mean your family. I meant the Cuban community. No, I don't mean that, either. I mean certain elements. Okay, let me spell it out. I found out there was a bolita operation going on at two of the Land O' Gocean restaurants. Several friends of mine told me they saw what appeared to be Cuban men escorted to a back room. That room in all of the stores is for banquets and parties. One said when he and his wife visited, the restaurant was full and they were waiting for a table when a man came to the desk and said something they couldn't hear to the hostess. She got the manager and he took the man to the back room.

"I went to that store and talked to the hostess. She said the manager had instructed her that if a customer said the word 'rumba,' she was to summon him. Every customer looked Cuban and the manager always took him to the back. A waitress had trouble with a customer at a table once, and the hostess went to the back to get the manager. She saw the Cuban holding a white ping-pong ball. The manager told her later it was a golf ball and they were making plans to go golfing, but she knew it was a ping-pong ball."

He paused and glanced at Alberto, who looked down and said nothing.

"I had to fire the managers of those two restaurants, Alberto. I couldn't have that kind of thing going on. Look what would happen if the police found out and raided them. It would be all over the news, and that would be the end of my restaurants."

Alberto downed the last of his drink. He looked at Kriger enigmatically for a couple of long seconds.

"You have to do what you have to do."

"Yeah," said Kriger. "The only thing is, I'm a little worried they might retaliate. They probably were raking in the dough from that operation."

He studied Alberto's face, and the Cuban guessed that his friend wanted something from him.

Kriger had heard rumors that Alberto bankrolled the organized bolita racket in Palm Beach and northern Broward counties. The restaurateur figured Alberto could pass the word without fuss that neither he nor his restaurants were to be harmed.

"I hope nothing happen," Alberto said.

"Hey, listen, Alberto. Jan and I have been invited to the home of a Democratic bigwig Friday night for a get-together with the governor. You and I are Republicans, but Andrews is friendly with both sides, and I think my friend would be happy to have you."

"Thank you, Rodger, but Lourdes and I already going to big Latino party. Thank you."

"Okay. Just a thought. Well, let's see how our catch is doing."

The two men walked up the stairs to the deck, where the marlin lay unmoving.

"The fight is gone out of him," Kriger noticed. "That baby put up a hell of a battle. He's going to look good mounted on the wall of my den."

Kriger gazed at the magnificent creature with the sword-like bill and tail that swooped in an arc like the wings of a huge bird, the distillation of might, grace, and symmetry.

It'll be a reminder that as big and powerful as we may be, we have to be careful or we could meet our demise.

The morning sun's slanting rays caromed off the large, bright, orange-and-green lettering of The Sporting Man sign, which beckoned as cheerfully as the store's clear bay windows. Welcome, everybody, they seemed to say.

The early-January air was crisp and breezy, and the men who trickled into the store at the Westside Mall just outside West Palm Beach were dressed in motley attire to ward off the chill—casual jackets, stylish light coats, a variety of pull-over sweaters, soiled denim jackets. Parked in front were vehicles that ran the gamut from older, cheaper models to newer, cheaper models to newer, expensive models to pickup trucks and ones with jacked-up bodies and oversized wheels.

The trucks outnumbered the others. Owners of the newer ones had not altered them: Their purposes were strictly utilitarian. Cheap trinkets dangled from rear-view mirrors in several older models, and their bumpers or rear windows displayed Confederate flags. They held a shotgun or rifle in the window rack. These conveyed less-than-subtle messages. A few sported bumper stickers that delivered in-your-face messages: "The South shall rise again!" "When guns are outlawed, only outlaws will have guns." "This truck contains Rednecks," printed over a Confederate flag.

A shiny, new, deep-green Jaguar drove up and parked at a spot away from the other vehicles. Two nattily dressed young men got out and walked with a rigid gait, as if certain of their mission, into The Sporting Man. Their dark hair and tan complexion suggested they were Hispanic.

"Mornin, gentlemen," the nondescript sales clerk greeted as they entered. "What can I do for you?"

"Guns," said the taller of the two.

"We want to see your selection of shotguns," the other explained.

"Of course. All the hunters come in on Saturday morning to get a jump-start on the weekend. Gonna bag some deer, are you?"

"Deer?" asked the taller man. His companion was standing close enough to kick the other's shoe without the clerk noticing. "Uh… oh, yeah, we're going deer hunting."

"I think Jorge thought you said bear hunting," the shorter man said.

"Yes, yes. That's what I thought you said. We weren't born in this country. Our father came here from Cuba to raise cattle. Sometimes we get the words mixed up and…"

"Jorge, I don't think this man is interested," the shorter man interrupted.

"No, that's okay. Let me show you where the gun section is. Walk to that counter, then go right and follow the aisle to the back of the store. There are three salesmen back there who will be glad to help you."

On the way, Jorge turned his head.

"Sorry, Miguel," he muttered. "I made a mistake. I'd better let you do the talking. I always get into trouble."

"I think that's a good idea."

Three long glass cases were filled with guns of every variety, and more rifles and shotguns hung on the wall back of the sales counter. Jorge and Miguel zeroed in on the shotgun display.

"Looking for anything in particular?" a gray-haired man wearing horn-rimmed glasses asked.

"We want something that's easy to load," Miguel said, "not too complicated, and very reliable."

"Well, let's see. We have this 12-gauge Winchester, a good overall shotgun, priced at…"

"We don't care about the price," Miguel interrupted. "We just want the best."

The salesman scanned Miguel's attire, then turned to similarly appraise Jorge.

"Certainly. Okay, then I think this is just what you're looking for. The Remington 870 pump with twenty-eight-inch barrel, and an extra barrel with rifle sights. If you don't mind the price tag."

"Do you have two of them?" Jorge asked.

"Hmm. Let me check in the back."

He left, and Miguel said, "If he doesn't have a second one, I'm sure we can get one at another store. I think this is just what we need. Papa is going to approve."

"We're in luck," the salesman informed the pair, returning to the counter through a windowless, swinging door. "Do you want these in separate boxes?"

"It doesn't matter," said Miguel. "And we'll need about thirty shells."

"You've got em. I'll pack those in a separate box."

He tallied the bill and Miguel paid with his credit card. On the way to their car, he gloated, "That was the easy part."

Chapter Eight

"So what'd you think?" said Kriger, driving the Lincoln Continental north on Flagler Drive in West Palm Beach toward the third bridge to Palm Beach. "Affable guy, Governor Andrews, but I had a hard time swallowing that usual Democratic baloney about how we're responsible for caring for the disadvantaged. How about the disadvantaged showing some responsibility for themselves?"

As the sleek black sedan crossed over the bridge, Jan looked out her window disinterested in the activity on a seasonal weekend night at the marina. The lights were on in many of the boats and yachts, their owners and friends walking to and fro on the finger piers. Once over the bridge, she gazed at the cars angle-parked in rows leading to the Royal Poinciana Playhouse around the corner. It was almost time for whatever show was playing to end, and she envisioned the show-goers rushing out the double doors like cattle released from a crowded corral.

"Jan? You sleeping?"

"Huh? No. You know I don't care much about politics."

"Well, I was getting kind of antsy to leave myself. But they were nice hosts, and the dinner was good."

They turned north on North County Road, drove the several miles to the Palm Beach Country Club in silence, jogged around it, and arrived a few blocks later at their home.

"I must admit, it felt a little stuffy," Rodger conceded, relaxing in the den with a bag of Fritos. He'd changed into his purple pajamas and slippers. Jan sat on the love seat beside him, clad in a pink robe. They absently watched *Columbo*, which had begun a few minutes earlier.

"Did you check on Barbie and Billy?" Rodger asked.

"Yes. They're sound asleep."

The doorbell rang. Rodger and Jan looked at each other, both frowning.

"Who do you suppose would come calling at this hour?" said Rodger. He looked at his watch. "It's after ten o'clock. Maybe it's Jodie. Maybe she left her key at home."

He walked through the living room to the foyer and called out, "Who's there?"

A shot rang out, shattering the window of the foyer on the west side.

Rodger doubled up in pain.

"The son-of-a-bitch shot me," he gasped.

A few seconds later, two more shot shots slammed through the thick wooden front door.

Kriger stumbled to the kitchen. Jan rushed to her husband's side and helped him to the floor. She hurried back to the den and was about to call the police.

A lot of people know about our fights over Rodger's affair with Stella.

She dialed the ambulance, then a neighbor, and finally her attorney, who told her to call the police right away.

A squad car with two officers arrived with siren blaring. One officer ran to the door and rang the same bell that the shooter had rung. An ambulance arrived seconds afterward. The crew stopped the bleeding, and rushed Kriger across the bridge to Flagler Drive and north several blocks to Good Samaritan Hospital.

At police headquarters, the dispatcher took a call from another officer who'd arrived at the scene, directing him to have the bridges over the Intracoastal Waterway raised. The dispatcher telephoned the three bridge stations, beginning with the north bridge, which was closest to the Kriger home.

Scores of friends, business acquaintances, members of Palm Beach society, and movers and shakers in Palm Beach County civic and government organizations came to Kriger's hospital room over the next two days. If they couldn't get in to see him, they visited with Jan in the waiting room. Many others called the hospital. All of these people either were unaware of Kriger's sordid associations at the Shore Club or didn't care.

Davey Ross, who sold drugs to Palm Beachers, watched the television news attesting to Kriger's popularity.

I wonder why rich and important people wink when members of their own class do sleazy stuff but common folks make people on their own level feel ashamed if they act that way. Hmm. Maybe it's because the higher-ups understand sin better. They do a lot more of it.

Over the next ten days, Kriger received thirty-one pints of blood. He drifted in and out of consciousness, often repeating the name of a Palm Beach police sergeant: "Jackson... Jackson... Jackson..."

The Palm Beach police chief, Jonathan Gurney, refused to allow Herb Jackson access to Kriger, telling reporters he was a personal friend of the Kriger family and would not be able to conduct an impartial investigation. But during one of Kriger's conscious periods, police showed him a list of written questions. He was unable to provide any answers helpful in identifying whoever was behind the shooting or the motive.

On the eleventh day, Kriger died, succumbing to bleeding and infection from multiple wounds to his internal organs.

"This is the most shocking thing that has ever happened in the fifteen years I've lived in this town," Palm Beach Mayor Evan Sanford, a retired U.S. State Department official, told reporters.

A steady stream of sympathy cards poured into the Kriger mailbox. The first was from Wallace Grey, president of the United States.

Without delay after the shooting, the town's entire force of twelve police detectives set about checking clues. They found two spent .12-gauge shotgun shells, one on the sidewalk near the front door and one in the grass by the foyer window. Two holes the size of fifty-cent pieces had shattered the heavy-wood front door.

If one shooter was involved, he shot first from the window, the blast hitting Kriger in his side, then hurried to the front and fired the other two shots, one at ground level and the other four feet above, both missing. The shots from the side window and the front door were seconds apart. Police estimated that was enough time for one shooter to fire from both spots.

Police could not find the third shell, and speculated that the shooter took it with him to confound detectives, perhaps to make them suspect each other of botching the investigation or of stealing it for ulterior motives. Either that, or one of them did indeed lose the shell.

Neighbors told the officers that within a couple of minutes after the shooting, they heard a car start up on the street south of the Kriger house. Another resident told police he saw a red Chevrolet Corvette speeding south about a mile south of the crime scene shortly after the shooting.

Almost all of the town's police officers were at the far north end of the town when the event occurred. A caller had reported a violent encounter between two next-door neighbors brandishing guns, and the dispatcher deemed the incident serious enough to send all officers on duty to the scene. The report turned out to be a hoax, and investigators believed the caller meant to lure police away from the getaway path of whoever shot Kriger.

Detectives interviewed dozens of persons. Kriger was an uncontested candidate for the Town Council, and they talked to each council member, including Barney Robbins. He told them his red Corvette was stolen the day of the shooting, and he suspected Johnny Traynor, his handyman and boat captain. Officers quizzed the family's attorney. They asked close friends if they knew whether anyone had a grudge against him. They contacted the board presidents of civic and municipal agencies he was a member of. They interviewed the managers of his restaurants.

All claimed to know nothing.

Friends of Kriger established a $10,000 reward for information leading to the arrest and conviction of the person or persons responsible, and donations raised the total to almost $40,000. Nothing came of it.

———————————

Bobby Gunder slept late on this Saturday after returning in early morning from a thirteen-day camping trip out West with several members of his platoon in Vietnam. Bleary-eyed, he stumbled into the kitchen of his apartment in the Northwood section of West Palm Beach in his T-shirt and jockey shorts, and set the coffee pot going. Returning to the bedroom, he changed into a pair of faded blue jeans, thick cotton sweat shirt, and socks to ward off the chill of a January morning. Back in the kitchen, he pulled a cup and saucer from the cupboard and placed it on the small square table.

While the coffee percolated, he went to the front door to retrieve the *Palm Beach Beacon*. He'd forgotten to have delivery withheld during his absence, and a pile of papers had accumulated on the porch. He gathered the folded editions in his arms and carried them to the kitchen entrance, pausing to decide where to dispose of them. He dropped them beside the table. Just to make sure he hadn't missed anything really important while he was away, he would glance at the front page of the first two sections in each issue. The degree to which they had yellowed indicated how old they were.

He poured the coffee into a cup, added a little milk from the fridge, and emptied a packet of sugar. While stirring, he picked up the most yellowed paper, scanned the two section pages, and flipped the paper onto the floor out of his way. He sipped the hot coffee and grabbed another paper.

A big first-section headline screamed: Unknown Gunman Shoots Palm Beacher In His Home. Leaning back in his chair with the coffee cup in his hand, Gunder read on.

He jerked upright, coffee spilling in his lap, as his eyes fell on the name and address of the victim: his parents' next-door neighbor, Rodger Kriger.

Gunder put the cup down, oblivious of the pain from the hot coffee on his pants. He sat transfixed, staring at the paper but not reading it.

Why would anyone want to kill Kriger?

"Oh my God," he muttered. "I'll bet they were after me."

He began pacing the living room. After several minutes, he hurried to his 1973 Chevrolet Vega GT and sped over to the north bridge, across to County Road, and south to the Palm Beach police headquarters. He rang the bell and was greeted by a sergeant.

"I have to talk to someone about the shooting a couple weeks ago," said Gunder. "I think I may have been the intended victim."

"Come on up," the sergeant beckoned, leading him to an upstairs office. "Sit down."

Gunder explained to the detective in charge of the investigation that he was staying briefly with his parents until five days before Kriger was shot, while a plumber made major repairs to his only bathroom and kitchen.

"Two guys and me smuggled cocaine out of South America. They thought I cheated them—I didn't—and I think they might be trying to bump me off."

He had kept his phone number and address unlisted, but surmised these guys may have found his parents' listing and discovered he was living at their house. They possibly intended to shoot him, he reasoned, but went to the wrong house.

"You realize you just confessed to smuggling drugs," the sergeant said. "We're going to have to arrest you."

"Yeah, I know. It's okay. I don't feel safe with those guys maybe after me. I was in combat in Vietnam, but over there we all looked out for each other. Here it's just me against these guys. I guess I'd better talk to my attorney about this."

"You want to call him?"

"Yeah. He told me he's at his office Saturdays till early afternoon."

Gunder and the attorney conferred at a desk in the police office. The attorney told the detective his client would be willing to assist in the arrest and prosecution of the others involved in the smuggling operation if he could be granted some sort of immunity. He felt that they would eventually find him, and he would be safer if they were locked up.

The lawman said he had no problem with that, especially considering that Gunder had risked his life for his country. They could arrange a meeting with the state attorney Monday to see if he were amenable to the plan. Meanwhile, Gunder could stay in his apartment if he preferred that to jail. If the smugglers were after him, they obviously didn't know where he lived, the detective noted. But he would instruct West Palm Beach police to keep a round-the-clock surveillance on the premises.

"I'm going to notify my parents about my suspicions, and I'm sure my father will want to hire a bodyguard for me until this thing is settled," Gunder said.

"All the better," replied the detective.

State Attorney Donald Bosworth agreed to ask the judge to grant Gunder immunity if he would cooperate with police in cracking the smuggling operation. The judge assented, and Gunder remained free.

Four law enforcement agencies continued investigating the Kriger murder, sending police to states out West and in the Northeast. The lead detective for Palm Beach interviewed more than two hundred persons over a period that stretched from weeks into months. But all leads to the identity of the killer or killers, or to a motive, ran into dead ends. It was an election year, and pressure was building on the state attorney and the sheriff.

"I have something to tell you," Diane Berglund said to her boyfriend, Mitt Hecher.

They sat on a wicker couch watching *Saturday Night Live* in her house a mile southwest of downtown West Palm Beach. She drew away from his arm around her shoulder and looked at him with a diffident smile, her head lowered. Hecher, who had been spending a lot of time in Diane's home, looked back at her. They locked gazes for several seconds.

"Uh-oh," he said. "Is it what I think it is?"

She nodded her head. "I think so. How do you feel about it?"

Hecher sighed and looked toward the ceiling.

"I think it's great, honey. I want to have a baby with you. But the timing is bad. The law in this county is out to get me. Can't say as I blame them too much. I've made it pretty tough for them. But they resent my popularity, the following I've got with all my karate students. They're going to throw the book at me. They could put me away for quite a while. And it won't be here. They'll send me to Raiford, up around Jacksonville. That's damn near three hundred miles from here."

"We both know you did a lot of bad things. But a lot of the people you beat up did something to deserve it. Like the lounge owners in Fort Lauderdale. If I was that entertainer and didn't get paid for a month's work, I might hire somebody to beat up those guys, too."

"Yeah, and we didn't even get the owners—just a customer who smarted off and told us they weren't around. Plus, I didn't even do the beating. Two guys from Fort Lauderdale who brought us to the place did the rough stuff. But I get charged with extortion along with them."

He flipped both arms in the air and looked vexed. "Why am I getting into that? It's history. You know all about it."

"But Mitt, you haven't been in any trouble going on a year now. Don't you think the jury will consider that when they sentence you?"

"Diane," said Hecher, drawing her closer to him, "you've been good for me. You made me think about the kind of life I was living—getting drunk in bars and picking fights. Remember how we met? At Spanky's, that neighborhood bar in Northwood north of downtown? Davey and me came looking for a guy I could beat up so I could get him into my karate studio, and then I spotted you at a table with your girlfriend."

"That's why you guys came to the bar? You never told me that before."

"No, after I met you, I didn't want to admit it. Davey wasn't turned on by your friend, and he could see I had the hots for you, so he left. We came in two cars. The last time, the cops hauled me in and he had to drive my car back to his place and park it in a vacant lot because his apartment lot was full."

"You tried to include Cindy in the conversation," Diane recalled, "but she could see you were interested in me and made an excuse to leave so we could be alone."

"And we started seeing each other. That's when I began slowing down—deciding that nothing good could come of the path I was going down. But it may be too late. I think the state attorney's office is going to pile on as many years as possible. The prosecutor will go for the max."

"I think you're imagining the worst. Let's just play it day by day and hope for the best."

"Okay, but regardless, I'm going to get hit with quite a few years. The judge is going to look at my arrest record and say, enough is enough. I've got to teach this guy a lesson. And I can't expect you to sit and wait for me. Especially when you have a child to take care of."

Diane cupped Mitt's face in her hands.

"You're forgetting something. I love you. I'm not going to abandon you. The next thing we're going to do is get married. We can find a justice of the peace. Let's do that next week."

———————

Despite Gunder's cooperation, police were unable to track down his drug smuggling partners after six months. While they were checking all the known drug dealers for any information about the possible mistaken identity in the shooting of Kriger, they received an anonymous tip that Mitt Hecher may have been the shooter. Hecher was facing prosecution for drug, weapons, and possession of stolen property charges. He was named as a suspect.

"Bobby who? Gander?"

"Gunder," snapped the detective, sitting at his desk in the central West Palm Beach police station. "Quit fakin it, Hecher. You're not a very good actor."

"Miss Ramsey would agree with you," said Hecher. "She was my seventh grade English teacher. Took me out of the skit we were working on. Said I had more talent writing than acting." He paused. "So why am I supposed to know this... who is it... Gunder?"

"We got a tip you were hired to kill him by two guys he screwed in a cocaine smuggling deal. His parents live next door to Rodger Kriger. Know that name?"

"Of course. He's the big shot in Palm Beach who got... woops, bad choice of words. He's the rich Palm Beach dude who got shot."

"You supposedly went to the wrong house to shoot Gunder."

Hecher stared open-mouthed at the detective, then burst out laughing.

"Sorry, detective. It ain't funny when somebody gets killed, but that's the most ridiculous thing I ever heard of. Who in hell came up with that wild-ass idea?"

"We don't know who the caller was and wouldn't tell you if we did. Must be somebody in the drug world who knows these two guys and knows you, or at least knows who you are. Every hoodlum in town knows who you are."

"Yeah. Maybe it's somebody I was hired to beat up. Somebody who has a grudge against me and wants to get even."

Detectives set about questioning Diane, who had just married Hecher, and friends. They checked his telephone records, searched his apartment thoroughly for any hidden evidence, talked to members of his karate studio.

Less than a month later, police dropped Hecher as a suspect in the murder of Rodger Kriger. Shortly afterward, a Circuit Court judge convicted him of the three other charges: unlawful display of a firearm, possession of marijuana, and possession of a stolen car radio.

The judge sentenced him to twenty-eight years in prison.

Chapter Nine

"Hello. Richie Gatson?" The voice on the phone was deep and slow.

"Yeah. What'ya got?" Gatson replied, his tone reeking with hostility.

"My name's Jim Scraponia. I'm the chief felony prosecutor in the state attorney's office. How are you doing today?"

"What're you after?"

"Well now, I've been doing a little checking and I understand that you're a pretty good friend of Mitt Hecher. Is that right?"

"We were in business together."

"What kind of business?"

"Let's just say we did bill collecting together. So what does that prove?"

"Oh, nothing, I guess. Except that you two have a lot in common, don't you? What I mean to say is that you both are in a lot of trouble with the law." Scraponia spoke in measured phrases, as if weighing his words.

"Mister Hecher is sitting in jail as we speak, convicted of several charges. And you. My goodness, you're up against a long list of criminal offenses: burglary, assault, armed robbery, loan-sharking, and on and on. I guess I don't have to remind you of that. In fact, I thought the judge would set your bail higher. Do you lose much sleep wondering how you're going to convince a jury you're not guilty of these things? An attorney would have to work miracles. Especially since I'll be the prosecuting attorney, and I have a darned good conviction record, Mister Gatson."

Silence at the both ends.

"Do you remember that murder in Palm Beach?" Scraponia asked. "The Rodger Kriger case?"

"Yeah, of course. Everybody knows about that. It's all over the news—every other day."

"Well, I heard a rumor that Mitt Hecher was the guy who did the shooting. And somebody told me that before Hecher was picked up and put in jail for this other stuff, you overheard a phone conversation in which he claimed to have shot a big blond guy in the north part of the island by mistake."

"Where you goin' with this?" Gatson asked, spreading the words out, his voice lowered.

"If I can get you to cooperate with me, Mister Gatson, I'm sure we can work something out regarding those charges against you. Because, wow, I'm afraid you're looking at a long, long time in the slammer, my friend." Scraponia spoke almost in a drawl.

He waited a moment. "How about it? Have we got a deal? You think you might have heard that conversation?"

Another pause.

"Okay, yeah, I guess that's what I heard him say."

"You guess? That's not going to be good enough. Aren't you certain, Mister Gatson? Let's see, that robbery charge alone ought to be good for about five years. Then there's maybe another four on the burglary and…"

"Okay, okay. I heard Hecher say he shot a big blond guy by mistake."

"There, Mister Gatson, you said the magic words. Now, let's work out the details. The way I understand it, last fall you were in Hecher's apartment in the north end of town on a Saturday afternoon while his girlfriend was out shopping, and Hecher had you pick up the phone in the other room and listen in while a mobster asked him to kill a Palm Beach guy who owed gambling and drug debts. Are you with me?"

"Okay, I gotcha."

"Then, the day after Kriger died in the hospital and it was in all the papers, you're at Hecher's place again, and he gets a call. And Hecher tells you the man said, 'You got the wrong guy.' Now, I think you know what a deposition is. You've been through more than one of them in your illustrious career, right?"

"Yeah, yeah. Let's cut the crap, okay?"

"What I'm going to do is order a deposition in which I will ask you about having voluntarily come to my office with information about the Kriger case. You will answer that you did indeed come forth. I will then ask you questions pertaining to what I just talked about and you agreed to. Think you can remember the story?"

"Sure. No problem."

"Now, what about the shotgun?" Scraponia asked. "I need to talk about material evidence. What happened to the shotgun?"

Gatson thought for a few seconds.

"I've got it," he enthused. "Hecher's family stores stuff in a warehouse where they live in Albuquerque, New Mexico. Mitt told me once his brother has a shotgun he uses for hunting and he keeps it there so there ain't no chance his kids can get their hands on it. I'll say the gun is in that warehouse."

"Sounds like a winner. We'll go over the story again before the deposition date. And then, of course, I'll need you to testify in court. You're going to go to jail for those charges, but not for long. I'll arrange to have them dismissed for your cooperation, and you'll be a free man. For some reason, I didn't think you would be suited for life in a gated community. Good day, Mister Gatson."

Scraponia leaned back in his swivel chair and gazed up at the off-white, acoustical-tiled ceiling of his office.

That son-of-a-bitchin Hecher has eluded me over and over. Hallelujah, I think I've got him nailed for good this time.

———————

"Good afternoon, Captain. I'm Jim Scraponia, chief felony prosecutor in the state attorney's office, and I'm here to see DeWitt Crimshaw." The attorney handed his identification to the jail officer.

"Yes, Mister Scraponia, I've been expecting you. If you'll just wait right here in the visitors room, I'll have the prisoner for you momentarily."

A lanky, smiling man in prison blues was escorted through the iron gate into the spare room with concrete walls painted light green. He was about thirty and had a thick mane of dark hair, parted down the middle, framing an oval face.

Scraponia reached forth his hand. "You are DeWitt Crimshaw the Third, I believe."

"Yes, but most people just call me Dewey," he said with a welcoming smile.

"Okay, Dewey. Let's sit down here at this table."

They took steel-framed chairs with plastic-covered foam seating on opposite sides of a small wooden table.

"We don't have a lot of time, so I'm going to get right to the point. You sure don't seem to realize when you have it made in the shade. Most people dream of the life you had—money to burn from a filthy-rich daddy whose wealth was passed from his own daddy. Your granddad was some kind of inventor, wasn't he?"

"Yes, I guess you could say my granddaddy invented doodads." Crimshaw broke into a big smile. Scraponia looked as though he were trying to keep a straight face.

The attorney sobered. "And with all that money, you go and try to cheat somebody in a yacht deal, and that's the end of your yacht brokerage. You get convicted of swindling, but you're lucky enough to get off on probation. And then you violate the terms and land here. I'm sure this does not have quite the ambience that you're accustomed to. Have you gotten used to it in the four months you've been here?"

"No, and the food is awful. But I try to stay busy helping the other inmates with their legal matters."

"I don't have to remind you that you're looking at five years."

Crimshaw's face darkened. "Yes. I guess I really messed up this time."

"On the other hand, there may be a way to get that sentence cut to a small fraction."

Crimshaw's face brightened. Scraponia stared at the table.

"Tell me more," said the convict.

Scraponia lifted his head and looked at Crimshaw.

"I have been aware of your activities on behalf of other inmates during your incarceration. Your adroit application of the law in their cases has earned you the reputation of an accomplished jailhouse lawyer. You may be able to assist me in solving an outstanding case of homicide. I am referring to the shotgun slaying of Rodger Kriger of Palm Beach. Are you familiar with that murder?"

"Yes. We have access to the news, and I keep abreast of things."

"It seems that Mister Kriger's neighbor has a son who thinks he may have been the intended victim but the killer went to the wrong house. The police have reason to believe the person who did the shooting was Mitt Hecher, who is confined at this institution for other misdeeds. You may know him."

"Oh, yes. He's the karate expert. Short, muscular fellow. Wiry. He tried to teach me a few moves, but I'm not very good at that sort of thing." An amiable smile.

"Hecher has been a real thorn in the side of law enforcement. He's very difficult to deal with. And he's a menace to society. He needs to be removed from the population for a long time."

"Isn't he serving twenty-eight years?" Crimshaw asked.

"Theoretically," Scraponia sniffed. "But with time off for good behavior, he'll probably be out a lot sooner than that. And with you helping him draw up appeals and prepare legal briefs, there's no telling how many years might be knocked off his sentence. We need you working for our side to keep him locked up—and get *you* out of here."

Scraponia paused, staring at Crimshaw, whose eyes widened.

"How can I help?"

"As I said, you would be doing a service to society, and redeeming yourself for the crime you've committed, if you could help convince a jury that Mitt Hecher shot Rodger Kriger."

"How do I do that?"

"I have a plan. As the jailhouse lawyer here, you gained the trust of the inmates. That much is known. What's not known is that Mitt Hecher sought your help in delaying sentencing for the crimes he was convicted of. He admitted to you that he shot Kriger, and he planned to plead insanity to avoid conviction for the murder. He said he had ingested mind-altering drugs after breaking up with his girlfriend. You advised him to write a confession. He wrote that he intended to shoot Bobby Gunder over his refusal to pay $10,000 that he owed Hecher in a drug deal. He learned the next day that he'd shot the wrong guy.

"How good is your handwriting?"

"My handwriting is excellent. In school, my teachers always praised me for it."

"Think you could forge Hecher's writing?"

"Do you have a pen and paper?" Crimshaw requested. "Write, 'My name is Jim Scraponia.'"

Scraponia pulled a pad and ballpoint pen out of his pocket, wrote the words on the back, and handed pen and paper to Crimshaw. He copied the words below and handed the paper back to the attorney.

"Well, I'll be a... you rascal, you," Scraponia jested, breaking into a big grin. "That better be the one and only time you ever forge my name, you hear?"

He slapped the wealthy playboy on the back.

"I'm going to bring you something Mitt Hecher has written so you can practice copying his style. Now, what you testify is that you thought about it and realized this wasn't going to help Hecher, so you just kept the confession and never presented it to the state attorney's office.

"Okay, here's what I'm going to do for you. I'm going to get that $350,000 bond cut down to something that's manageable so you can bail out of here. You said your family is upset with you for besmirching their reputation and is disinclined to help you."

"Yes, I'm afraid so. They want me to learn my lesson."

"So after that, for your cooperation, it'll just be a short while before I get your conviction overturned and this unfortunate interruption in your carefree life will be over."

"I'm through with Mister Crimshaw, Captain Danielson," Scraponia said into the wall telephone.

John Danielson was a gaunt man in his mid-fifties, stooped from an arthritic spine. Scraponia had a flashback to his college freshman class in Shakespeare and the conjured image of Cassius with his "lean and hungry look."

"How did it go?" the jail commander queried. "Is he going to cooperate?"

"All the way. Now let's try to get those other guys you thought had potential."

"I'll set you up. Anything I can do to nail that fucking Hecher. It's funny. He doesn't know it was my kid brother Kenny he decked at Patsy's Bar when Kenny and his partner were sent there to stop a brawl."

"Don't worry. We'll get him."

"Oh, Mitt. I can't believe they did this to you," Diane cried through the small window in the county jail's visiting room. "Twenty-eight years. For those minor crimes." Tears filled her eyes.

"Honey, it's okay. We'll deal with it. Look at you. What have you been doing, eating a lot of that apple dumpling? Oh, wait a minute. That's something else you've got in there."

Diane wiped her eyes and chuckled. "How can you be so cheerful when that judge did such a dirty, rotten thing to you? I'm so angry I want to strangle him."

"Look, they'll be sending me to Raiford, and I'll use the prison library to do legal research on how to appeal this. I think I've got an excellent case of cruel and unusual punishment."

"I ran into that reporter, Tom Palladin, when I was at the courthouse getting my driver license renewed. I told him I thought that judge must have been out to get you, and he said a lot of attorneys around the courthouse have been saying they thought the sentence was way too severe considering how light the offenses were. None of them were violent. They didn't even directly affect anybody. I told him I wanted to stir things up and get the public on your side so the judge would reconsider and reduce the sentence to something reasonable. But I told him I didn't know how to go about it.

"He said he had to maintain his objectivity, but pointed out that Martin Luther King and people against the Vietnam War brought about change by going into the streets and protesting. The news media couldn't ignore them, and they got movements going. I plan to get my friends to carry signs condemning that judge and march with me in front of the courthouse, so we can get some publicity."

Hecher looked at his wife for a few seconds, thinking.

"Sweetheart, that's wonderful of you. But I think it would be a big mistake. First, I built up a reputation around here, and there's a lot of people who don't have much sympathy for me. But more important, you don't want to be jeopardizing your job. You'd be putting your employer on the spot by advertising to the entire population that your husband is a convicted criminal. Besides, you have plenty of other things to do—like get ready for that baby. You know what? We haven't even picked a name."

"But we don't know if it's a boy or girl."

"Good point." He laughed.

"How about this?" she said. "You get to choose a boy's name and I choose a girl's name."

"It's a deal. Got one in mind?"

"I've always liked Helen. I love the story of Helen of Troy."

"Helen Hecher. You do like alliteration, don't you? Sounds good to me."

"Your turn."

"I kind of go for Pauley. You're not going to believe why. A guy like me doesn't seem very religious, and I'm not. But I do remember a little bit from my Catholic childhood. I always admired this guy Paul. He was such a mean bastard—just like me. And then something happened to him, and he changed. And he put up with all kinds of shit, and never got pissed off. Something happened to me. You. I'm facing a lot of crap. I'm pissed off, but I keep this dude Paul in mind and it helps me control my anger. I don't have to keep you in mind. You're always there. You're my reason for living."

Jim Scraponia finished writing a few words in a brief before laying the pen on his desk to answer the phone.

"George Demarco, eh? He's willing to talk to me. Well, why not? The guy's already been convicted of two murders and he's got a date with the hot seat for a third one. What's that? This line has static. I'll be there at three o'clock."

Danielson greeted Scraponia in the visitors room.

"He kept a diary," said the jail commander, his forward-leaning head bobbing like a duck. "He wrote that he killed eight people as a hit man for the Mafia. He's proud of it. He'd been a cop, but he didn't enjoy that. Being a hit man was his big ambition, like some people want to become doctors, or big league baseball players, or owners of businesses."

"Sounds like a charming fellow," Scraponia enunciated in his near drawl. "Just make damn sure the son-of-a-bitch is thoroughly frisked before you put him alone with me, okay?"

"Oh, yeah, no problem about that. I'll have him out here in a couple of minutes."

Danielson led Demarco into the room with hands cuffed in front, and ordered him to sit at the small table across from Scraponia. Scraponia put him in his upper thirties, straight dark hair combed back. The attorney looked into the man's eyes and felt a chill. They were gray and expressionless, like those of a dead man, or a fish, or a chronic alcoholic.

"Mister Demarco, I'm Jim Scraponia, assistant state attorney. I see that you have a rather heinous record of terminating people's lives. My boss has dealt with a lot more criminals than I have and he says no man deserves the electric chair more than you."

"These were not choir boys I bumped off," Demarco demurred.

"Perhaps not, but you apparently did them in with cold-blooded ease. I doubt you will find it so easy to enter the great beyond yourself. Are you prepared to die?"

Danielson shuffled his feet and pressed his shackled hands against his body.

"No. I have no desire to die." He lowered his head.

"Well, Mister Demarco, there may be a way out for you."

He raised his head.

"I'll put it to you simply: If you help Captain Danielson and I achieve what we want, we might be able to get the judge to spare the chair for you. Now, don't you think that has a nice ring to it?"

A glimmer of light seeped into Demarco's eyes and his sallow face took on a bit of color.

"What do you want me to do?"

"You know Mitt Hecher?"

"Yeah. Tough little shit."

"Okay. And you've heard about this guy Rodger Kriger of Palm Beach who was shot in January in his home?"

"Yeah, I've heard a lota buzz about it. Cops can't find who did it."

"Well, they don't have to look anymore. Mitt Hecher has confessed. He told an inmate he did it."

"Huh?"

"That's right. Only thing is, Hecher doesn't know he made that confession." Scraponia smiled slyly.

Demarco stared at him, bemused.

"Hecher will learn about that confession in court," Scraponia continued. "And he'll learn that he also admitted the crime to another inmate. You."

Demarco's mystified look metamorphosed into one of comprehension. "Oh, now I get it."

"I'm sure you'd rather see Hecher get the chair than you. Am I right, Mister Demarco?"

"No doubt about that." He paused. "But why do you want to get this guy so bad?"

Scraponia fought to suppress the thought of next year's Republican primary for the Forty-Seventh District of the Florida House of Representatives.

"Hecher is a bad actor who needs to be permanently removed from society."

"Oh." Demarco was puzzled. *I'm less of a danger to society than Hecher?*

He decided to keep quiet and do as he was told.

"Hello. Mister Palladin? Tom Palladin?"

"Yes," answered the baritone voice at the other end of the line.

"My name's John Danielson. I'm a captain here at the Palm Beach County Jail. I been reading them articles in the *Miami Gazette* you been writing about that Kriger murder. I got a real good story for you, if you're interested. I'll give you a exclusive because I been impressed with your reporting."

"What's your story?"

Palladin's tone was cynical. In his fifteen years as a reporter, he'd become wary of anyone holding a public position, lawmen included. In fact, the tall, lanky newsman had learned to question the motives of people in all walks of life. He'd witnessed over the course of his career the baser instincts of mankind manifested a thousand times.

"I got a prisoner on death row who's become a born-again Christian and is ready to meet his maker. Now I know what you're thinking. That's what they all say. They all get religion when they're gonna die. But this one is different. George Demarco is a changed man. He's full of good will. And he has artistic talent. He decorated the jail Christmas tree. You should meet him, and you ought to see that tree. I can arrange an interview. I think you will be impressed."

Palladin was silent while he thought. This might make a good human interest story. He didn't want the *Palm Beach Beacon* to beat him on it. On the other hand, he didn't want to be taken for a sucker. He'd have to be careful.

"Okay, when do you want to do this?"

"We can do it at your convenience, Mister Palladin."

"Hang on a minute while I check with my editor."

Palladin, who worked out of the *Gazette*'s West Palm Beach bureau, walked two desks over to the bureau editor.

"How about two o'clock tomorrow?"

"I'll have Mister Demarco ready."

George Demarco wasn't smiling. He was about to become an actor, but smiling wasn't in his repertoire. It was constitutionally impossible for him to effect.

"Good afternoon, sir," he said politely to the reporter, extending a hairy hand.

Palladin's grip was loose, and the two sat opposite each other at the visitors room table.

"Capt. Danielson tells me you're on death row for a murder you committed," Palladin intoned with a crisp air as he pulled a ballpoint pen and pad out of his sport coat pocket.

"That's correct. I am serving life sentences for two other murders, and have been sentenced to die for the third. If there was anything I could do to bring those men back, I would. It's a terrible thing to take another human life, and if you have done so, I believe you deserve to have your own life taken. I have made peace with the Lord Jesus Christ, who has forgiven me for my awful sins, and I am ready to be with him in heaven."

Demarco looked down at the table and portrayed a man so forlorn and pathetic that John Huston would have cast him on the spot.

Palladin studied him intently, saying nothing. He was skeptical, but didn't want to make a mistake. If the guy was a fake, he'd have fared better in a career shooting movie takes instead of human targets. Then too, Palladin was the son of a minister, and had been taught the redemptive power of Christ. He wanted to believe in the man.

The interview progressed, with Demarco tracing his boyhood in a broken home, his alcoholic father beating both his mother and him. Stealing hubcaps and bullying kids on the school playground evolved into auto theft, burglary, drug peddling, and finally, the big leap into killing for the Mafia. The first time made him sick, but each hit became easier.

As Palladin was winding up the interview, Danielson emerged through the iron gate.

"Let me show you the Christmas tree that Mister Demarco decorated for the entire jail," he said to Palladin.

"Oh, it's really nothin," Demarco shrugged.

The captain led the reporter and the inmate into the large mess hall. In one corner stood a twelve-foot fir tree, resplendent in silver icycles, red ornamental balls, various trinkets, candy canes, and a string of green, red, and white lights woven from top to bottom across the circumference of the tapered, deep-green tree. At the top was a large, silver star. The lights were on and the tree was radiant.

"We supplied Mister Demarco with the decorations, a crew of inmates, and two ladders," Danielson beamed. "He knew just how he wanted it to look, and directed the others in where to place everything."

"Were you always artistic?" Palladin asked.

"Well, yes, I liked to draw when I was a child. And I painted some as a teenager—mainly still lifes."

Palladin looked Demarco in the eyes. *He morphed from still lifes to stilling lives.*

"Mister Danielson, I think I have what I need," the reporter said.

"Thank you for coming, sir."

Back at the *Gazette* bureau office, Palladin rolled two sheets of paper with a sheet of carbon between into a typewriter:

"George Demarco, an inmate at the Palm Beach County Jail, grew up with the impulse to create but gradually replaced it with the urge to destroy. Now, he faces destruction himself, courtesy of the electric chair.

"But before he meets his fate, Demarco is trying to restore that old impulse. He's changed, he says. Facing death made him reflect on the lives he ended, and he's repented and accepted Jesus Christ as his savior. It's filled his heart with love, he insists, and he's drawn on his artistic talent to do a remarkable job of decorating the jail Christmas tree."

Palladin wrapped up his story and filed it with the bureau editor.

———————————

Convicted Killer Finds Christ, Festoons Christmas Tree.

Hecher stopped sifting through the sections of the *Beacon* and stared at the headline blazed across the top of the local front page. He pulled upright in his chair in the county jail library. A large photo of George Demarco gazing up at the star-topped tree accompanied the text. Hecher read.

"Oh, for Chrissake, I'm gonna puke," he muttered. "That cold-blooded snake suckered the socks off this reporter. I wonder who was behind this." He laid the paper on the table and looked into space. "And why."

———————————

"Mister Palladin, can I talk to you?" Dewey Crimshaw implored into the phone. "I've been doing some really juvenile things, and I want to publicly confess how childishly I've behaved."

Palladin had written stories about the sensational 1973 yacht swindle, for which Crimshaw got off with probation, which he then violated. Crimshaw was a colorful, high-profile person and Palladin knew people liked to read about such characters, whether famous or notorious. During his reporting career, he'd come to understand that common folks always were interested in the lives of the rich, which they experienced vicariously. Especially playboys, who seemed so carefree, flouting responsibility.

"Sure, if it's all right with Captain Danielson. I'll give him a call."

At the jail, which Palladin had visited two months earlier, he was annoyed by Danielson's obsequiousness and cut him off when he tried to explain Crimshaw's evolving attitude change.

"I'm pressed for time. Can you just bring him to me?" the reporter snapped.

"Oh, certainly." The jail commander's head bobbed forward in that duck fashion.

Crimshaw came forth, wearing his silly grin. He went into a narration of how his work with the other inmates as a jailhouse lawyer and his scaled-down lifestyle had made him realize how immature his behavior had been as a playboy. He understood it was time for him to grow up and accept the responsibilities of an adult.

"You know, Mister Demarco has found the Lord, and he reads the Bible a lot. He showed me a passage that says, 'When I was a child, I acted as a child. But when I became a man, I put away childish things.' He told me I was a man now and I needed to put away childish things."

Palladin left and told Crimshaw's story in the *Gazette* below the headline, *Rich Playboy Says He's Ready to Grow Up*

"Mister Crimshaw, please take the witness stand and tell the court what you know about Mitt Hecher's alleged involvement in the murder of Rodger Kriger," prosecutor James Scraponia instructed, glancing at the Grand Jury.

"Well, Your Honor," Crimshaw began unctuously, "while I've been an inmate at the Palm Beach County Jail, I've assisted other inmates with legal matters. Mister Hecher confided in me that he shot Mister Kriger by mistake. He meant to shoot his neighbor's son, Bobby Gunder, who owed him money in a drug deal. He planned to plead insanity over a very troubling romantic situation, and asked me how to handle it. I advised him to put the confession in writing, which he did. But I never turned it over to authorities because after thinking about it, it seemed to me that it probably would not help him."

Demarco took the stand. Appearing ever so humble with courteous and polite "Yes sir"'s and "I want to help in any way I can," he said Hecher told him of gunning for Rodger Kriger's neighbor but learning the next day that he had gone to the wrong house, and shot Kriger.

After the two jail thespians had strutted their hour upon the courtroom stage, Scraponia produced two more inmates, Alan Burns and Donald Gibbons, who poured fuel on the fire. Captain Danielson had proposed to the attorney that they add the two as insurance. They insisted Hecher told them the same thing.

Neighbors of the Krigers were called to testify, as were a number of investigating police officers including Sheriff's Detective Lt. Ronald Snopes, the lead investigator.

"I was brought into this case late," said Snopes, a smallish, nondescript man. "But I've come to the conclusion that there was no issue of mistaken identity in this shooting. Rodger Kriger was the intended victim. I think the jury ought to look into the possibility that vengeance over a business deal may have been the motive for the shooting. Another angle to pursue is a love triangle stemming from the Shore Club in Palm Beach Shores."

In calling the next witness, the select panel followed the detective's advice. The murder victim's widow, Jan Kriger, comprised a third of that love triangle. She testified how she had helped her husband stagger into the kitchen after he'd been shot, then called the police.

"I know this is difficult for you, Mrs. Kriger, but I have to ask you," Scraponia apologized. "We know your husband was having an affair with a dancer at the Shore Club in Palm Beach Shores. That must have been very upsetting for you. Did you play any part in the fatal shooting of your husband?"

Jan Kriger grimaced and appeared about to cry. After a couple of seconds, she composed herself.

"No," she murmured.

"That's all," said Scraponia.

At his arraignment in May, Mitt Hecher carried a sign made of cardboard, stapled to a board, with black lettering that read: "I am a scapegoat. Politics. Lies. Forgery."

The jury indicted him for first degree murder.

Chapter Ten

"You're going to have George Demarco testify that Hecher confessed to him he shot Kriger?" State Attorney Donald Bosworth asked in his Southern accent. A short man, his dark brown swivel chair engulfed him, and a shock of hair that matched the chair's color hung down on his forehead.

"I've gone over it with him," Scraponia told his boss. "He can seem pretty convincing. He sure put one over on the reporter for the *Gazette*. And that guy's a damned good reporter."

"Well, I hope you know what you're doing. But I have to tell you, I wouldn't trust that piece of vermin with his hand on a stack of Bibles reaching to heaven."

"It's all I've got. He and Crimshaw are my aces in the hole."

"Crimshaw!" Bosworth almost shouted. "That slippery sociopath makes Pinocchio look like Honest Abe. He makes me think of Charles Laughton in *Witness to the Prosecution*. 'Are you not, in fact, a chronic and habitual LIAR?!'"

"I'm going to try something," said Scraponia. "I'm going to use some reverse psychology on the jury. It's a bold plan, but it just may work."

The courtroom was filled to capacity. Hecher's bride, Diane, was seated in the front row, in back of the defense table. She cradled their infant son, Pauley. Next to her was Hecher's mother and brother, Dan, both of whom had come up from their homes in New Mexico. Well-heeled friends of Kriger and persons who had served on various civic and municipal boards with him were interspersed through the crowd. A number of reporters from local and regional media, and a few from the national press, were covering the trial. The rest were retirees and other curiosity seekers of diverse stations in life, judging by their grooming.

In the left corner of the courtroom, just ahead of the spectator section, stood a television camera mounted on a long tripod. A cameraman and a television reporter stood behind the equipment.

"Ladies and gentlemen of the jury," Scraponia began in a stentorian voice, his head and shoulders pulled back in the manner of a puffed-up preacher. "Through the testimony of some of society's most nefarious characters—killers, gangsters, scoundrels—I am going to prove to you that Mitt Hecher has admitted murdering Rodger Kriger."

The tall attorney strode slowly in front of the twelve jurors as he spoke, his eyes moving from one to another.

"These men have spent several months in the company of Mister Hecher at the Palm Beach County Jail and have come to know him well. By the time they have finished their testimony, you will not be able to come to any other conclusion but that Mitt Hecher is indeed guilty of the murder of Rodger Kriger."

Scraponia wrapped up his opening statement and took his seat at the prosecutor's table. Circuit Judge Timothy Schultz directed him to call his first witness. The attorney turned toward the bailiff.

"DeWitt Crimshaw, please."

The bailiff walked to the holding room and escorted the lanky inmate, clad in jail blues, to the witness stand with hands cuffed in front. After instructing him to identify himself and state the reason he was in jail, Scraponia asked Crimshaw if he had become acquainted with a fellow inmate named Mitt Hecher.

"Yes, sir, I did. Mister Hecher was explaining karate positions to two other inmates in the mess hall. I asked if I could listen in, and he welcomed me."

"Did you have any other association with Mitt Hecher during your stay at the jail?"

"Yes sir, I did. He asked me in the mess hall one afternoon if I knew about the Rodger Kriger murder in Palm Beach, and I said that of course I did because I paid attention to the news even while I was in jail. He said he had shot Mister Kriger by mistake when he meant to shoot a neighbor's son who owed him money for drugs. He said he was sure he would be charged with the murder, and asked me to help with his defense. I had gained a reputation among the inmates as a jailhouse lawyer."

"And did you assist him?"

"Well, he wanted to plead insanity over a fight with his girlfriend that caused him to go after the person who he claimed owed him money. That was Bobby Gunder. I advised him to put his confession in writing so I could present it to the state attorney's office. He did, but I later decided it might work against him if I turned it over to authorities."

"And what became of that letter?" Scraponia asked.

"Well, you convinced me I should hand it over to you to help with the conviction of a murderer."

"Is that all you provided me with?"

"No. I wrote a letter outlining what was in the confession, and also gave that to you."

"That's all, Your Honor," said Scraponia.

"Alonzo Seppish, would you like to question the witness?" the judge asked.

The chief defense attorney had straight, silvery hair that added age to the sallow skin on a tired face. He sat slumped in a rumpled, dark blue, pin-striped suit. He gazed transfixed at the table.

Here I was, good reputation as a Broward Circuit judge, and I fucked it up by screwing that slimeball defendant's wife. Why couldn't I have gotten prostate cancer before I let those tits seduce me instead of afterward? Then I'd still be sitting up there with a gavel in my hand instead of down here with the grunts. What a slut, ratting on me even after I cleared her guy of that robbery, which the bastard committed. There is no justice. Or maybe there is. A corner of his mouth twisted downward in a bitter smile.

"Mister Seppish?"

The attorney jerked his head and looked up at the judge.

"Pardon? Question? Oh... uh, no, Your Honor." Crimshaw was escorted back to the bench among the witnesses.

Scraponia requested that the captain who led the Palm Beach Police Department's investigation take the witness stand.

"Captain Richmond," Scraponia began, "Richie Gatson, an inmate at the Palm Beach County Jail, swore in a deposition that he was in the apartment of Mister Hecher when he received a phone call from a mobster who said the man Hecher shot was not the one he was hired to shoot. Do you know anything about this?"

"No, I'm unaware of that," said Richmond.

"Mister Gatson also swore that Mitt Hecher stashed the murder weapon in a warehouse he rented in Albuquerque, New Mexico. Do you know where that shotgun is now, Captain?"

"Yes," said Richmond. "We have recovered it in order to try to match it with shells found at the shooting scene."

"And do the gun and shells match?"

"We believe they do."

"Objection," Seppish interrupted. "Captain Blaine Richmond has not been presented as an expert firearms witness, and his opinion on this technical issue is irrelevant and inadmissible."

"Sustained."

Seppish said he wanted to call an expert FBI firearms witness.

The FBI man testified that the shotgun found at the warehouse probably was not the murder weapon.

Captain Richmond was called back to the stand for cross-examination.

"Captain," Seppish began, "are you aware that Richie Gatson admitted he lied about his deposition testimony after failing a lie detector test, and fled, violating the terms of his release from jail on bail?"

Scraponia leaped to his feet and shot his arm upward, fist clenched.

"Objection," he shouted, his face livid. "Testimony about a lie detector test is wholly inadmissible."

"Objection sustained," Judge Schultz pronounced. "The members of the jury are ordered to disregard the part of the question pertaining to the lie detector test." Pointing a finger at Seppish, "And if you ever again breach the rules of the court so flagrantly, Counselor, I will be forced to impose a severe penalty. Is that understood?"

"Yes, Your Honor," Seppish replied. "I apologize. I was not thinking clearly when I asked that question."

But he'd asked it deliberately, figuring it would affect the jury members, notwithstanding the judge's instructions to them to ignore it.

"Do you and others who have investigated the case for the Palm Beach Police Department have a theory as to how the murder of Rodger Kriger resulted?" Seppish continued.

"Yes, sir. We believe Rodger Kriger was a victim of mistaken identity, and that the intended target of the shooter was Bobby Gunder, the son of his neighbor. That is our speculation."

"And what is that speculation based on?"

"Solely on logic. It simply makes sense. We have interviewed countless persons and tracked down an enormous number of leads, and have found no reason why anyone would want to kill Rodger Kriger."

"Do you think that Mitt Hecher was the person who came gunning for Bobby Gunder and instead shot Rodger Kriger?"

"We have no information or reason which would lead us to believe that."

"Would you please repeat that, Captain?"

"We at the Palm Beach Police department have no reason to believe that Mitt Hecher shot Rodger Kriger."

"And when did the police department come to this conclusion?"

"About four months ago, shortly after Mister Gatson confessed that he lied."

"Thank you, Captain. Now, Captain Richmond, do you know what Rodger Kriger did the day before he was murdered?"

"Yes. He spent the day fishing with Alberto Francisco, the sugar baron."

"What was the connection between Mister Kriger and Mister Francisco?"

"As far as we could determine, they were just friends."

"Do you have any reason to believe they discussed something on the yacht which led to the murder?"

"We interviewed Mister Francisco and he indicated that the two of them simply had an enjoyable time fishing, and that Mister Kriger had caught a large marlin."

"Did you believe him?"

"We found no reason not to."

Seppish stood in front of the witness stand and placed his left hand on his chin, forefinger curled under his nose, head lowered in thought.

"I have no more questions."

"The court will adjourn for today and the trial will resume at ten a.m. tomorrow," Judge Schultz announced. "All parties please be present at that time. Ladies and gentlemen of the jury, I must admonish you again to refrain from speaking to anyone, and avoid all media reports, concerning the trial. Thank you."

At nine-thirty a.m., Scraponia met in the court anteroom with his next two witnesses, Alan Burns and Donald Gibbons.

"Let's review what you are going to testify, Alan," the prosecutor said. The jail inmate, whose arms were covered with tattoos, was muscular and had a large, square head that resembled a concrete block.

"Well, Hecher just talked about how this rich dude Kroger got shot in Palm Beach at his house and nobody knows who done it but they think he done it."

Scraponia stared balefully at his witness and swiveled his head back and forth.

"No, no, no. That's not what we discussed—not if you want to leave that jail early. First, let's get the name of the victim straight. It's Kriger, not Kroger. He owned a chain of restaurants, not a chain of supermarkets."

Alan Burns frowned, looking puzzled.

"Never mind. More important, Hecher asked you to carry notes to Dewey Crimshaw that were about the Kriger shooting. And you delivered them. Do you understand now?"

"Oh, yeah, now I remember."

"Do you think you can remember for another hour or two and repeat that on the witness stand?"

"Sure, sure. No problem."

"How about you, Donald? Do you have the story straight in your head?"

The thickset black man sat at the table next to his fellow inmate, a smile of amusement spread wide on his round face.

"I got it down pat," he assured. "You ain't got nothin to worry bout wid me."

Judge Schultz opened the trial, and Scraponia called Burns to the stand first, while their conversation was fresh in his memory. He had the witness identify himself as an inmate at the Palm Beach County Jail.

"Now, Mister Burns, did Mitt Hecher ask you to deliver notes to Dewey Crimshaw?"

"Objection," said Seppish. "Leading the witness."

Scraponia had led Burns on purpose to be sure he would testify correctly, figuring the damage from violating the procedural rule would be less than if his witness forgot what to say.

"Objection sustained," said the judge.

"Mister Burns, did you know Mitt Hecher while you were an inmate at Palm Beach County Jail?"

"Yes. I talked to him in the mess hall."

"What did you talk to him about?"

"Mitt Hecher asked me to deliver notes to Dewey Crimshaw."

"Did he say what the notes were about?"

"He said they were about the Kroger—I mean the Kriger shooting."

"And did you deliver the notes as Mister Hecher asked you to?"

"Yes. I passed them to Dewey Crimshaw."

"Thank you, Mister Burns. No more questions."

Seppish again declined to cross-examine, and Donald Gibbons was called to the stand. He testified that he overheard Hecher say he had mistakenly shot Kriger, intending to shoot his neighbor's son, who owed him money for drugs.

Seppish had not interviewed them, nor any of the other prosecution witnesses, before the trial. The night before this day, he sat at home watching a kick boxing championship fight on television.

The blond fighter feinted with his left, then paused and waited until the black guy moved forward. The white guy whirled and leaped two feet off the mat, striking out with his leg and connecting to the right of the black's nose, opening a bloody gash. The blow sent the black crashing backward onto the mat.

"Yeah!" Seppish shouted to an empty apartment.

The fighter lay there a few seconds while the referee counted, then shook his head and rose. The blond moved in and buried a fist into his opponent's midsection, doubling him up, then delivered the *coup de grâce,* a swift haymaker to the side of the head. The black fighter dropped to the canvas and remained there, unconscious.

Seppish rose from the couch and felt a surge of the manliness that the prostate surgery had stolen from him.

"Will the bailiff please summon George Demarco to the witness stand," the judge directed.

Back in the anteroom, Captain John Danielson turned off the television that he'd ordered a jail trusty to carry in. The trial was part of an experiment with cameras in the courtroom. Danielson had explained to the head bailiff that he, Danielson, needed the television to monitor the trial for law enforcement officials and advise them whether it compromised their efforts.

"I'm all ready to go," Demarco said to Danielson. "But it's a good thing I was able to watch the other three guys or I might have contradicted them in some details."

Demarco strode to the stand carrying a Bible.

"Mister Demarco," Scraponia began, "is that a Bible you're holding?"

"It is, sir."

"Why are you carrying a Bible, Mister Demarco?"

"Well, sir, while sitting on death row, I've been forced to think about the awful things I've done, and I've accepted the Lord Jesus Christ as my savior. I've become a born-again Christian and know that he has forgiven me. I am a new person, and I want to do what is right."

"Is that why you have agreed to testify in this trial?"

"Yes, sir, it is."

"Mister Demarco, what did Mitt Hecher tell you about the murder of Rodger Kroger—I mean Kriger"—Scraponia clenched his teeth and glowered at Alan Burns—"while you both were inmates at the Palm Beach County Jail?"

"Objection," Seppish shouted, shooting his arm up and pointing at the ceiling. "Leading the witness."

"Objection sustained," said Judge Schultz.

"Was Mitt Hecher a fellow inmate of yours at the Palm Beach County Jail?"

"Yes. I saw Mister Hecher frequently."

"Where did you see Mitt Hecher?"

"I ran across him in the gym and the mess hall a lot, and in the TV room."

"Did Mitt Hecher ever talk to you?"

"Yes, he did. He told me once when we were working out that he had shot Mister Kriger by mistake. He said that he meant to shoot the son of Mister Kriger's neighbor, Bobby Gunder, because Bobby wouldn't pay him money for drugs that Mister Hecher had supplied him with. But Mister Hecher accidentally went to the wrong house."

"Do you have any opinion about what kind of person Mister Hecher is?"

"Yes. He is temperamental and gets upset easily. The other inmates fear him, because he is a karate expert and has threatened to harm two or three of them. He seems like a violent man."

"No further questions, Your Honor."

"Mister Seppish, you may question the witness if you wish," the judge announced.

"No, thank you, Your Honor. However, I would like to call to the stand Nathaniel Hathaway, an FBI handwriting expert."

Hathaway came forth, and Seppish solicited testimony as to his résumé.

"Mister Hathaway, have you had the opportunity to examine the two-page confession allegedly written by Mitt Hecher?"

"I have."

"And have you examined the handwriting of DeWitt Crimshaw?"

"Yes, sir, I have."

"Have you come to any conclusions as to who wrote that confession?"

"No, I have not. I have found that it is impossible to determine whether either Mister Hecher or Mister Crimshaw wrote the confession."

"Thank you. That is all."

"I will not allow the written confession to be admitted into evidence," Judge Schultz pronounced. "However, unless the defense counsel offers a reasonable objection, I will permit the inclusion of Mister Crimshaw's letter outlining the confession into the evidence file as Exhibit A."

Seppish remained seating, saying nothing.

The trial recessed for the weekend. On the following Monday, Scraponia called the widow, Jan Kriger, to testify.

"Mrs. Kriger, did you have your husband murdered to gain possession of his business, or so you would be awarded his insurance, or both?"

"No, I did not."

"Did you have your husband murdered for any reason?"

Mrs. Kriger paused while struggling against tears. Then, in a tone resonating with anger, she spoke, spacing the words.

"No, I did not."

"Thank you, Mrs. Kriger. That's all."

Seppish stepped forward and waited a few moments while the witness composed herself.

"Mrs. Kriger, records we have obtained show that you are the beneficiary of a $200,000 life insurance policy taken out on your husband less than four months before he was shot. Was Mister Kriger aware of this policy?"

"It was Rodger's idea to buy the policy. We were planning a ski trip to Squaw Valley at Lake Tahoe, and he said I should have it in case of an accident."

"You also took over the management of the eleven Land O' Gocean restaurants that you and your husband owned. Is that correct?"

"Yes. I had assisted Rodger from time to time, filling in when he had to travel, that sort of thing, and I knew the business. It was no problem stepping in full-time. The challenge was juggling that and tending to our six children, some of whom are still in school."

Her lower lip quivered as she lowered her head, hiding the emotion that threatened to gain control over her.

"Mrs. Kriger, was your husband faithful to you in the weeks and months leading to his murder?"

"I'm going to interrupt here and direct that further interrogation of the witness be conducted in my chambers," Judge Schultz said. "The press and television cameras will not be allowed access."

In the judge's room, Seppish argued, "Your Honor, it's no secret that Rodger Kriger was having an affair with a dancer at a club in Palm Beach Shores, and that Jan Kriger was angry at him for it. This is a highly relevant issue."

"Excuse me, but this woman has been through too much already, and there is no indication that their marital troubles had anything to do with his death," Scraponia countered.

"Mister Seppish makes an important point," said the judge. "I know this is going to be very difficult for Mrs. Kriger, but I have to allow the defense to proceed."

As the three stepped toward the door of the chambers, Scraponia leaned into Seppish.

"You've got a lot of nerve pointing a finger at somebody else's sexual transgressions," the prosecutor said under his breath, out of earshot of the judge. "Maybe somebody should allude to yours."

Seppish walked to the witness stand.

"I have no further questions, Mrs. Kriger."

She walked with head bowed down the aisle and out of the courtroom, followed by her children. She sat on a bench in the hallway and sobbed.

"Do the prosecution and the defense wish to call any more witnesses?" Judge Schultz asked

Scraponia and Seppish both said they were finished.

Seppish never called Bobby Gunder. He had told police he didn't know Mitt Hecher and wasn't living with his parents when Rodger Kriger was shot. The defense attorney also declined to have Hecher testify in his own defense.

"Very well," said the judge. "We will move to the closing statements. Mister Scraponia, you may proceed."

"Ladies and gentlemen of the jury, I'm going to address you separately by gender to make my point in ways that are different in practice but identical in principle. Please hear me out and you will understand what I mean. Ladies, what goes into baking an apple pie—besides apples, of course? I believe you use sugar, and flour, and butter, and milk, and egg, and cinnamon. Am I right? Now, by themselves, these ingredients aren't terribly impressive, are they? They're banal, rather ordinary. Even the apple is nothing special. But what happens when you put them all together and bake the mixture? Aha. You get a delicious dessert that is much better than any of the individual ingredients by themselves.

"Now, gentlemen, I want you to consider the engine of an automobile. What are its main parts? Let's see… there's the block, the valves, the crankshaft, the pistons, and the spark plugs. By themselves, these components don't accomplish much. But unite them in a coordinated way, and they become much greater than five parts of an engine. They prove a principle taught to us by a very wise man a very long time ago. That man was Aristotle. He said, the whole is greater than the sum of its parts. And that has been shown to be true over and over throughout history. It applies in the case of the car and the principle of the pie.

"And it holds true in the trial of Mitt Hecher for the murder of Rodger Kriger. The men who testified against him were not, individually, strong witnesses. The defense will make much of the fact that I could not call the person who first identified Mitt Hecher as the killer to testify because that person, Richie Gatson, failed to appear in court and is eluding the law. Defense counsel also will note that Mister Gatson admitted to lying in a deposition about the location of the murder weapon. I would point out, however, that he and Mitt Hecher were fast friends, and he likely had misgivings.

"The crux of the matter is this: The testimony of these men, taken together, forged a steely finger of guilt that pierced to the heart of this case and left no doubt that Mitt Hecher is guilty of shooting Rodger Kriger through the foyer window and front door of his home on the night of January Fourteen, 1976. When Mister Hecher was charged with fatally shooting Rodger Kriger, he already had begun serving time for lesser, but nonetheless serious, crimes. In the case we have before us today, Mister Hecher crossed the line and intentionally took the life of another. He demonstrated that he is a menace to society and must be removed from its midst so as to never again present a danger to innocent citizens. I urge you to do your duty and find Mitt Hecher guilty of murder in the first degree in the fatal shooting of Rodger Kriger."

A weary-looking Alonzo Seppish walked with a little stoop to the front of the jury and leaned his right arm on the rail.

"Members of the jury, what you witnessed in these last few days was a charade, a show directed by a prosecutor who presented purely circumstantial evidence. He offered a parade of witnesses whose criminal backgrounds render them completely incredible. There was nothing to prove anything they said. You have been asked to believe witnesses who were, by the prosecutor's own admission, unsavory characters—jail inmates who were convicted of serious crimes. They had committed perjury in the past, and there was every reason to believe they would do so again to curry favor with the state. And don't believe the prosecutor's story about Richie Gatson. Once Gatson was on the run from police and had nothing to gain by lying, that's when he told the truth.

"Furthermore, no physical evidence was presented that would point to Mitt Hecher as the person who shot Rodger Kriger. The prosecution's own expert witness testified there was no indication that the shotgun produced by police as the murder weapon was the one used to shoot the victim. And a handwriting expert could not verify that Mitt Hecher's supposed written confession was his handwriting.

"Mister Hecher has not been a choir boy. He has been a brawler and has flouted the law. But no one, not even any of the police officers who responded to repeated bar fights he was involved in, has come before this court and said Mitt Hecher has the heart of a murderer. He's tough, but he's no killer. I implore you: Do not make a mockery of justice. A man's life is in your hands. You cannot lightly throw it away. You must find Mitt Hecher not guilty in the fatal shooting of Rodger Kriger."

Seppish took his seat.

"The jury will break for lunch," Judge Schultz announced, "and return at two p.m. to begin deliberations toward the goal of reaching a verdict."

Seppish leaned against the younger attorney assisting him in the case and fretted under his breath that he was quite tired and was heading to his home in south Broward County, since there was nothing more he could do. He said that he wanted to beat the Interstate 95 rush hour traffic.

As the afternoon wore on and no word came that the jury had reached a verdict, the courtroom audience gradually thinned. By five o'clock, almost everyone had left except for Kriger's and Hecher's family members and relatives. Friends of the Krigers bent down to Mrs. Kriger at her seat next to the aisle, patted her on the shoulder, and whispered words of comfort. Now and then, one of those remaining rose and walked down the outer hallway to the restroom.

Six o'clock passed, then seven, and eight. Attendees fidgeted, crossed and uncrossed their legs, and talked in low tones about family matters. Murmuring about the length of the deliberations began, first among the attorneys, and duplicated by the lay persons who had watched them and divined the nature of their chatting. Were they unable to reach a verdict? Was this going to be a hung jury? Why would the jurors be taking so long? Even those who wanted Hecher convicted had seen little chance of it happening. Now there was hope. Maybe a mistrial would be declared.

At nine p.m., Judge Schultz sent the court administrator to the jury room for a progress report. When she returned, the judge announced, "The jury foreman indicates that the jury has not reached a verdict and needs more time. Accordingly, I am ordering a recess until tomorrow at nine a.m., when the jury will resume deliberations. The court is adjourned."

"Well," Mrs. Kriger sighed as she turned to her oldest daughter, a college student, with a weak smile. "I guess there's hope. I thought this was going to be a slam-dunk innocent verdict."

In the morning, trial enthusiasts lined up early outside the courtroom, hoping to get a seat. When the room was full, scores were left to sit outside on benches or mull around in the hallway. Speculation about the pending verdict buzzed with the animation of a disturbed beehive. Strangers struck up conversations among themselves, beginning with the possible verdict and evolving into the merits of the case.

After two-and-a-half hours, the court administrator led the jury to the jury box. She opened an envelope and read: "The jury finds Mitt Hecher guilty of murder in the first degree in the shooting of Rodger Kriger on the night of January Fourteen, Nineteen-Seventy-Six, which resulted in his death eleven days later on January Twenty-Five."

A cacophony of gasps and exclamations of "What?" "Oh, no," "Impossible," "Are you kidding?" erupted as people leaped to their feet, their mouths open. Diane Hecher buried her head in her lap and sobbed. Mitt Hecher's mother sat motionless as tears slid down her cheeks.

Mitt looked back at them, his eyes meeting his wife's as she raised her head. He smiled and mouthed, "It'll be okay."

Police officers escorted him to the front row where his family members sat, and he hugged his wife and mother, assuring them that he would get through this. Then the officers led him away in handcuffs.

As they passed Seppish, Hecher turned his head and consoled, "I know you did your best."

Mrs. Kriger sat staring ahead, her face impassive. For almost a minute, she didn't move and said nothing.

Then, glancing at her children seated to her left, she murmured, "Let's go."

———————

Alonzo Seppish arrived just before the verdict was announced. In the hallway outside the courtroom afterward, he faced television cameras, radio microphones, and reporters brandishing pens and notebooks. He said that he would file an appeal to the Fourth District Court of Appeal within the fifteen days allowed.

At a hearing that afternoon, he chose not to allow the jury to determine whether his client should receive the death penalty.

"Mitt Hecher has seen how much he can trust these dozen dunces to act sensibly," he told reporters. "We'll put his life in the hands of the judge. I think he knows what a farce this trial was. It was apparent to anybody whose mind was halfway open. But the people who sat in that jury box came to this trial with their minds made up."

Scraponia revealed to Tom Palladin of the *Miami Gazette* that he would present reasons to Judge Schultz why Hecher should be sentenced to die in the electric chair. At a presentence hearing weeks later, the prosecutor listed what he called "aggravating circumstances" favoring the death penalty and argued there were no "mitigating circumstances." Shortly afterward, the judge announced that he had completed a background check of Hecher.

Considering the circumstantial evidence as the basis of the conviction, Judge Schultz said, he could not in good conscience condemn Hecher to death. Instead, he imposed the minimum sentence required by Florida law: twenty-five years in prison, to be served concurrently with the twenty-eight years the prisoner already had received for his other crimes.

Hecher took a deep breath. He turned to Seppish.

"Alonzo, do you think you could get the judge to let me spend just a little bit of time with the son I've never seen before I go?"

"I'll try," said the defense attorney. He approached the judge, spoke briefly, and returned to his client.

"This is a compassionate judge. He says you have ten minutes."

Two police officers led Hecher to the anteroom and removed the handcuffs, and Seppish escorted his wife Diane in with the infant, whom she handed to her husband.

"Hey, Pauley, you cute little guy." Hecher beamed. Pauley began to cry. "Hey, now, you cryin because I'm leavin or cuz you don't know who this strange lookin guy holding you is?" He tickled the tyke in the tummy, and the face that was contorted in fear and anger metamorphosed into wide-eyed joy and giggling.

"There, that's much better. Now you look like your mother. Before you looked like me, and had me a little worried, you little sucker. Because I don't want you to be like me, you understand? I want you to stay out of trouble, and go to school and get good grades, and help your mother. And one day I'm going to be back, and we're all going to be together again. I want you to never forget that. But until then, I'm going to be in contact with you, and find out about your progress. I can't be with you physically, but I will be with you in mind and spirit. You will always be in my heart."

He held his son close, and a tear escaped his left eye. The police officers walked toward him from the door.

"I'm ready."

He handed his son to Diane, hugged her, and whispered in her ear, "We're going to get through this."

The officer attached handcuffs and led him away.

———————

Like vultures hovering above their carrion, the five jailbirds who had collaborated with Scraponia to win the conviction of Mitt Hecher sent their attorneys swooping into the county courthouse on the very day the trial ended to file claims for reward money. Donors had offered $40,000 for information leading to the conviction, and the deal-makers weren't content with getting their jail sentences reduced or freed on probation. Even Richie Gatson, who remained a fugitive, sought a piece of the pie. The five soon agreed to split the money in order to move the process forward, and a judge approved a settlement.

But alliances built from an evil foundation are shaky, and this one had little chance of surviving. The first crack came after a few weeks when Alan Burns objected to his paltry share and demanded five times that amount. Days later, DeWitt Crimshaw argued in a letter to the court that he was entitled to the entire amount because time limits on claims by the others had expired. Furthermore, he was withdrawing his pledge to donate all of the proceeds to charity and would give only what, if any, remained after he paid legal fees connected with the case.

The judge withdrew his approval of the settlement and announced he would review it further.

Chapter Eleven

"Two, maybe three years ago, I am at party," the male, Latin-accented voice on the phone related. "I hear man who was manager of Land O' Gocean restaurant say Kriger fire him and he want revenge. His friends was calling him Carlos. He know about a guy they call Pat the Rat in gang of big drug sellers that very dangerous, and they work with Cubans. He say maybe he contact that guy. That all I know."

He hung up.

Vanessa Sanders, a private investigator whom Hecher hired before the trial, had gained media attention for her efforts to find evidence supporting his innocence. She had struck out.

Sanders checked state police records for anyone with the affectionate handle of Pat the Rat. She found him at Raiford prison, and examined the police files on him. He fit the description given by the tipster to a tee.

Pat the Rat was Pat Racoby, who was convicted of a car-bombing and sentenced in January 1978 to ninety-nine years.

Sydney Goldsmith left his swanky condominium in Hialeah early one evening in October 1974 to oversee operations at his Goldfinger nightclub a few miles away. He looked chic in a blue blazer and white slacks, a shiny gold chain around his neck. His sparkling appearance belied a vague sense of disquiet. Not long before, a frequent customer had become problematic. Goldsmith allowed the man to run a tab, which zoomed to $430 in five weeks. When he asked the man, Pat Racoby, to pay his bill, he became belligerent and left. A week passed and Racoby never returned, so the club owner had a bill collector track him down and threaten legal action if payment weren't made.

Goldsmith ambled up to his 1973 royal blue Cadillac Seville with gold trimming, parked in his end spot in the lot. The spot next to his was vacant until the couple it was assigned to would return from their Northern home.

Waiting in a beige, late-model Ford in a guest spot near the other end of the condo parking lot, between two other cars, was a man slumped in the driver's seat, peering over the lower edge of the passenger window frame at Goldsmith.

Goldsmith opened the door and climbed in. He turned the key in the ignition.

The explosion blew through the floor under him, ripped the console apart, tore the driver side door off, shattered all of the windows, and left Goldsmith a pile of bones, flesh, and blood all tangled with the disintegrated front seat.

"Now was that really worth four-hundred-and-thirty dollars, Mister Goldsmith?" Racoby muttered, smiling. "I'm not called Pat the Rat for nothing."

He raised himself in his seat, started his Ford, and drove out of the parking lot.

Residents tumbled out of their condos, and within three minutes police cars first, then fire rescue units, screamed onto the scene. Paramedics lifted what remained of Goldsmith onto a stretcher and began applying tourniquets to his profusely bleeding upper legs, which were hanging loosely, two sticks of torn flesh and bone. He survived, minus two legs, a hand, and an eye.

Goldsmith told detectives about trying to collect the overdue bar bill from Pat Racoby. Experts determined five pounds of dynamite were used in the bomb, and investigators set to work checking South Florida explosives dealers. They found a supplier where Racoby had purchased five pounds six days before the bombing. He'd asked what kind of damage that much dynamite would cause a car, saying he was a race car driver and wanted to test the strength of a car like the one he drove to get an estimation of how it would fare in a crash. The salesman had thought it was a bizarre and wasteful experiment.

In August 1977, Racoby was arrested. Investigators believed he also was a key part of a heroin smuggling ring that was suspected of several murders in the early 1970s. He had dealings with a hard-core gang of Cuban drug smugglers.

Vanessa Sanders contacted the Dade County state attorney's office, which asked the governor's office about the possibility of reopening the investigation of the Kriger murder in light of the new information provided by the telephone tipster. Aides of the governor said the office had no jurisdiction over the matter. But the Dade state attorney's office and Sanders announced they would continue to investigate.

State Attorney Donald Bosworth referred Sanders to an assistant state attorney, Joshua Whiteman. She recounted what she had learned. Whiteman said he was checking a claim by a county jail prisoner that the same Pat the Rat had killed Kriger.

The singing jailbird was a man named Jerry Cruddy, who was serving time for burglary. He told Whiteman that he often visited a convenience store near the Land O' Gocean restaurant managed by Carlos. Once the store clerk pointed to a customer at the beer cooler in the back and said, "See him? He's Pat the Rat. He killed that Palm Beach guy, Rodger Kriger, for some Cubans who worked for Kriger."

Whiteman talked to the clerk, who denied in a sworn statement ever having such a conversation with Cruddy. The attorney paid Cruddy a visit at the jail.

"Mister Cruddy, my boss in the state attorney's office has informed me that you volunteered the information on Pat Racoby in the hope of getting a better deal on your burglary charge. Of course, you wouldn't have to worry about retaliation from Mister Racoby since he will be spending quite a long time at Raiford. What do you have to say to this?"

"Well, sir, yes, I was hoping that for my cooperation, your office might recommend lighter punishment for me. What I have told you should help you find the real killer of Rodger Kriger."

"It so happens that what you told us hasn't helped at all, Mister Cruddy. Better luck next time. Good day."

Whiteman decided Cruddy had no knowledge of the case, and then another man called to suggest that Cruddy killed Kriger. Whiteman invited the man to his office to give a sworn statement. Cruddy asked him two weeks before the shooting to "do a job" in Palm Beach for someone angry over a business deal, he said, but he declined. On the night of the shooting Cruddy borrowed shotgun shells from him. Two friends of his gave statements saying they were at his house when Cruddy came for the shells, while Cruddy's friend Pete waited in the car. Cruddy's ex-wife also gave a statement, saying he spent a lot of money a few days after the shooting. She didn't understand how an auto mechanic could have that much money.

Whiteman was suspicious of the motives of the four. For one thing, they had waited two years to come forward with their accusation. On the other hand, their story seemed to jibe somewhat with one told two years earlier to Jim Scraponia and the Kriger family's attorney.

In a letter to the attorney and then in an interview with him and Scraponia, an admitted alcoholic said he'd overheard a conversation among two men and three women in a bar in Miami or Key Biscayne. He was drunk at the time and wasn't sure where. The men called themselves Jerry and Pete. They talked about how they'd done a "hit" in Palm Beach and afterward taken a dinghy across the Intracoastal Waterway to West Palm Beach, "deep-sixing" something in the water on the way. According to the alcoholic eavesdropper, the two men said they'd "souped up" a car so they could outrace police, and it awaited them on the other side.

Whiteman knew that Jerry Cruddy was an auto mechanic. The drunk's story seemed to fit with that of Jerry's associates and his ex-wife, and the more the prosecutor thought about it, the more convinced he became that Cruddy was involved in the shooting of Kriger. He had reviewed the inmates' testimony against Mitt Hecher and found them not believable. After completing his investigation, he sat on his findings for months until he had left for private practice, figuring his report would create much controversy.

It did. State Attorney Donald Bosworth called Whiteman into his office and asked him to delete from the report his concerns about how the case against Hecher was handled. Whiteman refused to change a word.

Jared Imwold, the news director of radio station WNQX, began his own investigation of the crime after reading all of the newspaper reports. Ever more questions about Mitt Hecher's guilt formed in his mind. He read the entire police file on the case and contacted the state attorney's office, which referred him to Joshua Whiteman.

Imwold realized that Whiteman had failed to consider why Jerry and Pete would have risked detection by neighbors as they walked from the Intracoastal to the Kriger home to do the shooting, then walked back to the Intracoastal, and then rowed across at one of the widest points along Palm Beach as police cars searched the area and in all probability scanned the Waterway with spotlights.

Wouldn't the two have been worried about residents walking down the block, tugged along by pampered pets, searching for discreet spots where their Pomeranians and poodles could poop, for somebody's yard where their Chihuahuas and schnauzers and Malteses and bichon frises and Lhasa apsos and shih tzus could shit? Surely, Imwold reasoned, Jerry and Pete would have checked and found that people took strolls along Palm Beach Lake Trail, sometimes late in the evening before heading to bed. Two men walking toward the waterway could have simply been a couple of gays, a common sight in Palm Beach. But carrying a shotgun? And boarding a boat at that hour of the night? There was nothing to indicate the two were that stupid.

And what about the car? Imwold remembered that witnesses reported a Corvette racing through Palm Beach, not West Palm Beach.

Whiteman discounted the later confession by the alcoholic that he had concocted the story of what he heard in the Miami-area bar, based on what he read about Jerry and Pete in the newspaper. The drunk said he wanted to collect reward money. No media attention had been given to the possible involvement of the two men in Kriger's murder. The drunk either was originally telling the truth or was linked in some way with the four—Jerry Cruddy's three associates and his ex-wife—who later implicated him.

Something was amiss.

Whiteman informed Jared Imwold that Cruddy's attorney had persuaded a lenient judge to release him on five years' probation. Cruddy told the judge that he feared elements in South Florida and wanted to move far away. Whiteman gave Imwold the name of Cruddy's parole officer, who put the newsman in touch with his client in Michigan.

"I'm not gonna tell you nothin," Cruddy told Imwold over the phone. "I'm scared for my life. I don't want nobody to know where I am. I'm afraid of what the Cubans might do to me if they found me. That's all I'm gonna say. Sorry I can't say no more. I want you to keep quiet about where I am. You don't know what town I'm in, do you?"

"No, your probation officer wouldn't tell me. He only gave me a phone number."

"All right. I don't want you to say nothin. I could get killed. Okay?"

"Sure. Mum's the word."

"Thanks. Gotta go now. Bye."

Imwold sat at his desk in a den in his house, back of a bulletin board thumb-tacked with newspaper stories in a neat arrangement. Copies of police reports, court documents, and other records lay in stacks on an eight-foot banquet table situated at a right angle with the desk, a waste basket in between. He leaned back in his swivel chair and propped his feet on the desk, his thighs and chest cradling an ample belly as though it were a basket of fruit. He removed the wire-rimmed glasses from his oval face and laid them in the crevice between his chest and belly.

Cruddy has done something to piss off the Cubans. And he knew they were mad at Kriger. If they thought Cruddy was the killer, they wouldn't feel so much animosity toward him. Could Cruddy have set it up to make it appear he killed Kriger? He probably figured the state attorney's office wouldn't conduct a real investigation, anyway, because they wouldn't go out of their way to prove they convicted the wrong guy. Nah, that's too far-fetched. Isn't it?"

PART II: BEHIND BARS; BATTLING THE BENCH

Chapter One

The light-green-and-white Palm Beach County Sheriff's squad car pulled up to the stone gates of Florida State Prison at Raiford, north of Gainesville, and continued to the Administration Building. The deputy driving got out, followed by a deputy in the back seat, then another deputy and Mitt Hecher, whose wrists were handcuffed together. Silently, they walked to the forbidding gray concrete building and entered the admissions office. Hecher's escorts handed him over to prison staff. The deputies exchanged a few pleasantries with the officials, who advised them of where they might want to dine in town before turning in to their motel for the night. The drive back the next day would take about nine hours.

The prison was near the town of Starke. Why state officials chose that site for a state prison is a matter for the history books. Surely the sparse population of the area was a factor: Nobody wants a penitentiary in his back yard. But fate must have picked the prison's proximity to a town with a name reflecting the institution's ambience so quintessentially that the two might have been one and the same. The prison's reputation as home to the hardest criminals in the state earned it a nickname of its own among the inmates: The Rock.

After a year-and-a-half in the Palm Beach County Jail, Hecher was savvy enough to know that Raiford, as the prison was known, would be both a relief and more daunting. At the jail, facing trial for murder, he'd been in virtual solitary for most of his term, stuck in a cell on the fourth floor and having contact with other prisoners only at meal times. At Raiford, he would be less confined, with more opportunities for activities involving interaction with his fellow inmates. On the other hand, Raiford was the final destination for a family of violent, predatory criminals, and their hopelessness only exacerbated those disorders.

"You won't last three months at Raiford, Hecher," Detective Lt. Snopes of the sheriff's department predicted. "You're not bad enough. Those guys are bad. They'll kill you."

Hecher stood in line with several other new prisoners who would join the community of 3,500. An inmate working in the processing office tossed his bedroll to him, and a guard led him to his cell. It had two bunk beds end to end back of the cell gate, and two single beds, one parallel with the cell gate to the right and its twin perpendicular to it. He would be sharing the cell with five others. The gate was open and he was free to roam until dinner at six p.m., and had to be back in the cell by eight p.m., when the gate was locked.

The toilet was under the television in the far corner of the cell, and at nine-thirty one of the cellmates used it for a bowel movement while the others casually looked over him at the screen. Hecher turned away out of respect for the fellow, and configured in his mind a different positioning of the beds to allow for an alternate location of the TV. He wondered if prison officials had deliberately designed this layout to humiliate the prisoners.

The lights went out at ten, and Hecher climbed into his upper bunk. After a few minutes, he heard movement below, coming from the single bed on the far side. Then, a near whisper.

"No, please, don't."

He saw a hefty black inmate crawl under the blanket into the bed of a smaller white prisoner who also had been admitted that day, and begin an up-and-down motion. Minutes later an odor of excrement drifted up to his bunk and became more powerful.

On his second day, Hecher approached the chin-up bar in the prison yard. A tall, raw-boned white guy, who appeared to be in his early thirties, stepped in front of the bar. A big grin opened to crooked, yellowed teeth separated at the top right by a wide gap where two were missing.

Hecher glanced up. *This guy must be some kind of alligator rassler from the Florida swamps.* He looked like an oversized version of the sodomizer in *Deliverance*.

"Hi there, li'l feller," he hollered at Hecher. "You new here, ain'tcha? Bet nobody done told you yet that ev'body gits nitiated in this here section of the prison. And I'm the guy who's in charge of the cer'mony. They calls me Big Dick."

Twenty or so inmates within earshot all stopped what they were doing and stared. The hayseed looked around at the men.

"Ain't that right, y'all?"

A few "Yeah, yeah"s. They were standing in rapt attention, awaiting the show, grinning.

"Okay, let's give the men some entertainment," Big Dick boomed, turning toward Hecher, pulling fully erect and leaning a little backward, grinning even wider. "They gits bored in this place. Never any fun."

"Sure," said Hecher. "We'll give them some entertainment."

"Huh? Yer gonna go along with me? Okay then. Here I come, pretty li'l guy. Pull your pants down."

"Listen, you pukey lookin scum. I don't like being called pretty and I don't like being called little. And if you as much as touch me, you're gonna regret it for a long time."

The other inmates jerked their heads in each other's direction, their faces mirroring disbelief. Nobody had ever talked to Big Dick like that, not even the bigger inmates.

The smile vanished from Big Dick's face.

"Now you done made me mad," he fumed, hustling up to Hecher.

Hands raised in the karate position, the much smaller man deftly stepped to the left as Big Dick lunged at him. The muscular Hecher swung his left hand sideways like an ax and caught the big guy in the windpipe. As part of his karate training, Hecher had spent hours beating boards and bricks, anything hard, with the edges of his hands to harden them. Dick clutched his throat and bent over gasping.

With his right hand, Hecher executed a powerful blow to the back of the man's neck, jerking his head up. The karate expert delivered an uppercut to Big Dick's nose, breaking it. Blood burst onto his prison blues. Hecher smashed a fist into the lout's solar plexus, doubling him up. Moving farther to the side, the smaller man leaped and shot his left foot at the man's kidney. As Big Dick was falling, Hecher swung a fist into the side of the man's head for the finishing blow. He crumpled to the ground, barely conscious and hardly breathing.

A large group of inmates had gathered to witness the event. For the initiation ceremony, it was customary for the inmates to gather closely enough to prevent guards from seeing what was happening, but in somewhat loose formation so as not to arouse their suspicion. Now, however, they had become transfixed and formed a crowd, attracting the attention of guards stationed at a distance. Two came running, and the inmates dispersed. The guards summoned medics, who raced onto the prison yard in a motorized cart, loaded Big Dick onto a stretcher, and sped back to the main prison building as inmates stood and gawked.

"All right, men, what happened here?" the captain in charge demanded.

The men shrugged and sauntered away.

"Gronowski's in damned ugly shape. It had to be somebody pretty big to beat him that bad." He surveyed the group leaving and called to a brawny, heavy black prisoner. "Packer, you do this?"

"Hell no, Cap'n. I wasn't even there when whatever happened happened. I just seen a bunch of guys and came up from over yonder"—he gestured back over his shoulder—"to see what was goin on, and there was Big Dick lyin on the ground, bleedin and lookin like he was dyin."

"Well, I guess nobody's going to talk. Okay then, it looks like you'd rather forfeit your freedom for today. Everybody will return to their cells now." He faced the other guards and ordered, "Fleming and Brogan, go to the east and west ends of the yard and tell the sergeants I've ordered everybody inside."

"Aw, man, you gonna punish us for somethin we didn't do?" a thin black man with a long, narrow face groused.

Others cursed under their breaths and cast baleful looks at the sergeant. They began trudging toward the gate to the prison interior. From a few mingling at the scene of the incident, a short inmate stepped up to the captain.

"There's no need for this, Captain," said Mitt Hecher. "I'm the one who beat Big Dick."

The captain looked at the inmate open-mouthed and appraised him—short, though strongly built. Still, he couldn't have been a match for the hulking Big Dick.

"You're the new guy, aren'tcha? What're ya tryin to do, get yourself in trouble right off the bat? No way you could handle that animal, so why're you taking the blame?"

"I'm telling you, Captain, I did it. I had to. He was trying to rape me."

The inmates had stopped their exodus and were watching intently.

"You're telling me you beat the crap out of that walrus?"

"He had it coming."

"He may have had it coming, but that's not my point. How the hell could a guy your size get the better of that gorilla? It's like David and Goliath."

"I know karate."

"You *know* karate? Holy Moses. You must be the world champion if you're not lyin to me." He turned to the other inmates. "Did you guys see this? Is he tellin the truth about what happened?"

They stared at the captain.

"It's okay. Nobody's gonna know anything."

One man nodded his head slightly, and one by one several others did the same.

"Well, I'll be a son-of-a-bitch," said the captain. "Okay, uh—what's your name?"

"Hecher. Mitt."

"Tell me exactly what happened, Hecher."

"The guy called me little feller and told me to pull my pants down. He said he and I were going to provide entertainment for the guys. I told him I didn't like his insults and warned him not to touch me. He came at me, and I caught him with a few blows. He went down hard."

"Men, resume your activities. You too, Hecher. I gotta go tell the sergeants to disregard my orders."

Hecher walked to the chin-up bar, leaped to reach it, and did thirty chin-ups as several inmates watched admiringly. Breathing hard, he walked off his exertion along the gravel path. A well-toned, young white guy, crew cut, a few inches taller than Hecher, joined him.

"Man, where'd you learn to fight like that?" he asked. "That was fuckin outa sight. I think Big Dick's fun times are over. I was almost his victim two years ago when I first came here. He'd just grabbed me when Danny Yankovich came jogging around the path. Danny was even bigger than the Dick. He happened to look in our direction. Danny hated queers, and he took off from that path and headed toward us. I looked up, and Big Dick wondered what I was seeing and turned to look, too. When he saw Danny, he got out of there in a real hurry. Danny yelled, 'You better git, you homo half-wit, or I'll kill ya.' Danny was paroled a year later, but Dick had lost interest in me."

"What are you in for?" Hecher asked. "By the way, what's your name?"

"Jimmy Rowen. Auto theft. I spent a few months in the Pasco County Jail for shoplifting and possession of pot, and they threw the book at me this time. I'm doing five years. But I'm hoping to get out in maybe two years on good behavior. So listen, where did you learn karate like that?"

"I began tae kwon do lessons as a kid. I owned a karate studio in West Palm Beach."

"You think, man—I mean, I prob'ly shouldn't ask you this—but I wonder if you could teach me some karate."

"Well, I'm not sure what the people who run this place would think about that. I want to get out of here as soon as I can, too, and I don't want to cause any trouble. I just got here the other day. But maybe after I'm here a few months and if the officials feel good about me, I can suggest that they let me teach a class in karate to the inmates. Whoever wants to join, I mean. See, I might as well make the best of my life here, cuz I'm gonna be here a long time—unless some people working for me can get a new trial, which I doubt."

"What you in for?" Rowen asked.

"First degree murder."

Rowen jerked back. "Geez. You don't seem like no killer to me."

"I'm not. I was framed. Yeah, I know. That's what they all say. It happens to be true. I'm not saying I was a choir boy. I did a lot of bad stuff. But I never killed anybody, and I wouldn't want to. Except maybe Big Dick. Certain guys ask for it."

"So who framed you?"

"A prosecutor who hated my guts. He was after my ass for years for all the shit I did, and the power brokers in the Palm Beaches needed somebody to blame for the shotgun murder of a rich Palm Beacher. He gave jail inmates leniency for lying that I confessed to the murder. He's planning to run for the Florida Legislature. He figured railroading me to prison would buy him a ticket to Tallahassee."

———————————

"Hecher," the portly corporal said on the inmate's fourth day, "we're going to assign you to the pastry crew. You're to report to the kitchen at three a.m. and you'll make pastries until six a.m. and then go to breakfast. After that you're free to do what you want for the rest of the day until eight p.m. lock-up time."

The lights were turned off at ten but three of Hecher's cellmates gabbed and laughed till way past that, and the noise from prisoners on three floors echoed through the institution.

Hecher had slept perhaps an hour when the guard came to the cell at 2:45 a.m. and called his name. He was so deep in sleep that he didn't hear it, and his cellmate below punched the mattress.

"Mitt."

"Huh? Whatsa matter?"

"The guard wants ya. Time for work, I guess."

"Oh, geez, sorry."

He scrambled into his prison garb and walked with the guard along the walkway and down three flights of stairs, then through a wide hallway to the huge kitchen. The kitchen manager, a resident of Starke, took him to the pastry supervisor, a fortyish white inmate whose pasty complexion conveyed to Hecher the sense that the man had an aptitude for this job. His serious demeanor enhanced that perception as he instructed Hecher in the process of making sweet rolls.

"You don't want to get so deep in preparing another batch that you forget to take the rolls out of the oven at just the right time," he cautioned. "Otherwise, they get dried out and lose their taste. Course, you gotta leave em in long enough, too, cuz there ain't nothin worse than bitin into a roll with uncooked dough. They gotta be just right. Think you can handle it?"

"No problem," said Hecher.

But it was hot, intense work, and he was tired by six a.m. quitting time. Back in his cell, he climbed up to his bed. The cell doors were opened at 5:30, but Eddie, his mate in the bed below, was still there.

"Man, am I pooped," said Hecher. "Think I'll skip breakfast and stay here and sleep."

"What?" exclaimed Eddie, a white guy who Hecher judged to have been a plumber or other craftsman. "Are you nuts? You do and there's a good chance you ain't gonna wake up again."

"What are you talkin about?" Hecher asked.

"Wow. You got a lot to learn. Soon's the guard cracks open that door, you gotta be ready to defend yourself. A lota these guys go around and steal from the weaker prisoners. You go to sleep and they'll come and stab you. And if you get the guard to lock the door, that'll piss em off and they'll come back with a jar of gasoline and throw it in the cell and flip a match on it."

"Holy shit. This sounds like a real fun place."

"Yeah, it's fun all right. Let me tell you somethin, and you better not forget it. If you wanna survive this place, you gotta be constantly lookin over your shoulder. When you're out on the yard, keep your eye on anybody who comes near you. Look at guys' hands to see if they're hidin a shiv. If you jog on the track, check to see nobody's comin up behind you. And if you pass up somebody and happen to touch him, make damn sure you apologize—even if he could barely feel it. Otherwise he'll think you disrespected him."

"They're that touchy, huh?"

"See, these guys are just lookin for stuff to take away the boredom. Most of em are in for a hundred years and some up to three hundred years. Obviously, for almost all of them, this is their home for the rest of their life. So they don't give a fuck. They got nothin goin for them. They'd kill for a joke."

"So what are you in for, Eddie?"

"Murder. I went crazy and killed my wife. Strangled her. I'm thirty-eight. Been here seven years and think about her every day. I'll never get over it. I loved her. I'd do anything in the world to live that night over. Not just to be outa here, but to have her back."

"I'm sorry, man."

"What happened to you?"

"First degree murder. Well, I had some small-time stuff, too. Then they pinned a rich guy's murder on me. I was framed. It's going to be appealed. It's a long story. Thanks for clueing me in about this place."

"We get about a killing a week. There's at least six assaults a day—I mean bloody ones. Just wait. You'll see the guards hauling guys on gurneys to the infirmary all day long. It's pretty amazing how bad this place is run. They let 3,500 violent guys run loose. It's like the Wild West in here.

"Now, they do have one floor where guys are in lock-down waiting trial if they hit somebody on the head or stab a guard, something like that, or get caught with drugs. If you kill another inmate, you go on death row in that facility over there"—he turned his head and gestured—"about a thousand yards from here and they keep you locked up twenty-three hours a day."

In time, Hecher was able to tune out all but the most calamitous night sounds, such as when cellmates became angry and yelled at each other. Sometimes a fight erupted and an inmate was bitten or stabbed, his screams piercing the cell blocks like bolts of electricity as the prison mimicked a haunted house in a Halloween horror movie. But he adapted and managed to sleep the five hours and even doze while watching TV before ten o'clock. Fortunately for him, his sleep requirements were minimal.

He quickly got the hang of the pastry operation and even began to enjoy the camaraderie of the other crew members. They became a cohesive unit, with everyone looking out for each other, much like soldiers in combat.

———————

Diane Hecher wore a snug-fitting, black skirt four inches above the knee and a yellow-and-red silk blouse that showed ample cleavage. Sultry eye shadow beneath seductive lashes contrasted with her pinned-up, blond hair. Ruby lipstick added to the sensuous appeal, culminating in a look that was both sexy and lovely. Thin, four-inch-heeled sandals featured her small, arched feet and painted nails as she sat cross-legged on the frayed, wood waiting room bench, leaning forward in anticipation. She beamed when her husband was escorted through the iron gate.

"Oh, Mitt," she cried, bounding off the bench and into his arms. Tears spilled out of her eyes, and she grabbed Kleenex out of her purse and dabbed them. "My make-up will run all over and I'll look like a hag." She laughed.

They kissed slowly for what must have been a minute.

"Honey, you don't know how much I've longed for this," Hecher said in his grainy voice. "It's been three months. I think of you before I go to sleep every night. You're what keeps me going."

"I missed you just as bad, darlin. I wish I could have gotten here sooner, but it's kind of hard finding somebody to take care of Pauley for two days. I'm a little hesitant about having him make the nine-hour trip up and back until he gets a little older. I left him with my girlfriend."

"Yeah, I think that's probably best."

"So what's it been like?" she asked as they sat on the bench. "I get your letters, but you don't talk a lot about what it's like here. I've been suspecting you don't want to worry me. Come on, now. I want to know the truth. I can handle it."

Hecher took a deep breath. "It ain't no picnic. Lota animals in here. First night, a guy in my cell was raping another guy after the lights went out."

Diane's hand shot up to cover her mouth in horror.

"Well, hon, we knew it was going to be like this."

"Yes, but not right in your own cell."

"Yeah, that kinda surprised me. Then I had to get used to being constantly vigilant against attacks from inmates, because most of these guys know they'll never get out of here and they don't give a fuck what happens to them. I'm just damn glad for my karate. Without it, short as I am, I don't think I could survive in this place. I had to use it the second day. I guess that perverted swamp monster did me a favor, because after what I did to him, nobody wants to mess with me.

"So it was kind of bad at first, but I've made friends with some of the guys, and it's going okay now. You don't have to worry about me. I like my job in the pastry shop. The prison staff respect me, and we get along good. How's it with you? Is Pauley growing?"

"Oh, yes. He's quite a rascal, into everything. Just like his dad. He's a livewire. And curious. I'm doing fine at the company. They're picking up more accounts, and that's good. Makes my job more secure. The boss complimented me the other day on how well-organized I am with the record-keeping, and I take accurate notes, and I'm a fast transcriber."

"That's great. I wonder what I'm going to do when I get out. Let's hope it won't be too much longer."

"The attorneys are working on it," said Diane.

They spent the rest of the brief time they had together discussing how he would deal with his prison record in trying to find employment. Or, he wondered, why not open another karate studio and start over? She agreed that was a possibility.

"Uh-oh," said Hecher. "Here comes the guard. I guess that's the end of our visit. What a long way for you to drive and then get to spend such a short time."

"It's worth it, Mitt. Let's hope a short time is all you have left here. We just have to have faith. I know you will be strong. You know I'll always wait for you."

In a voice huskier than usual, he said, "Love ya, babe."

He looked up as the guard approached.

"Okay, Sarge. We'll break it up."

He and Diane stood and embraced. They kissed, and she walked toward the door, turning to blow him a kiss.

Hecher was efficient at his job, and officials decided he should be given more responsibility. Just after his wife's visit, they transferred him to a job in the prison canteen, where he stocked shelves and maintained inventory. Weeks later the inmate in charge was released on parole, and Hecher became manager. Men gathered in long lines in front of two windows to order items.

"Hey, dude, I saw that," he called through one window. "No cutting in front. You get in line like everybody else. Back to the rear."

"You ain't big enough to make me."

"Now listen, pardner, let's not start any trouble. My job is to make sure everybody gets treated fairly. Nobody gets special privileges."

"Man, I wasn't cuttin in. I was standin here the whole time."

"No, you weren't. I saw you sneak in when the other guys were lookin the other way."

"Well, I ain't movin."

Hecher instructed one of the canteen workers to lock the door behind him and walked out to the obstinate inmate. He was Hispanic, average-sized.

"You're trying to cut in front of these guys who've been patiently waiting for maybe twenty-five minutes, and I ain't gonna allow it. Okay?"

"Fuck you."

With lightning speed, Hecher gripped the man's right arm with both his hands, threw his leg behind the inmate's hip, and flipped him onto his back. The wind was knocked out of him and he gasped for air.

"Now scram, and don't come back till you're in a more cooperative mood."

Eight or ten inmates who were in line where the incident occurred yelled at the guy in support of Hecher.

"I'm glad he wasn't too big," he said to three canteen workers who had watched. "Otherwise I'd have had to hurt him to take him down, and I didn't want to do that."

Hecher had to account for an average of $12,000 a week in receipts. He assisted other inmates in establishing lines of credit. In six months at Raiford, he had gained the respect of prison officials.

He also had become pals with some inmates, who wanted him to teach them karate. When he approached the officials about starting a class, they knew he was not a risk, even though the martial art could be used against the guards. Hecher had earned their trust. Besides, they figured inmates adhering to a training discipline instead of roaming free would be less inclined to cause trouble.

"I heard the news," said a beaming Jimmy Rowen, striding up to Hecher at the chin-up bar. "Eddie told me you're gonna start that karate class. Man, that's great. You're gonna let me in, ain'tcha?"

"Of course, Jimmy. There'll just be a few of us at first, and I'm sure others will join. We're gonna rock The Rock."

Signs bearing a head-and-shoulders photo of Jim Scraponia intruded like uninvited guests on tidy curbside lawns in front of homes. They cluttered median strips of thoroughfares, demanded attention on billboards and in store windows, and despoiled tree trunks. A folksy grin reached across his face and met a chute of hair running down either side from a thick, black, furry mat. Under the photo, in rows of large black letters, was: Jim Scraponia. A Prosecutor With a Record. Florida Senate, District 38.

"We need to put a stop to the violent crime that is running rampant in our neighborhoods, making our streets and sidewalks unsafe for law-abiding, hard-working citizens who worship God and love their country."

Scraponia had entered private practice a few months before and was speaking at a daylong Labor Day celebration at Greenacres City Community Park. Couples lounged on lawn chairs and families spread out on blankets, making picnics with coolers and baskets of sandwiches and chicken and potato chips and grapes and soda pop. Their children gamboled through the crowd, forming instant friendships with other children and spontaneously creating games. Between performances by musical groups of various pop styles, politicians delivered ten-minute pitches.

"I look out here and see these innocent, carefree children, and I realize that you, as parents, want to be sure that they are safe when they go to and from school," Scraponia droned on. "You want to feel secure in your homes, without fear of predators lurking somewhere in the shadows like wolves ready to attack. Yet we know all too well that law and order is sadly lacking, and we must constantly be on guard against those who would rob us of our property and cause us physical harm.

"Why, even the rich folks on the exclusive island of Palm Beach are not safe anymore from violent criminals who roam free amongst us. It was only two-plus years ago that a father with six children was murdered in his own home by an assailant who fired shotgun blasts right through a window and the front door. As a prosecutor in the state attorney's office at the time, I worked with law enforcement to uncover evidence leading to the identity of the killer. Once I knew who it was, I was determined to bring that person to justice. As a result, Mitt Hecher, the man who shot Rodger Kriger, is now serving time at the state prison in Raiford.

"Before I got Hecher convicted of first degree murder, he had been arrested dozens of times. But our laws are so weak that his attorneys always found loopholes and he was allowed to remain on the streets and continue with his violent ways. I promise that if you will elect me to the Florida Senate"—Scraponia's voice was rising— "I will get legislation passed that will close these loopholes and put criminals like Mitt Hecher behind bars before they can graduate to the level of committing murder. I'll stop them the first time they lay a hand on anybody."

He had crescendoed, and one knew this was the finale. Holding the microphone in his left hand, he raised his right arm and stabbed his forefinger skyward.

"And you good people of Greenacres will feel protected because law and order will reign once again. Thank you and God bless."

A smattering of light applause arose from the crowd of about six hundred, as if out of politeness. Here and there, a man was seen listening to the speech, which was punctuated now and then by a child's playful shriek. But most of the people ignored the speaker and chatted among themselves. An exception was a gaunt, disheveled fellow who stood unsteadily on the side far to the left of the stage and midway back into the crowd, and clapped loud and long as everyone nearby stared at him.

Scraponia's campaign manager awaited him on the grass back of the stage.

"Not much of a response," the candidate lamented. "I looked out and saw hardly anybody was paying attention to what I was saying. Maybe I've got the wrong message."

"Naw," said his manager, a recently retired newspaper editor. "This is just not a good forum for politicking. People are here to relax and have a good time. The others didn't get much of a reception, either. I don't know why the city officials invited candidates to speak. But you had to show up because if you didn't, your opponent would get recognition and gain ground on you. Nobody wins and nobody loses in a situation like this. Don't worry. Harry's not going to do any better."

Stage workers began setting up music stands and chairs, and about sixty members of a community pops band wandered to their seats with their wind instruments. For forty-five minutes, the band played an assortment of military marches, Broadway tunes, and light classical pieces. The finale was *The Stars and Stripes Forever*, which got a rousing ovation that had Scraponia envious as he waited backstage for his opponent to speak.

Then it was time for the opponent, Harry Canfield. Scraponia, a Democrat, was hewing to the law and order line in his candidacy. That was customarily the province of Republicans, and Canfield had to do something to one-up his adversary, who had become quite well-known through the constant attention that the case against Mitt Hecher garnered in the news media. Canfield needed to shock the public into paying attention to him. He decided on a huge gamble as his only chance of winning.

Canfield bounded from the back of the stage up to the microphone and boomed, "Good afternoon, ladies and gentlemen. How is everyone doing?" Tepid applause and two or three shrill whistles. "My name's Harry Canfield, and I'm running as a Republican for the District Thirty-Eight seat in the Florida Senate. If you're like me, you've been enjoying the music but tuning out on the windbag politicians. I'm sure you're tired of hearing them today, so I'm going to be brief and to the point."

Chicken drumsticks were arrested half way on their journey to picnickers' mouths, or clutched between teeth that stopped chewing.

"My opponent is that guy you just heard try to scare the wits out of you with malarkey about robbers and murderers hiding behind every other tree and bush, waiting to attack innocent people like yourselves. That's the same, tired, get-tough-on-criminals line politicians have been baiting voters with for as long as the game of politics has been played. Don't fall for it, folks."

Men exchanged looks of wonder with their wives.

"Jim Scraponia would have you believe that through his work as a prosecutor, a vicious killer was removed from the streets and locked behind bars for a long time. How long? The sentence was twenty-five years. Now I ask you, folks: If Mitt Hecher was that dangerous, don't you think the judge would have at least put him away for life, if not had him executed? But no. Hecher was given the minimum sentence allowed by law. Why? It's obvious. That judge had grave doubts about his guilt. And yet Mister Scraponia wanted him sentenced to die in the electric chair. Folks, you came here to be entertained, so I'm going to quit talking for a moment and wax a little musical."

Holding the mike, Canfield turned toward the back of the stage. "Can someone bring me my gee-tar and a chair?"

A young stage hand, wearing snug-fitting jeans and a tight, black tee-shirt that displayed his sculpted arms and torso, strode briskly up to the speaker carrying the instrument and a bar stool. Canfield positioned himself on it, propping his feet on the supporting cross spindles.

"I'm going to sing a couple of lines from a tune that was all the rage thirty years ago, but I'm going to take some liberties with the lyrics. It's a song titled *Caldonia* and it was written and first recorded by Louis Jordan in 1945. Some of you folks who have a few years under your belts—yes, and a few pounds, too; I see you patting those tummies"—the fiftyish politician was charming them, as attested by the audible chuckles… "some will remember the words and note how I have changed them to make my message clear."

Canfield strummed a few notes to warm up, then began accompanying himself as he sang.

Walkin with that baboon, he's got great big feet / He's long, mean, and cranky and ain't had no victims to beat / He's a baboon but he gained a lota fame / Crazy crafty is that torney cuz Scraponia is his name.

Scraponia! Scraponia! / What makes your stone heart so hard? / I'll lick him, I'll lick him just the same / Crazy crafty is that torney cuz Scraponia is his name.

Canfield stepped off the stool, bowed, and leaned the guitar against it. He'd captured the audience's attention as hearty applause, accompanied by a wave of laughter, followed his brief performance.

He took the mike and continued, "Have you been reading the newspapers lately? Mitt Hecher was convicted just over six months ago, and already there have been reports pointing to others suspected of committing the murder. Did any of you read the newspaper accounts of the trial? Hecher was convicted on the testimony of convicted felons, who got reduced jail time after testifying. One of them was scheduled for execution, and his sentence was reduced to life in prison.

"Folks, I'll lay odds that this thing is eventually going to come unraveled. Hecher's attorney represented him so badly that he didn't even challenge the confession Hecher supposedly wrote while he was in jail awaiting trial. Mister Scraponia was able to pull the wool over the eyes of a gullible jury with his slick talk and oily maneuvering. But that's all he is—an oil slick. If you send him to Tallahassee, you'll just get slimed.

"I'm concerned about crime, but I want to address it by having our police officers work more effectively with their communities on prevention. And unlike my opponent, I'm not one-dimensional. Education is a priority with me. I also think we need to make our roads better and our aging bridges safer. I could go on, but as I said, you're here to enjoy yourselves today, so I'll just close by urging you all to vote—intelligently. Thank you. You've been a great audience."

For the first time that day, a politician received a strong ovation. A smattering of people throughout the crowd even rose from their blankets and lawn chairs to applaud.

In the shadows near the rear of the stage, Scraponia muttered to his manager, "That son-of-a-bitch is going to be trouble."

———————

Not everyone agreed with Canfield's message criticizing his opponent's emphasis on law and order and ridiculing him for boasting about his successful prosecution of Mitt Hecher. But as more newspaper headlines and broadcasts blared reports that raised questions whether someone other than Mitt Hecher might have shot Rodger Kriger, Canfield gained credibility.

He continued poking fun of his opponent with his take-off on *Caldonia*, playing and singing it at every campaign appearance. That attracted television crews to rallies big and small, prompting charges of favoritism from Scraponia. It also elicited accusations of dirty politics from the candidate.

That only opened him up to more criticism, as Canfield retorted that the pot shouldn't be calling the kettle black. He allowed as how he couldn't compete with Scraponia in dirty tactics, considering the "scandalous" way his opponent had prosecuted Mitt Hecher.

In Palm Beach County, people who had never heard the song *Caldonia*, and those who once knew it, visited libraries to look up the lyrics and bought the sheet music from music stores, which had to order supplies. School children were singing it. A nationally broadcast radio program did a short piece on the oddball political campaign and played a recording of *Caldonia* by Louis Jordan, followed by Canfield's mocking rendition of the song.

By Election Day in early November, it was no longer a contest. Scraponia watched the televised coverage of the election with his manager and two campaign workers at Rex's Bar in downtown West Palm Beach, becoming more glum as the evening wore on. With seventy-five percent of the votes in, he walked up to a TV reporter and said something. She ordered her camera crew to focus on him, then signaled him to begin speaking.

"I want to thank my campaign staff for waging a spirited effort," he announced, forcing a smile. "It is obvious that my opponent is too far ahead for me to catch up with most of the votes already tallied. I congratulate Mister Canfield on a hard-fought campaign and wish him luck in representing the people of his district. My thanks to all of you who voted for me and supported me. Good night."

Scraponia buttoned his sport jacket and walked out into the chilly night with his manager, humiliation weighing on him like a drenched overcoat.

"That was the first and last time I'll ever run for political office," he said.

Canfield garnered sixty-two percent of the votes, Scraponia thirty-six percent.

"Hi son. It's good to see you."

Maria Hecher was a diminutive, nimble-footed woman in plain shoes with low heels, salt-and-pepper hair tied in a bun separating narrow shoulders. She wore glasses with bifocal lenses and was dressed halfway between businesslike and matronly. She wrapped her arms around Mitt as the guard walked out of the waiting room. She kissed her son on the cheek through a half-smile.

"You look like you're holding up pretty well."

"Hi Mom." He grinned. "I didn't lose any weight working in the pastry kitchen."

Her eyes sparkled. "But you're Italian, not French. They should have had you in the pasta department."

They both laughed.

"Sit down, Mom. How was the trip?"

"It was okay from Phoenix to Houston, about three hours. I had that blood clot less than two years ago, so I got up and walked around a couple of times. Then coming from Houston to Orlando, it got real bumpy in Florida. I don't like that—scares me." She grinned sheepishly. "I stayed overnight in a Ramada Inn, and the drive here was no problem."

She paused. "So… this place looked kind of dilapidated when they walked me in here. I don't like this, Mitt. You weren't behaving, and I figured a little prison time might do you some good. Get you to take life more seriously and act more grown-up. The odd thing is, I think maybe you were getting to that place when you got married and you and Diane had a baby. But all the trouble you caused caught up with you. That might not have been so bad. By doing all the right things in prison, following the rules and never being a problem, you probably could have shown that you were ready to be a good, law-abiding citizen and gotten paroled way before your time was up. Don't you agree?"

"I'm already getting the respect of the people running this place, Mom."

"That's good to hear." She clasped his arm. "But then they had to have somebody to blame for the murder of that Kriger guy, and my son was the ideal choice for them. You had quite a reputation as a tough guy, and the law knew it would be easy to make people believe you did it."

"You're not telling me nothing I don't know. You've got it in a nutshell."

"Well, we can't give up. The attorneys are working on it. Your grandfather, my papa, came to this country as a teenager, and through hard work became successful. From a single pick-up truck, he developed a whole fleet of sand-and-gravel haulers and made a small fortune. He never would have had that opportunity in the old country. He loved this country and believed in it. Never would he think that the American justice system would doom his grandson. He would have faith that it would eventually realize its error and correct it. We have to believe that, too, Mitt."

"I'm not giving up, Mom. I'll just make the best of the life I've been given until I can rejoin life on the outside."

"All right, men," Hecher barked, standing in the prison yard facing two rows of inmates.

A tall, black inmate in the second row shouted, "Stand up."

"Fuck you, wise guy," Hecher called back.

"Wise guy?" the inmate hollered. "Do I look Italian? You guys are the mobsters."

"All right, all right," said Hecher, "let's cut the crap and get down to business. Karate takes a lot of discipline. Any of you guys ever hear of Sonny Stratton?"

"Oh, yeah," one yelled.

"The best," another shouted.

"Greatest kick boxer of all time," the outspoken black said, his voice ringing with finality, as if his opinion were beyond dispute.

"He was totally disciplined," said Hecher. "I know, because I trained him."

"No," the black bellowed, sounding incredulous. "You trained Sonny Stratton? You guys hear that? This here's the man. He know what he be doin."

"Yeah. He sure do," said another, and the rest looked at each other and shook their heads in agreement.

"Sonny Stratton. Wow!" one exclaimed.

"The first thing we're going to do is get our muscles loosened and our lungs warmed so our bodies will operate smoothly when we get into the moves and the holds. All eleven of you volunteered for this class, so you're obviously motivated, and when I tell you it's important to go through these preliminaries, I know you'll follow my instructions, even though it may seem kind of boring. Everybody okay with that?"

"Yeah, man, let's do it," the boisterous inmate called out. The others mumbled or nodded their assent.

"So let's start out with fifty jumping jacks." Hecher threw his arms outward and above his head till his hands touched while jumping to a spread-leg position, and did fast repetitions. The inmates copied him.

That done, he yelled, "On your backs," and dropped to the ground, flipping his legs in the air, his hands and elbows propping his hips. He pumped his legs in a bicycle motion. The inmates followed suit, and they continued the exercise for three minutes.

"You're gonna love this next one," Hecher grunted, dropping to his stomach. "Let's see if we can do fifty push-ups. If you can't, do as many as you can."

Hecher breezed through the fifty, and only one other could finish.

"Okay, now we're ready to learn something." He glanced over their heads at the prison windows. "Hey men, we've got an audience. They don't know what they're missing, right? We oughta be charging admission."

The inmates in the karate class turned their heads to look at their compatriots watching them from the inside.

"Okay, let's work on our stance. I'm going to show you how to stand to best defend yourself from an attack. Remember, you're learning karate to protect yourself, not to start fights." Hecher paused, a guilty smile forming. "Although I guess I violated that principle a few times—*quite* a few. You don't want to do that."

He spread his legs two feet apart and went into a semicrouch. His left arm extended forward at an angle, with the fist pointing upward, and the right arm crossed his midsection, fist at the ready.

"You are now ready to block any blow directed at your body or head." Hecher pumped his arms to demonstrate. "Try it, guys."

The men assumed the position and, with proficiency that ranged from downright awkwardness to a modicum of athletic grace, pumped their arms, warding off virtual blows.

"Hey, dude," Hecher called to a white guy on the right side of the first row. "You've got your left fist pointed down. It's supposed to be up."

"Like this?"

"Yeah, that's it."

"Now we're going to put it into practice. I'm going to have one of you come at me like you're going to punch me out, and I'm going to block you."

Hecher surveyed the group. "Aha, I think I've found a victim."

He pointed at the teller of the Italian joke and mocked, "Come on up here, Mister Wise Guy."

The inmate smacked his hands on his chest in feigned horror.

"Uh-oh. My big mouth always gets me into trouble."

He shuffled to the front and stood, his five-foot-ten, well-toned frame facing the five-foot-six Hecher.

"Now don't beat on me," he pleaded, pretending apprehension.

"I want you to charge me as though you're pissed off as hell and you plan to beat the shit out of me," Hecher instructed. "Don't hold back."

"Now wait just a damned minute," the inmate protested. "That means you gotta do me some serious harm. Okay, I take back what I said about the mobsters."

The other inmates broke into uproarious laughter, bending over and slapping each other on their backs. Hecher turned away from the inmate, shaking his head and laughing with the others. He turned back to face him.

"Come on, you dildo. I ain't gonna hurtcha."

"Well, okay. Here goes."

The inmate walked backed ten feet, whirled, and came at Hecher in a walk-run, his fists raised. He swung his left fist in an arc at the side of Hecher's head, but the karate expert's right forearm deflected the intended blow and the inmate's midsection was left open. Hecher's left fist was pointed upward, and he delivered an uppercut to the man's jaw, checking his swing before connecting and yelling, "Stop!" Both men stood, immobile, and Hecher proclaimed, "Demonstration over."

"Whew," the inmate clucked. "You could have put me out cold."

"Yep," said Hecher. He turned to face the other inmates.

"That shows you how important the stance is. When you get a chance, you might want to practice that on each other. But be sure to let the guards and any of the inmates around you know before you do it, because otherwise they'll think you're serious and there could be trouble. And always control yourself. If one guy slips and the other guy gets roughed up a little—because that happens in practice sometimes—just know it wasn't intentional and don't get all pissed off. You have to stay cool.

"That's all for today. Next week we'll learn another move."

It was late afternoon, and the men meandered back to their cells. Hecher chatted with one, a slight black, who was in his cell block.

"See ya later," he said to the inmate as they reached his cell.

Hecher was several cells down the hall when he heard shouts from the direction he had come, one sounding like his student. He turned and half walked, half ran back toward the cell. A brutish, muscle-bound white had entered the karate student's cell and knocked him to the floor. The inmate, whose shaven head was one of the few parts of his body not tattooed, rifled through the black's locker in the corner.

"Hey, get outa here," Hecher shouted.

"Don't bother me unless you wanna die, fuckhead."

He turned to face Hecher, who approached with fists at the ready. The guy lunged. Hecher sidestepped and caught him with a vicious blow to the side of the head. The man staggered, and Hecher smashed him in the mouth. The inmate went down, but bounded back up and charged at Hecher, who struck backward with his left leg and hit the inmate in the midsection, doubling him up, then spun around and delivered a right-handed haymaker to the jaw. The inmate catapulted backward onto the floor and lay there a couple of seconds. He rose slowly, wiped the blood off his face with the palm of his right hand, and smeared it on his blue prison pants. He left silently.

"Now you see why karate is a good thing to know," Hecher panted.

"Yeah. Thanks, bro. Keep that class goin, will ya?"

Chapter Two

"Come in," Tom Palladin invited, escorting DeWitt Crimshaw to a couch in the reporter's living room. "I'm glad you called first, but how'd you get my number? Better not've been from the *Gazette*."

"I looked it up in the phone book."

It was now late 1979, and in the months since Crimshaw's release from jail, his dark hair had reached below the neck and darted in a line under his ears. It was as if the follicles had lain dormant and now sprang forth under their new freedom.

"Oh yeah, I guess I'm listed. How have you been making it on the outside? Are you straightening up, or are you still lying your way through life?"

"I'm not actually on the outside. Before they released me from jail, the judge had a psychiatrist interview me, and then they sent me to a psychiatric hospital."

"Where?"

"South Florida State Hospital in Pembroke Pines. I escaped just this morning."

"How did you get here?"

"I hitchhiked. It took me four hours. I caught four rides. Mister Palladin, since I've been out of jail, I've been feeling badly about what I did to Mitt Hecher."

"Why is that, Mister Crimshaw? You were a key witness in getting him convicted. Don't you think he deserved to go to prison?"

"That's just it, sir. He didn't deserve to be convicted for murdering Rodger Kriger. I made up that story about him confessing to me that he did it, and then I forged his written confession."

Palladin jerked his tall frame bolt upright, saying nothing as he stared at Crimshaw.

"That's a hell of an important thing you just said. Are you sure you're telling the truth this time?"

"Yes, sir, I am."

"Why did you lie in the first place?"

"It was the only way I could get out of that awful jail and sleep on a good bed and eat good food again. I hated being in that place. The place I'm in now isn't much better."

"Well," said Palladin, scratching his head. He paused. "I wish I could say, better late than never. But in this case—or in any court case, for that matter—it's too late. The damage is done. Recanted testimony almost never is grounds for a new trial. Not unless it's combined with new evidence. You did a man a grave injustice, Mister Crimshaw."

"Yes, I know."

"Why did you come to me with this? What do you expect me to do about it?"

"I was hoping you would write an article saying I admitted I lied and forged the confession. Then, even if Mister Hecher doesn't get a new trial, at least people will think he might not be guilty after all."

"Yes, it won't be any problem doing that article. But I'm going to point out that you lied to me in a previous article I wrote—so people can make up their own minds whether you're telling the truth this time."

"I understand."

"What are you going to do now?"

"I'm going to contact relatives and stay with them until the police come and take me back to the hospital."

"I can't give you a ride because I'd be aiding and abetting a fugitive."

"That's all right. May I use your phone to call them? I'll ask them to pick me up."

"I guess that won't hurt."

Crimshaw dialed and spoke briefly. He thanked Palladin, bid him goodbye, and walked outside looking glum. In twenty minutes, a chauffeur for an aunt drove to the front of the long driveway and took Crimshaw to the aunt's home in Palm Beach. Crimshaw called the state attorney's office and asked for Joshua Whiteman. Told that Whiteman had left for private practice a few months before, Crimshaw dialed information and called the attorney.

"Mister Whiteman, I know you were investigating the murder of Rodger Kriger and I want to get something off my chest."

"Is that so? Well, I'm no longer involved, but I'd be glad to hear what you have to say and forward the information to the state attorney, Donald Bosworth."

"Thank you. You know that my testimony about Mitt Hecher writing a confession that he shot Mister Kriger was critical in getting him convicted."

"Yes, of course."

"Well, sir, I lied. I made up that story, and I forged the confession."

Silence on the other end.

"Mister Crimshaw, I have two questions: One, why did you lie? And two, why are you telling me now that you lied?"

"I couldn't stand being in jail anymore, Mister Whiteman. And Jim Scraponia promised to get me out if I helped him convict Mitt Hecher. I'm telling you this now because I'm sorry and I don't want him to spend all of those years in that awful prison."

"Well, as I said, I'll pass along this information to Mister Bosworth, and I assume he'll investigate further. What you did was reprehensible, but at least you're decent enough to finally do the right thing. Thank you, Mister Crimshaw, and good luck."

———————————

Scraponia's political opponent proved prescient. Harry Canfield had predicted the witnesses' testimony against Hecher would unravel. Richie Gatson was the first to confess he had made up the story about Mitt Hecher's having shot Rodger Kriger. Emboldened by that admission and then Dewey Crimshaw's mea culpa that he'd forged Mitt Hecher's written confession, Alan Burns and Donald Gibbons followed suit. Soon after Palladin's article about Crimshaw's revelation of betrayal, Burns and Gibbons phoned Palladin and acknowledged that they, too, had invented stories about Hecher's confessions of guilt.

Palladin informed his readers about those admissions, as well. Hecher's attorney, Seppish, then got them to give sworn statements. Seppish called Scraponia.

"Your goose is cooked, Scraponia," Seppish gloated. "I'm going to file a motion for a new trial based on the perjured testimony of witnesses that you orchestrated in the most rotten scheme I've ever seen in all my decades in the courts. I've got two recantations and I'm sure I'll have a third shortly."

"Tut, tut, tut," Scraponia mocked in his slow baritone. "Look who's calling the kettle black. I seem to recall a perverse little act on your part whilst you held an esteemed position on the bench, Mister Seppish."

"Well, my nefarious deed may not have been in the interest of justice in that it favored the guilty, but at least it didn't harm the innocent, as did your scurrilous machinations. I'll be seeing you in court again. Good day."

Scraponia hopped in his car and drove south to the South Florida State Hospital. With a big smile, he told the doctor for Crimshaw of the need to discuss a case in which the patient had provided testimony. A nurse's aide escorted the attorney to a sun room with lounge chairs, and Crimshaw soon was escorted into the room by a male attendant. He sat on a chair in front of a round, off-yellow coffee table that separated him from Scraponia.

"Hello Dewey," Scraponia said through a pinched smile. "How have you been faring here?"

"Oh, it's not so bad. A lot better than jail, that's for sure. I'm getting some counseling, and I hope to become more mature."

"Well, you're not helping yourself by your behavior of late, Dewey. I'm going to be brief and to the point. Your statement to the reporter for the *Miami Gazette* that you lied in your court testimony is raising serious doubt among a lot of people that Mitt Hecher is guilty of the murder of Rodger Kriger. And it reflects very badly on my performance as a prosecutor.

"Now, Alan Burns and Donald Gibbons already have given Alonzo Seppish sworn statements taking back their allegations regarding Mister Hecher. Seppish is about to ask you also for a sworn statement recanting your testimony about Hecher's confession. I have a question for you, Dewey. You really don't like spending time in jail, do you?" He spoke it as a statement.

"No, I detested jail life. Uh-oh. Are you warning me about something?"

"I am here as an emissary of State Attorney Donald Bosworth, Dewey. He wants you to know that if you provide a sworn statement that you lied in your testimony, you will be charged with perjury. And I think you are aware that perjury is a felony punishable with jail time."

Crimshaw had listened without breathing, and took a deep breath.

"All right. I won't give a statement."

Scraponia broke into a fake paternal smile.

"I knew we could count on you."

Palladin visited George Demarco at the county jail, where he now was off death row and in the Federal Witness Protection Program. Scraponia had arranged the special treatment for Demarco to ward off attacks from inmates seeking retribution for his testimony against Hecher. Palladin showed Demarco the newspaper articles.

"Your partners in lying have fessed up, Mister Demarco," the reporter said. "How about it? Are you ready to admit publicly that you, too, made up that story you told about Mitt Hecher blabbing in jail that he killed Rodger Kriger?"

"I have to talk to you confidentially, Mister Palladin," Demarco insisted. "You have to agree not to write an article about what I tell you."

"I don't think I can let you go off the record," said Palladin.

"Okay. Here's what I will tell you that you can print: I do not admit that I made up that story."

"All right," Palladin acquiesced. "Anything else?"

"I'll tell you why I won't admit it, but you can't print that. Agreed?"

"Well, I guess knowing is better than not knowing. Okay, I won't print it."

"I can't admit it because I'm still hoping to get out of this place. If I admitted I lied, they might not put me back on death row, but I don't think they'd ever free me."

Palladin also visited Burns at the jail. He had nothing to lose by admitting he had lied, because he doomed his prospects for early release. Shortly before the date arranged by Scraponia, he got into a fight with another inmate and broke several of the man's vertebraes.

———————

"Okay men, let's keep the same spots you were in for the first session last week. So there'll be five men in a row, five rows. I know a lot of you were impatient for this class to begin, but I wanted to wait until it was big enough because I can't add people once it begins. The lessons build on each other, just like a dance class. I made that mistake a couple years ago with the first class when I started it with only eleven guys and couldn't add any.

"All right, let's do our warm-ups first, and then we'll learn a new move."

Led by Hecher, the men did jumping jacks, squats, and push-ups. Every window in the prison was open with men leaning on their elbows on the sills, taking in the drills, their live weekly show.

The exercise workout was strenuous, and Hecher waited several minutes for the men to catch their breaths.

"Last week you learned how to block a guy coming at you with his fists. But suppose you're in a stand-off with somebody wielding a pipe, bent on bashing your head in. Today I'm going to show you how to keep from getting hit in the head. You might get hit someplace else, maybe in the legs, and it'll hurt and you might get bruised pretty bad. But you won't be dead or brained. At first, I'll just demonstrate this move without a partner."

Hecher stepped back a few steps and crouched. He whirled, pivoting on his left foot and leaping in the air while kicking his right leg up and out. He landed on his hands and knees, jumped to his feet, and whirled to face the class.

"The idea, of course, is to kick the guy in the face and knock him down so you can then grab the pipe and make it a fair fight, which you will win once you become proficient at karate. Now, this takes a lot of practice. And you don't want to try it on anybody until you're damned good at it, or you're liable to do what you're supposed to do and break your partner's jaw."

Inmates turned to each other and shook with laughter.

"Do I have any volunteers for a real demonstration?"

A pause, then a hand shot up in the third row.

"Yeah, shit, I'll do it," a dark black with a slight amount of belly flab volunteered. "I've been eatin too much, anyway. This jaw needs a rest." He walked to the front.

"Naw, my foot's not going to touch you," Hecher said, handing the man a two-and-a-half-foot-long wooden dowel. "You notice it's made of wood." He grinned as his eyes shifted among the men. "Just in case somebody thought I exercised him too hard."

Returning his focus on the inmate before him, Hecher backed away.

"Now stand slightly crouched, holding the dowel up and back in a menacing way, as if you're about to strike me."

The guy complied.

Without warning, Hecher spun to his left, leaped and thrust his right leg at the man's head, missing it by six inches as the man stood mesmerized.

"Geez, I would'na had time to move outa the way," the inmate admitted. "I'd a been flat on my back. I gotta learn how to do that."

"Well, give it a try," said Hecher. "Not on me." A lot of laughs. "Later maybe."

The guy whirled, leaped, and fell on his face. That caused the others to double up, holding their stomachs.

The sound of hand-clapping came from the distance, and the inmate looked up to see several inmates at the windows applauding. He faced them and did an exaggerated bow while the others cackled.

"Okay, you guys," said Hecher. "Now it's your turn. Everybody spread out. We don't want anybody getting banged up."

For the next fifteen minutes, the men practiced whirling, leaping, and kicking. Gradually, they improved.

"Okay, men, you're making progress. Practice it during the week when you get a chance. I'll see you all next week."

Attorney Adam Sullivan filed for a hearing with the Fifth District Court of Appeal in Daytona Beach. He and two assistants set about preparing arguments to demonstrate that the truth did not prevail in the trial of Mitt Hecher. In mid-March of 1981, they faced the three-judge panel.

"Honorable justices," Sullivan began, "my colleagues and I beseech you to carefully consider the arguments we are about to make concerning what we believe to be egregious instances of disregard for the law, prosecutorial overreach, and a woefully incompetent defense, all of which conjoined to form an insurmountable wall blocking an honest answer as to whether Mitt Hecher fatally shot Rodger Kriger on the night of January Fourteen,

1976. We intend to show that the circumstances I just summarized did, in fact, effect the wrong answer as to Mister Hecher's guilt."

Sullivan walked from the podium to the table where his two colleagues sat. One handed him several papers, and he returned to the lectern. He removed his glasses, regarded the papers, and began.

"The plain fact, Your Honors, is that Mister Hecher was convicted purely on the basis of testimony by convicted felons, as the prosecutor himself volunteered to the jury. One of them admitted he had lied even before the trial, and he passed a polygraph test of that admission. Those facts were presented in the trial, and they were discounted by the jury. The four fellow inmates of Mister Hecher's at the Palm Beach County Jail who testified that he admitted shooting Rodger Kriger were all serving time for felony convictions. One had earned a reputation as a pathological liar. Another was facing execution in the electric chair for cold-blooded murder. He was given a reduction in sentence to life in prison in return for his testimony against Mitt Hecher.

"It seems superfluous to point out that he had a powerful incentive to say anything that he thought would spare his life. Similarly, if less dramatically, the other three were promised significantly shortened jail terms in return for what was described as their 'cooperation.'" Sullivan held up his hands and wiggled the forefinger and middle finger of each.

"I must emphasize that no material evidence was presented showing that Mister Hecher was guilty of committing this crime. Probably the most damning testimony came from one DeWitt Crimshaw, who is notorious for telling bald-faced lies. He presented two pages confessing to the shooting that he alleged were written by Mitt Hecher. A handwriting expert could not say that the handwriting was Mister Hecher's.

"Then there was the shotgun used to shoot Mister Kriger. A Palm Beach Police Department captain testified that a shotgun found in a warehouse in Albuquerque, New Mexico, matched the empty shells found at the scene of the shooting. But his testimony was ruled inadmissible because he was not an expert witness. He also testified that police didn't think Hecher was the shooter. And an FBI agent, an expert, testified that the shotgun and the shells didn't match.

"Further, the chief counsel for Mitt Hecher, for several reasons, exhibited breathtaking incompetence in representing his client. He insists that he was unprepared and the judge denied his request to delay the trial to give him more time. But that seems no excuse for his failure to object to the presentation of the confession allegedly written by Mitt Hecher admitting to the shooting. The judge did not allow it to be introduced as evidence, but the jury had heard the testimony and the damage was done.

"Finally, counsel inexplicably declined to call Bobby Gunder, the man whom the prosecutor alleged was the intended victim of Mitt Hecher when Hecher allegedly shot Rodger Kriger, the next-door neighbor of Bobby Gunder's parents. Mister Gunder has said he never even knew Mitt Hecher.

"Your Honors, I submit that added together, the complete lack of material evidence, the total reliance of the jury on the testimony of criminals, and the woeful incompetence of the defense counsel resulted in a verdict that made a travesty of justice in the case of the State of Florida versus Mitt Hecher. I adjure you to correct this injustice by reversing the verdict of guilty to not guilty. Thank you."

Sullivan took his seat at the appellant table.

The presiding judge focused on Jim Scraponia at the respondent table.

"Would counsel representing the prosecution like to respond?"

"Yes, thank you, Your Honor," Scraponia said, rising. He walked to the podium with a sheaf of documents.

"The counsel for the defense makes a sound argument." Scraponia stood erect with head tilted back, moving it from side to side like a spectator at a slow tennis match, his gaze shifting among the justices. "He says this was not a strong case, and he is right. We knew that when we decided to prosecute it. But we were convinced that the defendant was guilty of the crime"—he stabbed the podium with his forefinger—"and we were determined to present the most compelling case possible."

Scraponia paused for effect, then continued in a softer tone.

"Yes, there were weaknesses in the testimony of some of the convicted felons. But the jury found that, when taken in the aggregate, their stories jibed and were most persuasive. Jurors simply could not discount them based merely on the individual backgrounds of those relating them."

Through a cunning smile, Scraponia said, "I am reminded of an old joke: Just because I'm paranoid doesn't mean people aren't after me."

The justices chuckled, and two turned to look at each other with broad smiles of amusement.

"As for the written confession of Mitt Hecher, the judge followed the law by refusing to admit it into evidence. The jury was instructed to disregard that confession, and we can only assume that they did as they were told. We have no reason to believe otherwise.

"Concerning the argument that the counsel for the defense performed inadequately, the competency of an attorney is a matter for his client to assess. If the client feels he did not receive adequate representation, then it is his right to file a complaint with the Florida Bar Association. But it is not an issue that should concern this court."

With studied deliberation, Scraponia picked up the papers lying on the lectern with his right hand and placed them under those he held in his left hand, then tapped them on the lectern into a neat stack. He strode to the respondent table, handed them to an assistant, and returned to the podium.

He breathed deeply. "Your Honors, the path to justice is not always smooth. Obstacles that may seem impassable can present formidable challenges. Sometimes the way leads through dark passages that obscure the truth. But in the end, the jury was able to overcome the rough spots, get around the obstacles, and navigate the stretches of darkness into the light without losing their way. Ultimately, justice prevailed with their verdict of guilty on the charge of first degree murder against Mitt Hecher. Thank you."

"Hecher, I've got a letter for you," the guard called to the inmate, who sat on his cell bunk after breakfast. He was reading Larry McMurtry's *The Last Picture Show*. He'd seen the movie in 1971 and fallen in love with Cybill Shepherd, and always wanted to read the novel it was based on but was too busy being a bad boy. Now, doing time, he had plenty of it.

He laid the paperback book face down on the bed, open to the page he was reading.

"Thanks," he said, reaching to receive the letter. He glanced at the return address, which read, State of Florida Fifth District Court of Appeal, 300 South Beach Street, Daytona Beach, Florida 32114. He slipped the forefinger of his left hand under a corner of the flap and ran it horizontally, then lifted a single sheet of paper from the envelope.

Under the letterhead was one sentence: *By unanimous decision, the court has upheld the verdict of guilty of murder in the first degree in the case of Mitt Hecher vs. the State of Florida.*

Hecher stared for a few moments, shrugged, and replaced the letter in the envelope. He did not know that, following arguments before the panel, a second attorney had written the ruling after the first one assigned to it had refused. Susan Strickland was bothered by what she heard and took the case file home that night to study it. The next day, she told her boss she didn't believe Hecher was guilty.

Strickland, imbued with a passion for fairness, had left her career as an elementary school teacher in her late twenties and earned a law degree. She was a Southerner and a conservative politically, but to her, justice was neutral. Her first job was serving as a judicial aide with the appeals court.

Hecher tossed the letter in a collection of his belongings at the end of the bunk. His cellmate, Eddie, walked in.

"Hey man, why the glum look? Letter from home?"

"Naw. Appeals court turned down my appeal. It's okay. I would have been surprised if they hadn't. There ain't no justice, man. Those fuckin penguins in their black robes and white collars, you have to bow down and lick their shiny black Florsheims and Your-Honor em till you're blue in the face. That's why they ran for election to become judges—so they could hear people calling em Your Honor all day long. Most of em are on a big power trip. They don't know the meaning of the word honor. They think it means nothing more than interpreting the law the way they think it was meant. To them it's an abstract thing. They never think about how it affects human beings, which are like pawns to them. They've completely forgotten that laws are created to benefit people, and they make the law more important than the person. They have no humanity."

"I hear you, man. You know, I could be paying for my crime by helping the people I hurt. I been here seven years. The judge could give me three more years and then let me out to work. I was a tool-and-die maker, damn good at it, and they could take most of my wages and give them to our two children and my wife's parents. That way, I wouldn't be costing the state, and I would be at least doing what I could to pay for the pain I caused those I love. But that makes too much sense. It's using the law for the good of people. And judges don't know what that's all about."

———

Eight months later, the circuit judge who, at trial's end, had approved a settlement of the reward distribution and then withdrawn it, made a final decision after further review. He granted $20,000 in the reward fund to two of the felons who testified against Hecher, ignoring their admissions of perjury. Gatson received $15,000, but sounded almost apologetic in accepting it. Still eluding arrest for robbery, he told Palladin in a phone call arranged by his attorney, "I need this money, but I didn't testify against Hecher, and won't, either."

Burns got the rest of the money. Lawyers tried to ask questions that would show Crimshaw and Burns had concocted their testimony against Hecher, but the judge stopped the attorneys in their tracks. However, Crimshaw and Gibbons withdrew their requests for part of the reward.

Hecher's wife, Diane, mailed him newspaper clippings that told of the action by the judge. Despite his cynicism toward judges, Hecher was taken aback. He never expected that any judge would, upon knowing the witnesses had confessed to perjury, grant them the award money. His contempt for the honor of the black-robed men had been more than affirmed. This judge had rewarded these felons for committing perjury.

For perhaps fifteen minutes, Hecher sat on his single bed, to which he had graduated when one of his cellmates was placed in solitary for stabbing another inmate. He leaned against the wall, his legs stretched out ahead of him. Finally, he reached to his belongings on the floor at the end of the bed and grabbed a yellow, legal writing pad and a ballpoint pen.

After the judge's name, Circuit Court, Palm Beach County, he wrote:

Dear Sir:

I have read a newspaper account of your decision giving the award money to persons who provided information used to convict me for the murder of Rodger

Kriger. I am, sir, in disbelief. Can anyone expect justice from a court system that knowingly and willfully rewards criminals for committing perjury that keeps an innocent man behind bars? What terror must lurk in the hearts of men and women who read newspaper reports and hear broadcasts of what you have done? How can anyone know that such an egregious miscarriage of justice might not be visited upon him or her—that based on the claim of some pathological liar, such an innocent person might be snatched from his secure place in society, convicted of something for which he had no knowledge, and sent away to fend for himself in an institution controlled by predators? And that even after said liar confesses to his perjury, the innocent victim not only remains locked up but the perjurer is rewarded?

Is this what America is all about? If so, it would seem that upright citizens have more to fear from its justice system than from the miscreants in our society. I may be a karate expert and prison inmate, but I know something about history, and what you have done, sir, smacks of the French Revolution.

My hope was to persuade the contributors to use the money in the fund for an investigator to find the real killer. You have denied that possibility, and I am thoroughly disillusioned by your action. After the enormous injustice that has been done to me, I have come to expect the worst from our legal system. But what you did here has me at a loss for words, and I am plunged into despair at ever finding anyone in the system who cares about simple honesty and fairness.

Hecher signed and sealed the letter in an envelope, addressed it, and handed it to a guard the next day while walking to the canteen to begin work. Looking glum, he worked the combination on the safe, withdrew cash, and disbursed it in the compartments in the cash register. Then he began checking the shelves to see that they were stocked.

"Everything okay, Mitt?" one of his two assistants asked. "You're kinda quiet today."

"Huh? Oh, yeah. Just a little tired, I guess."

Lines had formed outside the two windows, and Hecher opened them for business. He went through the motions for six hours, then closed the windows and put the money away.

"See you tomorrow," one assistant said as he was leaving.

Mitt mumbled, "So long."

"Hey, Mitt," he said, "what's up?"

"Aw, it's nothin. Don't worry about it."

Hecher returned to his cell, took a shower, and sat on the bed, legs folded in front of him. Resorting to a practice he'd turned to in times of stress and depression since his early karate days, he meditated for a half hour.

But he was unchanged the next day: morose, barely speaking.

"Uh-oh, Mitt," said the other assistant. "We got a problem." He pointed to one of the lines. "That guy tried to cut in and that other one ain't gonna let im. They're fixin to fight."

Hecher looked through the window, then bounded through the door and up to the offending prisoner, a mixed-race guy confronted by a black. With both hands, he grabbed the guy by the scruff of the neck, looked up into his face, and shouted, "Listen, you mother fucker. Get to the back of the line or I'm gonna knock the shit outa you and have you on your ass faster'n you can say karate black belt."

"Karate, huh? I'll bet you're bluffin."

With lightning speed, Hecher flipped into his bulldog karate stance, and growled, "Try me, you fuckin asshole."

"Okay, dude. Holy shit, you don't need to get rough. I'm goin."

Hecher stared after him a couple of seconds while the man in line slapped his intervenor on the back and thanked him. He put his head down and walked slowly back to the canteen.

"Geez, you ain't in no mood to fuck with," said an assistant.

"Yeah. I think I just got something out of my system. Injustice strikes a raw nerve in me. People who aren't fair set me off—like certain judges. I'll be okay now."

Two months later, attorney Adam Sullivan requested an evidenciary hearing in Circuit Court to determine whether there was sufficient evidence to order a new trial and appoint a lawyer and investigator. Sullivan based his request on the confessions of the three prosecution witnesses who said they had lied and the proffered testimony of a Miami polygraph examiner who had administered two days of tests to Hecher and concluded he was innocent. The judge canceled the hearing, ruling he was obligated to grant such a request only in death penalty cases.

Sullivan was flabbergasted. Recent precedent contradicted that, he told the media, and he should have been allowed to make the argument.

An unsettling thought occurred to him: A silent, unspoken, unorganized conspiracy against Mitt Hecher had arisen in the justice system. Like roads during a flood, every route to exoneration proved impassable.

Chapter Three

Jimmy Rowen had Hecher on his knees, holding him in a headlock.

"Perfect," Hecher praised, as the younger inmate released his hold. Hecher rose.

"You executed that just right. You're getting pretty damned good." A devilish smile played on his lips. "I'm not sure I want to teach you anymore holds. You're liable to whip my ass."

He turned to the class. "Did you see how he blocked my punch, deftly side-stepped and kicked me back of the knee, forcing me to the ground so he could get a headlock on me? If you guys want to work on that during the week, pair off and give it a try. But remember, keep your cool. Okay, that's all for today."

Hecher and Jimmy walked on the track to wind down from their exertion.

"You've come a long way in—what, about two years, right?" Hecher said. "So when're you getting out of this place?"

"I thought about now. The parole board said I was doing good and if I kept my record clean, I should be out next year at this time. That's a long wait, though."

"Well, it's a hell of a lot shorter than I've got. The important thing is to keep yourself occupied. You have to keep active, physically and mentally. That's the only way to survive this place, I decided. Otherwise, it'll get you down. There's a guy on our ward, Joey Donato. A lifer. He's done thirty-two straight years in three prisons. He's fifty-eight, looks like he's eighty."

Jimmy's head jerked up, his eyes wide with recognition, as he turned toward Hecher.

"Yeah, I think I know who you mean. Guy kinda bent, quiet, looks sorta sad and hopeless?"

"That's him. Told me in the mess hall once that he used to be a fighter, but he doesn't have any fight left. After a while, he said, your cheeks sink, the lines grow deep in your face, your skin turns pasty, your hair turns gray and then it starts falling out. You just exist. You lose your desire for anything. After you've been here a long time, you get a certain respect from the other prisoners. But by that time, you don't care much what happens to you. That's what Joey told me."

"Mitt, we better move over to the right. That big dude who just jogged past us gave me a bad look. I think he wants us outa the way."

"Yeah, let's get off the track." Hecher stepped onto the dried grass. "Jimmy, I said to myself, holy shit, no way I'm going to let that premature aging and depression happen to me. So I keep as busy as I can. That's one reason I teach the karate classes. At night, when the other guys are watching TV, I read books my wife brings me, or newspapers or magazines the administration and the guards give me when they're through with them."

"Once I get outa here, I'm gonna make sure I don't come back," Jimmy vowed. "I ran with a pretty rough crowd on the outside, but this hellhole... Shit, man, this must be worse than bein in combat. At least in war, the other soldiers are your buddies. Here, almost everybody is your enemy. You never know when somebody's gonna try to stab you. Happens about every day. There's hardly a week goes by somebody ain't killed, right?"

"Yep. I never imagined it was going to be this bad. You know, come to think of it, you and me prob'ly woulda got drafted and sent to Vietnam if we hadn't got in trouble with the law. We screwed up. We'd a been better off over there. The Viet Cong weren't any more dangerous than the characters in this battle zone. And we'd a been home by now."

That night, Hecher tossed and turned. He was at the horizontal bar in the prison yard, doing chin-ups, when two Vietnamese, barefooted but clad in jungle combat uniforms, scaled the prison walls and headed his way, brandishing knives. Jimmy was on the ground near him doing push-ups.

"Let's take em, Jimmy," he shouted.

But just then the two Vietnamese turned from them and ran down the track toward Joey Donato, who was walking slowly with his head down, his back toward them. Hecher tried to run after the Asians but could hardly move. He tried to yell a warning to Joey, but his voice couldn't be heard against a strong wind blowing from the other direction. The two Vietnamese had their knives raised and were about to stab Joey in the back, when Hecher woke with a start. He lay on his back for several minutes, staring at the dark outlines of the beds and the iron door, myriad thoughts flitting through his mind. Finally, he turned on his right side and drowsiness overcame him.

He awoke at five-thirty, used the toilet and brushed his teeth, and dressed. As he was sitting on the edge of his bed, putting his shoes on, he heard screaming. Two guards carrying a stretcher came rushing down the walkway.

"The stabbings are starting early today," he said over his shoulder to a cellmate just climbing out of his lower bunk bed.

Three minutes later, the guards returned with an inmate on the gurney, his moaning wafting into the cells. Hecher had walked to the front of the cell, about to leave for breakfast. He glanced half-interested at the prone prisoner, who was on his back, his arms stretched parallel with his body. Hecher jerked his head toward the inmate as he passed in front of him.

"Holy crap," he yelled. "That's Jimmy."

Hecher ran out of his cell and followed the entourage to the stairway, down the stairs, and through the halls to the infirmary.

"Hold it, prisoner," a guard posted inside the double doors said to him. "Where you goin?"

"That's my buddy, Jimmy. He's a student in my karate class. I want to find out what's wrong with him."

The guard did a quick appraisal of Hecher. "Oh, yeah, I know you. You're the karate guy. Okay, go ahead."

Hecher walked to the emergency room, where a doctor was giving Jimmy a shot of morphine.

"What happened, doc? I'm a friend of Jimmy's."

"He your friend?" the doc asked Jimmy.

Jimmy smiled through a grimace, and nodded.

"Okay," said the doc. "Look at his hands. Somebody burned him badly with gasoline. There's nothing you can do now. The drug will take effect, and he'll get some sleep. He's going to be in a lot of pain for awhile."

The doctor motioned for Hecher to step back, and moved close to Jimmy.

"That right hand is never going to be the same," the doctor whispered, turning toward Hecher. "That was a vicious attack. Come back in a couple days and you can talk to him."

"Thanks," said Hecher.

When he returned, Jimmy's hands were in bandages.

"What happened, Jimmy?"

"After the guard cracked open the cell door for the morning, I closed it because I didn't feel like having breakfast—my stomach was a little upset—and I didn't want guys rushing me and stealing from me. Three shitheads on the ward musta known I'm pretty good at karate and they couldn't rob me by themselves so they had to gang up on me. When I shut the door, they got pissed off and came back with a can of gas and slung it at me before I knew what was happening. Then, poof, I was on fire."

"Cowards. They don't have the guts to take you on one-on-one. God almighty, this place is rotten. Guys got no principles. They're just evil. They don't care about nobody or nothin." Hecher paused. "Well, at least maybe some good will come of this. They might let you out of here early."

"I'm not keepin my fingers crossed. I can't."

"I hear you're starting a new karate class."

Hecher looked up from his plate at a six-foot white guy leaning on one leg.

"Yeah, the guys in the other two classes have been spreading the word, I guess. The program's getting pretty popular." Hecher took another spoonful of Campbell's pork and beans. "I don't think I've seen you before. You new?"

"Brand new. Mind if I sit down?"

"Hell no. Take a seat."

The inmate sat on the bench next to Hecher, who noticed an ungainly way of maneuvering, the right leg pulled along as if separate from the body.

"Name's Gary Lannon." He lowered his voice and said, "Listen, I gotta learn how to fight. Fast. Or I ain't gonna live long."

"Whoa. What's up?"

Lannon placed his forearms on the table and leaned forward. He looked surreptitiously around Hecher at two inmates toward the other end of the bench, who appeared ready to leave.

"Just a second till those guys go."

The men left after a minute.

"Okay, I can talk now. I s'pose I'm taking a big chance telling you this, cuz I don't know if I can trust you. But I got to trust somebody, and if the people who run this place allow you to choose who you're gonna train to fight, I figure you must be safe."

"I don't think you have to worry about me. As long as you're straight with me."

"Okay, here's the story. There's a contract out on me."

"Uh-oh. You mean you're a marked man? How'd you get yourself in that pickle?"

"Wait. You ain't heard the worst of it." He reached down and patted his right leg at the knee. "They figure I'm a push-over with this wooden leg."

"So that's why you were so clumsy sliding onto the bench. I thought maybe you were just favoring an old wound."

"Now here's why they wanna kill me. They think I'm a snitch."

"Are you?"

"I wasn't. That's why I lost the leg. Then these two bastards thanked me by turning on me, so I returned the favor. That's when the trouble started."

Hecher finished his beans, cleaned the plate with a piece of bread, downed it in two bites, and drank half a glass of water.

"Three months ago, I'm on the lam for stealing a coupla tires from a store after they overcharged me. That was my second offense. I burgled a warehouse eight years ago. So anyway, I'm at this highway rest stop in New York near the Canadian border when these two guys ask me if I can give them and their girlfriend a lift to the border. Hell, I say, why not? It was only a little out of my way and I was in no hurry. I was headed to a little town to see an old buddy and didn't set no time. Hop in, I says.

"Well, just before we get to the border, a highway patrol cop pulls me over. Saw my busted tail light. Asked for my driver's license and I gave it to him. He ran a check and told me to get the light fixed. Then he asked who my passengers were and where we were going. I told him they were Canadians and I was giving them a ride to the border. He asked to see their IDs. That's when all hell broke loose. The gal pulls a rod out of her purse and plugs the cop in the chest with two shots.

"'Git outa here,'" the one guy yells at me. "I don't know what that crazy broad is gonna do, so I hit the gas and leave the cop lying on the side of the road. I look in my rear view mirror, and he's on his radio. We're screaming down the highway, running cars off the road, damn near cracking up a couple times. It was only ten minutes till we got to the border check point, but man, they were waiting for us. There must have been a dozen cop cars, different agencies. The gates were down and they'd put barrels in front of em.

"'Let's ram it,'" the same guy shouts.

"You're crazy," I tell him.

"'Do it or you're dead,'" he yells. "He points to a little space between the guardhouse and barrels and tells me to slow down and then gun it."

Lannon let up on the accelerator as he approached the border station. Police officers peeked from crouched positions behind squad cars, their guns drawn. Forty yards from the guard station, he jammed on the gas. The car sped straight toward the road block, then swerved. A hail of pistol and rifle fire erupted, and the passengers dropped to the floor boards. Lannon felt a sting in his right leg, but rammed the car into the wedge. Metal debris and glass from the headlights flew into the air. The hood of the Buick sedan folded upward like a crushed cardboard box and shattered the windshield. The driver's door smashed inward against Lannon's left arm, but he hardly noticed. Beyond the barrels on the other side, two squad cars were parked end to end, perpendicularly across the road, and others formed blockades around them. Lannon had nowhere to go.

He jammed on the brakes and the car screeched to a stop. He stared into the cracked glass and croaked, "If you want to kill me, I might as well let you, because if you don't give up, we're all going to be killed anyway." They climbed up from the floor boards. "Put the gun on the seat, Sally," one of the men ordered in a reluctant tone. All three got out of the car and put their hands above their heads. Lannon did the same.

"They hauled us in to the nearest police station and right away took me to the hospital because my leg was bleeding pretty bad," said Lannon. "Two cops questioned me at the hospital about what happened in the shooting of the highway patrolman. They told me he had died of his wounds. I said I didn't know the people in the car and I had no idea who shot the cop. They said they didn't believe me. My leg was in bad shape, they said, and I needed surgery. But I wasn't gonna get any care until I spilled the beans."

The last of the inmates were filing out of the hall. Two were together and talked with animation, oblivious of Lannon and Hecher. A third made a furtive glance their way as he passed them, a subtlety that didn't escape Lannon.

"Did you see that?" he said.

"What?"

"That guy shot a look at us, and then real quick-like looked away, like he didn't want us to see him noticing us."

"You sure? You ain't gettin paranoid, are you? I wouldn't blame you if you were. Hell, this place'll make anybody paranoid. Especially in your situation."

"Yeah, maybe it was just my imagination. But he seemed suspicious. I'm gonna watch out for him."

"Prob'ly not a bad idea," said Hecher.

"Anyway, I didn't tell the cops nothin. I kept my mouth shut, and they kept me from having surgery. Fucking hospital managers and police worked together in this little hick town. So the next day, gangrene set in. Then the cops told me the two guys said the woman reached over from the back seat and handed me the gun after the patrolman turned on his siren to pull us over. The guys said I shot the cop when he asked to look at their IDs. The cops said they told them I said I was scared they were gonna get me for harboring fugitives. I knew the cops weren't making this up, because they knew the woman had the gun. They could only know that if the guys told them.

"I decided right then to tell the cops what happened. And then they allowed the hospital to take my leg off to save my life. All four of us got convicted of murder. The court sent me to a different prison, knowing I wouldn't have a prayer of surviving in the same joint with those guys. But they put the word out that I was a stool pigeon, and you know how it spreads."

Hecher sat with his hands held together in the praying position in his lap. When Lannon finished his story, the karate expert continuing appraising him for a couple of long seconds, drew a breath, and exhaled.

"Dude, looks like you really got screwed. You try to help these shitheads, and then they dump on you. Yeah, you need to learn some ways to defend yourself. I'll sign you up for my class this week. In the meantime, you better stick close to me whenever you can. I'll keep an eye on you. Where's your cell?"

"I'm in cell block E, number eighteen."

"Oh, hell, we're neighbors. I'm only a few cells away. Let's get back. We'll walk together."

Lannon swung his wooden leg over the bench, and they started out.

"You don't limp too bad," said Hecher. "You look like you can handle yourself on that pole. You might be able to use that baby to your advantage. We'll give it a whirl."

"Hey, my gosh, look who's here," Hecher beamed, as a small boy wearing a light-blue knit shirt, white shorts, and red tennis shoes bounded up to greet him. He swept the tyke off the floor of the first-floor reception area and into his arms.

"Wow, you're getting to be a big guy, Pauley," the inmate said, smooching his son.

Diane stepped forward and Hecher wrapped his free arm around her back and pulled her close. They kissed for several seconds while Pauley ran his hands through Hecher's hair.

"Come on," the inmate beckoned. "There's some lounge furniture here. Let's sit down and talk, and Pauley can run around."

They leaned back on a plastic couch, Hecher's arm around his wife's shoulders. The furniture was spaced far enough apart to afford privacy of conversation, if not of affectionate physical overtures. Two other couples sat to the right and catty-corner to the Hechers. One of them necked passionately, privacy be damned.

"You tell me what's happening in your letters," Diane noted, "but I sure miss seeing you. Somehow, you manage to keep looking good. I don't know how you do it in this hellhole."

"Well, I just stay as busy as I can to avoid feeling sorry for myself and keep my mind occupied. I just have to never give up hope that one day, somebody out there is going to do the right thing. I have to admit that was a low point for me when that judge gave the reward money to Gatson and Burns even though he knew they admitted to lying in court about me confessing to the murder. I'm still dumbfounded that any judge would see justice in that. We've really got a fucked-up... "

"Woops," he said, glancing at Pauley, "a messed-up justice system. I don't know if it's this bad in the rest of the country, but it sure as hell is screwed up in this state."

"I couldn't believe it either. Well, at least it got in the papers and TV, so the people could see how rotten it is. If I was a judge, I wouldn't want anybody to know I made a decision like that."

The two grew silent.

"Mitt, this may not be a good time to mention it, but I have to at some point, and there is no good time."

"Oh, shit. You've found somebody else and you want a divorce."

Diane broke out laughing. "No, Mitt. What's the matter with you? Don't you know I'm with you for as long as it takes? It's something else."

"Well, geez, what is it?"

She looked at him, then looked down and hesitated. "I have a disease—a serious one."

Hecher's mouth dropped open and he looked at her with widened eyes.

"It's called lupus, but it's not the usual kind. It's called systemic lupus, and it's what they call an auto-immune disease. It affects the vital parts of your body. It hits mostly women, up to about thirty-five."

Pauley had been inspecting the magazines in the rack against a wall, flipping through the pages and looking at the pictures. He came skipping up to his mother.

"Mommy, I want my crola book."

"You want your coloring book and Crayolas? Just a minute." Diane reached into her bag on the couch and retrieved a paperback book with brightly colored animals on the cover, and three Crayolas. "Here you are, sweetie. Why don't you sit on that chair over there where you can color and nobody will bother you?"

Pauley trotted to the chair fifteen feet away, hopped up on it, and immersed himself in the book, wielding the crayons.

"How long have you had this?" Hecher's voice was soft, almost pleading.

"I started noticing something was wrong about two years ago. I was feverish sometimes, and felt tired, and my joints ached."

"Two years!" Hecher retorted. "And you didn't tell me?"

"You've got more than enough to deal with. I didn't want to make life any harder for you. But I have to tell you so you can be prepared."

"Prepared? What are you saying? Shit, what are your saying?"

"It's… " She put her hand to her mouth. "I don't know how to say this. It's usually fatal."

"Oh, Christ. Baby."

He wrapped his arms around her and pressed her face against his. With his left hand, he held her head, while stroking her hair with his right hand. He remained that way for a half minute, partly because he didn't want her to see the glistening in his eyes. Finally, he drew back.

"Do you know how long you have?"

"There's no telling. It could go on for several years. Sometimes I feel okay. The symptoms come and go. There are periods when I don't feel well—days and weeks at a time. But let's be optimistic. Maybe God will be like Judge Schultz and won't give me a death sentence. It's not automatic."

"What are your chances?" Hecher's face brightened.

"Twenty years ago, about five percent. They think with the drugs they have today, it's around twenty percent."

Hecher's head dropped. He turned away and stared at the couple making out, swallowing hard against the lump forming in his throat.

"I'm sorry, darling. I didn't want to tell you. I just don't want you to be shocked in case the worst happens quicker than I expect."

"Hon, I'm glad you let me know. You should have told me earlier, just because I love you and need to, want to, share with you what you're going through. You need to tell me in your letters what it's like, how you're feeling. It will help if you don't have to suffer alone. Who knows? Maybe one of these days a decent judge with some common sense will hear my case and rule that evidence should decide a person's guilt or innocence instead of some fu… some stupid legal procedures or precedents and technicalities—and I'll get out of here so I can take care of you."

They kissed and held each other for several minutes. Pauley half walked, half ran to the pair, and Hecher hoisted him onto his lap.

"Hey, look at that picture. What a handsome horse. Did you do that?"

Pauley pumped his head up and down, holding his crayon up as proof.

"Wow. Maybe you're going to be an artist some day."

"What's a artis?"

"You'll know when you get older, Pauley. I'll just bet you've got artistic talent. It's that Italian blood in you."

Hecher grinned at Diane.

Pauley looked up at his dad with a blank look.

"I'm afraid the visiting time is about up," a guard announced, stepping through the gate.

"Oh, boy," Hecher said to Diane. "You come so far, and we have so little time."

"Yes, but it's worth it," she assured, rising.

They hugged, and Hecher lifted Pauley and kissed him.

"Why don't you come with us?" Pauley asked.

"I can't right now, Pauley. But one day I will. And we'll all be together."

He kissed Diane and managed a choked, "Goodbye, honey." He clenched his teeth and tightened his lips.

"I'll be okay, darling. You just take care of yourself."

Hecher couldn't speak. Smiling with effort, he waved as she and Pauley walked out the door.

The first session of the third karate class was winding up. Twelve men stood in three rows of four each. Lannon was to Hecher's right on the end of the first row. In the warm-ups, he did the jumping jacks by throwing his hands away from his body and above his head till his hands touched, forming an arc, coordinating each repetition with a jump on his good leg instead of the scissor spread. He had no difficulty with the bicycle pedaling exercise on his back, simply keeping his wooden leg raised in the air while pumping the right one.

Lannon handled the blocking defense move with aplomb, his handicap posing no problem.

In the next session, Hecher demonstrated the defense against someone attacking with a pipe, again using a wooden dowel. He had the men moving to their left, pivoting, leaping, and kicking at phantom attackers.

To Lannon, he said, "Gary, you move to your left and leap off your left foot. You can kick with your right. The dude who gets that pole in his face is going to be one surprised, sorry son-of-a-bitch. You better not practice that on anybody but me, cuz I know how to get out of the way."

The guards were little protection for the inmates from each other. An incident highlighted that reality for Hecher with the same harsh clarity as the clanging cell gate closing on him the first time he was thrown in jail, at age eighteen, for beating up a bar patron. He and a fellow inmate stood in the open space of the cell block, watching three medics run down the first-floor walkway bearing a white inmate on a gurney, heading for the hospital gate leading to the infirmary. From cells on either side, three black inmates ran up to the gurney with make-shift knives and stabbed the inmate on the gurney while the medics ran with him.

"Fuck this shit," groused the inmate with Hecher, short and vulnerable. He walked out to the yard, grabbed a fourteen-inch dumbbell bar, and slid it under his pants, along his thigh. "They come at me with them shivs, I'm gonna be ready."

Both Hecher and Lannon knew that the only viable protection for the marked inmate was the karate expert, for Lannon couldn't risk being alone with any other prisoner.

Chapter Four

"Here in this exclusive fantasyland of soaring grandeur, unrestrained opulence, and lavish lifestyles, the superwealthy have congregated since before the turn of the century to cavort amongst themselves with carefree abandon. Seldom have they had to worry about the kinds of crimes that concern ordinary folks in neighborhoods throughout America."

Jordano Rabona spoke into a microphone, connected to a cord, that he held in his right hand. He stood at the long driveway entrance to The Breakers in Palm Beach. A television camera of the American Communications Company homed in on the magnificent hotel in the background. The room windows covered the broad, mushroom-colored façade like dark, shiny boxes, and the two bell towers on the sides conjured sentries guarding against malevolence. A circular fountain in front bespoke classic European refinement.

"But this sheltered community alongside the Atlantic Ocean, rarely the scene of violence of any kind, was shocked to its core six years ago when a restaurant executive who lived with his family on the north part of the island was shot one night by someone who fired into the home from the outside."

As he spoke, Rabona switched the mike to his left hand and swept his right arm to the north, the camera following his pointing finger, to indicate the direction where Kriger had lived.

"The man was Rodger Kriger. He was barely forty-seven years old, and he died eleven days later. After two years, a young street fighter named Mitt Hecher, who was frequently in trouble with the law, was convicted of the murder. He was sentenced to a minimum twenty-five years in prison and sent to Raiford State Prison, where he remains.

"But questions over how the case was handled arose almost immediately, and the way in which the trial was conducted led to doubts as to whether Hecher received a fair trial, and even as to his guilt. Those uncertainties persist to this day. ACC's *Perfect Vision* examined the many troubling aspects of this case for two reasons: If Mitt Hecher didn't fatally shoot Rodger Kriger, then a gross miscarriage of justice has occurred and it needs to be corrected.

Second, if that's true, Mister Kriger's killer is still running around loose, and people have every reason to feel uneasy.

"We interviewed law enforcement officers, the prosecution, the defense, the trial judge, jury members, other persons associated with the case, and most important, the trial witnesses. At the end of the program, we go to Raiford Prison, where we talk to Milt Hecher and peek in on his five-year-old son and wife as they come to visit him."

The scene switched to a lavish, Mediterranean-style home on a wooded stretch of land several miles west in Loxahatchee. Rabona stood outside, microphone in hand, cameraman in front and to his right.

"A source whose identity we agreed not to disclose called us when he learned we were here investigating, and said two men who talked about being from Cuba bought two twelve-gauge pump shotguns at a sporting goods store in West Palm Beach a few days before Mister Kriger was shot. That is the kind of gun which was used in the shooting. The source said the two men behaved suspiciously. We checked with sheriff's police, who said they were familiar with the story and the two men checked out okay. The men agreed to talk with us."

The cameraman followed Rabona to the front door, where a young man granted them entry.

"Sit down." He gestured to an ornate, off-yellow, Italian sofa fronted by a glass-topped coffee table with artfully curved legs of the same color. Two leather-bound books rested atop each other on the shelf below. The table sat on an intricately patterned Oriental rug of yellows, blues, and browns. Classic European paintings, mixed with some from Latin America, adorned the walls. Miguel Francisco took a seat next to the interviewer.

"Miguel, you admitted to a sheriff's detective that you and your brother Jorge bought two shotguns of the type used to shoot Rodger Kriger just days before that event happened. And according to the source both I and the detective talked to, you two acted suspiciously when you made the purchase. Can you explain that?"

"Well... yes. I'm afraid we were going to do something we weren't supposed to. We are members of a club that used to shoot pigeons for sport. We would go out into the woods with cages of the birds and release them. Not all at once, but one or two or three at a time. When they fly into the air, we would shoot to try our skills. But that is illegal, so we were trying to be secret. We don't do that anymore. Now we use clay pigeons. We just do skeet shooting."

"So the sheriff's office cleared you of any suspicion in the Kriger shooting."

"Oh, for sure. That was terrible. He was fishing with Papa on his yacht the day before somebody did that awful thing."

"Yes, and because he was on the boat with your dad, Alberto Francisco, his name came up in the trial of Mitt Hecher, the man convicted of the murder. But the police official who testified said there was no apparent connection."

"Between Papa and the shooting? Of course not. Papa was a friend of Rodger Kriger. Why would he want to kill him?" Rabona detected irritation in Miguel's voice and face. He paused. "They put that guy Mitt Hecher in prison, but a lot of people don't think he did it."

"That's why we're here. We're trying to get to the bottom of whether he's guilty. Thank you very much for your cooperation, Mister Francisco."

"Glad to help you," he said as they rose and shook hands.

Rabona pinned down sheriff's department officials and got them to concede that Palm Beach police botched the investigation by pressing the same doorbell that the killer had rung, smudging the fingerprint. The cops also lost a cigarette found near the spot where the shots were fired, the officials admitted. Rabona exposed to the nation the mystery in which the town's police chief refused to grant Kriger's dying request to see a police sergeant who was a friend. But the broadcast journalist could only elicit from the chief his oft-stated response: Sergeant Jackson was "too close to the family" and would not be impartial.

"I would think his personal knowledge of the family would have been an advantage, if anything, Chief. That just doesn't hold water. Surely there wouldn't have been any harm for Kriger to see his friend before he died, would there?"

"I've told you my reason," Chief Gurney answered. "I have nothing more to say."

A West Palm Beach policeman, who spoke anonymously as the camera blurred his face, said, "Several of us who were investigating this case first thought Hecher must have done it, even though we were surprised because we didn't really think he was a killer. But within a month we realized he wasn't guilty."

"How did you come to that conclusion?" Rabona asked.

"Things just didn't add up. How could Hecher have mistaken the Kriger house for the next-door house of the Gunders, even if he didn't know that Bobby Gunder wasn't living there—which seems pretty stupid if you're coming to shoot somebody. There was a big sign in front of the Kriger house: 'The Krigers.' I know Hecher. He's a tough bast... woops, can't say that on TV, can I? Sorry. He's a tough guy, but he sure as he... uh, sure as heck isn't stupid. You think he'd come and blast away at this house without checking it out first and seeing that sign? Give me a break."

"So why didn't you and your fellow officers come forth and testify at his trial?"

"Look, he's got enough other crimes against him that he deserves to be behind bars a long time."

"If I'm not mistaken, he was convicted on weapons, possession of stolen property, and minor drug charges. Do you think those merited twenty-eight years? We've spoken with prosecutors in other Florida counties and they believe the penalty is excessive."

Officer Anonymous took a deep breath. "All right, I'll level with you. This guy has been a real pain in the... a thorn in our sides for a long time. He's a bad apple. Every time there's a bar fight, we ask the bartender on the phone if it's Hecher, and if it is, we take three extra men because otherwise we can't get him in cuffs and shoved in the car. A lot of us have been banged up scrapping with that little punk. It's time he got his."

The camera zeroed in on Alonzo Seppish at his desk in Miami. He leaned forward on his elbows, slicked-back hair a little more silvery than it was four years before. Head lowered, he eyed his inquisitor with a dour, suspicious look.

"Mister Seppish, lawyers have pointed to what they say were several glaring deficiencies in your method of defending your client. I'm going to list them and then I'd like for you to respond. First, you never called Mitt Hecher to testify in his own behalf. Second, you never objected to the prosecutor's mention of the confession that Mister Hecher supposedly wrote while in jail, even though the judge would have sustained your objection. You know that. I know that. I have a law degree. Third, you passed up the opportunity to pursue the love triangle element—Rodger Kriger's affair with a stripper—even though the judge gave you the go-ahead to do so. Fourth, you never called Bobby Gunder to testify, even though he was the person Hecher supposedly was gunning for. Fifth, you never interviewed the witnesses before the trial."

Seppish looked Rabona in the eye, expressionless and unmoving, as he made the charges. The attorney glared for a few moments after the journalist stopped, and Rabona wondered if he were going to pounce. Instead, he reared back in his swivel executive chair, threw his head back, and stared at the ceiling, appearing to have quickly changed his mind about his method of responding.

"My strategy was to allow Mister Scraponia to hang his own client by showing the jury just how noncredible his arguments and evidence were. Maybe it backfired on me. I hate to think so. I do know this: I was recovering from prostate surgery, and I asked Judge Schultz for a delay in the trial so I could have more time to prepare. He wouldn't grant my request. I think he didn't want to miss the chance to preside over the second televised trial in the state of Florida. Channel 18 in Miami told him they would televise a different trial if this one was delayed."

Rabona announced that Kriger's widow, Jan, declined to be interviewed. He then called on Mrs. Gunder at her residence next to the Kriger house. Milton Gunder had walked to his neighbor's house after hearing the shots and waited with Kriger until the ambulance arrived. He was out of town and unavailable for an interview.

"Bobby never even heard of Mitt Hecher before he was arrested," Mrs. Gunder said of her son. "He admits he got into drugs while he was in Vietnam and he bought some cocaine from two men from Brazil who thought he'd cheated them. He said he met the terms of the deal, but they wanted more money, and he was afraid they might come after him."

She waved an arm in the air, almost striking the *étagère* next to the Queen Victoria chair that she sat in, and exhibited a disdainful smile.

"But that had nothing to do with Mitt Hecher. We have no idea who killed Rodger Kriger, but it certainly was not a case of Mitt Hecher coming after my son, as the prosecutor made it out to be."

The scene switched to the Palm Beach County Courthouse in downtown West Palm Beach. Rabona stood on steps leading to the broad stone patio fronting the gray building of neo-classical architecture, built in the early part of the century. The camera caught the Roman columns in the background. The TV journalist turned sideways, pointed up at the horizontal entablature while turning his head toward it, then faced the camera as he read the Latin phrase carved into the frieze:

"Jusitiae via strata veritate. Translated: 'The way of justice is paved with truth.' But questions loom as to whether truth prevailed in the courtroom in this building where Mitt Hecher was convicted of first degree murder four years ago.

"As defense counsel Alonzo Seppish mentioned, the trial was televised. We're going to play for you the tape of the opening remarks by the prosecutor, James Scraponia."

The television screen switched from Rabona to the 1978 courtroom scene.

"Ladies and gentlemen of the jury, through the testimony of some of society's most nefarious characters—killers, gangsters, scoundrels—I am going to prove to you that Mitt Hecher has admitted murdering Rodger Kriger."

Exit Scraponia, enter Rabona.

"Ladies and gentlemen watching this program, through the testimony of those same nefarious characters, I am going to show that Mitt Hecher probably did not admit to murdering Rodger Kriger... " He paused a half-second, then, giving weight to each word, "and raise serious doubts in your minds as to his guilt."

The camera changed location again, zeroing in on Donald Gibbons in his shack in the black ghetto of Riviera Beach. He sat on a frayed, blue-gray couch, which rested on a soiled, light-green, shag carpet. A narrow beam of sunlight slashed a corner of a chocolate-brown, overstuffed chair with a torn armrest, which sat at an angle to one side of the couch.

"Mister Gibbons, how long have you been out of jail?" asked Rabona, sitting on a straight-backed bamboo chair that Gibbons had pulled from the dining table.

"Oh... " Gibbons turned his head down and to one side, then the other, frowning. "I guess it's been more'n three years now. Scraponia got me out a little while after I lied about Hecher. But he wad'n the only one who got me to lie. Cap'n Danielson, the jail commander—man, he put the fear of God in me. That guy was a bad

dude. He tol me I better cooperate—that was the word he used—or
he was gonna throw me into a cell wid some Ku Klux Klan guys.
You know how long a black man'd live locked up wid dem crazy
cross burners?"

"So what you said about Hecher confessing to shooting Rodger
Kriger wasn't true?"

"Oh, lordie, no, it wad'n true. I never even talked to Hecher in
jail—hardly even seen im."

Rabona interviewed Alan Burns at the Avon Park Correctional
Institution.

"Mister Burns, why did you get sent to this prison?"

"I got into a fight with another inmate and hurt him pretty bad.
They were gonna let me out after I testified against Hecher, but then
I fu… I messed up."

"You testified that Hecher asked you to pass written information
to Dewey Crimshaw, and you did that for him. Were you telling the
truth?"

"Nope, not at all. Nonea that happened. I made it all up so
Scraponia would get me out of jail early."

"We're going now to Laurent, Louisiana, where an ACC
associate found Richie Gatson at his hound-dog-breeding business."

"You received part of the reward money for giving a deposition
saying you had information that the shotgun Mitt Hecher used to
shoot Rodger Kriger was in a warehouse in Albuquerque. Is that
correct?"

Howls erupted from cages in the background as a young woman
clad in color-clashing tight slacks, a denim jacket, and leather boots
passed in front of the dogs with a bucket of pork bones with
remnants of meat.

"Yes," said Gatson, "but I later admitted that I lied about that,
and I refused to testify in court. I accepted the money because I was
strapped for cash."

DeWitt Crimshaw III sat cross-legged in a wicker rocking chair
in the sunlit, glass-enclosed patio of his aunt's home in Palm Beach,
smoking a cigarette from a long-stemmed holder. Rabona occupied a
wingback chair, facing the heir to an inventor's fortune at an angle
from behind a small coffee table.

"You have admitted that you lied in court when you testified
Mitt Hecher told you he shot Rodger Kriger and asked you to help

him plead guilty by reason of insanity over problems with his girlfriend. You also said you forged his confession. Are you telling the truth now?"

"Yes, I'm afraid so," the playboy answered calmly, looking squarely at Rabona. "I fabricated the whole thing."

"Why did you do that?"

Crimshaw took a long drag on his cigarette and blew the smoke out in slow wisps.

"It was a reprehensible thing to do," he said, looking pensive. "There's no getting around it. I simply was acting in my own interest. I detested my life in jail, and fabricating that story was my ticket out."

"Why did you decide to come forth and tell a newspaper reporter that you had lied, and then tell me the same thing?"

"I know how awful prison is, and I know that my testimony in court had a lot to do with the prison sentence Mister Hecher received. I am hopeful that my admission now that I lied will help him win a new trial."

Rabona stood outside the main building of the Palm Beach County Jail, several miles southwest of downtown West Palm Beach. The camera showed the drab, gray structure in the background.

"Only one of the inmates from this jail who testified against Mitt Hecher did not recant," he reported. "That is George Demarco, who remains here. Before his testimony that Hecher said he shot Kriger, Demarco faced execution for three murders. After his testimony, he was taken off death row and his sentence was reduced to life in prison.

"The chief jailer at this institution is Captain John Danielson. We're going to go to the home of Lester McCabe, a former trusty at this jail, and talk to him about the jailer."

Next scene, a ramshackle house in Riviera Beach, bordering West Palm Beach on the north.

"Can you repeat what you told me, Mister McCabe?" Rabona asked. He sat at one end of a marred, green-painted table off the kitchen, directly across from McCabe.

"Captain Danielson told me the trial of Mitt Hecher was going to be on television and showed me a television set and how to turn to the right station to watch the trial. And he ordered me to come with him and bring the TV set to a room in the courthouse and hook it up in a corner where nobody wouldn't bother George Demarco while he watched it."

Jim Scraponia sat erect in a high-backed, cushiony chair, his forearms on the armrests, and peered through horn-rimmed glasses beneath his thick, dark mane. A placard on the oak-paneled wall behind him contained a certificate that read, James Albert Scraponia, Honors Graduate, Class of 1972, Rutgers University School of Law.

"I was upfront with that jury from the outset," he insisted to the interviewer, who sat in a stationary chair across from his desk. "I told them they would hear testimony from criminals and scoundrels. And they chose to believe them. Who is to say when they were telling the truth, then or now? There was enough evidence on top of their testimony to believe what they said then. If they weren't telling the truth, they should be charged with perjury. They could have any number of reasons for lying now. It was their one chance for fame. Or they may worry about retaliation for having been snitches. All I know is that I did my job and I believe Mitt Hecher was guilty."

In his chambers in the downtown courthouse, Judge Timothy Schultz looked judicial against a backdrop of three shelves containing volumes of the Florida Statutes and various legal compilations, and scholarly treatments of historical judicial figures. A nondescript man, he was balding and bespectacled.

"I refused to follow the prosecution's request for the death penalty, and in fact meted out the minimum sentence of a mandatory twenty-five years in prison, because the basis for the conviction was inordinately flimsy."

Schultz's gaze alternated from Rabona to the TV camera above and to the right of the reporter.

"Did you refuse to grant the defense attorney's request for a delay in the trial because a delay would have prevented it from being televised?" Rabona asked.

"That suggestion by Alonzo Seppish is totally outrageous and false," the judge replied with raised voice, thumping his desk with his right forefinger. His face turned red and the veins in his neck resembled rivers on a map.

The camera zoomed in on Mitt Hecher walking through the gate to the reception area as his five-year-old son came running up to him, followed by wife Diane. After the kissing and hugging, the scene shifted to Hecher's cell. He sat on his bed, propped against the wall.

"I don't have the vaguest idea who killed Kriger, or why anyone would have wanted to." He looked at Rabona, ignoring the camera. "I'd never heard of the man before he was shot. I hardly ever was in Palm Beach, and never in that northern residential part where he lived. I popped in to the Shore Club in Palm Beach Shores with Richie Gatson and Davey Ross a coupla times, but my territory was West Palm Beach and Riviera Beach. I was a bar brawler, a street fighter. If I had any idea who shot Kriger, you can bet I wouldn't keep it a secret. But that's for the cops to find out. I sure wish they would, so I could get the he... Gotta watch my language on TV... so I could get the heck"—a grim smile—"the Hecher out of here."

Rabona stood at the foot of the stairs in front of the courthouse. On either side of him, people walked toward its wide, heavy, bronze, double doors. They were men and women who covered the age spectrum, their sartorial diversity hinting at their stations in life. The men in suits and ties carrying briefcases probably were their attorneys, Rabona surmised, the casually or inexpensively dressed persons their clients.

The camera crept forward, sliding off Rabona's half-turned face and climbing up the building to the Latin inscription, where it focused while Rabona intoned: "The way of justice is paved with truth."

A pause while the narrator's full, standing figure returned to the screen, microphone in hand.

"But if the case we have investigated tonight is any measure of the justice meted out in the courtrooms of this grand, historic building, the people walking in its path had better watch their step. That pavement may be laced with something sinister which subverts the truth.

"Thank you for watching, and good night."

Chapter Five

Hecher and Gary Lannon picked their trays off the table, both leaving half the spaghetti on their plates untouched, and headed for the kitchen. The karate expert had decided that if he were to stay in halfway decent shape, he'd have to restrict what he ate in the carbohydrate-heavy prison diet. Lannon emulated his mentor and body guard. They dropped their trays off at the counter and strolled through the double doors into the ward.

"Oh, holy shit," Hecher blurted, stopping.

Far down the ward, on the ground floor between the cell blocks, a group of about forty inmates were throwing excrement and food they had taken in plastic bags from the mess hall. One, who appeared to be the ringleader, a heavily tattooed white guy with a fu Manchu beard, brandished a metal pipe and yelled toward closed cells on all three floors.

"Come on out here, you mother fuckers. You know you're pissed off with the crap they feed us, but you let a few of us raise hell about it. Fuckin cowards." He shook the pipe in the air. "Come on out here and join us."

Twenty guards wearing helmets, boots, and protective vests wielded batons to defend themselves from the few make-shift knives and pipes. They formed a barrier to prevent the inmates from infiltrating other cell blocks and instigating a full-scale riot.

But the inmates were becoming more aggressive. One holding a knife lunged at a guard, who swung his baton. The prisoner ducked and barreled into the guard, catapulting him backward onto the floor.

"Stay here," Hecher said to Lannon.

He sprinted down the ward to the scene, where the inmate had climbed on top of the fallen guard, knife raised. The guard held his baton out horizontally with both hands, ready to parry the inmate's attempts to stab him.

"Hold it," Hecher shouted.

"Hey brother, stay the fuck outa this," the inmate demanded.

"This ain't gonna get you no place but solitary or death row," Hecher countered.

"You don't hear too good, do ya?" said the inmate.

He jumped up and, holding the knife aloft, rushed at Hecher, who went into his defensive karate position. As the knife came down, Hecher's left arm went up and deflected the movement while his right fist swung up into the inmate's midsection, doubling him up. Hecher then delivered a smashing chop to the back of his neck, sending him crashing onto the floor, where blood spurted out of his nose.

The guard leaped off the floor, placed handcuffs on the vanquished inmate, and thanked Hecher.

"Better get back to your guys while I get outa here," Hecher advised. "If this bunch thinks I'm siding with you all, I'm in big trouble. You're on your own now."

Hecher turned and hurried back to Lannon.

"Welcome back, Kemosabe. And now, hi-yo Silver! Away! The Lone Ranger rides again."

"Yeah," Hecher said with a wry smile, "let's scram. This thing might get worse, and we don't want to be a part of it."

Hecher accompanied Lannon to his cell, then walked to his own. The rioting continued, and he watched from his door as an inmate burst from a cell here and there and ran down the hall to join the rioters. The group grew to about sixty.

Fifteen minutes later, a contingent of twenty more guards brandishing batons and shields swept through the double doors and into the ward. As they stationed themselves, the loudspeaker blared a baritone voice.

"Men, this is the warden. I hereby order you to return to your cells immediately. If you do not, we will bring in the dogs. This is not a measure we prefer, but your actions leave us no choice.

"Regarding your complaint about the food served here at Raiford State Prison, I will tell you this: No amount of rioting, destruction of property, and violence committed against our security officers will accomplish your objective. We will not succumb to such tactics. However, you should know that the state Board of Correctional Institutions petitioned the Florida Cabinet just ten days ago to investigate the quality of the cuisine in our prisons and recommended measures for improvement. As the warden of Florida's largest prison, I already have made plans to provide input into what changes I think should be made. Now let's all calm down and go back to your cells for a while so the prison staff can clean up the mess. After that, you may go about your activities peacefully. You've taken out your anger, and so far nobody has gotten seriously injured. Let's keep it that way. Thank you."

Calls of "Bullshit," "More promises," "He's just fuckin with us," and "We ain't goin nowhere" erupted. But the yelling began to sound weaker and more like bravado. "Man, I don't like them fuckin dogs," one muttered.

The men began wandering back to their cells. When none remained, the guards stood by while staff came with buckets and mops, and cleaned up.

The warden returned to his office and fell into his executive chair. His assistant sat at a small desk in a corner, fiddling with an expensive-looking camera.

"I've got to talk to that board pronto and tell them I had to lie my ass off to stop that riot and they'd damn well better do something about the food in this rat hole," the warden grumbled. "They're not going to like it, so I'll show them the photos you took."

"Yeah," said the assistant. "I was up on the third floor and got a couple of good overhead shots of a guard down with an inmate on top of him with a knife, and another inmate rescuing him. Pretty dramatic. If this stuff doesn't convince these starched shirts with their heads in the sand, nothing will."

———————

Pauley wore light-blue shorts, a navy blue, short-sleeved shirt, and white tennis shoes. He walked briskly through the door into the reception area just as Hecher was entering from the gate. A small, brown imitation leather purse swung by a strap from his shoulder.

"Hi Daddy," he squealed, dropping the purse as the inmate hoisted him into his arms.

It was a toss-up as to whose face was the most radiant.

"Oh, my gosh, you have gotten heavier. I'm going to have to work out harder because I'm barely strong enough to lift you," Hecher mocked, kissing his son on the cheek.

The inmate's smile vanished, his face darkening, like a group of laughing people shocked into silence when a heretofore hilarious joke teller drops a mean one-liner. Hecher's eyes fastened on Diane for a second as she moved with obvious effort, her face screwed up in pain. He quickly lowered Pauley onto the floor and stepped forward, his arms up for an embrace.

"No, stop, Mitt," she protested, hands up and palms outward.

He halted in his tracks, mouth open.

"I'm sorry. It's too painful if you squeeze me. I'm afraid you'll have to treat me delicately, like a pampered prima donna." She smiled through a grimace. "You can touch me, but I can't let you show as much affection as I know you want to. Here. Put your hands on my arms, and kiss me softly."

Hecher stepped forward with hesitation, placed his hard karate hands on his wife's upper arms, and ever so gently touched her lips with his.

"Oh babe," he whispered, and fought to squelch the large lump growing in his throat.

"Let's sit," she said. "It's better than standing. There." She motioned toward a chair with a cushion, next to a plastic couch, and shuffled toward it. Hecher held his arm around her shoulders, almost without touching.

She turned and lowered herself into the chair, pain registering in her face. Hecher sat on the couch and leaned into her.

"How long has it been this bad?"

"It had been coming and going for some time, but lately when it comes, it doesn't want to go." She looked ahead at nothing. "Maybe if my body treated it like this place treats you, it wouldn't stay very long." She turned to her husband with a wan smile.

"Help me understand what you're going through," Hecher implored. "What exactly does it feel like?"

"Oh, Mitt, I didn't come here to dump my burden on you. You've got enough… "

"Stop that nonsense," Hecher said with pique.

Diane jerked her head back a few inches and looked hurt.

"I'm sorry, honey. I'm sorry. Your problem is my problem, and that's all there is to it. My God, I love you." He buried his head in his hands and stifled a sob.

Diane laid a hand on the back of his head.

"It's all right," she whispered.

Hecher drew his hands away from his face. "You don't need to worry about me at all. I can take care of myself just fine. Now tell me what exactly you're feeling."

Diane pondered. "It's like a toothache all over my body."

"But the drive over here—that's eight hours. How could you stand it?"

Diane breathed hard. "It took thirteen hours. I had to stop every hour and get out to get the blood circulating in my legs and relieve the pain in my back and my backside. That was actually better for Pauley because he gets restless."

Hecher was silent for several seconds. "I hate to say this, but making the trip here is too much of an ordeal for you. I can't let you keep suffering like this. I mean, when you leave here, you have to drive back and go through the whole thing over again. I'm going to ask for a meeting with the warden to see if I can arrange for us to talk on the phone."

"I have to be honest. It's not going to get any better—unless they come up with better drugs to fight it. You never know. They've made some progress over the last fifteen or twenty years. But until then, my condition is likely to only get worse. You're right. We'd probably better make this our last visit."

Her eyes moistened, and Hecher's lips trembled.

"But I'll be calling you, hon." His voice cracked. With utmost care, he placed his hands on each side of her face. "My God, I want to hold you and squeeze you."

Finally, a tear trickled out of his right eye, rolled down his cheek, and was pursued by another.

Diane's face brightened. "Listen, Mitt, I know we're going to see each other again. You're going to get out of here. You can't give up. Some new people are working on it. I waited till now to tell you so you wouldn't be too despondent when Pauley and I leave."

Hecher swiped his damp face with the palm of his right hand.

"What's happening?"

"Well, that private investigator who was working on your case, Jim, he's still digging, and he's come up with some new stuff. He's working with a prominent criminal attorney. And another big shot has gotten interested in the case. He's a lot better known than Kriger was, and richer, too. He's into all kinds of businesses and owns a lot of property. You have that saying, 'The bigger they are, the harder they fall.'"

A strained grin crinkled Hecher's lips.

"Every law agency in the county and even some on the state and federal levels accused him of wrong-doing in his business dealings and attacked him like pit bulls, never letting up," said Diane. "He says it was some kind of vendetta by a guy he did business with who had a lot of influence. They spent almost three years investigating everything about his business operations and his personal life. He was a big prize. But in the end, he stood tall. They came up with nothing."

"What does that have to do with me?"

"I made a copy of an article that was in the *Fort Lauderdale Ray*."

She called to Pauley and asked him to bring her purse. She had asked him to carry it because it was uncomfortable for her to deal with. He laid it on the floor in front of her, and she retrieved the article.

"Read this paragraph." She pointed.

Hecher read aloud: "The serious flaws and injustices of our justice system are no more clearly illustrated than in the case against Mitt Hecher, by which a person without the financial wherewithal to defend himself with the best legal resources is no match against an organized effort to subvert the truth and destroy."

He looked up at Diane, who wore a pinched smile.

"Do you understand where he's going with this?" she said. "He's been reading about your case and got ahold of Jim and said he wanted to know more. They contacted the attorney, and this wealthy guy is financing their work on your behalf. Read on. He's really angry at the way the criminal justice system works in our county, and he thinks there's a lot of corruption even in the state and the U.S. law agencies."

Hecher finished reading.

"Now here's what Jim has come up with," Diane recounted. "To start with, he uncovered the fact that when the grand jury charged you with murder, one of the jurors was the wife of the head of the county detective bureau, and of course he had a major role in the investigation. Big conflict of interest there. And now a member of the jury in the trial has given a sworn statement saying two other jurors made comments to her during the trial that showed they already believed you were guilty before the trial began."

Leaning back on the couch, Hecher nodded and rubbed his chin, looking pensive. A magazine in one hand, Pauley skipped up to the couch and jumped onto it beside Hecher. He threw his left arm around his son and pulled him close.

"Daddy, what's a bra?" he asked.

"What?" Mitt looked at Diane with both amusement and bemusement, then lowered his gaze onto the page where Pauley was pointing. He burst out laughing.

"Oh, Pauley, that an advertisement. That's something that women wear. We'll tell you about that when you get a little older. You're a little too young to understand it. How did you know how to say that word?"

"Mommy has been teaching me how to sound out letters so I know how to do it when I start to school next fall."

"That's great, Pauley. You're smart. You're going to be a good student. Your mother is helping you to learn, and she's going to need you to help her with things around the house, because she's not feeling well. Will you help her?"

Pauley shook his head up and down.

"Good. That's good, Pauley. I'm proud of you."

"So anyway," Diane resumed, "Jim said he learned that somebody called the Kriger house earlier in the evening and the Krigers' son answered. The boy said the man had a gruff voice and wanted to know when his parents were coming home, but the boy didn't know. Somebody called two more times but hung up when the boy answered.

"Jim says since you don't have a gruff voice, the police should have assumed that if you were involved, somebody else was working with you. So that means the case should be reopened.

"Also, it's mysterious that Mrs. Kriger made several calls after her husband was shot. She called an ambulance first, then a neighbor, then her attorney, and finally the police. She sure didn't seem in a hurry to let the police know. And it gave the shooter plenty of time to get away. Somebody already had called in a false report of a domestic disturbance way at the north end, which drew the cop there away from the escape route."

"Hmm." Hecher cocked his head back. "Interesting. Only thing, that stuff about Mrs. Kriger making the calls isn't going to help me, I don't think. Her motive is just speculation."

"Maybe so. But there's more. Jim says the side window that the shooter shot through was hidden by bushes, so he had to know ahead of time just where that window was. It must have been somebody who spent time in Palm Beach and somehow had gotten onto the yard near the window. Maybe he'd sneaked onto the property and checked it out at night when the lights were on in the house, and he could see the window through the bushes. That's just my own devious detective mind at work." She giggled.

"Good thinking. That makes sense."

"Now, here's something else that Jim came up with—something that seems pretty important. The first shot was through the window into the foyer. The next two shots were through the front door."

"Yeah, but we already knew that."

"Hold on. One of the two shots was about four feet high, and the other was only about one foot from the bottom of the door. Why are those different heights important? Jim says it shows the shooter was either a professional or a military man. He knew that the first shot would knock the guy to the floor, in case the shot from the side window hadn't floored him. Then he got in a kneeling position to have a better chance of hitting him at floor level. They teach them in the military to do that, according to Jim."

"Aha." Hecher's face lit up. "And I've never been in the military, and they can dig into my background all they want but they'll never find where I had any training to speak of in shooting."

"See, Jim and the attorney plan to combine all this stuff with a lot of other info that shows you couldn't have been involved with the Kriger murder. Oh, and Jim says the thing that has him most convinced of your innocence is the psychological stress test his friend had you take—you know, that retired Army intelligence general, or colonel, or whatever—where he asked you fifty questions and you never failed a single one. Jim thinks he's got a fighting chance for a new trial."

Jim had recruited his friend to come to the county jail where Hecher awaited trial, and conduct the test, similar to a polygraph exam. Attorney Seppish, recuperating from debilitating surgery, never tried to have the results presented at the trial.

A guard appeared at the gate.

"Five minutes."

Hecher nodded at him.

"Well, Diane, we'll keep our hopes up."

With much effort, she slid forward in her chair and rose. Hecher put his arm around the waist of her loose-fitting dress, taking care not to press against her body, and they moved in baby steps toward the door of the reception area.

"Come on, Pauley, we have to go," Diane called over her shoulder.

Pauley walked up beside his dad. "Daddy, why can't you come with us?"

"It's a long story, Pauley. But I'm hoping that before too long, I'll be able to join you." He bent down and kissed him.

They reached the door. Diane turned to face Mitt. He put his hands on her shoulders with care and kissed her tenderly for several seconds. He drew back and looked at her, his lips aquiver.

"It's okay, Mitt. The doctors will keep me as comfortable as possible. I'll manage. We'll try to talk on the phone. Surely the prison people will understand. As for you, people believe in you. You have to have faith they're going to get you out of here. It will happen."

Pauley held the door open as she walked through.

"Bye, Daddy."

Hecher swallowed hard. "Bye, Pauley," he managed, his voice gravelly. "Take care of yourself, and take care of Mommy."

Diane stopped, did a slow turn, and held her hand up, wiggling her fingers.

Hecher waved back.

Then they were gone.

He plodded back to his cell. It was empty. He sat on the edge of his bed, leaned forward with his elbows on his thighs, and rested his head in his hands. For the only time that he could remember, he wept.

Chapter Six

Hecher lay in his bed, twitching. Scraponia and several members of the jury that convicted him stood in the prison yard and laughed as he tried to subdue them with karate moves which proved futile.

"Hecher. Mitt Hecher."

The inmate heard his name as though from a distance. He lifted his head off the pillow.

"Hecher," the voice repeated from the cell door.

"Huh? What's going on? What time is it?"

"It's five-thirty," the guard announced. "I need to take you to the locker room so you can get your street clothes. You're being transferred to Avon Park."

"Oh geez," said Hecher, rubbing his eyes. "For a second I thought you were telling me I was being freed. But that's great news, anyway. Avon Park is a hell of a lot better than this dungeon. I'll be ready in a minute."

He walked to the sink in his boxer shorts, brushed his teeth, and donned the prison polo and pants that were draped over a wooden pole attached parallel with the wall. He slipped into his soft-soled, vinyl, black shoes. He opened a duffel bag lying under the pole, and stuffed his meager belongings inside: two books, a Checkers set, writing materials, several boxer shorts and pairs of socks.

"Okay, I'm ready," he said.

The guard accompanied him to the first-floor room, where he switched into a plain beige shirt, matching pants, and inexpensive leather shoes.

"Listen, Sarg, is there any way I can say goodbye to my buddy Gary. Gary Lannon, the peg-leg guy. I'm going to be worried about him. There's guys out to get him. They think he's a snitch, but they don't know the real story. He's straight up."

"I'll see if I can get him down here. But first, I think you'd better have some breakfast before they transport you. It's a long drive down there—five hours or so. Let's go to the mess hall."

They went through the cafeteria line and took a table. Hecher was excited about leaving and kept his head down at his plastic plate as he wolfed down the food. Only when he was almost finished did the guard speak.

"Looks like you might have some well-wishers."

Standing beside Hecher, he beckoned with a wave of his hand to a large group of inmates who had risen from their tables at the far end of the room.

"Huh?" said Hecher.

About thirty inmates paraded down the center aisle toward his table.

"Well, I'll be a son-of-a… How'd these guys know I was leaving?"

"Well," the guard confessed, a mischievous smile playing on his lips, "we sort of let the cat out of the bag—and told them to keep it quiet."

Ten feet in front of the table, the lead inmate jerked to a stop and dropped into the karate stance.

"Okay Hecher, we wanna know just how good you are. We're here to challenge you, all thirty-one of us at one time." Jimmy Rowen broke into a big smile, stepped forward, and grabbed Hecher in a bear hug. "Congratulations, man."

"Yeah, it feels great. But I wish you guys could come with me. I'm going to miss you."

"Mitt, it's lookin' good for me. I got high hopes of gittin outa here at my parole meeting in six weeks."

"Oh geez, that's terrific, Jimmy. Keep in touch with me, will you? Let me know how you're doing. I'm sure I'll be at Avon Park for awhile."

"I sure will, Mitt. I owe you a lot, man."

"Forget it, Jimmy. Take care of yourself."

The black inmate who had told the wise guy joke stepped up, grasped Hecher's hand, and pumped.

"You is the greatest, bro."

"Aw… " Hecher began.

"Stop, I ain't finished. And the wisest."

He and Hecher broke out laughing as the man walked away, waving.

The inmate who volunteered to wield the wooden dowel was next, pumping Hecher's hand.

"Ain't nobody gonna ever crack me wid no pipe. You be da man."

"You guys gotta cut this out, or I'm gonna get emotional," Hecher said.

One by one, the others came forth, shook his hand, and thanked him for teaching them how to better defend themselves. The last one to step up was Lannon.

"Hey, Gary. You gonna be all right? I hate to leave you at the mercy of these predators."

"Yeah, Mitt." He threw an arm around his protector's neck. "You taught me a lot. I think I can hold my own and fight off the wolves. I've just got to keep my wits about me and never let my guard down."

Hecher clasped the full length of Lannon's forearm and looked him in the eyes. "We're going to meet up again on the outside one day, brother man. Keep it going."

"The same, Mitt."

Hecher picked up his duffel bag and the guard led him out of the large dining area and down the long corridor into the prisoner intake area. Twenty-five guards were lined up on one side of the walkway leading to the exit doors.

"What the hell?" Hecher retorted. "They scared I'm gonna make a break for it?"

"I don't think so," said the guard accompanying him.

Hecher looked at him perplexed.

They reached the line of guards, and the first one extended his hand, smiling warmly.

"Good luck, Hecher."

The second did the same, and the third echoed him. It continued that way all the way to the end of the line.

Hecher turned.

"Gentlemen," he proclaimed, "I am touched by this. I will never forget it. I'll go through a gauntlet like this any day."

The guards smiled, chuckled, or laughed.

"Thank you very much."

Two other guards emerged from an office across from the walkway.

"We hate to do this," one said, "but we have no choice."

"Of course," Hecher assented. "I understand. No problem."

He handed his duffel bag to another guard standing by and held his arms out. The two guards placed a handcuff on each wrist, then led him through the doors to a waiting squad car painted royal blue and marked Florida Department of Corrections in gold on both sides and the rear. The guard holding the bag threw it into the front seat. The other two guards and Hecher climbed into the back seat, the prisoner in the middle. The driver piloted the car through the stone gates and onto the road.

Hecher twisted his head to the right and back.

"The Rock," he said. "Longest five years of my life. I don't know how I made it."

The two guards said nothing. The beefy one to his left had a crew cut and a craggy, weathered, stern-looking face, suggesting that he could have been a Marine drill sergeant.

After several seconds, he broke his silence.

"You claim you're innocent, and I'm not making any judgments about whether you're guilty of murder, or not. Half the population behind bars say they didn't do it. But if you're a killer, you're one of the most unusual ones I've seen in my sixteen years at this institution. And I've seen a lot.

"Not that you're the only one who didn't fit the profile. There've been three or four who I just couldn't believe were capable of murder. I observe them every day and get to know what they're like. And two of them got the electric chair. I probably shouldn't say this, but I think some innocent people have been executed."

"I wouldn't doubt it," Hecher concurred. "If that scumbag of a prosecutor had gotten his way, I'd be on death row. I won't bore you with all the details, but that bastard had me framed. There was no physical evidence. He spun a good tale for the jury. The judge gave me the minimum: twenty-five mandatory."

Silence.

"I think you're going to find Avon Park a lot easier to tolerate," said the guard on his right, the one who had apologized for having to handcuff him. "The really violent criminals don't go there. And they have a lot of recreational and educational programs that keep you occupied. It's a lot different from Raiford."

"That's what I heard. Good to hear you confirm it."

Hecher turned his head from left to right, gazing out the windows as the squad car rolled down State Road 121.

"It sure is good to see pastures again, and cattle, and trees, and fen... Nope, I don't like fences anymore."

The intake center at Avon Park was a drab, off-white, one-story building with a circular office jutting out like a tumor warning that all was not well within. Barbed wire atop this shrine to Spartan architecture formed progressive circles along the roof's edge. The rolling wire reminded Hecher of the Palmer method of handwriting he was taught in elementary school. As he stared, the barbs conspired with the imperfect circles to form the word "danger."

He shook his head.

"You okay?" asked the beefy guard.

"Yeah, just seeing things. It's been a long ride. My eyes are getting bleary."

The car slowed as it moved past a parched row of short scrubs next to the asphalt drive. It came to a halt on a broad patch for passenger accommodation, in front of the intake office.

"Oh, boy, what a beaut," Hecher sneered. "Real modern. Sprawling, one-story ranch style. I'll bet the interior is just as fancy."

He glanced at the guards with a sardonic smile. They smiled back.

"I don't think the guys who design these institutions are trying to make them so the people who come here want to stay or return," the hefty guard said with a wry grin.

"You got that right," said Hecher. "Nobody ever comes back to these places singing *Home Sweet Home*."

The other guard opened the door on his side, and the three men slid out. They entered the gate to the intake center, and it automatically closed and locked behind them, a deadbolt slamming into place with a resounding clang.

Two guards greeted them, and the escorting guards removed the handcuffs.

"Okay, Hecher, that's it," said the beefy guard, while the other one smiled. "Best of luck to you. If you're innocent as you say you are, I hope they figure it out."

"Good luck, sir," the other guard offered.

"Thanks, gentlemen."

Both guards shook hands with Hecher, and left.

The walls of the large, spare, windowless room were a faded light green. A sergeant sat behind the booking desk not far from the entrance gate, and a guard led Hecher to the desk for the admittance preliminaries. The guard then escorted him across the room to a partly open enclosure for finger-printing and photographing.

The next, and final, stop was his cell.

The Raiford guard was right. This prison was much different than Raiford. The inmates were less predatory, and Hecher found himself relaxing more. Exercising in the prison yard, he came to performing his routines without continually looking over his shoulder. Unlike the almost anarchic Raiford, this prison was run in a much more orderly fashion, with rules strictly enforced. As time passed, he shed his distrust of every inmate, and even began to enjoy their camaraderie.

For the first two weeks, Hecher was in the close custody cell block, which was automatic because of his murder conviction. Then, based on the high commendation Raiford officials had given him, he was switched to medium custody. He worked the cafeteria line for a month, then moved up to supervisor for supplying the line. A couple of months later, he was placed in charge of supply procurement.

Figuring he'd won the trust of prison officials, Hecher stopped the captain in charge of his cell block while walking to the dining hall, and asked if he could arrange a meeting with Lieutenant Andy Weller, the inmate superintendent.

"That shouldn't be a problem, Hecher. The lieutenant is pretty accommodating."

The next afternoon, the inmate sat in an armless, cushioned chair in front of a cherry wood desk. He faced a ruddy, heavyset, fiftyish man with a full head of blond-white hair.

"What's on your mind, Hecher?"

"Lieutenant, at Raiford I taught karate classes for dozens of guys, and I think it benefited them."

"I heard about it. The warden was pleased. He had to trust you a lot to train criminals in how to be even more violent than they already are." Weller spoke with his head lowered and eyes raised, which Hecher interpreted as skepticism.

"Actually, Lieutenant, I emphasized defensive maneuvers and instructed the men that offensive tactics and holds were to be used only to subdue attackers. And I picked guys for the classes who I had observed were not especially violent types.

"Understood. I'll bet you're about to ask if you can hold classes here."

"Yes sir, that's what I had in mind."

"Well, based on your past record, I'm going to let you give it a try, and we'll see how it goes. Most of the men here are medium and minimum custody, so we shouldn't have any trouble. You've been here long enough to get an idea of who you want to invite into your first class. Go for it."

He rose and reached his hand over the desk to Hecher, who shook it.

"Thanks, Lieutenant. I think you'll be happy."

Hecher had come to know two dozen or so inmates well enough to trust them for learning karate. In his two-man cell, he sat at his desk and jotted down the names, then chose half from that list whom he had the most confidence in. He decided to approach these twelve about joining his first class. If any declined his invitation, he would choose from the other list.

Over the next two days, in the cavernous dining hall and outside in the prison yard, Hecher conducted his recruitment efforts. Nine inmates signed up for the class, most of them without hesitation. He carefully considered the second list and selected three for invitations. The following day, he approached them in the yard. All they needed in the way of a sales pitch was a single short sentence, the one he'd used at Raiford and offered to the lieutenant: "I trained world champion kick boxer Sonny Stratton."

"Sonny Stratton? You?" was the usual, astonished reaction. They'd all watched the fighter's exploits on television. What followed was something like, "Yeah, sign me up."

Inmates jogging and working out in the yard gathered to observe the karate sessions, and increasing numbers besieged the instructor with requests to join the class. He told them he wanted to limit it so he could provide individualized assistance, but would see about forming a second class.

"Lieutenant Weller, a lot of the men want to join my karate class, but I have to limit it to twelve for it to have maximum effectiveness. I wonder if I could get your permission to open another class."

Weller leaned back in his executive swivel chair. He removed the cigar from his mouth and, head tilted in an attitude of appraisal, stared at the wet, dark end that he'd chomped.

"Hecher, I've been watching you. You're doing a heck of a job. Sorry for the pun. I'll bet you get tired of that." He smiled.

The inmate chuckled and said, "Yeah, you're right, I hear it all the time. But naw, I'm glad people get a kick out of it."

He paused. "That's a gentler kick than I've given some people."

Weller let out a hearty laugh. "Okay, you one-upped me. I know what you mean. I've seen you throw some kicks in that class."

He placed his cigar in the ashtray on his desk, propped his elbows on the arms of his chair, and rested his head against his fists while looking down, pondering.

"Hecher, how are you faring here at Avon Park?"

"Well, I feel less uptight. The security force has a lot better control than at Raiford. That place is pretty undisciplined."

"Maybe I shouldn't say this, but you've become pretty popular around here in a short time. You seem to be making a good impression not just with the inmates, but with the guards and the administration. It made me curious, and I've been checking your records not just at Raiford, but going back to your years in West Palm Beach when you were in a lot of trouble. You were popular then, too—but only with the bad guys. You had a lot of charisma. You were a leader.

"Hecher, take a look at yourself. Seems to me you're undergoing a metamorphosis. You're still leading, but you're pointing it in the right direction now. I know you're trying to convince the courts you're innocent and you should get a new trial, or the governor should throw out your conviction. Keep this kind of prison record going and it sure as hell isn't going to hurt your chances."

"It's good to hear that, Lieutenant."

"Listen," said Weller, "this karate thing seems to be going well. It's helping to keep the men occupied. I see them practicing the positions and moves and holds on each other between the sessions. Have you had any problems with tempers flaring—any of them getting into fights? I haven't seen any."

"No, I've warned them about that. I told them it wouldn't be tolerated and they'd have to leave the class if they couldn't keep themselves in line."

"Good. Well, then I can't see anything wrong with another class. In fact, I think it would be a good thing. We don't have a lot of hard-core cases in this institution, and they're all in another ward, as you know. So I don't think there'll be any problem expanding this thing with the prisoners available for you to choose from. Let's give it a whirl. Uh-oh, another bad pun."

A big smile showed teeth stained a faint brown by cigars. He reached a hand out to Hecher, who reciprocated, grinning.

The classes made the passage of time less onerous for Hecher, and the relief from continual vigilance against predators gave him extra freedom to pursue efforts at winning his release. Avon Park had a library with ample resources, of which he intended to take full advantage.

The guard cracked open the door of the cell where Gary Lannon had just finished strapping on his prosthetic leg. He occupied a single cell that the authorities had granted him, fearing attacks from cellmates.

"Ready for some eggs and grits, Lannon?" the guard called.

"Yep, Sarg. I'll be movin on down there in a minute. Gotta finish dressing and brush my teeth."

"See ya later."

Lannon pulled his pants over his peg leg, then the other leg, and hitched the belt. He slipped into his shirt and shoes, rose from the bed, and turned for the sink to brush his teeth. He heard the heavy clanking sound of steel and swung around. Three inmates were at the door, which now was slid all the way open. He pivoted on his good leg and hustled toward the wall several strides back of the foot of his bed.

The first inmate reached him just as he bent down, and he felt a sharp sting on the back of his neck as he grabbed the two-foot metal pipe he kept for protection. Hecher had gotten it from a guard, telling him he needed it for his karate classes. Hecher helped Lannon smuggle it into his cell in the pant leg of his prosthesis.

The shiv glanced off his neck as he bent for the pipe, and left a three-inch-long gash. Lannon back-swung his left arm and smashed the guy's nose, producing a fountain of blood, then rammed the pipe into his gut, doubling him over and sending him to the floor.

That seemed to instill caution in the other two, who halted their charge and assumed crouched, guarded positions. They began lunging and retreating as Lannon alternately swung the pipe to move them away and grasped it with both hands apart to ward off blows. One, who was smaller and wiry, had a knife and slashed Lannon along his right rib cage as he left that side exposed while swinging around with the pipe to parry a haymaker from the other inmate.

Uh-oh, should have blocked that with my left arm and kept my right side protected.

The pipe caught the bigger man on the top of his forearm, cracking the bone. He turned away, bawling like a calf under a branding iron. Now it was just Lannon and the knife fighter.

"Okay, mother fucker. One of us is gonna end up dead. Cuz if you don't get me first, I'm gonna make your head look like an egg that got dropped on a concrete floor."

The inmate faced off with Lannon, legs apart, holding the knife at waist level. Glancing to his right, the armed man saw his companions hobbling for the cell door, bent over, making guttural sounds. Without turning, he stepped backward, shouting, "We'll be back, fucking rat."

The three moved down the hall and out of sight.

Blood soaked Lannon's shirt in the front and back, and a tear opened to the long, deep gash. He made his way to the first floor and was met by a guard, who assisted him to the infirmary and summoned the lieutenant in charge of the ward.

Hecher ambled along the gangway toward the cafeteria. His sweet tooth was active this morning and he was hoping pancakes would be the main course. He was in no rush—as always, no place he had to be after breakfast. His peripheral vision caught someone with a bobbing gait gaining on him off to his right. The conditioned reflex engraved on him at Raiford had not entirely sloughed, and he jerked his head around. He stopped.

"Gary, you son-of-a-bitch." Hecher broke into a big smile and grasped his hand. "How the hell did you get here?"

Lannon beamed. "I almost didn't. If it wasn't for you, I wouldn't be here, number one. And number two, I'd be six feet under. Three guys bum-rushed me in my cell. They cut me pretty good in a couple places, but I was able to use what you taught me to chase 'em away. The warden figured he'd have another murder on his hands if I stayed, so the honchos got together and decided to transfer me here. It's almost like the damned Army, where you get wounded in battle and they send you home. I'm not complaining."

"Hell, you'll have to join one of my classes. I've got two going so far."

"Yeah, I'd love it. I'm going to be an expert one of these days."

"What ward they got you on?"

"Medium custody."

"Well, then, Gary, you shouldn't have to worry too much about using your karate here. They knew close custody with the hard-core guys would be too dangerous for you—a lot like Raiford, even though the security here is much tighter. But still, with that bum leg you're vulnerable anywhere. So yeah, you might as well jump in my second class. Come on, let's get some chow and I'll give you the details."

They passed through the cafeteria line and took a bench at a table, sitting opposite each other.

"Man, I got a weakness for pancakes," Hecher allowed. "Every time I have them I jog a couple extra miles that day. Easy to get a gut in the slammer."

He cut through the stack of three flapjacks and stuffed a sizable forkful in his mouth while Lannon lit into the scrambled eggs.

Hecher gulped a swig of coffee.

"How was Jimmy Rowen doing before you left? I thought he'd be out by now, but I haven't gotten any letters from him. He promised to write, and I'm sure he would."

Lannon held his forkful of eggs a few inches above his plate and stared at his fellow inmate.

Hecher sliced another hunk of pancakes, raised it to his lips, and stopped.

"What?" said Hecher. "Oh shit, what happened?"

"Maybe you better finish eating first, Mitt."

"Oh dammit to hell, Gary. I already lost my appetite. You might as well tell me now."

"Jimmy is dead."

"Oh fuck almighty." Hecher dropped his fork and flipped his tray aside. He threw his elbows on the table and dropped his head into his hands. For fifteen seconds, he said nothing. Finally, in a quavery voice not much louder than a whisper, "Those animals get him?"

"You got it. There was a big fight in the yard. Jimmy didn't have anything to do with it but was working out right next to the five guys in the brawl. These two guys who'd thrown the gasoline at him way back when happened to come by at the same time. They used the brawl as cover and grabbed him. One had a blade and stuck it in Jimmy's ribs, and they took off. The guards finally came and broke up the fight, and had Jimmy carried off to the infirmary. They thought at first he was involved in the fight, but other guys in the yard told them what happened. Jimmy died in surgery. The knife cut an artery. I was sent here three weeks afterward, and I don't know what they did to the two guys who did Jimmy in."

"He was a good kid," Hecher said quietly. "I talked to him. He was a lot like me when he was a kid—full of adrenalin, fighting a lot with his parents and pissing off his teachers. When his parents divorced while he was in high school, he pretty much didn't give a shit about anything anymore and started doing drugs and stealing hubcaps, vandalizing public property—anything connected with authority. He got thrown in jail a few times, and finally they tied him to a string of car thefts and sent him to Raiford."

Hecher gazed up and into the spacious cafeteria, seeing nothing, his mind's eye in a more distant place.

"I knew how he felt. I had so damn much energy I drove my dad and mom nuts. I was into everything. But I was little, and I had a slight speech impediment, and the kids picked on me. I came home from first grade one day and cried about being teased and punched, but my dad was a tough little Italian, and that didn't last long. He yelled at me to be a man and stand up to those bullies. So I did—and got the crap beat out of me. At least I got a couple of licks in, and it was only the biggest and meanest guys I had to worry about after that.

"One day I saw an ad in a Super Man comic book for a jujitsu book. I bought it with money from my paper route and practiced on my older brother. We were getting pretty good, and then one day I took a different street from the newspaper office to my paper route and passed a karate studio. I saw these guys, and some kids too, dressed in these pajamas, doing these really fast moves and kicks. And I said, I want to do that. So I got my parents to help me pay for lessons."

He took a swig of coffee.

"Then my dad got killed in a car accident, and I started acting up bad in school. I was angry and all torn up, and I'd race through my paper route so I could get to the karate school and fight like hell. I got good at it fast, and went after the big mean bastards at school who'd bullied me. I knocked the shit out of them. Everybody respected me now. They feared me. And I went wild.

"By high school, I was the meanest, toughest kid walking the halls. The teachers were constantly expelling me. My mother couldn't control me. I got into one brush with the law after another. Good as I was with my hands and my feet, they were no match for somebody with a gun, so I learned about firearms from my buddies on the street. I smoked pot and I boozed, but I never did tobacco. Karate taught me to take care of my body."

Hecher threw his arms up and out. "It all finally caught up with me, as it did Jimmy. I still have a chance. For Jimmy, it's over."

Hecher pulled himself up from his chair, then Lannon rose, and they carried their trays to the big metal rack on wheels against the half wall separating the cafeteria line from the dining room. They trudged down the gangway en route to the ward, Hecher buried in thought, where the cell block formed a right angle and each man's cell was in a different direction.

"See ya later, Mitt. Sorry to be the bearer of bad news."

"Yeah... well, I might have figured something had happened. I guess I just didn't want to face the possibility. It's tough. Thing is, he almost made it. He would've done just fine on the outside. They spend a lot of money to keep guys like Jimmy and you and me locked up, guys who have gone through a rough phase and had to learn to straighten out. And they release criminals who you know can't fit in with society and are going to be back. I guess we just have to keep convincing them we're ready. It's easy for me. I'm just doing what comes natural."

Hecher returned to his cell and showered. Then he meditated. Into his mind crept Diane. He felt the pain that racked her body.

How is she going to tolerate it as her condition worsens? Will the doctors keep giving her more pain medication? What a terrible way to die. Talk about injustice... what happened to me pales in comparison. And I at least brought on my problems through my history of bad behavior. Diane did nothing to deserve this awful fate. She is goodness personified.

She must be finding it difficult to do the simple day-to-day chores. Surely Cindy and other friends are helping her. And Pauley is older now and able to help out around the house. This must really worry Pauley. He sees his mother getting worse all the time. His dad is not around to care for him, and now he's afraid he's going to lose his mother. Wow, did I ever screw up?

Chapter Seven

Hecher spent much of his afternoon time in a class in accounting and one in computer programming, an emerging vocation that technology experts touted as having a bright future. He also enrolled in a typing class and spent an hour each afternoon plus a half-hour in the evening practicing. He made quick progress.

Shortly before lunch daily, he hustled to the mailbox, hoping to find news about efforts to get him freed. Letters from Diane always made his heart race. On this day, he decided to hold off opening it until after lunch, worried it might contain upsetting reports about his wife and son that would cause indigestion. Nonetheless, he couldn't stifle the butterflies, and ate faster than he knew he should, then hurried to his cell.

Hi Darling,

From your last letter, it sounded like things were going a lot better for you at Avon Park. I am so glad. That makes it easier for me to cope with my situation, which I'm sorry to say isn't getting any better. But you knew it wouldn't. I can handle my problem, but it's not easy to watch Pauley try to deal with the kids at school who are picking on him, making fun of him and calling him names because his dad is in prison. I'm wondering if I ought to enroll him in a karate class so he can defend himself against these bullies. He's quick and athletic like you, but they're bigger than he is and he needs some skills, I think.

How do you feel about that? He doesn't understand why you have to be in prison if you haven't done anything. I explain to him that a terrible mistake was made and we're trying to get it corrected, but there are a couple of people who caused the mistake to happen and they are working hard to stop us. I tell him to just wait, you will be out one day, and then we'll all be together again.

Honey, the case took a step backward a month ago. I had written a letter to tell you, but just when I was going to mail it I got some better news. Here's what happened. Jim, the investigator, thought he had a good lead when a guy told him he overheard a conversation in a bar and thought he heard this younger fella say he knew who killed "the rich Palm Beach dude". That's the way he put it. Jim spent a lot of time hanging out at this bar with this guy waiting for the young guy to show up, and he finally did. Jim tailed him for a long time and finally questioned him, but was convinced the guy misunderstood the conversation. Nothing was happening with the investigation, and the wealthy backer lost interest in financing it, so the attorney dropped out too. He wasn't finding out anything anyway.

But Jim wanted to keep working on the case, even though he wasn't being paid, so he went to two other criminal attorneys with big reputations, Jeremy Mancbaum and Rick Larbin. They went through the entire file and Mancbaum told a newspaper reporter that what happened to you was "outrageous". You can read about it in the article I enclosed. You can see where that guy who wants to keep you locked up, the state attorney, Donald Bosworth, tried to keep from talking to the reporter but she kept after him and he finally told her the case was closed and he didn't have anything to say. His job is to see that justice is done, and he's doing the opposite. These two attorneys called it a "travesty of justice" and are so mad they're going to make court appeals for you without charging any fees. So we have reason to hope again, Mitt.

I've had to go on part-time on my job, so I only work twelve hours a week now. I'm on partial disability. The company actually likes that because they hired another part-timer and get by without paying a lot of the benefits full-time employees get.

Well, Pauley just came home from school, so I will close. He says, "Hi Dad. I love you." Did you hear him? Do you hear me? I love you, Mitt—forever.
Diane

Hecher's cellmate, a quiet, uncommunicative young man doing three years for burglary, spent as little time in his cell as required, and was away now. Hecher allowed two tears to spill out of his right eye and one from his left, and didn't bother to wipe them from his cheeks. He stared at the floor, vacillating over whether Pauley should take karate lessons. He didn't want him to end up a street fighter like his dad. On the other hand, his son needed the self-confidence to stand up against bullies.

Diane hadn't talked much about her condition. Probably didn't want to upset him, he figured. Gosh, he hoped the pain wasn't too awful. Those two attorneys. He'd heard of Mancbaum, but Larbin, he was damned good. But he couldn't just sit and wait, and hope their efforts paid off. God helps those who help themselves. He'd have to knuckle down and be resourceful. This place had what he needed to communicate with the people who had the power to make things happen. And he had the time. He wasn't going anywhere. That was the problem he needed to solve.

His business classes over for the afternoon, Hecher headed for the library. He asked the armed library custodian for a pencil and several sheets of paper. Seated at a table, he began scribbling a point-by-point outline of his case: 1) the murder, 2) his targeting as the prime suspect while he sat in jail on three relatively minor charges, 3) his indictment, 4) the lack of material evidence presented at the trial, 5) the accusations by four jail inmates that he confessed to the crime, 6) the reduction of their sentences afterward, 7) his conviction of first degree murder, 8) the subsequent confession of two of the inmates to a newspaper reporter that they had lied about his confessing, 9) the confirmation of those confessions and addition of a third on a national television show less than two years later.

Over the next two days, he penciled revisions, then committed the final document to five type-written pages. Who to send the packet to? He established categories: state officials, U.S. officials, civil rights organizations, human rights agencies, antideath-penalty groups, political organizations, television advocacy programs. Next, he combed through the library's resource directories for names of persons and entities, and their contact information.

He began with the members of the Florida Legislature from the district where he lived in Palm Beach County, the U.S. representative from his district, and other politicians on a state and national level, from both parties. He targeted them after reading about their records and concluding they were more responsive than most politicians to abuses of power in government and in the courts. And he figured organizations such as the American Civil Liberties Union would take up his cause.

Hecher spent weeks researching the list of those he wanted to contact, and jotted down their names and addresses. He used the printer in the library to make five hundred copies of his five-page document—2,500 pages total. When he was finished, he had a pile ten inches high. On each five-page packet, he had left a space at the top and a smaller space at the bottom. At the top, he typed the name of the prison and date in the middle and the name and address of the recipient on the left, followed by the salutation. On the bottom, between the copied, typed words "Yours truly" and "Mitt Hecher," he signed his name. The entire process took five months. He ran up a bill for the substantial costs of printing and mailing them, and pledged to pay it.

Hecher mailed the packets out as he finished them, figuring he didn't want to cause confusion and resentment in the prosecutorial offices from inquiries pouring in all at once. But as the weeks wore on, he came to realize that he needn't have worried. Almost all of the responses were to him, not the prosecutors. They usually were form letters expressing regrets that they were unable to help him.

However, he found encouragement in eight or ten. Four state legislators, two U.S. senators, and an ACLU official informed him they were calling on Florida Governor Rob Garner to intervene. A state senator wrote in her letter to Garner, *I receive many letters from prisoners claiming they are innocent, but this one is different. A series of horrendous errors seems to have resulted in the murder conviction of a man who was in no way involved in the event. I implore you to review this case.*

Diane sent her husband a newspaper article in which the local ACLU director said, *We have appealed to State Attorney Donald Bosworth to correct this injustice, but it just seems as though he needed to convict someone of this high-profile murder and Mister Hecher was convenient.*

In the same article, a spokesman for Governor Garner's office said the governor was checking into the case. Hecher read at his desk, his eyes growing wide. He tried to suppress his hopefulness. The next lines made it easy: *The governor is of a mind that if a court, whether it be a judge or a jury, has found a defendant guilty, and that verdict has been upheld on appeal, then the person is guilty.*

"So why are we wasting our time?" Hecher muttered. He kept reading.

However, he is open-minded enough to realize there could be rare cases in which everything goes awry. He is looking at this one to assess whether it falls in that category and he should take some action.

"Yeah, yeah," the inmate said wearily to an empty cell, tossing the clipping on the floor. "Better chance snow falls on Fort Lauderdale Beach this Fourth of July."

Mancbaum and Larbin maintained contact with Diane to apprise her of their progress. She told Mitt in a phone call that they indicated their work was proceeding at a snail's pace because the state attorney was stonewalling their attempts to have the voluminous file copied. They considered filing a writ of federal habeas corpus to test the constitutionality of his conviction by the state.

"Hi Mitt." Maria Hecher glowed and opened her arms wide to embrace her son.

"Mom, you don't get any older," a radiant Hecher bubbled, hugging her. "And what about this feller?" He reached down and lifted Pauley from his armpits. "I think this is the last time I'll be able to do this. You are just getting too big." He smooched his son and set him down.

"Dan, it's great to see you, man. Wow, I'm glad you made the trip."

"You're looking good, Mitt. It must be the discipline from that karate."

"Yes, you sure keep yourself in shape," said Maria. "It's going on eight years now, nine counting the county jail. And you don't let it defeat you."

"Come on," said Mitt. "Let's go into the visitors reception lounge. This place is a lot nicer than Raiford, don't you think?"

"You can say that again," Maria agreed. "It's not nearly as depressing. I'm glad."

They sat on two short imitation-leather couches facing each other, with a plain wood coffee table in between. Pauley sat next to his dad, who draped his arm around the boy's shoulders.

"I work out hard. First thing in the morning, I jog around the track. Then I knock myself out on the parallel bars and do chin-ups on the horizontal bar. In the evening, I often do calisthenics. That's before I settle down with a good book. I was too full of pi..."—he looked down at his son—"full of pickle juice and vinegar to go to college in my younger days, but now I'm enjoying fine literature."

"Why did you drink that stuff, dad?"

Hecher laughed, and Dan smiled.

"That's just an expression, Pauley. It means I was too rambunctious, too unsettled. But I want you to study hard and get a good education so you can have a lot better life than I've had. Okay son?"

"Yeah, dad." He twisted his torso toward Hecher, jerked his head up at him, and said with mild defiance, "I'm doing good in school. I get good grades. Just ask Mom."

"Oh, I know. Your mother brags about you every time I talk to her. You just keep it up."

Pauley's dad noticed that his son looked reassured, and the boy scooted off the couch.

"I'm going to go and look at the magazines." He bounded off to a rack in the far corner.

"So how was the flight to Tampa?" Hecher asked.

"Pretty smooth. It took only three hours after we landed to get the rental car and drive to West Palm Beach. A lot shorter than Raiford. Nice scenes of cattle in wide pastures as the sun was dropping in the other direction. Pleasant. But it wasn't pleasant to watch Diane move around. It's a lot of effort for her. She doesn't complain, but you can see she's in pain. She said she has her good and bad phases, and right now it's kind of in limbo."

"I told you in my letter we decided she shouldn't try to come and see me anymore," said Mitt. "It was best for both of us."

"Yes, we talked about that. She thinks that was a good decision."

"No sense in her going through any more pain than she has to, and seeing her suffer like that just made it so much harder for me to cope with. I got so depressed, it took me three days to get back on track."

"Well, here's something that should make you feel a little better. Pauley is following in his dad's footsteps and getting good at karate. My, has that child grown. I couldn't believe how much bigger he'd gotten since the last time I saw him."

Mitt frowned.

"What's the matter? I thought you'd be delighted he's taking karate."

"Diane and I discussed whether it was a good idea, and I reluctantly agreed to it because he's having trouble with the kids at school picking on him. You know—his dad being in prison. It makes me furious, but it's partly my fault he's in this predicament. I feel so bad for him. So if he can show these kids he's not going to take any crap from them, that's good. What worries me is that he might end up like me—with a swagger that gets him into trouble because he doesn't have a dad around to control him and keep him on the right path. And as Diane's condition gets worse, it's just going to make life tougher for Pauley."

"But Mitt, your dad was gone."

"Yeah, and Dan was in the same situation, but he turned out all right, so I'm not sure what that proves."

"But you were a hell-raiser. Dan was quieter. He just let things roll off his back."

"Yeah. I should have been more like my brother and I wouldn't be here."

Dan smiled.

"Everybody's personality is different, Mitt," said Maria. "The point I'm making is, you can guide Pauley on the phone and in letters. He knows you care a lot about him, and that makes all the difference in the world. I think he'll be all right. You just need to keep after people to get you out of here. Diane told me all about what that investigator and these two new attorneys are doing. But that State Attorney Bosworth is making it as hard for them as he can."

"Yeah, and you know what I've been up to with my contacts to everybody I could think of who might have the power to make the wheels turn—and care enough to. But the woman with the ACLU—you know, the Civil Liberties Union—flat out told the press that that bastard Bosworth didn't care if I was innocent or not."

"Mitt, I can't tell you how angry I am at that man. I have fantasies about blowing him up. When I do that, I go out and walk real fast around the block till I've burned off my energy. Him and that snake who did the dirty work in the trial—Scraponia. Those guys are worse than the criminals behind bars, because they lie and cheat and sacrifice innocent people for their own personal gain. They hide behind the law they're pretending to uphold. At least most of the ones who commit crimes that get them in prison don't go around posing as upstanding, moral, church-going members of their community. Those types hardly ever get caught."

"Don't do anything rash, Mom. We don't need two Hechers in the hoosegow." Maria's son looked at her with an admonishing smile.

She chuckled.

"Governor Garner is looking at the case," he said. "I've got about this much hope." He lifted his right hand and held the thumb and forefinger a quarter-inch apart. "His aide said the gov believes if both a jury and an appeals court find a guy guilty, he's guilty, except in rare cases. I think he's just going through the motions, bowing to pressure, making people think he's serious. He had his mind made up before he even looked at this case."

"Well, you're doing all the right things," Maria reassured. "As you keep drawing attention to this miscarriage of justice, your chances of somebody finally making something happen increase. There's a lot of publicity about your case. The press doesn't forget it."

"Yeah. They have to keep their neutrality, but I think those reporters are savvy enough to know what's going on."

Mitt faced Dan. "How's the computer business shaping up?"

"More people are getting interested all the time. It's catching on. I think computers are going to be big."

"I've started teaching a computer class in the afternoons," said Mitt. "Lieutenant Weller—that's the inmate superintendent—he asked if I could help out. The prison staff instructor told him I was his best student and too many guys were enrolling to fit in his class. He needed to start another beginning class."

"Hurry up and get out of here," Dan urged. "I need you in my business."

"You always were smart in school," said Maria. "Just think what you could have done with your brains if you hadn't gotten off on the wrong track."

"But you know what?" Mitt pondered. "Maybe I had to land here. I think I've done some good things in prison. I've used my time well. But yeah, I'll be making up for that. But first I have to get out of here."

"You're a fighter"—Maria Hecher shook her fist in a feminine way—"and you just have to keep slugging."

"You know that I will, Mom."

"This isn't going away," she said. "It may take awhile yet, but one day it's going to happen. I know it."

———————————

"And now we come to electing the president," an inmate announced. "Do we have any nominations?"

Thirteen men sat in office chairs at a conference table in a paneled room adjacent to the library, six on one side, five on the other, and one on each end. Styrofoam cups of coffee and plastic glasses of water left spill stains here and there on the glass top. But for their prison garb, the men might have passed for prison officials holding a staff meeting.

A hand shot up. "I nominate Mitt Hecher."

"Is there a second to that nomination?"

"I second the motion to nominate Mitt Hecher for president," came a voice from near the opposite end. It was Gary Lannon.

"Are there any other nominations?"

The inmates turned their heads toward one another. Hecher, seated in the middle on the odd-numbered side, kept his head down.

"Since there are no other nominations, Mitt Hecher is the new president of the Avon Park Correctional Institution Prisoner Jaycees. Congratulations, Mitt."

All stood and reached across to shake Hecher's hand.

"Speech, speech," someone shouted.

"Yeah, speech," another joined.

"Come on, Mitt," said a third.

"Well, gentlemen, I am truly honored. I pledge that I will do my best to work with both the inmates and the prison management to make our time here as bearable as possible. None of us wants to be here, but the best way to handle it is to play the hand we were dealt rather than wring our hands and wish things were different."

He hesitated, hand on chin. "I've kept this quiet because people are pretty cynical about prisoners who get religion. But I do a lot of reading in the library, and I've been checking out the Bible. I already knew a little about it because I had to go to mass as a kid."

A hand shot up half-way down the table on Hecher's left.

"Scuse me for interruptin," the guy sneered. He was an average-sized white in his forties who wore a perpetual scowl. Are we about to hear a sermon? Cuz if we are, I'm outa here. I've had it up to my eyeballs with religion. It's what holy-ass judges and prosecutors practice as they go about merrily punishing poor bastards who never had a chance in life, never doin a damn thing to see they don't turn out that way. These bastards parade to church Sunday morning and fill the pews with their stinkin hypocrisy. I don't wanna hear nothin from the fuckin Bible."

"Hey, jerko," said a white on the other side of the table. "Who asked you? You ain't the president. Shut up and let him talk."

"Who you tellin to shut up?" the guy challenged, rising.

"Whoa," Hecher admonished. "Hold it right there." He looked at the antireligion inmate. "You've had your say. If you want to leave, fine. Otherwise, sit down and let me finish."

The guy shifted from one foot to another, glared at the inmate who told him to shut up, and sat down, looking at his lap.

"He makes a good point," Hecher said. "But just because some people use the Bible for bad purposes doesn't make the Bible bad. A lot of rich people would never give to charities if it didn't lower their income taxes, but that doesn't make the charities bad. They're just used for the wrong reason sometimes.

"Anyway, I was starting to say, I've been reading about this guy Paul. That dude was a mean son-of-a-bitch until something changed him—something just knocked his socks off, or I guess it was his sandals, while he was hiking one day. It just hit him all of a sudden that, man, this ain't workin. After that, he wasn't pissed off about people and things anymore. He just accepted whatever came his way. He said, 'In whatever state I am, I am content.' Course, I admit, he wasn't in Florida."

A few of the men laughed.

"They threw him in prison, put his feet in stocks—at least they don't do that here—and even there, he didn't bitch. Now this guy was something superspecial, no doubt about it. But what I'm sayin is, we're all a lot happier, or at least less unhappy, if we can accept what we can't change and try to make some good come out of it. We can actually improve our lives in here, so that when we get out, we'll be better off than before we got here."

He paused. "All right, shut me the fuck up. I got carried away." A diffident smile.

Applause erupted, along with shouts of "We hear you, Hecher," "You be da man," and "Yeah, Mitt."

"Buncha horse shit," the religion cynic said over his shoulder as he left.

———————

Among the inmates Hecher had come to know at Raiford was a rapist sentenced to a life term. He wanted to enroll in a karate class as recreation and to have the means to defend himself from other inmates. The administration accepted Hecher's argument that there would be no harm in his learning karate because he would never be outside of prison where he could use it. In conversations during mealtimes and out in the yard, the inmate disclosed to Hecher his methods for preying on women.

Hecher knew he was facile with the English language and had put that ability to good use in drafting his appeal for release from prison. He had admonished the Jaycees to use their time in productive ways. He needed to practice what he preached.

An idea struck him one evening when, while he was reading a book, the Raiford rapist invaded his consciousness. The book and the sexually violent inmate connected. Hecher needed to use his talent for communicating via the written word to author a book on how women could protect themselves from rape attacks. It could accomplish two goals: help women, and produce income to pay his bill for the printing cost of the packets calling for his conviction to be overturned.

He began work in earnest, setting aside one hour in late afternoon weekdays and one-and-a-half hours in the evenings. Devoting the first several sessions to drafting an outline, he then began to fill in the pages.

Over the next few weeks, he became more absorbed with crafting the book. He relied on his memories of the extensive conversations he had with the rape convict on how he would stalk women, lure them, and catch them in locations where they were especially vulnerable. Narrating these stories, he explained how to avoid such situations. But if a woman were attacked, she could ward off the assailant with certain moves, using her hands, feet, and sometimes her mouth. Personal items such as hairpins could be used as weapons.

Hecher found an inmate who was an accomplished artist to illustrate the physical ways of deterring would-be rapists.

In his preoccupation with the book, Hecher forgot about the operations for his potential release occurring behind the prison gates. He was almost startled at mail call one day when a letter arrived with a preprinted return address: Executive Office of the Governor, 400 S. Monroe Street, The Capitol, Tallahassee, FL 32399-0001. A frisson flitted through him, and just as suddenly reason gained control. Without rushing, he lifted a corner of the envelope flap with a fingernail and slid his finger under it. Removing the single page, he read:

To All Concerned:

I have completed a review of the lengthy file in the case of Mitt Hecher vs. the State of Florida, by which Mr. Hecher was convicted of first degree murder in the fatal shooting of Rodger Kriger of Palm Beach on January 14, 1976.

It is a complex case, and there are aspects of it that I found troubling. The contention by the defense that little or no material evidence implicating Mr. Hecher was presented at trial appears warranted. Similarly, the reliance on the testimony of four incarcerated felons and a fugitive seems a flimsy basis for the conviction of first degree murder. That decision by the jury was further undermined by the later retraction by four of the five of their testimony that Mr. Hecher had confessed, while in jail, to shooting Mr. Kriger.

However, prison convicts may have various motives for reversing their testimony following a trial, and it cannot be relied upon to automatically alter a verdict. Appeals courts have reviewed the arguments calling for a new trial, and have found them wanting.

I do not feel that it is in the best interest of justice for me to circumvent the courts, simply because I have the power to do so and have an emotional, or even rational, response to a particular case. Unless I have found something egregious in the disposition of the case, which I haven't, I must have faith in the integrity and competence of our judges, who have been schooled in administering the law and whose command of jurisprudence has been forged in many years of experience.

If solid evidence casting serious doubt on Mr. Hecher's guilt should be forthcoming in the future, he will want to petition the courts for a hearing. In the absence of any such evidence, however, I must decline to take any action in this case.

Very truly yours,

Rob Garner, Governor of the State of Florida

Hecher folded the letter and inserted it into the envelope.

"He hasn't found anything egregious?" he muttered.

Gary Lannon limped up and stopped at his mailbox nearby.

"Uh-oh Mitt, you're talking to yourself. Bad sign. But not too bad. I haven't heard you answering."

"Yeah, well, if I didn't think it might put me in jeopardy I'd give Governor Garner an answer to his letter. He just let me know he's not going to interfere in my case. He didn't think anything egregious was done. Just what the hell does he call egregious? Maybe the prosecutor bribing a couple of jurors? It's the same ol same ol. At least I got a lot of important people realizing that state attorney's office is rotten and I got screwed. That can't do any harm."

"And the governor didn't make himself look good, either," said Lannon. "You had a lot of important people rooting for you. You've gotten a lot of notoriety. Garner was in a tough spot. He caved, and people who make a difference aren't going to forget."

"I think you may be right. Hey, let's get over to the cafeteria."

The two ambled down the long walkways and around corners to the dining hall. They passed through the cafeteria line, where servers placed a lunch of an open-faced tuna sandwich, two hard-boiled eggs, and a bowl of chicken soup on their trays.

At their table, Hecher said, "I've been thinking about what we could do to improve the recreation here. I came up with this crazy idea. Did you ever play tennis?"

"Tennis? Geez. No... yeah, when I was a kid in Biddleton, Georgia. Me and my sister batted the ball around with our cheap rackets. There was a beat-up court in the town's public park. That was before my dad lost his job at the textile mill and took to drinking and started knocking Mom around. He finally took off. Mom was a supervisor at a supermarket in Athens and making enough to support herself and my sister, so I quit school and took off, too. That's when I started getting into trouble—stealing in order to survive, then stealing to pay for drugs and booze. But that's history. Tennis. You want to get tennis going here?"

"Why not? I think the men would enjoy it. And it would help them assimilate into middle-class society once they leave this place."

"But man, tennis courts have got to be expensive. Who would pay for them?"

"We would."

"Who's we?"

"The entire prison population. We'd get—we is the Jaycees—the Jaycees'd campaign to get everybody onboard in supporting the project. I'd map out an organizational plan and assign each member to cover a particular section of the prison. The artist doing the sketches for my rape book could draw up a rendering of the tennis courts that would make the guys' eyes pop out. I figure we'll want three of them. I think if we can get the men to each donate a small amount, once these things are built they're going to be very popular.

We'll probably have to hold a referendum first to see if there's enough support. If there is, we go ahead with it."

"Some guys are going to balk at paying," Lannon surmised. "They're going to say they'd never use the courts. And we can't force them to pay."

"I think we can convince almost all of them they're going to feel pretty lonely watching the others enjoying the hell out of themselves and talking about it in the cafeteria. And there'll be tournaments that the whole prison will come out to watch. These guys will feel left out. And they'll be told every inmate who pays will be issued a tennis card that he has to show to use the courts."

Lannon smiled and said nothing for a few moments. He took a deep breath.

"Sounds ambitious, but maybe it'll work. I'm sure it'd be the only prison in the whole damn country with tennis courts. I can hear the law-and-order crowd hollering now: 'We're running a goddamn country club for them criminals at Avon Park.'"

"Let the bastards yell," said Hecher. "All they know is punishment. They think rehabilitation is for wusses. And then they piss and moan about the recidivism rate. What the hell do they expect? These places are basically no more than training grounds for criminals to perfect their trades. Maybe not Avon Park. It's a cut above."

He looked around the vast dining hall, which had mostly cleared of inmates. Prisoners assigned to work detail were wiping tables and sweeping the floor.

"Anyway, I'll have to get approval from the administration, of course. If the Board of Jaycees is up for the idea, I'll see the superintendent."

———————

"So that's my idea."

Hecher sat at the head of the table in the conference room.

"I think it would go over great. The guys would love it. The biggest problem would be too many guys wanting to use the courts. They'd have to reserve court time. It would give them something to look forward to as a break from the everyday routine. We already have baseball, but you need too many guys to make a team. It's harder to organize. You have to plan quite a bit in advance before you can hold a game. Basketball... that's fine. I know you black dudes, that's your sport. Ever since you started taking over the game, you're making us honkies look silly. Especially me. I can't even see up to the rim without glasses."

The four black board members howled with laughter, and the eight whites joined in.

"Hecher, you too much, man," beamed a tall, lean black near the opposite end of the table from which the Jaycees president conducted the meeting.

Hecher's self-deprecating smile evaporated. "But you need a bunch of guys for a basketball game, too. And it can get pretty rough. There've been problems with guys building up grudges against each other. Next thing they act them out inside the walls. But tennis, there's no contact, it requires only two people, but you can have four if you play doubles. What do you think?"

He allowed time for the men to reflect, his eyes moving from face to face to study their reactions.

"Here's what I don't like," said a black near Hecher. "Tennis is a white sport. I won't say it's a rich people's white sport, but you don't see too many poor whites playin it, far as I can tell."

"Exactly," said Hecher. "The only black tennis players I know are Arthur Ashe and Althea Gibson. They were both great. And the only reason there aren't more like them is because they don't get a chance to play. Having tennis at the prison would give blacks here the opportunity to learn the game, so when they get out, it'll help give them respectability. It'll do that for all of us. Help us hold our heads up high."

"Hmm," the black pondered. "Well, when you put it like that, I guess it makes sense. Hell, why not? Okay, let's do it."

"What about the rest of you?" Hecher asked.

"Let's go for it, Mitt," said a white.

"I'm with you," another chimed in.

"Let's take a vote," a black suggested.

"Okay," Hecher signified. "The motion is on whether I, as president, should petition the prison superintendent for permission to hold a referendum of the prison population on whether all should pay for building three tennis courts."

"I second the motion," Lannon said.

"All in favor raise your right hand," Hecher instructed.

Eleven men raised their hands. One, a husky white inmate, declined.

"The motion has passed," said Hecher. "Today is Thursday. I'll ask for a meeting with the lieutenant on Monday."

_____

"You again," Lieutenant Weller said with mock dismay, stretching his hand across the desk. "How ya doin, Hecher? What are you up to now? You're one busy inmate."

"Yeah, Lieutenant. I'm trying to make the best use of my time. Makes it pass faster. I've come up with an idea that may seem pretty far-fetched at first, but I hope you'll give it some thought after the initial shock wears off." A sheepish smile.

"Uh-oh. What'ya got up your sleeve now, taking the whole damn population on a world cruise or something?"

Hecher chuckled. "Nope, nothing quite that drastic, Lieutenant. I want to build tennis courts."

Weller sat upright in his swivel chair, his forearms on the armrests. He stared at Hecher.

"Damn, you're right. That's a wild-ass idea. I think I like the world cruise better. Now what the hell makes you want to do *that*?"

Hecher explained that he thought learning to play tennis would elevate the self-esteem of the inmates. He presented his plan for holding a referendum on whether to collect an assessment from each inmate to pay for three courts, and for issuing a tennis card that would grant permission for each paying person to play.

"I don't know if that referendum would pass," said Weller.

"It'll take a marketing effort," Hecher conceded. "Each member of the Jaycees will be given a part of the prison population to try to sell the idea to. As I see it, this thing will have benefits beyond recreation. It will get a spirit of community involvement going in the prison population. It will generate discussions. There will be agreements and disagreements. The Jaycees might have to serve as intermediaries, and they will let the men in their sections know they're always available to answer questions. They need to be ready to help resolve disputes. It'll be great for the Jaycees, especially. Give them responsibility for helping people. That'll be a huge benefit on the outside."

"You've thought of all the angles, haven't you?" Weller sighed. "Let me think it over. We're not talking about tinker toys here. This is a pretty big undertaking. And if the whole thing goes awry, it could be my undoing. I'll need the undertaker." His cheeks crinkled in a tight-lipped smile.

"I don't want to do anything that will get you into trouble, Lieutenant."

"Nah, nah. Don't worry about me. I'll decide whatever I think is best for the inmates and the prison. Give me a few days. I'll get back to you."

Hecher devoted more time to his rape defense book. He met frequently with the artist to work out sketches of a would-be rapist stalking and luring, then attacking, a woman. They designed artwork of the physical ways the woman thwarted the attack: striking him with the sharp heel of her shoe, kicking him in the groin, stabbing him with her hairpin, poking him in the eye, biting him.

After nine days, Lieutenant Weller summoned him.

"Okay, Hecher, here's what I did. I decided I needed to go a little higher up the ladder with this, and took it to the assistant warden. I had to twist his arm a little, but I got him to see the merits in the idea and he came around, as long as the inmates would pay the bulk of the cost. I made some inquiries, and building three courts would run twenty to twenty-three grand. So you'll need a hell of a lot of participation in order to keep the assessment low enough for the men to go for it. You've got the green light to see what you can come up with. Keep me abreast of how this thing is going. Any major problems come up, I need to know about em right away. Okay?"

"Sure enough, Lieutenant."

"I've got confidence in you, Hecher. Go to it."

"Thanks. I'll do my best."

He called a special meeting of the Jaycees. They discussed a reasonable assessment and decided on twenty dollars. Reviewing a map of the cell blocks, Hecher designated an area for each member to canvass. They went about their assignments with enthusiasm, cornering inmates in the cafeteria, the hallways, and the yard. Sometimes a Jaycee would talk to more than one man at a time and get a discussion going.

"I think it's a great idea," a white inmate having lunch with a black said.

"Yeah, you white guys like it cuz it's whitey's game," said the black. "Real nice'n clean, dudes wearin them shiny white shorts and shirts."

"Horseshit," the white rejoined. "Poor whites don't get to play tennis no more'n blacks. Nobody ever played in my neighborhood, that's for sure. You ever hear of Arthur Ashe?"

"No."

"He was the world's number one player just a few years ago, one of the greatest players ever. He was from Virginia, and he was black."

"Oh yeah, another Uncle Tom," the black inmate sniffed.

"Bullshit," said the white inmate.

Bam! The white lay on the floor beside the table as surrounding inmates turned to look.

"Don't bullshit me, mother fucker. I don't cotton to no ass-kissin Uncle Tom. I don't care how fuckin good he was."

The white, who was four inches taller than the man who had struck him, sat up, rubbing his jaw.

"You know what, man? I wanna get these tennis courts, so I'm gonna give you a pass. Otherwise, I would beat the livin shit outa you. What the hell got into you? Now just let me talk and don't go poppin off like that before you even know what I'm gonna say."

He rose to his feet and stood over the man who had punched him.

"Now, I'm tellin ya, Arthur Ashe wasn't no Uncle Tom. And if you take another shot at me, you're gonna be the one on the floor and you're gonna be there for a long time. So listen the fuck up, you got me? Arthur Ashe started playing tennis because there happened to be a court in his neighborhood. And he showed that if blacks have the chance to play this game, they can be just as good at it as whites. And probably better, because with hardly any of em doin it, the odds are not many of em's gonna get very far in the game.

"And this dude Ashe gets to be the best player in the United States, and even the whole fuckin world. If as many blacks was playin as whites, how many do you think would be at the top floor of the game? They'd be kickin ass. Does that make sense to you, or are you too fuckin stupid to figure that out? Same thing with Althea Gibson before Ashe. Ever hear of her? Prob'ly not, cuz you don't seem to know nothin, dipshit. She was the first black ever to make it to the top in tennis. She was one of the greatest ever. And get this: She also played professional golf."

He looked up at the windows that faced the yard. "I don't think we want to be taking up golf here. The point I'm makin is, don't pass up the chance to show whites you can do what they can do, and maybe better."

The black eyed him with head lowered, looking doubtful.

"Come on, man. We wanna get these tennis courts in here. It'll be good for everybody."

"I'll think about it."

"Yeah, you think about it. You think real hard, cuz I'm gonna be thinkin about what you did to my face. And I ain't gonna forget about it till I know you voted for the tennis courts."

The campaign continued for six weeks. Jaycees collected signatures of the men who said they'd vote for the courts. Of the total population of 925, about 850 indicated they were in favor. Most of the others said they'd consider it, and only thirty or so were adamantly opposed. Almost all of those were in the low-population, close custody division of the prison, where Jaycees expended little effort at recruitment. A lot of these were in for very long terms or life, and had little or no interest in ways to enhance assimilation into society on the outside. They also had greater antisocial tendencies, and were more likely to cause disruptions, some of which might spill outside the courts into other parts of the prison life. Jaycees offered them the opportunity to join, but didn't try to sell them.

Hecher typed a simple ballot stating the referendum issue. Below it was a box and next to it the words: In favor. Below that was another box and next to it the word: Opposed. Near the bottom of the ballot was a signature line. At the bottom were instructions for where to deposit the ballot—a slotted wooden box in the cafeteria—and the deadline.

He typed three copies on a page and gave it to Lannon, who printed 320 pages. Using the paper cutter in the library, he sliced the pages into 960 individual ballots.

Hecher and Lannon met with the prison sergeant in charge of the mail room, whom Lieutenant Weller had apprised of the ballot initiative, and discussed their plan to place a ballot in each mailbox. Lannon carried the ballots to the mail room in a large paper bag and, with the help of five other Jaycees, inserted them into the mailboxes. The deadline for depositing each ballot with the vote marked and signature provided was three days later.

Late on the morning of the third day, a guard accompanied Hecher to the cafeteria, where two inmates rushed to deposit their ballots.

"Hey, man, I hope we ain't too late," one said.

"Nah, I figured there'd be some who procrastinated or forgot, so I waited a few hours. You made it in the nick of time. Stick it in the opening."

He carried the box, which an inmate in the lowest-custody Community division had crafted in the shop, into the library and left it with the prison librarian. After lunch, he returned and set about counting the votes. The totals were very close to the results of the preliminary survey: 856 in favor, thirty-six opposed. The rest didn't vote.

Hecher presented the results to Lieutenant Weller, who pulled a calculator out of a desk drawer and punched some numbers.

"Seventeen-thousand and one-hundred-twenty dollars." He rubbed his chin. "If you can collect almost all of that, I think the prison board will approve the rest. I'll take it to them. Don't do any collecting till I get back to you."

Eleven days later, Hecher faced Weller.

"Seventeen thousand is the bottom line," said the lieutenant. "The prion will pay for the rest out of the general fund. That's cutting it pretty close."

"Men, we've got our job cut out for us," Hecher notified the Jaycees board. "We have to collect from all but six of the guys who voted in favor. I think we should set a deadline of five days from today to pay. Otherwise, they don't get a tennis card. They will deposit their money in the library, in the same box used for the ballots. The librarian will check their names on a list. The money will be secure with the librarian. Is that okay with everybody?"

The others nodded or verbalized agreement.

The Jaycees fanned out through the prison, touting the good outcome of the vote and cajoling the inmates to follow through with their payments so construction of the courts could begin right away and they could get their tennis cards. By the deadline, eleven of the inmates had failed to pay, and refused, saying they had reconsidered.

But something unexpected happened. Two who had not voted came forth and said they wanted to participate if it wasn't too late. The effort was still three short of the number needed to raise seventeen thousand. The next regular meeting of the Jaycees was in four days, and a decision on what to do would be made. By then, five more inmates changed their minds and asked to become part of the tennis program. Their contributions put the amount needed over the top.

Hecher brought the money to Lieutenant Weller.

"Look at this," Weller said, holding up a copy of the *Orlando Standard*.

Hecher stared at the headline: Tennis Coming to Avon Prison. The subhead read: *For inmates, courts without judges.*

"Apparently somebody in the administration called the paper," said Weller. "I don't know who. The article talks about how the Jaycees organized a fund-raising campaign to pay for the courts. Good publicity for the prison. Congratulations."

"Thanks. Glad they wrote something good about us for a change."

But before the prison board could approve the project, another article appeared in the paper, this one quoting State Rep. Ronald Cransdale, Republican of Orlando.

"This is an outrage," he fulminated. "I've never seen such a blatant example of coddling criminals. We're turning the Avon Park Correctional Institution into a country club. Tennis courts. How genteel. Next thing they'll be asking the Legislature to pay for white shirts and shorts and sneakers. Oh, and don't forget the sweat bands to keep perspiration out of their sensitive eyes. How are we supposed to keep people from committing criminal acts if they know their punishment is going to be whiling away their time in a luxurious institution where they can hop on out to the tennis courts for a little volleying anytime they get bored? I, for one, am not going to stand for this. Warden Pickering is going to hear from me."

Hecher saw the article in the library and wondered if the project were doomed. He expected to be called into Lieutenant Weller's office at any time and instructed to have the Jaycees return the money to the inmates. Hecher was unaware of the phone conversation between Rep. Cransdale and the warden.

"If you don't stop this from happening, Warden, I'm going to bring the matter before the House prison finance subcommittee when the Legislature convenes in a few months and ask that funding to Avon Park be slashed."

"Rep. Cransdale, I must remind you that the inmates are paying for all but $3,000 to $5,000 of the cost of these courts out of their own pockets. And the rest of the money is coming out of funds already allocated to the prison. The taxpayer is not being saddled with any extra burden. On the other hand, learning to play tennis will help build self-esteem in these inmates and make them feel that they belong when they return to civilian life, that they are a part of mainstream society. And that can only work toward lowering the recidivism rate. Or don't you want that, Rep. Cransdale?"

"Of course I want that. But... I don't think that's the way to make it happen."

"Very well. Then, why don't you do what you have to do, and I'll do what I think is right for this institution, and we'll let the chips fall where they may? It was nice talking with you, sir. Call me anytime you have a problem."

"Uh, yes. Well... goodbye."

Within days, the administration hired a contractor, and the work began soon after. The courts were ready for playing in six weeks.

Chapter Eight

The tennis court project was as big a challenge as any karate opponent Hecher had ever faced. Its success gave him a deep feeling of satisfaction. Yet, when he left the activities of the day for the quiet of his cell in the evenings, Diane and Pauley haunted his thoughts, and his sense of well-being dissolved into anxiety and sadness.

In his meditations, he concentrated on every part of her body, imagining that his eyes cast penetrating rays deep beneath her skin, subduing the overwrought cells that were wreaking havoc on her nerve endings. He hoped fervently that the living, breathing matter would receive the energy he willed her way. In his earnestness, he became transfixed, nearly entering a hypnotic state.

The spell would be broken when the lights were turned off. He climbed into his bed and wondered what it would be like helping Pauley with his homework and being there for him as the father he wanted and needed. His eyes finally grew heavy, and his fantasies segued into oblivion.

Attorneys Mancbaum and Larbin filed an application with the appellate court in West Palm Beach to review Hecher's case on the basis that three witnesses who testified against him at trial later recanted. They wrote:

The evidence presented at the trial had reasonable doubt written all over it in huge black letters, and the jury ignored it and returned a verdict of guilty. But the jury did not know at that time what is now known—that the testimony was false. It consisted of outrageous fabrications of DeWitt Crimshaw and others.

Four months later, the appeals court rendered its decision. It would not hear an appeal.

"I didn't think there was much chance this would work," Hecher said to Lannon at lunch. "Judges don't think it matters much if a witness changes his testimony. You'd think three out of four reversing themselves would make a difference, but these guys don't give a damn. Hell, it's only a guy's life. They just rap their little hammers, and poof, that's one more pesky item off their docket."

"I doubt the attorneys had high expectations either," said Lannon. "They're just getting started, don't you think?"

"You're probably right. Even though I knew in my head it was likely going to fail, in my heart I couldn't help hoping for a miracle."

"The grand opening of the tennis courts is tomorrow. That'll get your mind off it."

"Hey, yeah, I almost forgot."

At two p.m., Warden Sloan Pickering stood before a microphone on an eighteen-inch-high wooden platform in the yard. The assistant warden, Lieutenant Weller, Mitt Hecher, and three prison board officers sat on metal folding chairs back of him. Members of the Jaycees sat on chairs flanking the platform, two rows of three on each side, angled twenty degrees inward. The entire population of inmates stood in various postures, facing the platform. Guards kept vigil at key points.

One-hundred-fifty feet to the right of the congregation, three side-by-side tennis courts gleamed with the freshness of bright green and rust-orange paint in geometrical patterns divided by white lines. The sun's intermittent disappearance on this partly cloudy day temporarily diminished, but failed to nullify, the sheen.

"Good afternoon, gentlemen," Warden Pickering welcomed. "This is indeed a wonderful occasion—one that I am proud to be a part of. I'm not going to be long. I just wanted to say how pleased I am that you all could join together in a spirit of cooperation and make a small sacrifice for the common good. Nobody wants to be here, and I think you've done something to make the experience a little more tolerable. And without any further ado, I'm going to turn the mike over to our inmate superintendent, Lieutenant Andy Weller."

A smattering of applause.

"Thank you Sloan," said Weller, stepping up to the mike. He motioned to Hecher and said, "I'm going to ask Mitt Hecher to come up here. I'm sure a lot, if not most, of you men recognize him. He's the guy who's been teaching those karate classes."

Hecher, clad in whites, strode up to Weller, who shook his hand.

"This is the guy behind this whole thing," Weller declared, looking down at the shorter inmate. "When he came to me with the idea, I have to admit I was skeptical. I had my doubts whether he could pull it off. But Mitt's got a good head on his shoulders. He organized his team of Jaycees here..." Weller swept his arms to his left and right... "and they got you men to understand how a tennis program could benefit you not only here at the prison, but on the outside, as well. As construction was nearing completion, more men came forward and said they were willing to pay the assessment so they could be included in the program. We now have almost unanimous participation.

"The board matched the additional money to add to the number of tennis rackets, and we now have fifty of decent quality and a range of grips to fit different hand sizes. We also have a good supply of Wilson tennis balls. Just don't hit them over the wall, because you're not allowed to go after them."

A roar of laughter erupted from the crowd, with men doubling over and slapping each other.

"Mitt, do you have anything to say?"

"I just want to thank Lieutenant Weller for having the faith in me to get this done, the whole administration for their cooperation and going the extra mile for the project, and the Jaycees for their hard work. And I want to thank all the men for having the good sense to realize that these tennis courts are a sound investment of their meager savings. Beyond that, I just want to say: Tennis anyone?"

He stepped back from the mike with a droll smile. Weller moved in front, his chuckles blending with the light laughter of the others on stage.

"I'm sure you'll have plenty of takers, Mitt. That's it for today, everyone. Thanks for your attention. And enjoy yourselves on the courts."

Lannon was right: The two attorneys for Hecher, in making the appeal that the appellate court rejected, had just gotten started. The ink on the ruling was barely dry when they got to work on their next strategy. In a few weeks, Hecher received a letter from Mancbaum, who said he and Larbin had filed a request with the Florida Supreme Court to invoke discretionary jurisdiction, based on the same grounds: that witnesses had admitted lying in court.

A month passed, and another letter arrived from the attorneys. This could only be bad news, Hecher thought. The court usually took longer to make a decision, and must have dismissed this appeal summarily. He opened the envelope and learned that Palm Beach County Circuit Judge Walton Oren had granted permission to have a handwriting analyst test the confession letter that DeWitt Crimshaw accused Hecher of writing.

"If this guy is any good, I've got a chance here," Hecher mumbled, standing by the mailbox.

Mancbaum filed the results of the test by a retired FBI handwriting expert with shining credentials that showed many differences between Hecher's writing and the letter. He concluded Hecher didn't write the letter. The state attorney's office argued before Judge Oren that he should not grant Hecher a hearing based on that testimony and Mancbaum's argument that Seppish provided incompetent defense. Oren rejected the prosecution's attempt and scheduled a hearing.

"Way to go," Hecher almost shouted, as inmates at nearby mailboxes turned to look. "That son-of-a-bitch'n lawyer is kickin ass."

"Good news?" one asked.

"Well, who knows? I'm probably getting excited for nothing again. But there's some hope. My lawyer's pushing for a new trial."

Weeks went by, and the state Supreme Court voted not to accept jurisdiction.

"Keep your chin up," Mancbaum wrote to Hecher. "The state court almost never considers recanted testimony as a basis for taking another look at a conviction. But we had to give it a try. We have a much better chance with the local court on the new handwriting analysis and poor-defense claim."

Near the end of the year, Mancbaum and Larbin, plus an idealistic lawyer they knew in Gainesville, Samuel Jackson, teamed up to argue for a new trial before Circuit Judge Oren. They laid out several reasons why Seppish provided ineffective counsel. He failed to call key witnesses to testify, and didn't even put his own client on the stand, they pointed out. Further, he didn't object to permitting the jury to hear DeWitt Crimshaw's testimony about the alleged written confession, nor to admission of Crimshaw's letter outlining the confession into evidence.

Scraponia argued all of those were tactical decisions by Seppish.

However, the trial judge in the case, Timothy Schultz, testified that, if he had been the defense attorney, he would have questioned the witnesses.

After several hours of arguments and testimony, Judge Oren adjourned the hearing and announced that he would render a decision by the spring on whether to grant a new trial.

At the time of the trial, during a recess period, Judge Schultz appeared so certain the jury would vote to acquit that he joked with reporters about not knowing what he'd do if it found Hecher guilty.

"We wanted to get Judge Schultz to testify that he thought you were innocent," Mancbaum wrote to Hecher, "but were unsuccessful. The only thing we can do now is wait for Judge Oren's decision. Keep the faith."

Hecher shrugged, slid the letter under his waistband, and walked to his cell. After lunch, he attended his business classes, then hurried out to the tennis courts, where he had a match scheduled with Lannon in late afternoon.

"It's coming back to me a little bit," the peg-legged prisoner called over the net. "Course, I moved around a little better when I was a kid."

"You're covering the court pretty good, man. I thought I'd have to baby you—hit the shots right at you. And I'm not good enough to put em just where I want to."

"Yeah, I can stretch… whoa, couldn't reach that one," he said as the ball shot to his left a foot inside the line.

"Gotta keep you on your toes—so to speak," Hecher yelled.

"Wise ass," Lannon hollered back.

A spirited doubles match was under way in the center court. It was the prison version of mixed doubles: a black and a white on each side. Two blacks played a singles match on the other end court.

The program was proving more popular even than expected, with the courts in use throughout the day. The period of least use was midafternoon, when classes were in session.

Tennis, teaching a karate class once a week, working on the rape book, leading the Jaycees. Hecher had a full schedule, and the months passed quickly. He was too occupied to dwell on the outcome of his current court appeal.

So the letter that arrived in his mailbox in late April took him aback. It was from attorney Mancbaum. Hecher fumbled in his haste to open it. He read:

I regret to inform you that Judge Walton Oren has rejected our appeal for a new trial. As the basis for his decision, he held that the letter outlining the confession contained basically the same information that DeWitt Crimshaw provided on the witness stand. Therefore, admitting the letter into evidence didn't change the outcome, Judge Oren decided. We think he has made a very serious mistake. The letter contained critical details of the supposed confession that Crimshaw did not reveal to the court.

Accordingly, we will file for a petition of rehearing within 10 days. Such a request is very rarely granted, but I have hope that because of the egregious nature of this shortcoming, an exception might be made. As for the incompetency of Seppish, the judge ruled that his performance was adequate and he was using stratagems that didn't work. There's nothing we can do to change that opinion.

Hecher raised his head and looked into space, holding the letter in his right hand and the envelope in his left.

"Here we go again," he said to no one.

"Where we goin?" asked a member of his karate class, looking up from the mailbox he was opening.

"Huh? Oh… nothin."

He went to his cell and lay on his back on the bed, head propped on the pillow, hands clasped behind his head with arms akimbo, staring at he ceiling. Lannon walked by.

"Hey Mitt, let's go to lunch."

"Nah, I think I'll skip it today, Gary. I'm not hungry."

"The way you look, that's because something's eatin ya."

"Yeah. Another appeal turned down. I thought this one had a decent chance."

"I'm sorry, man."

"I'll get over it. I just need a little time by myself. I'm going to meditate in a little while, and I'll come out of it. I'll be ready for that doubles match tomorrow."

"Okay, brother. Catch you later."

He closed his eyes.

Maybe I'm beating my head against the wall. We've tried just about everything, and nothing works. Seems like these judges don't want to rule against each other. It's like a brotherhood. How long has it been now? Nine years counting the year in jail before the trial. Sixteen years to go before my release.

Oh no, I've got to keep fighting.

Seven weeks later, Judge Oren pounded the nail into the coffin, upholding his original decision to deny Hecher a new trial. In his order, the judge wrote: *The counselors are correct in asserting that the so-called letter of confession does more than merely duplicate what Mister Crimshaw testified to on the witness stand by providing details not contained in the testimony. However, they failed to prove that, had Mitt Hecher's trial attorney, Alonzo Seppish, objected to introduction of the letter, the verdict would have been different.* Oren cited a 1984 U.S. Supreme Court ruling that decided if a defendant's lawyer committed specific acts that would indeed have affected the outcome of the case, then the defendant should be granted a new trial.

"Huh?" Hecher howled, tossing the letter in the air.

"Whoa," said a guard passing by the mailboxes. "Take it easy, Hecher. I've never seen you like this before."

"You're right, Sergeant. I am one pissed off dude. I wanna pretend that fuckin judge is a wooden box and put my fist through it. And if I was on the outside, I would. This guy just made it obvious he had no intention of making an impartial decision. It was just a nonsensical ruling. There is no way I can get any justice through the courts. Here's what's really infuriating. Listen to this."

Hecher reached down and picked the letter off the floor. He ran a finger down the lines, stopped, and read: *There was substantial evidence of defendant's guilt.* He looked up at the guard.

"He just made that up. There was no evidence at all. The only evidence was the testimony of those jailbirds, and they admitted later they lied."

"I don't want you doing anything that'll get you into trouble, Hecher. You've been a model prisoner at this institution, and it would be a shame to ruin your record."

"I know, I know, Sarg. Guess I'll just go bang the ball around on the tennis courts."

Mancbaum and Larbin had been working pro bono on Hecher's case and were as exasperated as he was. Two weeks after Judge Oren's final rejection of a new trial, Hecher received a letter from them.

"We regret to inform you that after shooting several arrows at the process in which the trial was conducted, we have reached into our quiver in search of more with which to attack the outcome and

win a new trial or overthrow the conviction, and found it empty. At
this point, therefore, we have no choice but to suspend work on the
case. We are extremely disappointed in the decisions of the judges
and do not concur with them. It goes without saying that you must
be frustrated to the point of hopelessness with the judicial system.
We cannot blame you.

"What we can do is continue to hold out some hope. Our
colleague, Sam Jackson in northern Florida, will remain on the case as
he drives to Tallahassee to seek redress from Governor Rob Garner.
Mister Jackson will ask for clemency within a few days. Florida law
requires that no action can be taken until the governor and at least
three members of the Cabinet review the case."

"The gov doesn't give a crap about whether I should be in
prison or not," Hecher said to Lannon as they walked away from the
courts after finishing a match. "His office said he was looking into it
almost two years ago, and he hasn't done a damn thing. That was
when some important people raised a stink. But he just let the
hullabaloo die away. Politicians. They only care when there's
something in it for them."`

A reporter for the *Palm Beach Beacon* phoned Hecher, who told
him: "State Attorney Donald Bosworth, the prosecutor Jim
Scraponia, and Ronald Snopes, chief of sheriff's detectives, all put a
conviction ahead of finding the person guilty of the murder. These
people are hungry for political power."

Both attorney Jackson and Hecher accused the prosecutors and
sheriff's officials of manipulating evidence to convict him.

"What about the fact we uncovered that Richie Gatson couldn't
have listened in on that supposed telephone conversation from a
mobster asking Hecher to kill a Palm Beach man who owed drug and
gambling debts because Hecher didn't have a phone in his
apartment?" Jackson lamented. "Mister Scraponia mentioned the
deposition, but never disclosed the absence of a phone. Why didn't
the prosecution disclose that Hecher's fingerprints never were found
on the confession, while DeWitt Crimshaw's were? Why has the
prosecution kept quiet about Crimshaw's failing a lie detector test
about the confession?"

Jackson told Hecher that a woman attorney in Orlando had
refused to write the Fifth Circuit ruling in 1981 denying his appeal for
a new trial because she didn't think he was guilty.

Her name was Susan Strickland and she was an idealistic person who had a strong record as an appeals attorney in private practice.

Hecher decided to write her a letter and ask if she would help him. They exchanged several letters, and she agreed to use her experience with the appellate courts, making calls to her connections in Tallahassee, and use her high-powered law firm as a resource.

After Jackson filed the petition for clemency, he sent a copy to the Florida Parole Commission. Four members of that six-member body investigated Hecher's file and his record in prison, and forwarded a recommendation for clemency to Governor Garner.

The governor's term in office was due to expire at the end of the year. Though the case had been presented to him two years before, he only now announced that he would make a decision soon. The commission members had to rush to review the case, and two had insufficient time, leaving no possibility of the desired unanimous recommendation of the commission.

Cabinet clemency aides assured the prosecutor representing the state attorney's office that they would try to delay a clemency vote beyond the twenty-six days remaining in the governor's term. A hearing before the governor was scheduled for the next day.

Attorney Jackson sat at the defense desk and surveyed the hearing room before the proceedings began. His eyes fell on Jan Kriger and her six children. All seven had flown to Florida's capital to attend the hearing. They had written to Garner and the Cabinet urging them not to grant clemency. Jackson stared at the matriarch.

Why is Mrs. Kriger so eager that Mitt Hecher's guilty status remain intact that she would cart her entire family all the way up here from West Palm Beach? It's almost like she's making sure her children don't have any doubts. I wonder why. If he's found innocent, that means somebody else is guilty. And she acts like she doesn't want that to come out. Could it be she knows who that somebody is?

Jackson argued that State Attorney Bosworth allowed perjured testimony and had kept secret an investigation after the trial that suggested another man may have committed the murder. The governor allowed the investigating attorney's testimony over the objection of the prosecutor.

"I am Joshua Whiteman," the fortyish man with thinning hair announced as he took the witness stand. "I was an assistant Palm Beach County state attorney and investigated the murder of Rodger Kriger. Three months after I left office, I turned in my report, which

I knew would meet with much resistance because it went contrary to the finding of Donald Bosworth and Jim Scraponia that Mitt Hecher committed the murder. My work brought me to the conclusion that a man named Jerry Cruddy either shot Kriger or was outside the house when he was shot, and that Hecher was not involved in any way. I am convinced that if the state attorney's office had disclosed my report, this case would have taken a very different turn and we wouldn't be here today."

"That's tommyrot," the prosecutor objected, almost shouting, fair skin turning crimson. "You have no proof of any of that. It's just supposition, and it's irresponsible."

"You weren't even around at the time," Whiteman parried, his voice also raised. "You're the one who's engaging in supposition. If State Attorney Bosworth thought my conclusions were not sound, then why didn't he probe further instead of just quashing the report? The reason is because he didn't want to learn that he might have been wrong. He had the conviction he wanted."

"There you go again, making wild accusations." The prosecutor stood at his table, shifting from one foot to the other on his lean frame, his neck veins prominent.

"All right, all right, let's move on to the next witness," said the hearing administrator.

The prosecutor testified that Hecher should remain in prison regardless of his murder conviction because of his lengthy arrest record before then.

"By granting clemency to this man, you would be giving him the green light to go out and commit more crimes against the people of Florida," he warned.

But a former parole commissioner countered by noting that Hecher had received not a single disciplinary report while in prison.

"Mitt Hecher is not a menace to society," she concluded. "In fact, a review of his entire arrest record shows that all of the acts in which he was charged with an offense against someone involved a person who also was a lawbreaker."

She was persuaded to testify at the hearing by Susan Strickland, who volunteered to assist Mancbaum and Larbin. She contacted officials of both the Raiford and Avon Park prisons to learn about Hecher's record. She asked them for names of former parole commissioners who consistently offered a second chance to inmates who had demonstrated a willingness to be a part of civilized society without flagrantly flouting its laws and rules and displaying hostility toward others.

Garner's staff and the parole commission urged him to make a decision rather than let the matter die. The governor promised he would make a recommendation to the Cabinet, sitting as the Clemency Board.

Eleven days later, Governor Garner announced his decision in a brief written statement.

I find no cause to recommend, to the Clemency Board, clemency for Mitt Hecher from his twenty-five year prison term, nor any reason to propose a reduction in his sentence.

The governor offered no basis for his decision or comments on the testimony presented at the hearing.

"I'm obviously quite disappointed, and vexed that the governor would allow this charade to continue," Hecher told a reporter for the *Fort Lauderdale Ray* who called the prison. "The politicians have no reason to do the right thing. Their power robs them of their humanity. But I'm not giving up. I'm optimistic that one day the truth will see the light of day."

It was pure bravado. He knew that Scraponia and Bosworth would be delighted, and the worse he felt, the better they would feel. He was at war with them. They had won another battle, but he was fighting on.

"Hecher is up against a judicial system that is flawed," attorney Larbin contended to the reporter. "It does not afford any means by which a conviction can be overturned if doubts about the defendant's guilt come to the surface. The only way for that to happen is if it can be shown that a legal mistake was made during the trial. Otherwise, if all the trial rules have been followed, it doesn't make any difference if new evidence shows the defendant may not be guilty after all."

Mancbaum telephoned Hecher to offer encouragement.

"The governor had no intention of freeing me," Hecher said. "I saw on TV he said he'd make a decision instead of letting the time expire till he was out of office. He did that just to make it look like he was being fair. He knew before the hearing what he was going to do."

"You may be right, Mitt. But we can't worry about him anymore. I don't think we stand much chance with the next governor, Ronald Montez. He's a heavy-duty law-and-order kind of guy. But we have to give it a try. At the same time, we need to make an appeal to the U.S. District Court. That's our best shot."

"Yeah," Hecher agreed, "I think that's the route to justice."

Though both Hecher and his attorneys had virtually given up on the state courts, one more avenue remained open and the lawyers girded up for a last-ditch effort. They filed a petition for a hearing before the Fifth District Court of Appeals in Daytona Beach, listing once again recantation of witnesses' testimony and incompetent representation by Hecher's trial attorney.

Hecher concentrated all his efforts on completion of his rape-defense book. It was growing into a compendium that was both attractive and easy to understand. Hecher was articulate in describing the threatening situations women faced and the ways they could both elude attackers and overcome them with various physical means. He and his illustrator agreed the volume should not be so thick that buyers would worry it might be arcane and dull. But it shouldn't be too slim, either, they reasoned, because that would give it a flimsy, superficial appearance.

"Your illustrations not only bring my words to life, but make the book visually appealing, and I know a lot about appeals," Hecher said, his mouth crinkled.

The artist looked bemused.

"Never mind. It's a personal joke."

A month later, the book was ready for publication, with the title, *Practical Ways to Foil a Rape: The Preying Man Won't Have a Prayer*. By Mitt Hecher. Illustrated by James Fazio. A girlfriend of Diane went to the Palm Beach County Library and wrote down names of publishers in the categories of Self-Help, How-To, Illustrated, Sociology, and Women's Issues/Studies in the thick *Writer's Market* guide. Diane mailed the list to her husband at Avon Park, and he set about typing a query letter, making copies, and filling in the information for each publication, in the same way he had set up mailing of the five hundred packets declaring his innocence.

The tennis program was so popular that inmates clamored for tournaments. Hecher brought the issue up at a Jaycees meeting, and the group decided to establish a ladder by which players could challenge each other to climb in rank. In three months, the top sixteen players remaining would be paired off in round-robin competition leading to the finals. Hecher delegated the organizing of the ladder and the tournament to volunteer Jaycees and put Lannon in charge. He typed a notice about the plans and assigned four of the Jaycees to make copies and put them in the inmates' mailboxes.

A growing number of inmates also asked Hecher about joining his karate classes. He sought permission for a third class from Lieutenant Weller, who gave his approval for a group limited to fourteen. The ever-present, gratuitous violence at Raiford, along with the years of frustration and disappointment of continually seeing his hopes of obtaining justice dashed, had diluted the hostile aggressiveness in Hecher. He had become like Buck, the heroic dog in Jack London's *The Call of the Wild*. Buck was beaten into submission by the lawgiver, the man with the club, but never was cowed or conciliated. Hecher was driven to the reality that the law, resistant to justice for him, was master. Yet he remained unbroken.

Hecher had come to accept the futility of raging against the law and society, and brought that cognizance to his karate classes. He emphasized to the men that the martial arts should be used for defense, rather than offense. Physical violence should be avoided if possible, he preached.

He worried that his son would become vengeful against his schoolmates who taunted him for having a father who was in prison, and use the karate he was learning in the same way Hecher used it. He didn't want Pauley to suffer the same fate, to go through a long period of rebellion and hostility before finding satisfaction in working with, instead of against, the community in which he found himself.

"You sound weak, babe," he said by phone to Diane. "How are you feeling?"

"Oh, honey, I'm sorry to tell you, it's just getting worse. The company is being really good to me, but I'll have to stop working soon. I'm too weak, and it's too painful."

Hecher took a deep breath while he composed himself. "You put my problems into perspective, sweetheart. I'm a lot better off healthy in here than you are in your condition on the outside. How's Pauley doing?"

"Oh, you should see him do his tae kwon do. He's getting quite good at it. And the teachers have only good things to say about him. He's here. Let me get him."

"Hi Dad."

"Hey. How's my boy? Fifth grade. Your mother tells me you're doing well in school."

"Yeah, I guess so."

"Listen to that modesty. What subject do you like the best?"

"English—and math."

"That's great. Keep it up. How do you like the tae kwon do?"

"I like it a lot. We have matches in the studio and I always win mine."

"Are the kids at school bothering you?"

"Not anymore. I told Jimmy Jansen to stop making fun of my dad because I wasn't going to stand for it anymore. He just laughed at me and called you a jailbird. I walked up to him and used holds I learned and flipped him on his back on the ground. He looked really surprised. A bunch of other kids saw it, and nobody pokes fun of me anymore."

Hecher felt a surge of pride and wanted to lavish praise on his son.

"Well, it looks like that worked out for the best. That's what the martial arts are for—defending against bullies. If that's the way you use the skills you learn, Pauley, I'm proud of you. Just don't use them to become a bully yourself. Then you're no better than they are. Do you see what I'm saying? Use the tae kwon do for good, not for bad. Okay?"

"Okay, Dad."

"Good. Listen, Pauley, I know you're worried about your mother. Especially with me being away and unable to take care of you if something happens to her. I want you to know that whatever happens, you are not going to be alone. I don't know how much longer I'll be here. But regardless, other members of the family love you a lot and will take you into their home if your mother is too sick to care for you. Do you understand that?"

"Well… I guess so."

"Trust me, Pauley. You don't need to worry. Now you just keep up the good work in school, and keep winning those tae kwon do matches, and everything will work out. Let me talk to your mother now. Bye Pauley. I'll talk to you again soon. I love you."

"Love you too, Dad. Bye."

"Better finish that math assignment, Pauley," Diane called. "He always acts so cheerful after he talks with you, Mitt."

"Well, I feel a lot better, too. And one day I'm going to get out of here and be with you and Pauley again. Governor Garner was a joke. He was just going through the motions. And the state courts are stacked against us. We're going to push it in the federal courts now. Okay, the guard is signaling I have to give up the phone. Do whatever you have to in order to be as comfortable as possible, sweetheart."

"I will, Mitt. I love you, honey."

Silence. Then, in a cracked voice, "I love you too. Bye."

PART III: BOMBSHELL

Chapter One

"You know, Tom, I've been chasing that Kriger murder for seven years, running to my den at home from the station and digging into files, pinning papers onto a big bulletin board."

WNQX radio's Jared Imwold spoke to Tom Palladin as they sat, Palladin's tall frame hunched a little, on a reddish oak bench in the hallway of the Palm Beach County Courthouse in downtown West Palm Beach. The reporters waited for the opening of the trial of a semiwealthy North Palm Beach man charged with murdering his wife.

"The thing has consumed me," Imwold divulged. "I've become obsessed. My wife has had it with me. She told me the other day, 'Jared, you have spent hardly any time with me for years now. You're going to have to let go of this thing, or let go of me. I can't stand it anymore.' So I'm pulling in the reins. If something comes my way, I'll go with it. But I'm through busting my ass trying to solve this case."

"I don't blame you," said Palladin. "It's awfully frustrating. I've felt the same way sometimes."

"This issue with the wife came up just when I felt I was onto something big. I don't want to let it go down the drain, so if you want to pursue it, be my guest."

"What have you got?"

"Okay." Imwold leaned forward, elbows on thighs. "I was thinking Joshua Whiteman was right. You know who I'm talking about: the former assistant state attorney. He thought Jerry Cruddy shot Kriger or at least was present at the scene. I thought the same thing and sent a letter to Bosworth urging him to investigate. I also told Robert Gusse what I knew."

"You talking about the agent in charge of the FBI Regional Office in West Palm Beach?"

"Yeah. You know him?"

"I've never talked to him."

"He doesn't think Cruddy did it, and he told me why. I don't want to violate the confidence of a source, so I'll just say this: Get ahold of Gusse. Tell him you think he knows who shot Rodger Kriger. If he asks you where you got that idea, it's okay to say I referred you."

"Hey, man, thanks. I'll jump on it."

Palladin filed the story on that day's murder trial and was at his desk midmorning the next day. He searched his Rolodex and found the number of agent Gusse. The FBI man's secretary took a message. Palladin grabbed his note pad and pen and headed for the coat rack to don his sport coat for the second day of the trial. The phone rang and he scurried back to answer it.

"Oh, yes, Agent Gusse." Palladin thanked him for his prompt response and asked to meet with him for a few minutes. "Yes, nine tomorrow would be perfect. This should only take about fifteen minutes. I'm covering that high-profile murder trial you might have heard about—William Jones. Yes, that's the one—but it doesn't begin until ten every morning. I'll see you at your office."

Gusse was the picture of a conservative federal lawman. He wore a white, wrinkle-free shirt and green paisley tie that matched close-cropped sandy hair highlighting a strong jaw, a straight nose that extended slightly too far, and ears in proportion to his head. For a man of five-foot-ten, he had a strong hand grip, doubtless due to workouts that also kept his build trim and sinewy, as revealed by the snug fit of the shirt against his torso and his telephone-pole posture.

"So what's on your mind?" he asked of the taller reporter with the dirty-blond hair, himself an imposing physical image. "Sit down."

It was a small office on the second floor of an adjunct federal building on the outskirts of downtown West Palm Beach. Gusse sat on an ordinary black chair on wheels at an inexpensive metal desk. His guest took a straight-back chair next to the agent's desk.

"I've been covering the Palm Beach murder of Rodger Kriger since about a year after it happened in 1976, reporting and investigating. That's been… what, about eleven years, I guess."

"I know. I've been reading your reports. It looked like you got bamboozled a couple of times by the people running the show, but I think you generally did a good job letting people know what was going on."

"Thanks. I've been frustrated trying to get to the bottom of who was behind this shooting. I've got several sources who I think know the answer, but I get the feeling they're afraid to talk. I'm wondering if you might have come up with anything on your end and can point me in the right direction."

Elbows on the chair's arms, Gusse raised his hands to his chin and rested his two forefingers on his lips. He studied the reporter.

"Now you didn't just suddenly decide for no reason that I might know something," the FBI man said with a twisted smile. "You heard something."

"Okay, yes. Jared Imwold of WNQX told me I ought to call you."

"Aha. Yes, I shared something with Jared. He's a good man. Worked his ass off on this case. So have you. Here's what I'm going to do. I'm going to give you some information on condition that you do not reveal me or the FBI as your source. You have to make me that promise. You can take what I give you and investigate, and try to confirm what I told you from another source or sources. Is that a deal?"

"You got a deal. I hope it'll lead to something."

"It should. It's pretty hot. Get out your pad and pen."

Palladin pulled a reporter's note pad out of his left sport coat pocket and a ballpoint pen out of his right pocket.

"Our agents had an electronic listening device implanted in the home of Frankie Campanella in Memphis, Tennessee. I think you know Campanella."

"Yeah. Mobster who operates out of the Shore Club up in Palm Beach Shores. Lower level Mafia figure."

"The agents were looking to nail him for book-making, small-time drugs, extortion, prostitution, loan sharking—that sort of thing. And they're listening to the tape. Lo and behold, Frankie and his cohorts start talking about this murder in Palm Beach. They mention the name of an associate of theirs who is hired to come down from Orlando to do the hit."

Gusse paused. "Okay, write this name down."

"I'm ready."

"Generoso Gagliardi."

"How do you spell it?"

"Yeah, good thing you asked. I didn't think of that. It's spelled G-a-g-l-i-a-r-d-i. But you don't say the second g. It's pronounced Gall-ee-ar-dee, like I said. So… you got it?"

"Yeah, I got it."

"The agent in charge of the bugging operation said it came across clear as day. They checked the guy's record, and it fits this crime to a T."

"This is a great lead," Palladin said, his voice uncharacteristially revealing mild excitement. "I'll jump on it."

"Now remember, you didn't get it from me."

"What did you say your name was?"

Gusse winked. "Good luck."

"Davey Ross?"

Silence.

"Do I have the right number? Is this Davey Ross?"

"That depends. The voice sounds familiar. I had to hear it again. Who is this?"

"Tom Palladin. I used to be a reporter with the *Miami Gazette*. I'm with the *Palm Beach Beacon* now."

"Yeah. That's who I thought it was. Haven't heard from you in a while. You still workin that Kriger case?"

"That's what I'm calling about. I'd like to meet with you."

"What's in it for me?"

"A free lunch."

A big horselaugh. "Oh, wow. Where we gonna eat, The Breakers?"

"That's beyond the *Beacon*'s budget—and mine. How about the Blue Pelican? That's convenient for you—not far from your hangout, the Shore Club. Good food, too."

"Yeah, it's kinda nice by the water. Why not? I never turn down a free offer."

"Can you make it tomorrow, say, one o'clock? I'd rather wait till the lunch crowd has thinned out so we have a little privacy."

"Sounds good to me. I eat breakfast late, anyway."

Palladin took a parking spot and paid the meter. He walked up the sidewalk to the overhang, and waited out of the sun. Even so, he began to sweat in his brown-green herringbone sport coat, which he wore to stash his note pad and pen.

A few minutes later, Ross drove up in an older model silver Honda Civic. Wearing a black-and-blue polo shirt and blue-gray denim pants, he casually approached Palladin. The reporter reached out his hand.

"You don't remember too good, Palladin. I don't shake hands with guys. No offense."

"Ah, yes. So you don't. Last time we talked was… maybe five years ago—at a bar in Riviera Beach. The Pussycat, I think."

"Was'at it? Maybe your memory ain't so bad."

"Where do you want to sit?"

"On the patio so we can look at the water and catch the breeze."

"Can you seat us over there toward the end, waiter, where the tables are empty?" Palladin requested. "We need a little privacy."

"Certainly. That's no problem."

Ross ordered shrimp scampi, Palladin lemon sole.

"And let me have a Bud," said Palladin. "What are you drinking?"

"Bud? That's horse piss," he blurted, cackling. "Gimme a Miller. Regular. Not that lite crap."

"The Pussycat," said Palladin as they munched on rolls and butter. "All the bar stools had a pink cat painted on the back side— up on its haunches, a long, curled tail."

"Yeah, I remember. Me and Mitt used to go there and smoke grass outside and go in and get drunk, and Mitt would start fights and all hell would break loose."

His laugh turned heads.

"The cops would come and haul Mitt away, but it took three of em to get him in the car. Man, them was the days." He smiled at the bobbing green waters of the Intracoastal Waterway.

Over their main courses, the two talked about the repeated rejections of Hecher's appeals to win a new trial.

"Mitt didn't have nothin to do with killin that guy," said Ross. "He was framed—pure and simple. These scumbags come out and admit they was lyin, and the fuckin judges, they don't give a shit. What a buncha cocksuckers."

He downed his last shrimp, guzzled his remaining beer, and swiped the cloth napkin across his mouth.

Palladin polished off his sole and washed it down with a swig of Budweiser.

"That's why I took you here," he revealed.

"I knew there was no free lunch," Ross snickered.

"I don't think Mitt Hecher shot Rodger Kriger, either. And I think you know who did. You hang around the Shore Club a lot. You hear things. I think somebody who operates out of the Shore Club arranged that shooting. You've been leading me down blind alleys and dead-end streets all these years. Come on. How about it? It's time you told me who shot Kriger. You were Mitt Hecher's good friend. You owe it to him."

Ross gazed at the table. He said nothing for several seconds. Then he reached to his right, picked up an extra beer napkin, and motioned to Palladin for his pen.

Palladin drew the pen from his pocket and gave it to Ross.

Leaning forward, he printed with care on the napkin. He laid the pen on the table and handed the napkin to Palladin. The reporter stared at it. His eyes widened and his pulse quickened, but he said nothing.

Generoso Gagliardi.

Ross rose. "Thanks for the lunch."

Palladin looked up, as if coming out of a trance.

"My pleasure."

Palladin drove back to the newspaper office. He called Muriel Sandefer, the madam who ran a brothel in Palm Beach Shores.

"Ms. Sandefer, this is Tom Palladin of *The Beacon.*"

"What do you want?" She sounded hostile.

"I'd like to talk to you about the Rodger Kriger murder. I suspect the Shore Club was involved somehow, and thought you might have heard something."

"I can't talk to you." Palladin could hear the voice was anxious, even fearful. "What do you want to do, get me killed? I've got to go now."

She hung up.

Palladin dialed Davey Ross.

"Davey, sorry to be a pain in the butt, but I want to talk to an old acquaintance of yours, Johnny Traynor. I called, but it's been a long time and he's not at that number anymore. You know how I can reach him?"

Ross told him to wait, then gave him a number.

"Thanks, Davey. Next time, I take you to lunch at The Breakers. If I win at Las Vegas."

Palladin pulled the phone away as a resounding belly laugh hurt his eardrum.

———————————

The Fifth District Court of Appeals in Daytona Beach denied the petition for a hearing, and no more opportunities for state appeals remained. The new governor, Ronald Montez, was a conservative with a tough-on-criminals reputation, and Hecher's attorneys held out scant hope for getting him to even review the case. Mancbaum and Larbin geared up for a run at the federal court level.

Hecher's book on how to prevent a rape found a publisher, Datstaff Publishing Co. Sales were slow at first, and then the publisher's promotions staff landed an interview with Hecher on a radio program at a liberal station in Atlanta. The show host interviewed him live by telephone.

The show had a wide regional following of women, and sales of the book increased appreciably. In a few months, royalties totaled enough to pay off Hecher's debts from compiling and mailing the packets pleading his innocence to politicians, prominent persons, and public and private agencies.

———————————

"Johnny Traynor?"

"Who's this?"

Palladin did not remember him sounding timorous.

"An acquaintance from way back. Tom Palladin."

"Oh, yes. I remember. Haven't seen you around for a long time."

"I had a little difficulty finding your new number. Finally got it from a friend of yours, Davey Ross."

"Oh, yeah, I moved inland a few years ago."

"You used to live near the Shore Club. I thought you liked hanging out there. Why would you want to leave the neighborhood?

"Well... to tell the truth, things got a little dicey."

"You talking about the Kriger murder?"

"Well… uh… yeah, sort of."

"I'd like to get together with you and chat about that. I have some new information."

"Yeah, I guess so. I don't know if I have anything that will help you."

"Where do you live?"

Traynor gave directions to a duplex apartment on the west side of West Palm Beach.

"How about two p.m. tomorrow?" Palladin asked.

"Yeah, that's okay. I'm working on a guy's car, and I've got plenty of time to finish it."

"See you then."

The neighborhood was seedy. Most of the houses were small, run-down, wood-frame structures. Early-model cars and trucks, the paint usually fading, occupied driveways, littered lawns, or sat on the street in front. Patches of dried grass sprinkled with pale green contrasted with splotches of bare, sandy earth, like the shabby clothes of a tramp with tatters that revealed his skin.

Traynor's duplex was the only property on the block that didn't look slummy to Palladin: a white, concrete-block structure with sidewalks leading to two screen doors opening to wooden front doors. Prosaic, but the grass was mostly green, and the car in the driveway, only a few years old, looked well-cared-for.

He parked on the street and walked to the unit on the right. Opening the screen door, he knocked.

It struck Palladin like a light flipped on in a dark room. Something was different about the man who opened the door.

"Come in," Traynor said. He gestured toward an armless, cushiony chair. "Sit down. Want a beer? Or Coke? I mean, you want a Coca Cola?"

He seemed shaky.

"Thanks. Are you renting here?"

"No. I bought the duplex and rent out the other half. Gives me a little income."

"Your place doesn't look bad. Best one on the block."

"I've gotta keep it up in order to rent it out. I rent it month-to-month and charge a big rate. A lot of my renters are people with criminal backgrounds like me who can't find anyplace else. That's why I bought this place. Nobody would rent to me."

Palladin could see what had changed in the man. No longer exuding cocky self-confidence, he appeared timid, almost frightened. Sitting on the couch, smoking a cigarette, his hand trembled. Then it hit Palladin. Coke. The quick clarification of the offer of Coca Cola. Traynor was a cocaine addict.

"Let me tell you why I called. I found out something from a couple of sources. I know who shot Rodger Kriger."

Palladin saw Traynor blanch. He looked without seeing at Palladin, then raised the cigarette to his lips with a shaky hand and took his time inhaling. He turned his head to blow the smoke away from his guest.

"I think you know who it is, too."

Traynor leaned forward to the glass-topped coffee table and snuffed his cigarette out in a small plastic ash tray. He straightened and looked away from Palladin, who noticed his face was grave.

"If it gets out that I told you this, I'll prob'ly get killed." He turned to look at Palladin. "You understand? You have to agree not to publish this."

Palladin said he wouldn't publish Traynor's name, but would use the information he provided to dig for details about the murder. Traynor said he was okay with that.

"I drove the getaway car."

Palladin's pulse quickened.

"It was Barney Robbins's Corvette. Neighbors couldn't see me on the property when I came to get the car because it's hidden by tall hedges. Richie Gatson dropped me off. I knew Robbins wasn't around because his Buick was gone. Getting the door open could have been a little dicey, but I'm good with a coat hanger and was inside in two minutes. I hot-wired it and took off. After the job, I drove it to a garage I rented and took the license plate off. In a couple weeks, an exporter bought it and shipped it overseas out of the Port of Palm Beach."

"Who did the shooting?"

"I'm not gonna tell you that. You said you already knew, anyway."

"What was the reason for the shooting? Why did someone want Rodger Kriger killed?"

Traynor rose and slinked, limping a little from his Vietnam injury, to the bay window in the front of the room. He peered through a crack in the curtain, bending his head right, then left. Returning to the couch, he lifted the pack of Pall Mall cigarettes from his shirt pocket and withdrew one. He dug into his right pant pocket, pulled out a lighter, and lit the cigarette. He inhaled and blew the smoke out, looking thoughtful.

"I'll tell you this much, and you draw your own conclusions. Barney Robbins owns a boat—a fifty-foot Bayliner cabin cruiser. I was the mechanic and captain for the boat. Him and Kriger used to set up Republican politicians from Washington with prostitutes for fun times out on the ocean in his boat. Well, this one time they had a real important... not a politician, but a politician's son, come down for a good time. Here's the shocker. The kid was Shane Grey."

"You don't mean President Grey's son."

"You got it. He was only nineteen. Now, I just thought his dad was sending him here to celebrate something. But it became pretty obvious the kid was..."

A smile of mixed amusement and contempt formed as he held his hand out and wiggled it.

"I'm gonna be polite: He wasn't straight."

"How did you know this?"

"Hell, the hookers came up to the deck and told Barney he was totally uninterested. They did everything to arouse him. Nothing worked. I heard it all."

"So then what happened?"

"Barney told Kriger and his buddies who came to the Shore Club what happened, and they made all these jokes about the kid. They got real loud. The whole place knew about it. It was the talk of the club for days. And what I heard, the pres got word about it. And he wasn't happy. Fact is, he was fuckin furious."

"How did Grey learn about Kriger insulting his son?"

"A guy from Washington came down here and set the whole thing up. Name was Jack Varney. He had me get ahold of Robbins about the boat and paid for two prostitutes. Me and Richie worked out a deal with Muriel Sandefer for the whores. You prob'ly know about her—the one who owns the brothel near the Shore Club. Jack met Kriger at the club. Jack came back to the club after the boat trip to check on how it went, and Ginnie the barmaid spilled the whole thing to him. She had no idea how serious it was."

Traynor picked the ashtray off the coffee table, held it in his lap, and flicked the ashes off his cigarette.

"Two weeks later, I get a call from Jack, and he's down here and wants to see me. We meet in the lobby of the Hilton. He starts telling me the people at the Shore Club seem like tough characters, and he wonders how much I know about em. I tell him what I say has to be confidential. I talk about how Frankie Campanella—you know, the mobster—I tell him Frankie and his group operate out of there. I say I'm on good terms with these guys."

"Where are you going with this?"

"I'm gettin there. Keep your pants on. So he says, the pres heard about the jokes Kriger told about his son and he was not amused. He said the guy he took his orders from, one of the president's assistants, told him his boss rarely got angry over anything, but he was so pissed about this it scared him."

"So what did Jack want from you?" Palladin asked.

"He kind of hemmed and hawed, but in a round-about way he asked if I would introduce him to one of Frankie's gang—whoever I thought would be best for finding somebody good with a gun to do a favor for the president of the United States. What he was looking for was a hit man, but he didn't say it directly. He did say the guy would get paid.

"I told him to give me a coupla days. I arranged a meeting between Jack and somebody in the gang. After they met, the guy got back to me and said an associate of Frankie's group out of Orlando would come down and fire a weapon into Kriger's house. He asked me to drive the car since I used to be a race car driver. I said okay. I got ahold of Jack and told him everything was set up."

Traynor paused, looking at Palladin. "And that's how it all happened."

Traynor lit another cigarette, and now his hands shook worse than before.

"If you print any of this, you damn well better not say it came from me—or even give any clue that would make somebody suspect you talked to me."

Palladin closed his notepad, put his pen in his pocket, and rose.

"I'll try to be careful," he promised, heading for the door.

"Wait," Traynor said, jumping off the couch. He slinked, limping, to the bay window and carefully peeked through the slit in the curtains.

"Okay, good luck."

Chapter Two

Palladin returned to the *Beacon* office and answered two phone messages. Based on information provided by an attorney on one of the calls, he dashed off a seven-paragraph story about a lawsuit a condo resident planned to file against the homeowners association. The resident claimed negligence when a pool cue fell from the rack on the clubhouse wall and smacked him in the mouth, opening a gash that required six stitches and causing it to swell so badly he could hardly talk. He became the butt of jokes as other residents gossiped that his wife, who had a reputation for aggressiveness, must have popped him. The attorney planned to demand damages for pain and mental anguish caused by acute embarrassment.

The reporter sent his story from the word processor screen to the printer, ambled over to pick it up, and delivered the copy to the city desk. City Editor George Catlin sat with his head buried in a story, making changes with a pencil.

"George, here's a cute one that might grab you," Palladin said, depositing it in the wire rack for incoming stories.

"Yeah? Good."

"You're on deadline, so I'll be quick. What time will you be in tomorrow?"

"Around ten. You need to see me?"

"Yeah. I've got something hot. Really hot. The Rodger Kriger case."

Catlin, fortyish, balding, lifted his head from the copy, leaned back in his swivel chair, and stared at Palladin.

"I'll give you the whole thing tomorrow. I think we'll have to run this past a couple other people. I'm not just talking about Walker."

"Whoa. It has to go higher than the managing editor? You think we need to get Sanders involved?"

"I don't think Harry Walker will want to make this decision on his own. But nobody else has it, so I don't mind waiting. I'll see you in the morning. Any problems with the short, you've got my number. I'm going straight home."

Palladin picked the day's newspaper from a stack along the wall near the city desk as he entered the newsroom. He thumbed through the sections and stopped at the local section to peer at a four-column, double-deck headline: Condo Owner Speaks Softly But Carries Big Stick Against Association. The subhead read: *Attorney Ready to Sue on Cue.*

He smiled.

"Tom, I already talked to Andy Sanders about this," said Catlin from behind the city desk. "He told me to let him know when we're ready and we can meet in his office."

"Okay. Anytime."

Catlin shuffled out the newsroom and left past the elevator to a row of offices, stopping at one with a door that was half frosted glass. The words Editor in Chief were painted in black in the middle. He knocked.

"Come in."

Catlin opened the door and leaned in. "Are you ready to see us, Andy?"

"Yes, sure. I've got two extra chairs, but let's see… it's you, Harry, Tom, and me. We can ask Nancy in the marketing office next door to let us borrow one."

Catlin summoned the others, and they sat down as Catlin got the fourth chair for himself.

"So you've got something big on the Kriger case," Sanders said to Palladin. "What's up?"

"I found out who shot him."

All three men gawked at Palladin, their mouths open.

"Did I hear you right?" said Sanders. "Are you sure?"

"Positive. I got the name from two completely independent sources, neither of whom have anything to do with each other. One is the local FBI agent, and the other… "

"The what?" Harry Walker interrupted.

"That's right. And I confirmed it with one of my longtime sources familiar with the same hoodlums the federal guy had the goods on. Let me start from the beginning."

Palladin recounted the story of how he came to know the name of the hit man who shot Kriger.

"So that much I'm sure of. Now, why would the Mafia want Kriger dead? I don't think they did. I think they did it as a favor to somebody. Somebody very important. A politician. Out of Washington. Are you ready for this?"

"Let's have it," said Sanders.

Palladin paused. "Wallace Grey."

"Oh, come on," Walker uttered, looking disdainful. "Grey wouldn't do something like that. He's such a gentle soul."

"I went to the library last night and spent a couple hours researching some historical stuff on his presidency. He surprised people a few times—got really tough when he was pissed off, and even when somebody did nothing to upset him. But we never heard much about these incidents. The guy who told me about the president's alleged involvement in this is a frightened cocaine addict. What he said made sense to me. A lot of loose ends started coming together. But the guy is unreliable and his story would never be admitted in a court of law."

"Let's get to it," Sanders pressed. "What did he tell you?"

Palladin related the story of the president sending his teenage son for an excursion on the ocean with prostitutes to alter his homosexual tendencies, and Kriger's mockery of him at the Shore Club when it didn't work. His source knew all of this because he was the boat captain, the reporter said.

"The source told me Grey was so incensed that he had the agent who arranged the boat fling see about wreaking vengeance on Kriger and hushing him up, Palladin said. So the agent contacted a mobster at the Shore Club, and paid him cash, and this guy talked to some capo or don. They hired an associate out of Orlando to do the job. Guy named Generoso Gagliardi. And the cocaine addict was a race car driver, so they used him as the getaway driver."

Walker and Catlin looked blankly at each other. Sanders sat with his left elbow on his armrest, his chin resting on his fist, looking down and away. No one said anything for several seconds.

Finally, Walker chimed, "Sounds like Palladin has the shooter nailed down. The rest of it… like he said, it could never get in a courtroom. And if it couldn't get in a courtroom, I don't know how we could put it in our paper."

"What about you, George?" Sanders asked.

"Yeah, I'm inclined to agree. We don't know just what was on that tape where the FBI heard the conversation about the guy coming down from Orlando to shoot a Palm Beach guy. And Tom agreed not to do a story saying he got that info from the FBI man. And he also can't name his other source for the name of the killer. So what does that leave us with? Not much, if you ask me "

"I think I'm in the same camp," Sanders concurred. "The only thing we could do is say two independent sources named the same person as the shooter of Rodger Kriger. I guess we could say the shooter was a Mafia hit man. And maybe we could say one of our sources is a member of a government agency and the other is acquainted with people at the Shore Club, but that kind of puts him in jeopardy. Do you think it would, Tom?"

"Yes, that bothers me. It borders on violating his confidence. And the FBI agent's."

"Yeah," said Sanders. "And I'm not even sure it would be smart to identify the shooter as a Mafia hit man if we're giving hardly any clues about our sources."

He paused and looked back and forth at the other three. "Anybody see it differently?"

"I think you've raised valid points," Palladin conceded. "If we're not going to do any story with this information, let me throw this out. How about if I talk to Robert Gusse—the FBI agent—and see if it's okay if I turn over what he told me to the sheriff's office? I'll also turn over that my other source gave me the same name, and I'll give them the whole story about the president's alleged involvement and the assassination. I'll deal with Detective Lt. Ronald Snopes and insist that if they issue subpoenas, which they should, that I'm notified before any of the other media. Then we can do an exclusive story or stories on that."

"Hmm." Sanders' face brightened. "That sounds like a good way to handle it. What do you guys think?"

The editors looked at each other.

"I'm for it," said Walker.

"Let's do it," Catlin echoed.

"Great work, Tom," said Sanders, rising. "Let's hope we can get a big exclusive out of this."

"The only thing that could throw a monkey wrench into this plan is if Snopes sits on the information and does nothing with it," Palladin worried.

"You don't think he'd be that dirty, do you?" said Sanders.

"He's in bed with the state attorney's office—Bosworth and the ex-prosecutor, Jim Scraponia. He's smart enough to know Hecher never committed that crime. There's just no evidence, and he understands that. And he's familiar enough with Hecher to know he's not a killer. These guys wanted Hecher convicted, no matter what. And they don't want to change that. But now we've got solid evidence that somebody else did it, and we've got that person identified. This will be a test of just how far these guys are willing to go to subvert justice."

———————————

Palladin called Agent Gusse.

"Doin great. I'd like to come over and see you. I have some new stuff I want to run past you. Yeah, tomorrow at two would work well. See you then."

Palladin wound through the city streets to the small federal building.

"I got the same name of the shooter from a longtime source of mine—a guy who sort of hangs around the fringe of the mobsters at the Shore Club. But I got a lot more than that. A guy associated with him told me a fantastic story, one that's hard to believe but makes sense to me because the pieces of the puzzle start fitting together."

Palladin related the story told by Traynor and said the *Beacon* editors had decided to turn the information over to the sheriff's department and, assuming subpoenas would be issued, the paper would get a scoop.

Gusse said he, too, would turn in his information.

Lieutenant Snopes told Palladin he would review the materials and "take them under advisement."

Gusse visited Snopes two days later, left an envelope with the information, and attached his card. Days passed, then a week, then two weeks.

Palladin called and was told the lieutenant was unavailable. The reporter left a message. The next afternoon, he called again, and left another message. He left five messages over the next ten days, none of them returned.

Palladin called Gusse. "Have you heard from Lieutenant Snopes?"

"Not a thing," said Gusse. "How about you?"

"He's not returning my messages."

"Guess he's not interested. Nothing I can do about it. I've done my job. They're transferring me out of organized crime to economic crime. I'll be moving to Miami. Good luck with this."

Chapter Three

Jeremy Mancbaum used the same basic argument before Magistrate Lorna Stowe of U.S. District Court in Fort Lauderdale that he waged in trying to persuade state courts to grant Mitt Hecher a new trial: The defendant's attorney was woefully incompetent.

But Mancbaum refined it, imparting a logic that Magistrate Stowe perceived as razor sharp for its clarity and compelling: Had Alonzo Seppish successfully objected to the jury hearing the contents of a letter outlining the four-page confession that Hecher supposedly had written, there would have been no conviction, the attorney argued. The letter, he said, contained details that questioned DeWitt Crimshaw's veracity.

"The jury would have had to rely mainly on the testimony of one witness: George Demarco, convicted of three murders and facing the electric chair. Are we to believe that the jury would have found this man credible enough to convict Mister Hecher based on what Demarco said about him? It's preposterous."

A new attorney represented the state attorney's office. As his predecessors had done, he argued that Seppish allowed the letter to be read as a "reasonable strategy" to show the "absurdity" of the confession's existence.

Mancbaum noticed that Ms. Stowe appeared to be listening intently. But she revealed nothing about her thoughts. She announced that she would issue a ruling at an undetermined date.

Shortly afterward, Judge Timothy Schultz wrote a letter to the Florida Probation and Parole Commission.

"As the judge who presided over the case of the State of Florida versus Mitt Hecher, I am writing to inform you that I have from the beginning had serious doubts about the verdict," Schultz wrote. "A salient reason is that I found the testimony of the four primary prosecution witnesses to be highly questionable. Another is that this trial was televised, and I think it affected the jury in ways detrimental to fairness for the defendant.

"I would, therefore, have no objection if the commission found that justice would be best served by releasing Mitt Hecher from incarceration. I would emphasize, however, that I believe Mister Hecher received a fair trial."

Subsequently, the commission recommended that Governor Ronald Montez and the Cabinet consider a pardon for Hecher.

Magistrate Stowe set about reviewing the case with a fine-toothed comb. After a few weeks, she recommended to U.S. District Judge Norbert Ridder that Hecher be released from prison and a new trial scheduled. She called the trial a "case of justice gone awry." Seppish's defense strategies were "abominable" and "incredibly ill-conceived," she said. And she said Judge Schultz should have delayed the trial to allow Seppish time to recuperate from surgery.

The next step in the process was for Judge Ridder to act on the magistrate's recommendation. He would rule either to grant a new trial or to deny one.

Dear Mitt,

I'm going to be brief because it's gotten painful for me to write. I'm enclosing a letter to the editor that the Kriger family sent to the Palm Beach Beacon. It made me angry. I don't think they care whether you are guilty. They want everyone to forget about you. They don't want to find the real killer.

I'm afraid to be hopeful, but the actions of Judge Schultz and the federal magistrate give us more reason than ever.

Pauley is doing better. Nobody dares to poke fun of him anymore—he's shown a couple of the boys how good he is at karate.

Think of you always, darling.

Love you,

Diane

Hecher sat at the desk in his cell and unfolded the newspaper clipping:

We feel that, in light of recent recommendations by members of the courts regarding the future of Mitt Hecher, it is time for us to break our silence. The State Attorney's Office has shown no interest in following up on new leads or holding a new trial. We think that justice demands all new information be investigated thoroughly, no matter what path is the ultimate outcome.

For a dozen years, I and my children have been continually run through an emotional wringer as Mister Hecher makes appeal after appeal, insisting his trial was unfair and he should be granted a new trial or released. The news media have consistently favored him in his efforts. Yet hardly a word has been uttered about the devastation all of this has wreaked on us, the victims.

Short of a new investigation by State Attorney Donald Bosworth, we intend to conduct a blitz aimed at finding whoever is guilty of the murder of our husband and father.

The letter was signed by Jan Kriger and her six children, three of whom had different last names from having married.

Hecher placed the clipping back in the envelope and reread Diane's letter. His eyes focused on "painful for me to write." It's getting worse, he thought, staring into space and wondering how much longer she had to live.

For the next two days, he felt disconsolate, canceling a tennis match and staying to himself in the dining hall. Then he went to the office room and sat at a typewriter.

Dear Diane,

I feel so helpless that you're going through this pain and I can do nothing to help. Yes, I'm stuck in prison, but my situation is far better than yours. Don't be shy about asking people to help you with cooking, cleaning, etc. Pauley is at an age now that he can help around the house and do things to make your life easier. I'm glad to hear that he has control of the situation at school.

You are right, Diane, that the Krigers don't want to find the real killer. That letter to the newspaper was phony. Mrs. Kriger and her oldest daughter want Bosworth to open a new trial because they're afraid the Clemency Board might release me. When Judge Schultz wrote to the Board saying he would have no problem with that, the Krigers suddenly decided they needed to act. Why did they wait until now? They showed how they really felt when they urged Governor Garner and his Cabinet not to give me clemency. And they know that if I get a new trial, Bosworth will do everything in his power do get me convicted again— twist the facts, get false testimony, invent evidence, whatever he has to do.

Why do the Krigers want to keep me in prison? Because then the murder of their husband and father is resolved. If I'm exonerated, that means the killer is unknown, and that is too difficult for them to accept. They want finality. At least I think that's what Jan Kriger's motive is. But I'm beginning to wonder if she doesn't have a more sinister reason. Maybe she has something to hide. It's possible.

They wail about the anguish they've gone through. But even though they have no reason to think I'm guilty, they care not a whit that I'm spending all of these years in prison. And if they knew about your condition, and the problems that

Pauley faces with his father a convict, I'm sure it wouldn't make a bit of difference to them.

They bitch that the media have been biased in favor of me. Diane, you and I and my attorneys together have read every newspaper article and heard every radio and television broadcast about my case. There hasn't been a single instance where I've been shown any favoritism. In fact, that reporter who used to be with the Miami Gazette wrote a couple of stories praising those scumbags who testified against me when they and that crooked jailer hoodwinked him. Except for those, all the media have done is factually report what has happened in my case over the years, never taking any sides. I guess the Kriger family just wants the media to ignore the case and not report anything new that happens with it.

I hope we don't have to wait too long for this U.S. District judge, Norbert Ridder, to decide whether to accept the recommendation of that magistrate, Lorna Stowe, to give me a new trial. Mancbaum said he was a hard ass, so it's a long shot. But if he does, I think Bosworth might be less likely to pull some hanky panky than if he ordered the trial himself. This Stowe woman, she's a doll—the only one in the whole judicial system who's seen this case for what it is and shown some common sense.

I'll be talking to you on the phone soon, sweetheart.

Love you, babe.

Mitt.

Two weeks later, Hecher called Diane.

"Hi hon. How are you feeling?"

"Well, not too bad at the moment. In fact, I was just getting ready to call you. The pain has let up a lot. It started turning around right after we last talked. See what an effect you have on me? I can move around easier now."

"Oh, wow, that's great to hear."

"Yes. Sometimes this disease spontaneously goes away, you know. I don't want to get any false hopes up, but it's possible that's happening."

"Oh my God, would that be wonderful? I've been meditating real hard on it. Trying to give that spontaneity a boost with a little mind over matter."

Diane laughed. "I got your letter. You're so clever. You read between the lines of that letter to the editor Jan Kriger wrote and saw just what she was up to. I didn't see that. I do now. There's been two articles in the *Beacon* since then. Let me read just a little what they say:

'The widow and her oldest daughter met with Bosworth recently'—
the meeting was before the letter-to-the-editor was published—'and
told him again that they thought Hecher was guilty. Jim Scraponia,
the man who prosecuted Hecher, was at the meeting and agreed with
the Krigers.'"

"Of course," Hecher said. "The Krigers and the state attorney's
office are working hand-in-hand to keep me locked up."

"Now, listen to this. Another article came out a few days later,
and the reporter wrote that the daughter said, and this is a quote, 'her
family continues to think that Mitt Hecher shot her father, and
therefore he should not be retried.'"

"You gotta be kidding," Hecher gasped. "So that letter-to-the-
editor where they called for reopening the investigation no matter
what the outcome was a lie, a bald-faced lie. They just wanted to put
one over on the public. They're just as dishonest and conniving as
Bosworth and Scraponia."

"Oh Mitt, at least the stuff you did in your rowdy days, you were
open about it."

"Yeah, too open, I guess. Well, we just have to keep on hoping.
Let me talk to Pauley. Is he there?"

"Yes. He just took the garbage out. He's being wonderful,
helping me in every way he can. Just a minute, I'll get him."

Hecher heard her calling, "Pauley, your dad's on the phone."

"Hi Dad," he said in a few seconds, panting.

"Hey, big guy. You sound out of breath."

"Yeah. I ran from the dumpster across the street. But I'm in
good shape because my karate keeps me that way."

"How is that coming?"

"I've won two medals."

"Wow. Oh, that's great. I'm proud of you. The kids at school
giving you any more trouble?"

Pauley giggled, and Hecher detected a shyness that he liked.
"Not really. They found out I wasn't going to stand for it. I have a lot
of friends."

"Terrific. How are your grades?"

"I'm doing good. I like my subjects."

"Pauley, your mother told me you were really helping her out a
lot. That's very good of you, Pauley. She needs you. I hope you
continue being so unselfish. You're the man in the family. I hope I

can come home not too far in the future, but until then, you're all your mother has. I'm glad she can rely on you. You're a good son, Pauley."

"Thanks, Dad. I'll do the best I can."

"Take care, Pauley. Let me talk to Diane, will you."

"Sure."

"Okay, I'll have to give up the phone."

"Maybe it won't be too long."

"We just have to keep the faith, babe. Take care, now. Love you loads."

"Bye, darling. I love you forever."

———————

Hecher headed toward the dining hall, an extra bounce in his step. He shot his hands out and away in the manner of karate chops, and did a little leap, kicking his left leg sideways.

"Mitt," Lannon called as he hobbled up from behind almost at a run. Hecher stopped and turned.

"What the hell are you doin," Lannon said, "fixin to fight somebody?"

Hecher let out an embarrassed laugh.

"No, I'm just feeling pretty damned good. I talked to Diane, and she's doing a lot better. She's been in such awful pain. It's really been eatin at me."

"Well, I've got some good news, too. Let's go through the line and sit down. I'll give you the scoop."

They took their trays of macaroni and cheese, green beans, hamburger patty, and fruit jello to a table.

"So here's what's happened," said Lannon. "That bitch I picked up with those guys—the one who shot the cop—she confessed."

"How does that help you?"

"That ain't all she did. She told the district attorney for that little county that I gave her and her friends a lift to the border and I had nothing to do with killing the cop and they forced me to try and escape."

"Ooh. Now that is good news. What happens next?"

"They're going to recommend to the parole board that I be released. It may take a while yet, but I've got something to look forward to."

"When's your next parole hearing?"

"Not for another year-and-a-half. But hell, I been locked up going on nine years now, so I guess I can deal with that. Meanwhile, I've got to keep my record clean."

Lannon put his fork on his plate and finished chewing his bite of macaroni. His face brightened.

"Do good works," he said. "I was raised a Protestant and that's a Catholic thing. Doing good works will get you to heaven. I think I need to convert." He chuckled.

"I'm not so sure," Hecher differed, squeezing a packet of ketchup onto his hamburger. "I grew up a Catholic, and I've been doing good works my entire twelve years behind bars. Perfect record. See what it's got me? I think the Protestants have it right. You can't earn your way to heaven. Faith is what gets you to heaven. It hasn't gotten me there yet, but things are happening. I'm not giving up. And maybe we can get out together. I still have faith."

"Hi, Mom. Hey, it's only one-thirty. You usually call in the evening."

"Mitt, I think you're going to want to sit down," Maria Hecher said softly.

"Huh? Why, what's the matter? Is Diane in the hospital or something?"

Maria didn't reply.

Mitt hesitated, then continued in a slow, deep voice. "Oh, no. Mom. You're not telling me…"

"Diane died at ten-thirty this morning. We took her to Hospice just two days ago. That was Tuesday. Pauley called me Sunday because she couldn't get out of bed. She had him call one of her girlfriends, who came over and took care of her until I could get there. I caught a plane and got to West Palm Beach after midnight and took a cab to her house. First thing next morning, I called her doctor. A visiting nurse came, and after consulting with the doctor, they had an ambulance take her to Hospice."

Mitt couldn't speak. He sat in a lounge chair in the prison intake center.

"I can't… " His voice trembled.

"It's okay, son. Take your time. I'll wait. Whenever you're ready."

Mitt put the phone in his lap, bent forward with elbows on thighs, his head hanging above the linoleum-covered floor, and sobbed. Racking, heaving spasms surged through his body as the pent-up pain of dealing year after year with never-ending disappointments, of coping with the horrendous conditions of prison while feeling helpless to help as his wife suffered and his son struggled, burst through the floodgates.

It was almost two minutes before his emotions were spent. He picked up the phone.

"Mom," he quavered, "it was all my fault."

"Mitt, don't say that. What are you talking about?"

"If I hadn't been such a bad actor before I met Diane, the state attorney's office wouldn't have had it in for me, and they wouldn't have been able to pin this on me even if they had. And I wouldn't be here and I could have taken care of Diane and Pauley."

"Mitt, dear, the past is over. You had some growing up to do, and you did it a long time ago. Bosworth and Scraponia are doing everything to keep you in prison because they're evil people. It's a good thing I'm not a karate expert, because I'm so angry at those two I'd probably do something that'd put me behind bars, too. Mitt, Diane was suffering. It's over now."

"How is Pauley taking it?"

"Naturally, he's broken up. He's a wonderful boy, and he loved his mother dearly. But he's going to get over it. He knew this was coming. And of course, we were preparing for it."

"But I just talked to her less than two weeks ago and her condition had suddenly improved. She wasn't in near as much pain, and she thought she might be recovering."

"That happens sometimes with terminal illnesses. People rally just before the end, and it causes false hopes."

"Yeah. I sure had my hopes up."

"I'm taking Pauley to live with me in Albuquerque. He'll have to adjust to new schoolmates, but he has new-found confidence with his karate, and I'm sure he won't have any trouble."

"That makes me feel so much better, knowing Pauley will be secure and well-cared for and loved."

"Mitt, Diane said something just before she died. It was the last thing she said."

Maria paused.

"Tell Mitt I love him."

Chapter Four

Six weeks after recommending a new trial for Mitt Hecher, U.S. Magistrate Lorna Stowe set bail of $150,000 pending the trial. However, U.S. District Judge Norbert Ridder nullified her order and required Hecher to remain in prison while he determined whether the convicted murderer should be retried.

Seven months later, he still had not decided, and Mancbaum issued a request for a status hearing. While conceding that a federal judge would have a lot on his docket, Mancbaum said it still seemed far too long to render a decision.

"I am hoping that the judge will see fit to convene a conference of the attorneys for both sides so we can assist him in making a determination," Mancbaum told the *Beacon*.

Ridder denied the request for a hearing.

Three months later, Susan Strickland, the attorney who assisted in the clemency hearing before Governor Garner, wrote a lengthy letter to the new governor, Ronald Montez, asking that he appoint a special prosecutor to review the case. She accused the office of State Attorney Bosworth of inducing the main witnesses against Mitt Hecher to commit perjury in order to gain a conviction.

"The office of the state attorney is guilty of suborning four primary prosecution witnesses in its determination to have the jury return a verdict of guilty of murder in the first degree against Mitt Hecher," Strickland wrote. She alluded to the recantation by three of the witnesses, including DeWitt Crimshaw's admission that he had forged Hecher's letter confessing to the murder.

The long delay by Ridder in making a decision convinced Hecher that the judge had no intention of awarding him a new trial. He decided to preempt the judge with a public announcement, in the form of a letter to his attorney, predicting the negative ruling and criticizing the delay.

"U.S. District Court Judge Norbert Ridder is delaying his ruling on whether to grant me a new trial as a way of using time to allow the public's interest in the case to wane," he wrote. "The judge has no intention of ruling in my favor. His mind was made up from the beginning."

After eleven months, Strickland asked the Eleventh Circuit Court of Appeals in Atlanta to force Ridder to make a decision.

A month later, one year after he had received the request for a new trial, Judge Ridder issued a ruling.

After reviewing thousands of pages of transcripts and pleadings, I have come to a decision. I am convinced that the jurors in this trial considered all of the evidence before deciding, correctly, that the defendant, Mitt Hecher, was guilty. Therefore, his petition for a retrial is denied.

Ridder also wrote: *Mister Hecher was familiar with particular aspects of the murder that could only be known to someone who was at the scene when it happened.* He wrote further that attorney Seppish never asked for a postponement so he could recover from illness.

Asked about his supposed familiarity with murder details, Hecher told the *Beacon* on the phone, "What in God's name is that man talking about? When did I talk about details of the murder—or anything about the murder? I didn't even testify at the trial. I didn't talk to police about the murder because I knew absolutely nothing about it. This judge is flat-out biased. He just plain lied. He was determined I would stay in prison.

"What does it say about our judicial system when a man so dishonest occupies a position as important as a judgeship in a U.S. District Court? I fully expected this ruling. I predicted it. But I didn't think the judge would stoop to making stuff up like this."

He sighed, then added with a lilt, "You know what? I'm relieved this is finally out of the way. We had to go through the motions with this judge. Now we can move on. I still have hope. My attorney, Susan Strickland, is going to appeal this to the Eleventh Circuit Court of Appeals. We're not done yet."

Jean Wade, the oldest Kriger daughter, spoke to the same reporter.

"I'm happy with the ruling, but I expect another appeal. This thing just keeps evolving. Our family would so much like to put it to rest."

Ms. Wade proved prescient. Three months later, Strickland filed a brief with the appeals court in Atlanta, again arguing ineffective counsel for Hecher as the reason he deserved a new trial.

The state attorney's office countered the argument with its usual assertion that Seppish employed a strategy which, while perhaps unwise in the opinions of many attorneys, nonetheless was valid.

Oral arguments followed. The lack of credibility of witnesses and their recantation was regurgitated with the same gray contention that the defense counsel was ill. It was the same concoction that no judge had deemed palatable in the long line of appeals.

If District Judge Ridder took a long time to rule, his response was expeditious compared to that of the Atlanta appeals court. Almost one year and eight months passed from the time of the filing to the court's decision, in early spring 1991.

The three-judge panel, sitting as the nation's second-highest court, denied the appeal of Hecher's conviction.

Strickland said she remained convinced Hecher was not guilty and was unjustly tried. After reviewing the opinion, she said, she and the other attorneys would decide whether to appeal to the United States Supreme Court.

But Florida had a new governor. As Hecher's attorneys had expected, Governor Ronald Montez never acted on the Parole Commission's recommendation for a clemency hearing. Nor did the governor answer Strickland's request that he appoint a special prosecutor.

In November 1990, Floridians voted to replace Montez with Layton Childers. He took office in January 1991. After allowing him time to settle in, Mancbaum and Larbin filed a request for a hearing with the governor and the Cabinet for clemency. In such a hearing, they would sit as the Board of Executive Clemency.

In mid-July, the clemency board agreed to hold a hearing in December. Aides in the governor's office asked the staff working for the Parole Commission to review the case and the bases for Hecher's request for release from prison. After interviewing the concerned parties, including the Kriger family and Hecher, the staff would turn its findings over to the commission. A recommendation then would be made to the clemency board whether to grant clemency.

———————

"Whew, Gary, you were all over the court today. You're getting good on that piece of lumber. You had me chasing. I've never seen you play like that."

"I wanted to wait till the match was over to tell you. I'm outa here."

Hecher's mouth dropped open. "You're shittin me. For real?"

"I got the word yesterday afternoon. The Parole Board looked at the confession of the woman who shot the patrolman and decided to release me. You been getting more disappointments from the courts so I didn't want to be jumpin for joy while you were feelin crappy."

"Oh, hell no. I'm happy for you, brother. Besides, things are looking a little more optimistic for me."

"What's happening?"

"I just found out the clemency board's going to give me a hearing with the governor and the Cabinet in six months. The Parole Commission has to first do a lot of checking to see if they want to recommend I get released."

"Oh, wow, that sounds like your best chance yet."

"Yeah. So when are they letting you go?"

"My sister is picking me up tomorrow at eleven. She's divorced and living alone in Georgia, near Athens where we grew up. I'll stay with her till I can get... I was going to say, get on my feet, but that'll be a little hard to do." He laughed. "That peg leg is going to keep me from jobs like construction. And the prison record will be an even bigger handicap."

They walked from the courts to the cell building and stopped at the juncture where their wards went in different directions.

"Gary, listen, write and give me your address. And when I get out of here, we'll meet up."

"For sure, buddy."

"I hope I'm not here too much longer, cuz it's going to be pretty dismal around here with you gone," Hecher said. "Well, that's life in the big house." He shrugged.

"I got a feeling the Lone Ranger is going to ride again real soon."

Lannon and Hecher stood facing each other.

"I owe my life to you, brother," Lannon said. "I wouldn't have survived."

"And you made life locked up tolerable, good buddy."

Lannon grasped Hecher's hand.

"See you soon, Kemosabe."

"Hecher."

He looked up from the novel he was reading, Graham Greene's *The Power and the Glory*, and dropped his feet off the desk. He stared at the guard standing outside the cell gate.

"Yeah, Sarg?"

"Tomorrow morning at ten, be at the superintendent's office."

"Okay, sure. What's up?"

"They never told me. I'm just supposed to give you the message."

"Righto. Thanks."

Lieutenant Andy Weller's office door was open. The inmate hadn't seen the affable prison official for a while, and it struck Hecher how the years were taking a toll on the man who treated him favorably. His midriff always was ample, but now it was beginning to spill over his belt. His hair, once blond-white, had turned mostly white.

"Hi Hecher. Grab a chair. Haven't had occasion to run into you lately. I did hear about the passing of your wife. I'm awfully sorry about that. I wish there was something we could have done for you."

"Oh, thanks, Lieutenant. I appreciate that."

Weller turned to a small table to his right, pressed a button, and spoke into a microphone.

"Sergeant Miller, Lieutenant Weller here. Would you send the two parole officers to my office, please? Thanks."

He pushed the button again and faced Hecher.

"These two gentlemen are on the premises, talking with various inmates who will eventually come up for parole. They just wanted to chat with you for a minute or two. It's more or less a formality, a matter of routine."

Two men, one about Weller's age and the other perhaps fifteen years younger, clad in civilian attire, arrived at the door.

"Come in, gentlemen. I've got a couple extra chairs here. Anybody want coffee?"

The two declined, the older one saying they wouldn't be long. They introduced themselves and shook hands with Hecher.

"We're officers with the Florida Parole Commission," the older officer said. "I'll be asking you a few questions. My partner has been a corrections officer for more than a decade and is now learning the ropes as a parole officer. Now, Mister Hecher… would you rather be called Mitt?"

"Sure. Mitt is fine."

"Okay, Mitt. I've reviewed your prison record, both here and at Raiford, and it's quite impressive. Sterling, as a matter of fact. Not only have you not had disciplinary issues in your thirteen years of incarceration, but you have distinguished yourself in several ways. I'd like to ask you if you've thought about what you will do when you're released."

Hecher was taken aback. *When I'm released? Doesn't this guy know I'm serving a minimum of twenty-five years? Why does he have that hint of a smile? Is that sarcasm, or does he mean something by it?* He took a deep breath.

"Well, I haven't had much reason to think about that, to be honest. My attorneys have made twenty-five appeals for a new trial, and we've been turned down every time. You try to keep up hope, but my possibilities have just about disappeared, and I've got a lot of years left to serve."

"I understand what you're saying. But you never know what's going to happen. I think you should be thinking about what you will do on the outside, just in case. Do you have family members who can support you in the beginning?"

This is strange.

"Yes. My mother lives in Albuquerque and my son Pauley lives with her. And my brother Dan lives there, too. He's just getting started in the computer business, and I've become knowledgeable about computers through my course here at Avon Park. There aren't very many people who have that knowledge, and he told me that if I'm released, I've got a job waiting."

"Do you think you would want to settle down to a quiet life like that? It'd be a lot different than the one you were leading before you were sent to prison."

"I'd already changed by the time I went to jail in Palm Beach County. My wife Diane did that to me. Now she's gone. But the worst thing I could do to her and for our son would be to go back to my old ways. No, I'm past that forever."

"Excellent. All right. Well, you've told us what we need to know. Best of luck."

The parole officer extended his hand, which Hecher grasped. The officer noted his nonplussed look. Hecher thought he appeared eager to say more.

———————

In November, the Parole Commission issued its recommendation on clemency. The verdict: The governor and Cabinet, acting in tandem as the Board of Executive Clemency, should commute the remainder of Mitt Hecher's sentence.

The news media trumpeted the startling development, and attorney Susan Strickland optimistically spoke of "justice finally within reach."

But one of the board's options was to reject the recommendation and leave Hecher to serve at least twelve more years. Otherwise, it could commute those twelve years or grant a pardon, and release the prisoner. Three of the six Cabinet members would have to join the governor in voting for a commutation of his sentence.

Strickland told the media that Hecher felt optimistic because parole officers had recently asked him if he had made plans for his life upon gaining freedom. He'd never been asked that before.

The December hearing date arrived. Another attorney, who was not on the state attorney's staff when the case was prosecuted, presented that office's usual argument: Every court which had reviewed the case found there was no reason to grant Hecher a new trial.

The youngest of the Kriger children, Randy, rose from his seat in the Tallahassee courtroom next to his mother and four of his sisters, and provided testimony wrought with emotion but devoid of factual argument. He spoke of how, at age eleven, he watched his father bleed on the floor and how he missed him. He also talked of the fear he felt for years when the doorbell rang, and the unease at walking by the windows inside the family's house at night.

Randy said he remembered the videotape of a television documentary three years previous that showed Hecher's son telling his dad during a prison visit that he hoped his father would be out in time to celebrate the boy's birthday.

"But I'll never be able to see my dad again," Randy bemoaned.

He didn't say how that had anything to do with whether Hecher was guilty. He only insisted that the convicted man was, indeed, guilty and should be kept in prison. But he offered no facts to support Hecher's guilt.

The Krigers' neighbor, Milton Gunder, had a different opinion.

"This idea of the state attorney's prosecutors that Mitt Hecher meant to shoot my son Bobby over a drug deal and mistakenly went to the Krigers' house is nonsense," Gunder said. "Bobby didn't even know Hecher. He didn't know anything about him. And these two South Americans he had this drug deal with never bothered him. I think this shooting was done by a professional hit man for a mobster who had it in for Kriger because he was seeing the guy's lady friend. We know that was happening."

Henry Murray, who spent considerable time investigating the shooting for the Palm Beach Police Department, also testified that he thought it was a professional hit, but said he didn't know who did it or why.

"Law enforcement was under a lot of pressure to solve the murder," Murray said. "We had to name somebody. And it's eating at my conscience, because I know Mitt Hecher didn't do that shooting. It's wrong that he should be sitting in prison for something he's not guilty of."

Hecher's four attorneys had conferred to determine which should argue their case. Samuel Jackson of Gainesville, who had joined the team in the later years and was a friend of Strickland, felt she could deliver an emotional punch that would sway the board members their way. She wanted the job, and her colleagues gave it to her.

It was Strickland's turn to testify.

"Eleven years ago, when I was a judicial aide for the Fifth District Court of Appeal, I was assigned to write the ruling denying Mitt Hecher's appeal for a new trial," she began. "I took the case home that night, studied it, and concluded that this man was not guilty. I told my boss that I could not in good conscience draft that ruling. Someone else did. I went on to become an appellate attorney in Orlando and argued successfully for the death penalty in sixteen cases. If I had thought Mitt Hecher were guilty, I would have had no hesitation in writing a denial of his appeal.

"The word of what I had done got around and eventually reached Mister Hecher. In 1985, after the state Supreme Court had rejected yet another of his appeals, he wrote letters to me in desperation, asking for my help. I agreed to, and my firm supported me, paying the bills. I never talked to my client on the phone, never visited him in prison, never even read media accounts of his case. I didn't want to be influenced.

"My law firm has allowed me to put its name on the line in the interest of justice. I put my own job on the line back in 1981. There is no way I would do that if I had one iota of doubt about this man's innocence. I have looked deeply into my heart and mind. I don't know Mitt Hecher. I have never met him, never spoken with him. All I know is there is no evidence whatsoever that under the influence of drugs and alcohol, he mistakenly went to the next-door house where he thought the person he meant to shoot was staying, and shot the wrong man. What evidence there is—plenty of it—is that Mitt Hecher was framed. I'll repeat that. Mitt Hecher was flat-out framed."

The room was stonily silent, save for the background droning of the air conditioning system. No one stirred. Governor Childers and the Cabinet members looked at Strickland as if hypnotized.

"The real murderer remains on the loose, and he must be asking, 'Why should I care about the law when the people who run the legal system are willing to let a man rot in prison for something he didn't do? It's all a big joke.' And you can bet he's laughing.

"It is in your hands whether this travesty of justice will continue, or, after fourteen years, finally be corrected. I implore you to do the right thing.

"Thank you for your time."

The hearing officer announced that the hearing was adjourned. He gave no indication when the board would rule.

Six weeks later, in February 1992, Governor Childers and the Cabinet, sitting as the clemency board, met again, this time to make a final decision on the fate of Mitt Hecher. The meeting was brief.

"It is the unanimous decision of the Florida Board of Executive Clemency," the chairman read, "to commute the remaining eleven years of the twenty-five years in Mitt Hecher's sentence to the time already served."

Mancbaum, Larbin, Strickland, and Jackson broke into beaming smiles and reached past each other to grasp one another's hands. Strickland's eyes glistened.

"We looked at a number of factors before arriving at this decision, but the critical one was this: The motive for the shooting as delineated by the prosecution—that the shooter mistakenly went to the house next to that of his intended victim—quite simply overlapped all limits of believability. We don't know who shot Rodger Kriger, or why. That is the reason we are not overturning the conviction and granting a pardon, but only a commutation of sentence."

The four attorneys for Hecher sat back in their seats.

"The board further rules that Mister Hecher may not reside within the state of Florida for a period of one year. Additionally, he may never carry firearms on his person. If he violates those conditions, the commutation may be reversed and he may be returned to prison."

Looking stern, Strickland whispered to Jackson, "I'm going to make sure that doesn't happen."

"At this time, the session is adjourned."

A guard looked through the bars of Hecher's cell door, wearing a big smile.

"Hecher, the superintendent wants to see you. I think you'll want to get there right away."

"Mitt," Lieutenant Weller sang, beaming from ear to ear, "it's finally happened. You're outa here. I got the phone call a half-hour ago. The governor and Cabinet commuted your sentence."

Hecher stared at him, unable to speak. Weller stepped forward and draped his arm around the shorter man's shoulders.

"That's all right. You don't have to say anything. You'll be released the day after tomorrow. One of your attorneys, Susan Strickland, will pick you up. Now, why don't you just go back to your cell and let all your emotions out? Go on."

Head lowered to hide the tear spilling out of his eye, Hecher thrust his hand out and grasped Weller's. Then he pivoted and walked briskly to his cell, where he sat on his bed and wept.

"Congratulations, Mitt," Tom Palladin said on the phone the next day. "I understand you're headed to Albuquerque. I'd like to talk to you after you get there. Can I have the phone number?"

"Sure." He recited the number.

"I'll be calling you soon."

No sooner had Hecher returned to his cell than a guard summoned him to the phone again.

"Hi Mitt," said the pert female voice. "We finally get to talk. I imposed a rule on myself that I wouldn't speak or meet with you until the case was resolved."

"This can only be Susan Strickland. I can't believe you did it. I'm eternally grateful to you. And to the others—Jeremy Mancbaum and Rick Larbin. And Sam Jackson and Adam Sullivan helped out. You all never gave up."

"Well, it's over now. Lieutenant Weller told me you were planning to go to your family in Albuquerque. You've been locked away for fifteen years. I didn't like the idea of your entering society by yourself and having to deal with everyday issues. It'd be like entering a foreign country and not speaking the language. I have too much invested in you to let something go wrong and have you end up in jail again. So I advised Weller that I'd drive you to your home. I'm ready for a vacation anyway and I've never been out West. I'd love to get a look at the scenery."

"Terrific. I think it's a great idea. It'll give me a chance to breathe real deep."

"See you in two days."

Chapter Five

The gates of darkness opened, and Mitt Hecher, carrying a suitcase, walked into the bright light of a crisp February day. The sun's rays, the now ex-convict's gleaming white shirt, pants, and shoes, and his beaming smile synthesized into a dazzle like a believer's vision of paradise. In fact, Hecher felt as though he had emerged from hell and entered into heaven in the twinkling of an eye.

Standing in front of him, wearing a beige, knee-length skirt, violet blouse, and sand-colored heels, was a woman he judged to be his age. He'd never seen her.

"We've never met," he said, putting the suitcase down, "but I'm sure I know you. I'm Mitt Hecher."

"I know. I'm Susan Strickland."

They embraced.

"There's nothing I can do to thank you enough," Hecher said, his voice trembling. He worked to control the quiver in his lips.

Strickland smiled.

"Yes, there is. Once we drive outside these walls, you can make sure you stay outside them. You can use your new-found freedom wisely and do nothing that would get you tossed back behind bars."

"I can promise you that's not going to happen."

"Because we both know there are some people who would like nothing better than to see you screw up. And if there's anything they can do to facilitate that, they will."

"You got that right. The clemency board didn't need to order me out of the state. There was no way I was going to stick around."

"So what are we waiting for? My car is in the nearest lot. Can you carry your piece of luggage that far, or shall I drive up?"

Hecher let out a belly laugh. "If I couldn't carry that bag a couple hundred feet, I wouldn't have survived two days behind bars—at Raiford for sure."

He lifted the piece as though it were an Easter basket, the sinews in his forearm rippling.

With Strickland driving her 1989 black Camaro, they headed out the gates in front of the prosaic, one-story intake center. Hecher looked up at the roll of barbed wire that had mesmerized him when a squad car carried him to this place nine years before. The prison wall disappeared behind the passing car, and he didn't look back.

They drove down the prison entrance road to the main highway, then followed a network of state and federal highways until they reached Florida's Turnpike going north, and in a few hours were moving west across the Panhandle. She wanted to know what prison life was like, and he told her story after gruesome story about the violence that was a routine part of existence at the Raiford facility. She listened with eyes wide.

"Wow," she finally said, breaking her silence. "I guess the public has no idea what goes on behind those walls. Even I didn't realize it was that bad."

"It's a nightmare."

"Speaking of night, we're in a different time zone now. It's an hour earlier. But we've only stopped once, and I'd just as soon not drive after dark. So why don't we pull off the next exit we see a motel and eat something and stay for the night? Then we can get an early start tomorrow."

"Sounds good to me."

He paused. "Avon Park wasn't nearly as bad as Raiford. Much more controlled, so you weren't in constant danger. The inmates weren't as violent, either. And they offered classes to keep you occupied and stimulate your mind, and also to help you find employment when you got out. At Raiford, it was anarchy. The inmates ran the place. You had to protect yourself any way you could. Prisoners who became friends looked out for each other."

"Sounds like the state Legislature needs to step in and make some reforms at that place."

"Are you kidding? They're politicians. They don't give a damn about what happens to the people in these dungeons. They only care about getting elected. And they know that all most of the voters want is revenge for what criminals have done. Punishment is all they're interested in, and the worse the prison conditions, the better. Rehabilitation is a bleeding-heart liberal idea that makes them seethe. So these guys enter prison with a chip on their shoulder, and by the time they re-enter society, there's a big solid block of wood on it. And that's what these simple-minded tough-on-crime fanatics don't get. Their attitudes just cause crime to get worse."

Strickland frowned, and Hecher wondered about the meaning of her pensive look as she kept her eyes straight ahead on the highway.

"What these people need is to hear the stories of the guys who land behind bars and what got them there," he said. "I don't have much excuse. My wife loved me. My mother loves me. My son loves me. And I love them. I guess I just always had to prove how tough I was because of my size. Kids always wanted to beat up on me. And then when I got so I could lick anybody, I overcompensated and turned into this supercocky dude who thought he was invincible. And when I got to prison, I wasn't, and it helped me to turn myself around.

"But these other poor bastards, their old man beat em and knocked their mom around, or their mom was strung out on drugs and never cared about them. They've all got terrible stories, every one of them, and it would be a miracle if they turned out any different than they did. They're consumed with anger, and they take it out on anything and everything. They don't consider whether the objects of their rage deserve it. Venting that fury is all that matters to them.

"And you've either got to kill them, or keep them locked up forever, or reach inside them to get them to understand their rage so they can deal with it. Otherwise, they're just going to come back out into society and hurt somebody again."

He went quiet.

Strickland looked pained, Hecher thought. She said nothing.

Finally, "That sign said six miles to a Comfort Inn and a McDonald's. I think we should get off at that exit."

"Good by me."

"We've made good progress. We're well into Louisiana."

"Time flies when you're having fun." Hecher smiled. "This is pure joy for me."

They ate and took separate rooms at the motel.

At eight a.m., they were on the road again, driving through a drizzle for an hour before the clouds parted and they crossed into a sunny Texas.

"You know, what you said got me thinking," Strickland said, glancing to the right at a vast, flat pasture strewn with hearty, brown-red Hereford cattle. Their white heads lazily chewed under the warm sun or skimmed the short green grass as they grazed. "As awful as your prison experience was, maybe it saved you. You know the joke about an awful tasting medicine: If it doesn't kill ya, it'll cure ya. If you hadn't gone to prison for supposedly killing somebody, you might have ended up in prison for really taking somebody's life."

"I don't think so, Susan. I'd found a woman who was setting me in the right direction. And we had a son on the way, and that made me realize more than anything why I had to straighten out. But yeah, I had no choice in prison."

By evening, they entered a new time zone and gained another hour, enabling them to make it through Texas and then north to Albuquerque by twilight. Hecher remembered the route to his mother's house and directed Strickland there.

Streamers decorated the windows and doorway, and a limousine waited on the street in front. The Camaro pulled into the driveway, and the pair got out and walked up the sidewalk. A half-dozen persons spilled out of the front door, yelling, "Welcome home, Mitt." Maria Hecher stood on the stoop, waiting for her son, who hugged her, then introduced her to Strickland. The two likewise embraced.

A teenage boy appeared in the doorway.

"Oh my gosh, who is that?" Hecher beamed. "That can't be my son, can it? Lordie, Pauley, you're taller than me. And better lookin, too."

Everybody laughed.

"Hi Dad," Pauley said, as the two embraced.

"How are you doing? Do you like your teachers here? Do you have a lot of new friends?"

"Yeah. I'm getting along well."

Hecher lowered his voice. "I know losing Mom had to be terrible for you," Pauley. "It was for me, too."

He threw his arms around his son, and they both shed a few tears.

"I couldn't study and didn't care much about anything for a few weeks, and I didn't get very good grades that semester," Pauley said, wiping his face. "But I gradually came out of it."

"Well, I'm here for you now. They'll never have an excuse to take me away again."

"Come inside," Maria said. Hecher's brother, Dan, walked up to Hecher with a glass of champagne in each hand. The others already were carrying glasses.

Dan raised his. "To a great future full of happiness for Mitt."

"Folks," Hecher announced, "I want to introduce you all to Susan Strickland. This lady is the reason I'm here tonight. She began working on my case without a fee six years ago because she was convinced of my innocence. And it was her passionate argument that persuaded the governor and the Cabinet to release me. When I walked out of that prison, she was there to greet me. She knew that fifteen years separated from society would leave me a little unsure of how to deal with the little issues of everyday life—kind of like Rip Van Winkle waking up after twenty years and finding that everything had changed. She wanted to make sure I got here okay, and had her car waiting. She's an angel. Let's raise our glasses in a toast to Susan."

"Yeah, Susan," someone shouted.

"All hail Susan," another joined in, and they all clinked glasses.

Maria showed Mitt and Susan separate bathrooms.

"Why don't you both go and freshen up? I'm sure you'll want to after that long drive."

One of the young women in the group began passing hors d'oeuvres as they all continued putting away the champagne.

After forty-five minutes, Dan said to Mitt, "Well, that limousine driver doesn't want to wait all night. Let's go out and celebrate."

He grabbed his brother's arm and they headed for the door.

Strickland stepped in front of Mitt.

"No, you don't. You're staying right here. You think I'm going to let you go out and end up in a brawl? That's all you'd need to be back in the slammer. You can't be doing anything reckless. That kind of life is over for you."

Hecher looked at her like a chastised child. "You're right. I'll stay here. Sorry, Dan. It was real generous of you, but I hope you understand."

"Mitt, no problem. I wasn't thinking. Susan is right. I'll send the limo driver on his way."

The party broke up, with the others congratulating Mitt and leaving. He and Susan watched television for a short while, and then Mitt told her he was going to his room and turning in.

Susan changed into pajamas in the bathroom and went to sleep on the couch outside his room.

———————

Strickland stayed for two more days, then drove back to Orlando after admonishing her client to stay out of trouble. Don't drink heavily or do drugs, and absolutely never carry a firearm, a condition of his release, she warned. She said she would be in touch.

The next day, Hecher called Gary Lannon. Before Hecher's release, his fellow inmate had sent a letter giving his new address and phone number near Phoenix, where a friend of his sister had a brother who needed someone reliable to work at his junk-car parts business. They discussed getting together.

The phone rang at noon the following day, and Maria answered.

"Mitt," she called from the living room to the kitchen, where her son was finishing a fruit salad after sleeping late. "It's for you. A reporter named Tom."

Hecher picked up the extension in the kitchen.

"Is this Tom Palladin?"

"Congratulations, Mitt. I'm glad you finally got justice."

"Yeah, thanks man. It feels great. It's going to take me a while to get used to this freedom. Getting up late. Going to the fridge whenever I went to. It's just exhilarating."

"I'm really happy for you. A couple of things. I'm doing a short freelance piece for a small paper around West Palm and wanted to ask you how you felt about those attorneys spending all those hours working without pay to get you freed because they believed in you."

"Oh, these people are the best. Lawyers have a bad reputation, and they get it from guys like Scraponia. Then these gems come along and show that you have to judge each person individually, because that guy and the bunch who worked for me are on opposite sides of the same coin. I'll never be able to repay those folks for what they did for me. Like Susan Strickland said, all I can do is make sure I justify their faith in me by never going astray."

Hecher heard a keyboard clacking in the background as Palladin said nothing.

"Okay. I have a couple of other questions, but we can get to them later. There's something I've been wanting to tell you for four years but couldn't because, obviously, you were in prison. And as a newspaper reporter, I was ethically restricted from getting involved in your case. But I'm freelancing now, so my hands are untied."

"I hear you. I've been wondering what this is all about since you called me at Avon Park."

"You might want to sit down."

He paused. "I found out who shot Rodger Kriger."

"You what?" Hecher's voice reverberated with disbelief. "No way. You gotta be shittin me."

"In 1987. The FBI got the name accidentally in a bug on Frankie Campanella's house in Louisville. One of the guys who hung out at the Shore Club gave me the same name. A hit man. Generoso Gagliardi. Looks like Kriger insulted Wallace Grey's gay son when the president sent him down here to get straight with a couple of party girls on a boat owned by Kriger's friend, and it didn't work. According to the boat captain, Johnny Traynor, the pres heard about it and was furious. That's what led to the murder. My editors at the *Beacon* didn't think we had enough to go on for a story, so I turned my information in to the sheriff's department. So did the FBI agent. The sheriff's lieutenant—you remember Detective Lt. Ron Snopes— he did nothing with it."

"Holy crap. Do you know where the killer is?"

Palladin sighed. "Yes, I do. He's still in Florida. West-central part. I checked the Florida state law enforcement records and found out the guy was released from Raiford a year ago after doing two years for weapons violations. He had a rap sheet that makes him a good fit for the Kriger murder: aggravated assault, attempted murder twice, conspiracy to commit murder, other stuff. He also did time in a couple of other East Coast states."

Hecher was silent while the wheels spun in his head.

"Do you think...?" He hesitated. "I mean, I was just thinking how great it would be if this guy was caught and my name would be cleared. Because you know what? As long as I live, people are going to wonder in the back of their minds if I might really be guilty, even if I live totally clean."

"Yes, I suppose you're right."

"How am I going to prove this... what's his name?"

"Gagliardi. It's spelled G-a-g-l-i-a-r-d-i, but you pronounce it Gal-ee-ar-dee."

"How do I show he did it?" Hecher asked.

"Your attorney would have to subpoena Robert Gusse, the FBI agent, to give an affidavit that the wire tap on Campanella's house revealed Gagliardi did the shooting. I'd do a story on it, and now the *Beacon* would have a story the editors could use. The other media would pick up on it, and the sheriff's office wouldn't have any choice but to have him arrested."

"Yeah, yeah." Hecher spoke as though thinking. "That sounds like a helluva plan. Let me talk to Susan, and I'll get back to you. Give me your number. Hold on. Where's a pen? I just got out of a pen and now I'm looking for one." He chuckled.

"Sounds like your sense of humor is intact."

"I developed that when I relaxed and stopped being a tough guy. We joked around, the inmates who were friends. It was either that or go insane. Okay, here's one. Shoot."

Palladin recited his phone number.

"One more question," Palladin said. "How does it feel to be out of prison after all these years?"

"Oh... I can't put it into words. To have no restrictions, no time on when you're allowed to leave the house and no hour when you have to be back. In prison, you're like a child. Here on the outside, you can eat at home if you want, anything you want, or go out and eat. Nobody can dictate any of these things to you. It's the strangest, most foreign, most wonderful feeling."

Hecher waited five seconds until the keyboard clacking stopped.

"Is that it?" he asked.

"There's just one thing," said Palladin. "This guy has been running away from the law for a long time and he's a pro. He could elude the police trap."

"What then?"

"Then we have to try to figure out where he went. And I don't know how we do that. Let's not worry about that unless we have to."

"I'm with ya. I'll let you know what Susan Strickland decides on this."

"Please do. Good luck."

―――――――――

"How was the trip?" Hecher sat at the breakfast table, using the kitchen phone. "You must be done in after all that driving."

"I'm fine, Mitt. The question is, how are you adjusting to your new life?"

"I'm still in heaven, Susan. I wouldn't change this for anything. But there's something that's been bothering me. Happy as I am to be free, I still want to clear my name so there won't be any question about my guilt in anybody's mind."

"That would be great, but I don't see how it'll be possible."

"I think it is."

"Huh? What are you getting at?"

"The newspaper reporter who covered this case from the beginning called me the other day. You ready for this? He found out in 1987 who the killer was."

"Oh, my God." Susan stretched out the words.

Hecher related the story to her.

"This is an incredible turn of events," she enthused.

"I need your help, Susan. The reporter is Tom Palladin. Here's what he suggested."

Hecher told her of their plan.

"On the face of it, I don't see what we'd have to lose. But let me sleep on it. I'll get back to you tomorrow."

"Okay. If I'm not here when you call, about the only place I could be would be the grocery store. With my mother driving, of course. I've got to apply for a license. See? A simple thing like that, my record is going to make it difficult."

"Don't forget, murder isn't the only thing on your record."

"Yeah, but murder is the big enchilada. It's the one that throws up the red flags."

"And what if this plan doesn't work?"

"That has occurred to me. I'm working on plan B."

"And what might that be?"

"If you don't mind, Susan, I'd rather not get into that unless it becomes necessary. Can we just worry about plan A for now?"

"All right. I'll call you tomorrow."

"Thanks."

At eleven a.m., Strickland called.

"Good timing," Hecher said. "We just came back from Safeway."

"I'm okay with this. I'll draft an affidavit and track down Robert Gusse in South Florida. He might try to claim exemption under federal security laws, but I doubt it, because when he turned his information over to the sheriff's department, it became public property. He turned it in because he was expecting something would be done with it. So I think he'll sign the affidavit. And then we can contact the reporter and he'll let the world know what happened."

"Great," said Hecher. What's next?"

"I'll get to work on it right away. It shouldn't take long."

Three days later, a four-column headline below the fold on the front page of the *Beacon* screamed. FBI Agent Names 1976 Kruger Killer. The subhead read, *Sensational Palm Beach Murder Work of Hit Man.*

The *Beacon* had whacked the competition on this story. The *Miami Gazette* asked Lieutenant Ronald Snopes, chief of sheriff's detectives, for an interview as a way of scoring a secondary exclusive. Snopes agreed. Then he called attorney Jim Scraponia at his firm's office and asked for help in countering Hecher. They devised a scheme.

"Don," said Snopes, squinting. He sat across from State Attorney Donald Bosworth, buried in his swivel chair. "Hecher thinks he's outfoxed us. He wants to make us look bad—force us to nab this other guy so everybody will know we made a big mistake. I think we can foil the son-of-a-bitch's plans."

Snopes provided the *Gazette* with the detailed strategy for apprehending Gagliardi that the lieutenant had worked out with a cooperating police agency, and the paper published it. The wire services picked it up, and newspapers across the state carried the story while radio and television news programs broadcast the information. It was almost impossible for Gagliardi not to read or hear about it.

A Manatee County sheriff's SWAT team would conduct a stakeout of the apartment where Gagliardi lived. The officers would watch him leave his residence and wait until his return, then swoop in and arrest him.

They went to the apartment complex management, which supplied the location of the wanted man's parking spot. In a plain car, wearing civilian clothes, two officers drove to the apartment parking lot to identify his car and obtain his license number. The car was gone. They radioed the other team members, parked nearby in other unmarked cars. It was five p.m. They waited until four a.m. The sergeant in charge radioed the others that he was radioing headquarters to call the relief team in. At five a.m., the replacements arrived. Gagliardi still had not shown.

The twelve-hour stakeout shifts continued for three days, and Gagliardi never returned to his apartment. The captain leading the stakeout brought the ten men in the two shifts together at the sheriff's office in suburban Bradenton.

"We've wasted our time, men. The guy has flown the coop. That jackass in West Palm Beach made our job impossible when he advertised to the whole world how we planned to corral this guy. I should have realized our mission was hopeless. Sorry to put you through this. That lieutenant down in West Palm is a fucking idiot."

The captain couldn't know that Snopes was in fact a fucking fox.

A brief story in the next day's *Bradenton Blade* told of how Gagliardi had slipped away, under the headline: Murder Suspect Eludes Police. In the article, the captain excoriated Lieutenant Snopes. The wire services sent the story to their member papers across the state. The *Beacon*'s headline over it read: Snopes' Snafu Lets Suspect Scram.

―――――――――

"Have you heard what happened?" Palladin asked, phoning Hecher.

"Yeah. Susan called me. And those guys are supposed to be fighting crime. They're on the side of the criminal, man."

"It sure seems that way."

"Look, Tom, I got a buddy who knows Johnny Traynor and these other guys who hung around at the Shore Club. I'd put money on it that he knows where Gagliardi went. I know this would be awfully risky, and it's asking a hell of a lot, but… do you think you and my buddy could lead me to Gagliardi?"

"Risky's not the word for it. You sure you would want to do this?"

"I got another pal who'll help, too. Lives down here. I protected this guy in prison and taught him karate. I can't carry any firearms, and neither can he. Condition of his parole. He's got a wooden leg, but he knows how to use that sucker as an asset. He can set you on your ass."

"You don't want to do anything that's going to land you back in prison."

"Yeah, I'd have to be careful. Come to think of it, I'll have to run this scheme by Susan Strickland first."

"Well, to be truthful, I kind of anticipated your wanting to do this. I've already thought it over. I'm game."

"So what are you going to do now?" Susan Strickland asked when Hecher phoned.

"I've got no choice. Plan B."

"Okay, let's hear it."

"I called my old buddy Davey Ross in West Palm Beach, and he thinks he knows where Gagliardi has gone. A guy Davey said is reliable told him Gagliardi is holed up with Johnny Traynor. Remember I told you he was the guy who drove the getaway car? Davey knows where he lives—somewhere between Sarasota and Bradenton. I've devised a plan."

"Mitt, I don't like the sound of this. This is extremely dangerous, confronting such a vicious person. How can you possibly do this without a gun when he'll very likely have one? Or two."

"I promise I'll be very careful. Gary Lannon and I will drive up from Albuquerque over to the Bradenton area. Gary is my prison buddy and he lives in my area. We'll meet on the Gulf Coast with Davey Ross and Tom Palladin, the reporter. I called Davey and he said he was the one who gave Generoso Gagliardi's name to Palladin. He said it'd be like old times. Don't worry, I told him it wouldn't be the same. Palladin and Davey will drive across the state to meet us. Davey is going to lead us to this guy."

"Well, like I said, I'm not in favor of this. You know, of course, that you're not allowed to live in Florida for one year. But I realize there's nothing in the clemency ruling that prevents you from visiting in the state. Nonetheless, I'm going to check with the governor's office just to be on the safe side. You have to do what you have to do. Just please be ultracareful."

"I think it's good we'll have the reporter along. Tom will help us keep our heads screwed on straight."

"Keep me up to date."

"Susan, you and I are both smart enough to realize Snopes deliberately threw a monkey wrench into this. He did not want Gagliardi captured. And I'm as sure as Albuquerque is in New Mexico that it wasn't just him who planned the screw-up. Bosworth at least knew about it, and I'd be surprised if Scraponia didn't have his fingerprints on it. Those three have always worked as a team to mess me up."

"I read the record, Mitt. I don't doubt you a bit."

Chapter Six

"My buddy Davey Ross…"

"Davey Ross?" Palladin interrupted Hecher on the phone. "I didn't know you and him were that friendly."

"Yeah, we go way back," Hecher allowed.

"He's the one who confirmed Gagliardi's name after I got it from the FBI agent."

"I know," said Hecher. "He told me. Anyway, Davey knows where Traynor is living, and he heard Gagliardi is holed up with him. He's quite confident in his source.

"Here's what I've got in mind. I can't carry a gun, and I'm sure as hell not going to let you carry one, whether you know how to use it or not. Too dangerous. Davey Ross can, and he's handy with handguns. Traynor and Gagliardi are going to be armed, and we need an extra man. So my peg-legged prison buddy, Gary Lannon, is coming over from Phoenix, and he'll drive me and him down to Florida in my brother's car. My brother and his wife have two cars. I still don't have a driver's license. We'll meet you and Davey up by the Gulf Coast."

"I think that'll work."

"Yeah. We'll have a posse of four. Partly armed and partly legged." Hecher couldn't resist chuckling at his pun. Palladin, usually reserved, let out a big baritone laugh.

Palladin pulled his black semisports car into the apartment complex southeast of Bradenton at three-forty-five p.m. Davey waited while the reporter asked the office person for the unit number of Johnny Traynor. Palladin drove past the apartment, looking up at the third floor, while Ross scanned the numbers on the parking blocks.

"There it is. It has to be that red Mustang, I'd say '87."

Palladin drove into a spot near the end of the third row, far enough from the Mustang so its owner wouldn't spot them but affording a good view of the apartment.

"You want to take a snooze?" Palladin asked. "One of us needs to keep a lookout."

"Yeah, okay. We'll take turns." Ross reclined his seat in the Dodge Charger and soon dozed off. He awoke after forty-five minutes as the descending sun cast wider shadows over the parking lot.

"My eyelids are getting heavy," said Palladin. "I'll let you spell me." He reclined and slept for an hour, awakening as dark was setting in. He switched on the radio. "Listen to whatever you want."

Ross fiddled with the dial until he landed on a station with a woman wailing about how she slammed the door shut on her cheatin man and told him to hit the road when he came beggin to be let back in. They waited.

Shortly before seven o'clock, Ross jerked upright.

"Uh-oh, they're leavin. Shit. But they ain't got any bags."

"We'll tail em," said Palladin.

The men rode the elevator to the ground floor and walked to the Mustang. With Traynor driving, they took the streets leading to I-75 and headed north. Palladin waited until they wouldn't have seen his Charger pull out of the lot, then pulled to within a hundred yards.

"It's kind of hard to keep sight of their car in the dark," he said.

"I see it," Ross chimed. After the first exit, the Mustang moved into the right lane. "Looks like they might get off at the next exit."

They did, and Palladin followed them up three streets to a tacky looking bar-and-grill. The Charger pulled into a Walgreens across the street, and the two waited. More than three hours later, their adversaries emerged, walking unsteadily.

"Seventy-five bucks," the man they assumed to be Gagliardi bellowed. "Them fuckin guys didn't know I was a pool shark. I even beat em with five beers in my belly."

"They're not going anywhere tonight," said Palladin. "Not in that condition. We're going to have a hard time finding a restaurant open at this hour. Why don't we just have a burger and a beer at this place and head for the motel."

"I'm good with that," Ross agreed.

The next morning, Ross watched in Palladin's Charger in the small commercial plaza of shops and professional offices across the road from the apartment complex. Gagliardi emerged from the apartment in midmorning and left in Traynor's Mustang. Should he follow him, Ross wondered? Naw. The hit man would have to return, not having his own car or a place to stay. Now would be a good time to go back to the motel and get Palladin, who had awakened with a splitting headache.

The two returned to the complex and waited in the plaza two-and-a-half hours until Gagliardi returned. He walked around to the passenger side and pulled two large pieces of luggage from the rear seat, then drew a smaller bag from the front seat.

"He's by himself," Ross noted. "Now's our chance to grab him."

"All right, let's do it," said Palladin.

Ross patted the gun in his shoulder holster and the two jumped out of the Dodge. They hustled toward the road.

A car pulled into a spot two spaces from the Mustang, and a man who appeared to be of retiree age got out and approached Gagliardi. Palladin and Ross overheard him.

"You're the fella's been staying a couple doors from me on the third floor. I'm going up there. Let me help you with that luggage."

"Oh, yeah, thanks. I couldn't get my hand around both the big one and the little one. If you can carry the small piece, I'll be fine with the other two."

"Let's get back," Palladin said under his breath. "We don't want him to see us."

They returned in haste to the Charger.

"Fuckin son-of-a-bitch," Ross grumbled. "We had that bastard."

"Those bags looked used," said Palladin. "He probably picked them up at a thrift store and went to several stores. That's what took him so long. So at least it looks like they're getting ready to move out."

"What do you think?" Ross asked. "They ain't gonna be leaving at night."

"No. Highly doubtful. But maybe one of us ought to keep a watch out a while longer."

They drove to the Waffle House at the Fifty-Third Avenue exit of I-75. Ross picked up a couple of snacks and returned to the complex, leaving Palladin to meet Hecher and Lannon, who were due soon.

Hecher and Lannon arrived in a Chevrolet Impala, famished, and ate at the Waffle House with Palladin.

"Ya know," Lannon pondered, "I was thinking. I'm just playing devil's advocate here, so if I'm fulla shit, let me know."

"You're fulla shit," Hecher said, chuckling.

"Thanks, smart ass, but I forgot to tell you. I already knew that."

"All right, come on, let's hear it."

"If we know Gagliardi is in that apartment with Traynor, why don't we just call the cops and let them come and arrest him?"

"Nope," Hecher objected. "We can't chance it. The Manatee sheriff's office might call the Palm Beach County sheriff's office to check us out, and Snopes would talk them out of doing anything. That guy is a snake. He'll get together with Bosworth and Scraponia, and they'll fuck us over again. We've got to bring Gagliardi to the Manatee office—and Traynor, too, if we can."

"I think Mitt is right, Gary," Palladin agreed. "That triumvirate in Palm Beach County will do anything to keep Mitt's murder conviction intact so they don't have to admit they were wrong."

"Okay, no problem. You convinced me."

Palladin looked at Hecher. "You and Gary find a place to stay yet?"

"No. We just got here."

"Davey and I are at a Days Inn just down the road. Their vacancy sign was on. It would be a good idea if we all stayed at the same place."

"What say, Gary?" Hecher asked.

"Good by me."

"I wonder what's taking Davey so long," Palladin fretted. "I know you guys are dog tired, but maybe we ought to run over there and check."

"Let's do it," said Hecher.

Lannon drove, and they pulled in to where the Charger had been parked.

"Holy mackerel!" Palladin exclaimed. "He's gone. And look, the Mustang is, too."

"Let's see if I can reach Davey on the CB radio," said Hecher. He picked up the mike.

"Mittster to Pal Tom. Come in, Pal Tom."

They waited several seconds.

"He's out of range. Either that or he tried something stupid and they're holding him. Or they did him in."

"Damn, I shouldn't have left him there alone," said Palladin. "Only thing we can do now is wait a while and hope he comes back.

If he doesn't, we'll have to notify the police. We won't have any choice. It'll be our only hope of rescuing Davey. If he's still alive."

In Bradenton, Ross drove the Charger down a thoroughfare, surveying side roads and parking lots.

"Shit, I lost em," he muttered.

I wonder if they're gone for good. They didn't have any bags, but they might've put them in the car while Palladin and me drove to the Waffle House. Damn, they have to be around here somewhere. I saw em make that turn, and then they disappeared. Where the... ah, what's that? In front of that massage parlor. That's a Mustang. What's the license read? Last two numbers are 43. Zoweee! That's the car. I remember those numbers. Oh man, I feel better. I'll just park and wait.

"It's been an hour," said Palladin. "We can call the cops or we can try something first. Why don't we head into downtown Bradenton? At this late hour, maybe these guys just got bored and went to a strip joint or an X-rated movie house, and Davey followed them. That city's not very big, and traffic will be light this time of night. We might just spot them. We've got nothing to lose."

"All right, let's go," Hecher said.

As Lannon pulled the Impala up to the south end of the city, Hecher got on the CB.

"Mittster to Pal Tom. Come in, Pal Tom."

Ross banged his knees against the console and grabbed the mike.

"Mittster, Davey here. You scared the crap outa me."

"Good. Then we're even. Cuz you scared the crap out of us. Where the hell are you? You okay?"

"Yeah. Shit, I lost these bastards for a few minutes, but I found em again. They're inside a massage parlor gettin banged. I'm waitin outside, and when they've had their jollies I'll make sure they come home and go straight to bed like good boys. When'd you guys get here?

"Oh fuck. I'm talkin to you guys and I took my eyes off the joint. They're gettin in their car. Damn, I gotta follow em."

"Where the hell are you?" said Hecher.

"Damned if I know. Downtown someplace. Main Street. I don't even know what direction I'm goin. No problem. I'm sure these guys are headed back to their apartment. I'll tail em."

"Okay. We'll pick up your trail somewhere."

Palladin, Hecher, and Lannon were waiting in the Impala parked in the commercial plaza as the Mustang pulled into its parking spot. Its occupants got out and walked to their apartment.

The Charger with Ross drove up beside the Impala a minute later as the drivers communicated by radio. The four then left for the Days Inn, feeling assured that their prey weren't going anywhere that night.

——————————

At six a.m., Palladin drove the Charger into the commercial plaza. Ross hunkered far down in the passenger seat, his tall frame no hindrance because Palladin had set the seat as far back as it would go. At six-foot-three, three inches taller than Ross, the reporter sat with his hair brushing the roof of the low-slung car. He pulled into an inconspicuous parking spot between two other cars in the second row, not far from the plaza entrance to allow for a swift departure.

A half-hour later, the Impala entered the plaza. Lannon held his left thumb up to let Palladin know he saw him and continued to the third row, then left almost to the end, where a vacant spot caught the edge of a shadow cast by a Florida sugar maple rising just beyond the asphalt.

After forty-five minutes, Palladin spoke into his CB mike. "Hey Mittster, this is Pal Tom. Thought we ought to check to make sure these things are working properly. They worked fine last night. Do you read me?"

"Loud and clear, Pal Tom."

"Okay. Let the waiting begin."

Hecher turned to Lannon. "Why don't you lay your head back and catch a few winks, Gary? You can't be recovered yet from all that driving. There's enough of us keeping watch."

"Good idea. I'm feelin sleepy already."

The four men in the two cars went silent. Palladin turned on his car radio and played a rock 'n' roll station at low volume. Palladin saw out of the corner of his eye that Davey's eyelids were beginning to droop.

An hour-and-a-quarter passed. Hecher grabbed his CB.

"Mittster calling Pal Tom. Do you see that?"

"Pal Tom here. I sure do. Looks like they're moving out. Wait a minute. I'm not so sure. They've only got one bag—a big one, but Gagliardi came back from the store with two of those. Where are they going? They stopped by the elevator. They're getting in."

"Maybe we ought to go for them," said Hecher. "We'd catch them totally by surprise."

"I don't think so," Palladin demurred. "I'm sure they're both armed—probably wearing holsters under their jackets. Or a pro like Gagliardi might have a gun strapped to his leg. People are coming and going in that parking lot. We can't risk injuring or killing others."

"They're on the first floor," Palladin said a minute later. "They're heading for their car. Mittster, a space has opened up two cars from mine. Tell Gary to drive up and park here so he can leave before me. The Impala stands out less than my Charger, and we don't want to attract attention. I'll bring up the rear."

"Gotcha, Pal Tom."

Lannon drove into the second row, headed toward the plaza entrance, and parked in the space. Three minutes later, the 1987 red Mustang left the parking space near the apartment building. Reaching the road, it turned toward Fifty-Third Avenue. Lannon waited until it had gone a block, then moved onto the road. The Ford turned east toward I-75, and Lannon followed several blocks behind.

"We're lucky their car is bright red," said Hecher. "If we lose them, it shouldn't be hard to spot again. Traynor likes hot cars."

As they neared I-75, Lannon sped up.

"Pal Tom, come in."

"What's up, Mittster?"

"They're about to enter I-75. Better get your buggy in gear so we don't lose them. He doesn't drive slow."

"Okay, Mittster. You guys stay with him. We'll be there pronto."

The northbound entrance ramp was empty, and Traynor tromped on the gas pedal, reaching sixty-five miles per hour.

"Uh-oh," Lannon uttered. "He's takin off like a bat outa hell. He might get suspicious when he sees a car in his rear-view mirror going as fast as he is."

Lannon accelerated onto the interstate highway. But the Mustang wasn't far ahead. Traynor hadn't sped up.

"What's he up to?" Lannon said.

"Strange," Hecher said. A moment later, "Oh, I get it. The speed limit. It's only sixty-five on the interstates in Florida, not seventy like New Mexico. Those two want to make damn sure they don't get stopped by the highway patrol."

"Yeah, you're right," Lannon concurred. "That'll make things easier for us. Another thing in our favor is the light traffic. It's Sunday."

Hecher turned his head to look through the rear window. "Here comes Tom and Davey. That fuckin Charger deserves its name."

"Hey, what's going on?" said Lannon. "They're headed for the exit."

"Oh shit," said Hecher. "What the fuck are they up to. Ya think they know they're being followed?"

He got on the radio. "Mittster to Pal Tom. They're getting off at the third exit. We'd better keep our distance or they're going to know something's up. They may suspect something already and they're doing this as a test."

"Yeah, Mittster. I think you two should tail them from a far enough distance that they won't think they're being followed, and we'll just hang here for a while and then turn back."

Lannon slowed and allowed the Mustang to turn onto the exit road before he entered the exit ramp, so the criminals wouldn't see the Impala following them. Then he drove onto the ramp.

"Look," said Hecher. "He got back on the southbound ramp. He's going back." He lifted the mike. "Mittster to Pal Tom."

"Come in, Mittster."

"They're headed back south on I-75. We took the exit and will follow at a distance. I think you'd better get off too and get behind us."

"Good idea, Mittster. We'll speed up and catch up to you."

Lannon stayed in the far right lane of I-75 so the Impala wouldn't be directly behind the Mustang's rear view mirror. He and Hecher watched the car exit at Fifty-Third Avenue and head west toward the apartment complex.

Lannon pulled off and followed, driving into the commercial plaza across the road and parking in a secluded spot between a van and a truck. He and Hecher watched as Traynor jumped out of the car and half-walked, half-ran back to the building, and swayed his arms impatiently while waiting for the elevator. He made a beeline to the apartment, entered, and came out a half-minute later carrying a medium-sized bag.

"They forgot something," said Hecher. "Geez, I really thought they were onto us." He got on the CB. "Mittster to Pal Tom."

"Come in, Mittster."

"It's okay. They just forgot something. Keep out of sight, and I'll radio you when we're headed down Fifty-Third again."

"Gotcha Mittster."

The Mustang sped away, and Lannon took off when it was well down the road, allowing a car to get between so the Ford's occupants couldn't see the Impala following.

"Mittster to Pal Tom."

"Come in, Mittster."

"We're approaching I-75. He's going like hell. But he'll have to slow down for the speed limit. No problem."

"I'm not far behind you, Mittster."

Six minutes later, Hecher called, "Pal Tom, can you see ahead? They're exiting. What the hell do they want in this subdivision, unless they're heading back again? We'll have to follow and find out."

Lannon drove the Impala onto the exit street, keeping seventy-five yards back of the Mustang. It turned a corner in the subdivision, and Lannon also made the turn.

"Where'd he go?" said Lannon. He drove three more blocks and stopped. He and Hecher looked left and right, and back from where they had come. Hecher radioed Palladin as the Charger entered the subdivision.

"We lost them. I'm stymied. Where the hell did they go? We'll have to drive around."

Both cars raced through the streets of the housing development, to no avail. After fifteen minutes, Palladin spotted the Mustang on the street leading to the I-75 ramp.

"Pal Tom to Mittster. We found him. He's headed to I-75."

Both cars followed, but the four men noticed the Mustang had only one occupant. It headed south on I-75, exited on Fifty-Third Avenue, and continued to the apartment complex. The Charger pulled into the commercial plaza first, and Palladin and Ross saw Traynor get out of the Mustang and walk to the apartment. Lannon and Hecher arrived in the Impala, and the men talked by radio.

"Traynor had to have dropped Gagliardi off at one of those houses," Hecher hypothesized, "but I sure as hell can't figure out how none of us saw it."

"Yeah," Palladin acknowleddged. "That is a big mystery. Traynor must be a magician."

"We'll just have to keep an eye on Traynor now and hope he leads us to Gagliardi," said Hecher.

They decided a round-the-clock vigil was necessary because of the unpredictable movements their two nemeses had shown. Both cars always would be staked out in the plaza, one man in each car. If Traynor left, one car would follow him while the other rushed to the motel to pick up the other two. That car with three men would join the first car in the pursuit of Traynor.

The two cars parked in different parts of the commercial plaza so that frequent visitors to the plaza wouldn't notice their constant presence.

Traynor occasionally left his apartment, and the Impala and Charger went after his Mustang. But he always went to the grocery and drug stores, never to the subdivision. The four were tiring of the continual false alarms, and realized this could go on for weeks or months. They also feared that plaza businesspersons and apartment residents, including Traynor, might begin to notice their presence. After three days, Ross conceived an idea to get Traynor and Gagliardi together.

"This guy who tipped me off that Traynor and Gagliardi are here has got a beef with Traynor," Ross told Palladin and Hecher on one of their pursuits of Traynor that led to a supermarket. "Says Traynor cheated him on a cocaine deal. But he never bitched about it cuz he's scared of Traynor. Traynor don't know the guy is pissed at him. I can call the guy. I'll ask him to get ahold of Traynor and tell Traynor the cops are about to question him cuz they think he might have information about where Gagliardi is. It'll be like leading a scared bull out of a thunderstorm into a slaughter barn."

"Sounds like a good plan to me," said Hecher.

"Yeah, why not?" Palladin agreed. "We have to do something."

Ross made the call from a drugstore telephone. His source said he would love to help out to get even with Traynor. He said he'd call Traynor right away.

The four men positioned themselves in their two cars across the road from the apartment complex. They had to wait only a half-hour. Traynor hurried from his apartment with the other large suitcase, and drove out to I-75. The Charger and Impala followed, and the Mustang got off at the third exit and entered the subdivision. The pursuers kept far enough away to avoid arousing suspicion in Traynor, but close enough to keep the red car in sight. Nonetheless, when it turned a corner, Palladin and Ross could not find it when they made the same turn.

Palladin told Hecher via CB to have Lannon drive around the streets in the area. Both cars raced up and down, screeching around corners in wild pursuit of the elusive Mustang.

"Damn it to hell, where does that fuckin red bantam rooster hide every time?" Hecher lamented to Pal Tom.

"Danged if I know," Palladin radioed back. "This is the case of the Phantom Ford. Oh, wait, there it is—coming out of that alley. There's two guys. Now it makes sense. He must have been in something like a garage apartment. Let's wait and see where they go. Okay, they're heading back toward I-75. Mittster, you guys move on up and get behind them. No doubt they'll be heading north out of here. We'll follow you."

"Gotcha, Pal Tom."

The Mustang occupied the middle lane of northbound I-75 and Lannon drove on the inside lane three hundred yards behind. Palladin held to the outside lane a hundred yards behind Lannon. Neither car communicated for the next fifteen miles.

Then, "Pal Tom, this is Mittster."

"Pal Tom here, Mittster."

"Twenty, maybe twenty-five miles ahead, there's a junction with I-275. If they stay on I-75, it'll take them on the east side of Tampa, and that'd mean they probably plan to hide there. If they do that, nabbing them will be tough because we'll have to wait till they're separated and act on the spur of the moment. I hope they turn onto 275 and head for the big bridge. If they do, I think you ought to pull out ahead of them. Your Charger has tinted windows, so Davey can watch them through the rear window without them knowing it. Here's my plan."

Hecher laid out his strategy.

"What do you think, Pal Tom?"

"Well, we knew from the beginning you guys were at a disadvantage with only one gun, so all the pieces will have to fall in place. But that'll have to happen in any scenario. I think this is as good a plan as any. What say you, Davey?" He looked at Ross, who nodded.

"Let's do it, Mittster," Palladin answered.

"All right," said Hecher. "You take the outside lane. If he makes the turn, we'll all follow him and you gradually move ahead of him."

No one spoke for the next twenty minutes.

"Mittster to Pal Tom. Less than a quarter mile to the junction. He's getting into the right-hand lane for the turn-off. Thank God. We need to get to the right, too."

All three cars took the I-275 exit, which led them on a fly-over above criss-crossing roads before turning west toward the four-mile-long Sunshine Skyway Bridge rising 190 feet above Tampa Bay. Palladin accelerated and passed the Impala, then the Mustang, moving to a quarter mile beyond it.

"Pal Tom to Mittster."

"Mittster, Pal Tom."

"You guys pull ahead of the Mustang and get behind me. Mittster, draw your baseball cap down low so Traynor won't recognize you when you pass them. Gary, make sure no cars get between us. We want the Mustang back of both our cars when the traffic stops on the bridge. We'll be there in a couple of minutes."

"Gotcha, Pal Tom," said Hecher."

"Here goes."

The Impala passed the Mustang, Hecher hunkering down in his seat. Traffic was light as they drove onto the bridge and began the long ascent. Both the Charger and Impala had gone a good distance beyond the Mustang, as its occupants were careful to keep within the speed limit. Three cars passed it, but couldn't pass Palladin or Lannon because they occupied both lanes, close together.

Approaching the top, Palladin sped ahead, then screeched to a stop with the Charger parked at an angle crossing both lanes. Lannon pumped his brakes to signal the cars behind of a problem ahead, and they slowed. Traffic came to a halt. Ross got out of the Charger and raised the hood. Palladin circled the front of the car to the passenger side and climbed in the back seat, where he pulled a blanket over him and lay curled up.

Behind them, people exited their cars and peered up the bridge roadway to see what the matter was. Traynor was one of them. Ross walked down the bridge road between the cars.

"Johnny!" he yelled, arriving to within seventy-five feet of the Mustang. "What the hell are you doin here?"

"Goin to get a little sun on the beach. What about you?"

"I'm headin over to see an old girlfriend in Clearwater. Man, am I glad to run into you. An expert car mechanic is just what I need. I was lookin for somebody with a toolbox. I think the brakes locked or somethin. Come on up here and take a look, will ya?"

"I'll be right back," Traynor said to Gagliardi.

Traynor and Ross hurried up the bridge to the Charger.

"Get behind the wheel and pump the brakes, and see what it feels like," Ross directed.

Traynor climbed in and put his foot on the petal. Ross crouched with his back to the other motorists, reached under his sweatshirt to the side of his chest, and pulled out a pistol.

"Stay right where you are and don't move or you're dead, Traynor. I've got a Glock 21 pointed right at your head."

"Why, you bastard. What are you up to?"

"You'll find out real quick. I'm gonna reach over to Tom in the back seat and hand him the gun to keep you from tryin anything while I get in the passenger seat."

Palladin threw the blanket off, rose to a sitting position, and accepted the gun. Ross scurried to the passenger side of the car and got in front. Palladin gave him the gun. "Now we'll just all wait and enjoy the water view," said Ross.

Lannon got out of the Impala and walked down the bridge. Hecher followed a step behind, to his side. He and Gagliardi had never met, but newspapers had frequently carried Hecher's photo with stories that would have interested Gagliardi. Hecher kept the baseball cap pulled low on his forehead. Gagliardi had exited the Mustang and come over to the driver's side, where he stood beside the open door, searching for his partner at the top of the bridge. Lannon could see the concerned, quizzical expression on his face.

Lannon and Hecher stopped beside Gagliardi. He was five-foot-eleven, lean, and muscled, with dark, thick hair, a sharp nose, and an elongated face. He wore a gold chain around his neck.

"Hello, Mister Gagliardi," said Hecher as he took his cap off and stuffed it in his back pocket.

Gagliardi, concentrating on the Charger up the bridge, was startled. "Who the hell are you? You look familiar."

"I should. My picture's been in the newspapers quite a bit. They've been telling about my fights to convince the courts I didn't shoot Rodger Kriger in 1976. I spent fifteen years in prison for a murder you committed, you fucking slimeball. Now I'm taking you in and setting the record straight."

Gagliardi lunged inside the car and grabbed a revolver from the floor of the passenger's side. He scrambled back out, pointing it at Hecher.

"I don't know what's happened to Traynor up there, but you two are gonna march on up and we're gonna find out. Then we're comin back down here and me and Traynor's gonna tear-ass around that little road block and be on our way."

"You're a little late," said Hecher, motioning with his head up the bridge. "The fuzz have arrived."

Gagliardi jerked his head to look, and Lannon leaped off his left leg and cracked Gagliardi in the forearm with his wooden leg.

"Yeeoww!" he howled as the gun went flying. He took off running full-speed up the bridge, with Hecher in pursuit. Lannon could only retrieve the gun and walk-hop after them. Hecher was in superior physical condition from his prison workouts and caught up to his nemesis just past the summit. He moved in, taking up the karate position.

Gagliardi backed up to the three-foot-high wall on the edge of the bridge, reached down to his left leg, and pulled a knife from a holster strap.

"Karate, huh? I took some karate back in my younger days. You ain't big enough to handle me, cocksucker."

Hecher sensed the bravado in the man's voice and detected fear in his face.

"That's what they all say, dirt bag."

Wielding the knife with his uninjured arm, the killer slashed with the knife, and Hecher jerked his torso inward while nimbly hopping backward. He allowed Gagliardi to continue swinging the knife, knowing he was less adept with his left arm. He would eventually become reckless and give his foe the opportunity to take the weapon away.

Hecher sensed Gagliardi was becoming desperate as he lashed out ever more wildly. When the knife opened a superficial cut in Hecher's chest, he grabbed Gagliardi's arm with both hands and smashed it across the karate expert's upraised thigh. The knife fell to the pavement as Gagliardi clutched his arm.

"Now it's a fair fight—except for four or five inches. You said I wasn't big enough. Prove it, asshole."

Hecher moved in closer. Gagliardi jabbed at the head with his left and Hecher jerked to the side, then ducked to avoid a right cross as panic overcame the pain Gagliardi felt from the injury. That left Gagliardi open, and Hecher threw a vicious punch to the abdomen. When the assassin bent to grab his midsection, Hecher smashed him in the face with a left, then a right. Gagliardi staggered backward against the short wall. Hecher rushed forward and grabbed his belt to keep him from plunging 180 feet into the bay. He held him with half his body bent over the edge.

"I think I'll throw you over, you piece of vermin."

"No, please. Don't."

"Oh, you don't like the idea of dying, huh? Well, guess what. Neither did Kriger. His wife didn't like the idea of him dying, either. Or his six kids. And the idea didn't appeal to me when that prosecutor wanted me to get the electric chair.

"You know what else? My wife didn't like the idea of dying without her husband there to comfort her because he was locked up in prison for a murder you committed, you cowardly shithead. What kind of a yellow-bellied sapsucker would sneak up in the night and shoot a defenseless man for money? I'll tell you what kind: the lowest of the low. You sure as hell don't deserve to live. I'm going to do the world a favor and take you out of it. I'm counting to three, and you're history. One, two, three. Okay, into the drink."

"No, no, I beg of you. I'll do anything."

"Mitt!" Lannon yelled from fifty feet away as he hobbled toward them. "Don't."

"What's that I hear?" Hecher glanced to his right. "Here come the cops. Looks like you were saved by the siren. For now, that is. You'll either get the chair or life behind bars. Either way, you're going to look back and wish I'd pushed you over the edge."

He pulled Gagliardi up from the wall and placed a karate hold on him. Lannon waved to the Florida Highway Patrol squad car. The car stopped and two patrolmen got out, one with pistol drawn.

"I've got a prize for you, gentlemen," said Hecher. "Meet Generoso Gagliardi, the killer of Rodger Kriger of Palm Beach. He's the one who slipped away from the Manatee sheriff's men—thanks to a big tip-off from Palm Beach County lawmen. You'll find his accomplice in that black Charger over there."

He motioned his head toward the Dodge.

"My buddies are holding him."

The officer with the gun out holstered his pistol and slapped handcuffs on Gagliardi, then led the prisoner to the patrol car, shoving him in the back seat. The other patrolman asked Hecher for his identification.

"Mitt Hecher? Oh, you're the guy who just got out of prison. The governor commuted your sentence."

"That's right. I spent fifteen years for a murder I didn't commit. Now you've got the real murderer. You can verify it with the FBI office in West Palm Beach."

"And who are you?"

"Gary Lannon. Mitt and me were prison buddies. He kept me alive."

"You two come and wait in the patrol car while my partner and I run a check."

"Certainly," said Lannon. He got in the back seat with Gagliardi, and Hecher climbed in the front seat.

Twenty minutes later, the patrolman smiled. He waited until the other officer got in next to Hecher, then drove the squad car seventy-five yards to the Charger. Palladin got out and approached the patrolman exiting the driver's side.

"Hello, officer. You'll find the driver of the getaway car in the Kriger murder in the driver's seat. It's my car, but the guy in the passenger seat is the one who captured him. He's Davey Ross, a friend of Mitt Hecher. I'm Tom Palladin."

"Where do you fit in?" the patrolman asked.

"I reported on this case for two newspapers and finally learned from the FBI agent for that area that the guy Hecher just handed you was the real killer. I also found out that Johnny Traynor—Davey is holding a gun on him—he drove the car."

"Let's see your ID."

The patrolman studied Palladin's driver's license.

"What papers did you work for?"

"The *Miami Gazette* till six years ago, then the *Palm Beach Beacon*. I've been freelancing the last few months. You can call both papers for verification."

"You know the numbers?"

"Sure." Palladin recited both phone numbers without hesitation.

"That's good enough for me. Looks like you're not faking it."

The other officer opened the passenger door and looked at Ross, slouched in his seat, gun in hand, his head facing Traynor. Ross turned and cast a quick glance at the officer, then back at his prisoner.

"How did you get involved in this?" the officer asked.

"I'm just helpin out my buddy Mitt. We go way back."

The officer walked around to the driver's side, ordered Traynor out of the car, and slapped handcuffs on him. He placed him back in the car and returned to Ross.

"I'll take that gun from you now."

Ross handed the Glock to the officer.

"Get out of the car, please, and hand me your ID."

"Yeah. I got a concealed weapon permit, too. The permit is in my wallet in my back pocket, with my ID."

He withdrew both and handed them to the officer, who inspected and returned them.

"You're okay," he said, returning the gun. "You can put that away now."

He leaned inside the car. "What's your name?"

"Johnny Traynor."

"Where do you live?"

"My wallet is in my back pocket."

The officer came around and pulled Traynor out of the car. Slipping his wallet out, the patrolman inspected the driver's license. He escorted Traynor to the squad car, told Hecher and Lannon they could get out, and deposited Traynor in the back seat with Gagliardi.

The officer radioed the Manatee sheriff's office and a detective said he had the right guy.

"Good work," said the officer, shaking Hecher's hand.

The cop frowned.

"We probably should charge you and your buddies with obstructing traffic, but I think justice has been well-enough served today. We'll take it from here and you guys can be on your way."

The four stood facing each other.

"Geez, I don't know what to tell you guys," said Hecher, smiling at Palladin, then Ross. "You all pulled this off like pros. We mapped out a real piece of strategy, Tom. The army could use us."

"Well, you and Davey won the battle," Palladin responded. "And Gary... you're going to need a concealed weapon permit for that leg."

Everybody laughed.

"Yeah, that thing is potent," said Hecher. "Gagliardi's gun was no match for it."

"Guys, the cops are getting ready to open the bridge up," said Tom. "That traffic is backed up as far as you can see. We'd better be going."

"You and Davey want to stop on the other side of the bridge and have a bite to eat?" Hecher asked. "I'm buying."

"I'd like to, but I've got to get back to West Palm and turn this story in as soon as possible," said Palladin. "That okay with you, Davey?"

"Yeah, sure. I'm just glad I could help my old buddy out. I want to get back to my stompin grounds and relax. I can't take excitement like this the way I used to."

"It did seem like old times, Davey," Hecher reflected. "Only this time, we're the good guys. It's a nice feeling."

Hands in his pockets, looking down and away, Ross shrugged.

"I s'pose so."

"And now, Kemosabe," Lannon chirped, "hi-yo Silver! Away! The Lone Ranger rides again."

EPILOGUE

Florida Attorney General James Bidwell appointed a special prosecutor for the trial of Generoso Gagliardi, charged with first degree murder in the fatal shooting of Rodger Kriger on January fourteen, 1976.

The trial before Circuit Judge Timothy Schultz lasted less than a half-hour. Gagliardi's attorney had plea-bargained with the prosecutor, a retired judge. Gagliardi confessed to the shooting in exchange for immunity from the death penalty. Schultz sentenced him to life in prison with no chance of parole.

In the bargaining session, Gagliardi said he was paid to shoot Kriger, but refused to reveal who paid him or who ordered the murder. The prosecutor offered an even lighter sentence, the possibility of parole, if Gagliardi would provide verifiable information about who was behind the crime.

"I'd never survive in prison if I told you," he said.

The former judge also prosecuted Johnny Traynor and told him he likely faced life in prison. But the prosecutor dangled before the defendant the prospect of talking Judge Schultz into a reduced sentence of twenty-five years if Traynor supplied the name of the person who decided Kriger should be killed. Traynor's response was similar to Gagliardi's.

"I can't," he objected.

The prosecutor saw fear in his face.

"They'd kill me. I may not make it, anyway."

Schultz sentenced Traynor to life in prison, but didn't exclude the possibility of parole.

The trials of Gagliardi and Traynor occurred on consecutive days. Tom Palladin covered the proceedings for a follow-up to the news feature he wrote about the capture of the two men.

––––––––––

"In light of the convictions of Generoso Gagliardi and Johnny Traynor for the murder of Rodger Kriger of Palm Beach in 1976, we have reviewed the trial record of the State of Florida versus Mitt

Hecher," the Florida attorney general announced before television cameras. "We have, of course, overturned the conviction of Mister Hecher for first degree murder.

"In addition, we have found that the prosecutor in the case, James Scraponia, suborned critical witnesses to commit perjury in testifying against Mister Hecher. Our office has indicted Mister Scraponia on a charge of perjury, a first degree felony, and we have forwarded the case to the Palm Beach County State Attorney's office for prosecution."

Scraponia sat at his desk in his law office and read the five-count charge against him detailed in the letter from the attorney general's office. He grabbed the phone and dialed.

"If I'm going down, you're going with me, Bosworth," he yelled. "You're in this just as deep as I am. You approved everything I did, and you know it."

"Jim, I have no idea what you're talking about. You mean what those appeal attorneys said all along was true? You got those inmates to lie? That's a grave offense."

"You needed to get somebody convicted, Don," Scraponia said, more restrained. "The pressure from the community to find somebody guilty of that crime was intense, and you wanted to pin it on Hecher as badly as I did. And I'm going to make sure everybody in that courtroom knows it."

"I can't believe you're saying these things, Jim. Now, I think we'd better not go any further with this. If you make any more threats against me, I'll have to add to the charges you're facing. You'd better start thinking about how you're going to defend yourself."

"Oh, I am, all right. With a good offense. Same way I got Hecher convicted."

At the trial, Bosworth called the inmates who had received lighter sentences in return for fabricating confessions by Hecher that he had shot Kriger. The state attorney also called Hecher and the appeal attorneys. They and Hecher spoke with each other and agreed they thought Bosworth was guilty along with Scraponia, but would hold their noses and cooperate in the effort to convict the one they were sure was most blatantly and callously guilty.

"There can be no doubt," Susan Strickland testified, "that James Scraponia orchestrated a massive plot of suborning fellow jail inmates of Mitt Hecher to perjure themselves in testimony before the jury. That was revealed in their subsequent recantations and, of course, in the discovery of the real perpetrators of Rodger Kriger's murder. Obviously, Mister Hecher had no reason to make any confession of guilt to any inmate. The lighter sentences that these inmates received after their testimony adds to the evidence of Mister Scraponia's Machiavellian maneuverings."

With the evidence overwhelmingly against him, Scraponia pleaded no contest and testified that Bosworth knew of his plans and helped him obtain reduced sentences for the lying inmates. The state attorney denied the allegations, but it didn't matter either way because he wasn't on trial.

The judge found Scraponia guilty on all five counts. Five days later, he sentenced him to eight years at the Avon Park Correctional Institution. Tom Palladin was in the courtroom.

"Mister Scraponia, I understand you're an avid tennis player," Palladin called to him. "They have tennis courts at Avon Park. Mitt Hecher was responsible for getting them installed. Would you like to thank him?"

"I'd like to tell him to go to hell," Scraponia growled.

Before filing his story with the Florida News Service, Palladin decided to get a comment from Hecher and called him in Albuquerque.

"He deserves every minute of that sentence," said Hecher.

Told about the exchange regarding the tennis courts, Hecher said, "Geez, I didn't know the man was *that* low. What ingratitude."

They laughed.

"Mitt, stay in touch."

"You too, dude."

Donald Bosworth escaped punishment for his complicity in the conviction of Mitt Hecher. But Scraponia's courtroom testimony created strong suspicions throughout the community that the state attorney played a role, and his reputation was sullied. He saw the handwriting on the wall and decided not to run for re-election.

Politically and socially, Donald Bosworth faded into the shadows. His glory days in the spotlight of power were over.

———————

The electronically operated steel gate clanged shut behind Scraponia with a sound akin to that of a sledgehammer swung full-force against a clock tower bell. He lurched up and to the side, the handcuffs digging into both his and the sheriff's deputy's wrists. Fear knifed through the former prosecutor like a bolt of lightning.

The deputy turned him over to the sergeant at the booking desk, not far from the entrance gate to the large spartan room with walls painted a faded light green. After the preliminaries, a guard took him across to a partly open enclosure for finger-printing and photographing. Then it was on to his cell in the medium-security section of the prison.

His cellmate was a man of grim demeanor, about Scraponia's age, in for blackmail and extortion. He asked what Scraponia's offense was, and the latter answered that he'd committed perjury to get a conviction against a child molester. Scraponia knew that prison inmates detested those offenders, and figured he'd be safe with his cellmate and the other prisoners if they believed that story.

But he forgot that the convictions he'd won had sent others to this prison, and they were aware of his skullduggery in the Mitt Hecher case. The word began to get around the prison population. Inmates Scraponia had struck up conversations with were gradually shunning him. No one would agree to a tennis match with him.

The ex-attorney noticed some beginning to eye him in the cafeteria and the recreation yard. His uneasiness increased, and grew into apprehension as inmates made no attempts to mask the hostility in their stares.

He began to have nightmares that took various forms, but always with inmates, usually in groups, taunting or threatening him. Waking up in cold sweats, he would sit bolt upright in bed, staring into the gray.

He grew more depressed and lost weight as he ate ever less, speculating that the inmates in the kitchen were poisoning his food.

After six weeks, as he was jogging on the track in the prison yard, he felt someone slam into his left side from behind, and struggled to keep from hurtling onto the cinders.

"Oh, sorry," a hulking inmate mumbled, smirking, as he passed, barely pausing.

Scraponia cut short his recreation period and returned to his cell. He sat on the edge of his bed, gripped by fear. He quick-stepped to the guard station and asked to see the superintendent.

"He has a lot on his plate. I don't think he can just drop everything to see you, Mister Scraponia."

"Tell him it's urgent. Please."

"What seems to be the problem?"

"I'm in danger."

"In danger? Is the sky falling, or something?" The guard looked up.

"You don't understand. I need help."

"Hmm." The guard cocked an eye. He noticed the inmate's hands trembling. "You may be right about that. I'll see what I can do. Why don't you just go back to your cell and wait for me? Try to calm down."

"Thank you, thank you."

The guard came to Scraponia's cell fifteen minutes later. "Lieutenant Weller said he has two appointments, but he can see you for a few minutes. Let's go. We'll have to hurry."

They hustled down the gangways to the lieutenant's office.

"Sit down, Mister Scraponia. What's the problem? You look a little frazzled."

"They're trying to kill me."

"Whoa there, whoa. What's this all about? Who's trying to kill you?"

"Everybody. The prisoners."

"How do you know this?"

"The way they look at me. They don't talk to me. They won't play tennis with me."

"Well, Mister Scraponia, word has gotten around the prison grapevine as to why you're here, and it's true you're not going to win any popularity contests. But I don't know that anybody's out to kill you."

"I tell you they are. I saw the kitchen inmates whispering. And one guy ran into me on the jogging track just an hour ago and tried to give me a brain concussion."

"You're quite thin, a lot thinner than when you arrived here. Don't you like what they serve in the cafeteria?"

"I have to be very careful what I eat. They're poisoning my food."

Scraponia sat hunched over, his shoulders pulled in. Weller noticed his hands shaking, and his eyes appeared glassy.

"Have you been getting adequate sleep?" Weller asked.

"I'm having nightmares all the time about the inmates. I can't sleep right."

Weller rested his chin in one hand, his elbow on the office chair's armrest, and looked at Scraponia with raised eyes for several seconds. He picked up the phone.

"Let me speak with Doctor Andrews. This is Lieutenant Weller." While he waited, he said, "Don't worry. We're going to see that you're protected."

He swiveled his chair until it faced the wall, away from Scraponia.

"Doctor Andrews," Weller said in a hushed tone, "do you have an extra bed in the ward? You do? Good. I'm taking an inmate down. I think you'll want to admit him. Yes, now, if that's all right. He's in pretty bad shape. Thanks."

"Okay, Mister Scraponia, why don't you just come along with me? We're going to see a doctor who can give you something to help you with those bad dreams. And we're going to place you in a location where no one can harm you."

"Oh, wonderful, Lieutenant."

Weller didn't tell the inmate he had been scheduled for transfer to the minimum security section in two days. The superintendent realized he needed hospital care.

Weller, Scraponia, and the guard made their way to the psychiatric ward.

"Hello, Mister Scraponia," Doctor Andrews welcomed. "Why don't you relax on this comfortable couch and tell me what's bothering you?"

Scraponia repeated what he had told Lieutenant Weller.

"I'm going to give you something that will make you feel a lot better," the psychiatrist said.

He injected the inmate with a sedative.

"I think you'll be happier in this environment than out there with the general prison population. The attendant is going to take you to the dormitory and show you your locker and bed. I'll see you in the morning."

At seven a.m., Scraponia sat on a plastic-coated couch in the ward and listened to an attendant in green garb summon a different inmate to an adjoining room every twenty minutes. Then he heard his name called.

The attendant led him into the room. A green, cylindrical tank supported on wheels occupied a corner, and a long, narrow surgical table covered with white paper was in the middle.

"Just lie down here, Mister Scraponia," said Doctor Andrews. "This won't hurt a bit. Open your mouth, if you will."

The inmate complied, and the doctor inserted a chunk of wood. A nurse stood back of him and rubbed his temples with a cool jelly while the doctor inserted a needle into his arm.

"Raise your left hand and lift each finger one at a time, a second apart."

Scraponia began with his forefinger, continued with the middle finger, and progressed to the other two. He started to lift his thumb, and his arm fell to his side.

The doctor attached a pair of round pads to his temples and pressed a button on the machine. Scraponia's body convulsed for almost a minute. He awoke a half-hour later.

"Where am I?" he asked.

"You're in the Avon Park prison hospital," Doctor Andrews said. "How are you feeling?"

"Just fine."

"A few more of these ECTs and you'll be as good as new," the psychiatrist promised, smiling. "You won't be worried about inmates out to harm you anymore."

Scraponia underwent two more electroconvulsive treatments over the next four days.

"Why are you giving me shock treatments?" he asked after the last one.

"You've been feeling pretty stressed out, and your mind has been playing tricks on you."

"Doc," said Scraponia, "Just because I'm paranoid doesn't mean people aren't after me."

"That's right," the doctor said, smiling in a reassuring way. "And we're going to keep you here where you're safe."

Scraponia turned and walked toward the dormitory.

Rolling his eyes at the nurse, Doctor Andrews said, "They don't come any sicker than that."

The End

Bob Brink is a journalist who worked with the *Palm Beach Post*, The Associated Press in Chicago, *Milwaukee Journal*, *Tampa Tribune*, *Joliet Herald-News*, and Palm Beach Media Group (magazines). His byline has been on thousands of news stories, features, and entertainment reviews.

He has been a freelance writer for several years, and now has embarked on writing novels. He has won numerous writing accolades and several awards, including three for *Palm Beach Illustrated*, which won the Best Written Magazine award from the Florida Magazine Association after he became copy chief and writer.

Brink was a reporter for the *Palm Beach Post* when the crime this novel is based on occurred. It was an enormously sensational event that was featured six years later on a national TV show, and made newspaper headlines for 15 years.

Besides dabbling in short-story writing over the years, he has immersed himself in learning to play the clarinet and tenor saxophone. He performed many years with an estimable, 65-piece community symphonic band, and played a few professional big band gigs. He relegated music to the back seat after embarking on writing novels.

A product of Michigan and Iowa, he has a bachelor's degree in English from Drake University in Des Moines and completed graduate journalism studies at the University of Iowa.

CPSIA information can be obtained at www.ICGtesting.com
Printed in the USA
LVOW01s0741230315

431559LV00002B/2/P